ETERNITY AND THE OMEGA SHIELD

Future Navigator Compass

By

D. M. YOURTEE

INTRODUCTION

This is a book about Eternity and the rise of human kind within it-to their ultimate place in the cosmos---as they reach their stellar development, their highest evolutionary phase, their "Omega Point".

It is for those who may be searching for higher meaning in their lives witnessing the value of life ignored through the cruel and thoughtless actions of others in today's complicated world. It is addressed to those who realize the simple fact that the future of their children's children is dependent on our behavior now! It is hoped that those who have not grasped this reality will awaken and join the others who are awake, our Future Navigators.

The following gives an overview of the writings that may help, all Future Navigators.

"Eternity and the Omega Shield" is a work that unfolds an unyielding challenge to rational thinking about the value and future of the Human Being.

Beginning with Part I, "Challenging Forever", the reality in which humans exist is illuminated, making clear the need for a new kind of humanism based upon rational thinking.

In Part II, "Armor for Omega", thoughtful people properly called "Future Navigators" show how to protect the essential core of human benevolence as humans rise to their final rest in the cosmos.

DEDICATION

If in reading this book you are looking for gratuitous sex and violence, war like ideas, defense of a demanding faith, or even an excuse not to think--- you will be disappointed. Rather this work is dedicated to more universal ideas, for example the following.

Einstein said…"I never think of the future, it comes soon enough." Even so, he also said, most directly to us and obviously very concerned about the future…"We cannot solve our problems with the same thinking we used when we created them!"

In much the same era, it was Eleanor Roosevelt who said…"In the long run, we shape our lives, and we shape ourselves. The process never ends until we pass on. And the choices we make are ultimately our own responsibility!"

So, this book is dedicated to those among us who realize this, who do want to place the best thoughts toward the future, ours and others, all who because we are a human family must touch ours.

Clearly related is this question: *Are the past, present and future connected in an unexpected way- one that we can see directly, even change so as to solve problems with deeper forethought? Further, is there an aspect of human future evolution that may be in danger, and can that be aided to make it a safer climb?*

You know this is important! You are human, this is your story, you are a part of it - past, present, and future.

The Empires of The Future Must Become The Empires
of The Mind!
From Winston Leonard Spencer-Churchill

PATHWAYS

PART 1: CHALLENGING FOREVER

CHAPTER 1: TIMELINES

WITHIN A MICROSCOPIC SLICE OF SPACE-TIME!

On a mountain desert much resembling those in an area of Afghanistan, against a background of constant machine gun fire and the cascading noise of helicopter blades is this event.

A navigator has been on a quest born from his rational concerns wanting to find a true and lasting guardian for those who are at mercy of brutal monsters. Yet, at this time there is what seems to be a beast staring at him!

Frozen, not moving a muscle, not even his eye-lids, he looks into glaring heated seeming irrational eyes, eyes set in deep, deep hatred. He knows from his times of combat that there are moments like this where time compresses. All the visions of his life are there still held in his brain, and one sorts rapidly through them, to find what matters most in such a time, a time of mortal terror, a time when life most likely will end!

Reality is! He knows this! He is able to recognize at this moment his simple mortal needs, his mind craves for release. He could resist in a final battle that surely given the odds he could not win. But he knows that would mean he must kill again and in his heart he does not want to kill!

Is he odd? Perhaps, everywhere in every creature he knows, in everything he has learned, every living organism, lusts to stay alive, to eat, and to kill to that end, to relieve physical pressures, to secure a safe place, to guard immediate kind. Even so, at this moment, being in the end hominid like, he craves to know where there is for him---a guardian or is it necessary? For he is now no different than any other of those poor souls for whom he sought the guardian in vain.

We can stand above this scene, we see most of the others, in a Schadenfreude, one against the other, knowing full well that there may be blood, carnage, horror, that we will not experience, that in a relief---it is not us, not our fate, but, we observe in sickening fascination. He knows from his unique military experience that he could be the subject of that Schadenfreude!

We can though leave the beast for now and study the victim the kind of being whom some among us will understand. We can from experience gained in living long enough to reject cruelty enter his thinking, his heart and soul.

He is young, of good self-control, his bearing is charismatic. He is standing in this insanity with tattered uniform, bleeding here and there, with burns on arms and hands. He is very badly wounded, just able to stand upright! He has been in a terrible battle, a war created in the bowels of entrenched faith, fear and greed.

Born after the last Great War and between the futile ones of insurgencies and terrorists, he begins. In his formative years you might say he was existing abstractly, unlike so many of his generation who are addicted to this or that. Unlike many others, however, he progressed to adulthood, first holding counsel not being implanted into dogmas. On his way to maturity he was given all the tools of life, the way to build the way to sustain nutrition, the way to study, and understand his world, he was allowed to form his own mind! And through that, a deep freedom

and confidence - he found love for those so struggling around him. His strength he saw was the means to help others succeed in greater goals. He became ultra-vigilant. Getting used to his hungry body, nonetheless, he found it senseless to fight or challenge others. And it should be said he was repelled at the thought of so doing. There had to be a very great reason, indeed, for that. It was as he grew up first necessary to learn the tools basic for survival, to try to know others. Quite simply, he became wise enough to see the main tool, that without others he would not go on!

Practicing this sense of benevolence he knew would come about only by methodical observation and practice. Because on his planet there was a deeper imbedded agenda that virtually none of the others understood!

First recognitions for this, he gleaned from the creatures around him. He knows all are outshoots of the same basic sub-cellular biology. Yet, he learned, across the board of *the species need*! It is on his planet, survival of the fittest among them. Within that agenda he observed deeply, seeing the devotion of parents from the smallest to the largest creatures. What is more, most of the species he studied do not have to kill their own young! So it is the irrevocable priority, the survival of a species is the inherent absolute design, most must go on! This for all species, even the great many without a sense of future, is a reflex, but much, much more - it is a kind of love, is it not, that is for one's own kind?   At least, yes at least, there is that!

Of course the main issue, to evolve is - what about *his kind*? Their killing rarely has excuse to preserve the species. The matter of "One's Own Kind", is distorted, is miniaturized. It becomes localized failing to see all the others that are indeed, of "One's Own Kind". There are so many who maim and kill without remorse on irrational excuses, failing to see all the others, all the suffering. That is certainly the record of history on his planet!

Yet in the worst of times there has almost always been an effort by some to preserve, be it religious foundation, a new form of government, a new – yes -

benevolent document. Though there has been this, there is not yet discovered a broad guardian spirit for all, an inherent - principled benevolent heart.

Although the evil persists there is a momentary kind heart in most of his kind. It is driven by survival, but it is there! It surfaces each time one looks at one's child, that is, those that have it developed above their greed. In those actions they have the feeling of species need. It is the same kind of love that animals have.

In the end he has learned that it is the only path to a universal benevolent heart.

Simply put the young must learn to be the guardian of their own soul, and as they grow be given a chance to see, to let that spark of childhood protective love whelm up and secure the promise of the species.

He contemplates, In fact, there is no need for the bombs, no need for the suffering witnessed by all those he knows, no need for horrible cruelty felt by millions upon millions of children.

Mercilessness cruelty, terror, and senseless killing is triggered by individuals! However, peace on the planet cannot be obtained until those acting on their faith and personal philosophies act only on their benevolent ideas, and cease with dogma that instills the ideas of uniqueness to them, their "unique assembly". Then and only then can the young who are brought into these groups become benevolent members within them and totally for all others of their species.

Even so, with those thoughts persisting, now at this instant - he faces the one with evil eyes, in deep anger, approaching with knife in hand!

Yet, he knows what matters most. Although the eyes and the stance of the one approaching promise him unbearable suffering, he holds, not a return threat to be seen! He looks forward his own eyes glowing into that one's eyes. He knows those are of a kind that have never before really seen! Now though those evil eyes look into a different world, that of one who is at peace in the life he has lived and in his humanity!

Although this appears an ending, he knows he will, if so, fade back into star stuff - the place of angels, of cosmic eternity.

So he stands still and lifts his arms up in a warm gentle gesture and holds courageously.

Because he remembers, that she the Vistavien said "Should it come, Love and understanding will control the force of Death"!

TIME SLICES "RECENT"

And, as she the Vistavien[1] said, "One's life continues as long as does the life of Homo sapiens".

Schooled in that idea, a University Professor's Laboratory is in process of creating living cells from scratch as it were (using off the shelf biochemical). The research objective is to create cell replacements, aimed at enabling people to live healthier longer lives, so that they can help others into the future. In short this he saw as his role as a "Future Navigator", that is - improve chances for human kind to achieve immortality.

The Professor, (known fondly by staff and students as "Dr. Why" because of his eternally inquisitive personality), first name Daniel, made a call just as he sat down at this desk in the University Lab. It was a call to his old Navy friend, formally surname Skellan. Every one including "Daniel" called this dear friend "Hawk", because of the wound across his face, giving him a somewhat "hawk beak shaped nose".

However, given circumstances, there was just voice mail possible, leaving message…"Hawk, How about a beer tonight down at the Newport Bar? I have something I'd like to run by you, and it's been a long time since we got together. (Although the Professor was deep into things "scientific" he would always run his troubles by his old friend, simply because the Hawk was more schooled in living than anyone he knew.)

"Right now I'm on my way to the Osbern Crime Lab, some damn thing I have to check on. Once again, its's something unbelievable, this case about a baby in a toilet!"

The assignment was too typical. He was still on faculty teaching and researching, and still had an active doctoral program, but was a consultant to Osbern to review crime cases as their "Drug Man", checking to see if drugs had to do with events before prosecuting attorneys' went to court. Usually this was a review of police records and the autopsy, but he had a worry about this one, because it surely would require some personal contact. The "mother" had only some traces of "thc" in her blood meaning he had to go on scene to see if there were heavy users of meth, etc. in the home, that might have created such and insane tragic incident. That would require he thought a team with him because the location was in the slum area near the docks. They would sure have to leave the

---

1. A visionary for the future. The beginnings, her lessons are told in the books "The Final Human" and summarized in "The Future Navigator", ISBN: 978-0-69-240588-8

Research lab for a bit, meaning nowadays the near final experiments and the difficult decisions that must be made on continuing those biosimulaters cells, they label "BIOS+".

Looking over at the lab benches he could not help but wonder about his good fortune. His recent assistants were a bit odd as they go, but the most talented ever with him over all the years. And this said something as he was a director of new Ph.D. candidates in their research programs for some twenty-two who had obtained the degree.

Piper, who all called appropriately "Pi", was a math and physics major, now completing her dual Ph.D.'s in physics and biophysics. Pi was tall and so thin he was afraid she would disappear when she turned side-ways. Though quite beautiful, all that physical was just the smallest part of her. Frankly, she could be described as "a primitive social", but she was absolutely brilliant. Even so, she had a quirky aloof personality appearing to all to be "unconcerned" about anything the rest of us do care about. Or, he liked to think, she was just coldly academic about everything, even the value in drinking a cup of coffee.

Over in the corner lab at the chromatograph was "The Bean". Calling this robust young man "The Bean" fit as Tim James Bean was the most capable Post Doc biological science-biomaterials specialist he knew. Pi and Tim sometimes acted as a pair, whether it was minds or just sex, he could never tell, because Tim's close brushes with her in the Labs always met with a side-step from Pi.

Well, finding out about the drugs and that poor little one, he wants both with him to serve as "Snoopers" using their marvelous powers of observation, and also along must be the case detective as protection.

So, this Friday, just after lunch, near one, they gathered up notebooks, cell phones, cameras, rubber gloves and sample packages and were all on the way in a Police Van.

\`\`

Meanwhile, just as they left the Medical School and the Professor's lab --- Hawk called back…leaving message..."No Bar time tonight Daniel….explaining he was on the continent, working on a bomb left at a Worldmart Super Store, in Nice."

This man is, indeed, really surname "Skellan". His wife Angelei (yes, so spelled but all called her Angel) is with him on this trip with their eleven year old son Andrew. She usually does not go on his trips, the danger, but their oldest son a Navy Corpsman named Gabriel is sadly missing in action, presumed dead and she feels the need to comfort her husband, knowing full well the danger in his work. Even so, while Skellan is "working" Angelei and Andrew are sent away a bit, and are touring the hills around Nice, following the flowers and perfume creators.

The reason for all that caution is that Skellan is a Navy Master Chief by job description an explosive ordinance demolition expert (an "EOD"). Even though retired, his experience brings him back frequently as a special investigator. As said before, he is known as 'The Hawk" for his beak like nose. There is, however, a reason the cut across his face resulted from an underwater demolition when a cable broken from a mine explosion whipped viciously through the water slashing his nose and cheek.   This was on one of his many missions, (In the Yellow Sea) long ago.

After retirement the "Chief", saw his role as a Future Navigator clearly. He would travel the world discovering and disarming the millions of mines left in fields maiming or killing children in countries once in war. So he was totally willing to be called up when needed. Now he is recalled to lead this Worldmart demolition.   To it Hawk brings the experience of some 200 bomb removals. Yet, he has put himself on hyper mind control because he remains deeply troubled by the disappearance of his son Gabriel!

Before suiting up, though he felt it 'mandatory' to return the call to Daniel. These two it would seem are a curious pair, an "egg-head" college teacher-researcher, and a sailor who disarms bombs! However, they have history as friends, sailor buddies. Many years ago they were in the Navy stationed together in Newport Rhode Island (the Professor was Corpsman, i.e. Medic). Then by coincidence almost 20 years later they renewed that once deep friendship when the Hawk attended a special class on "Clearing the Mind" at the University were the Daniel was a tenured professor.

Although an incredible, but true story, both men received special training, from a teacher Jehan, who in turn had received it form a most remarkable African woman named See-ela who many thought of as a "Vistavien", the most capable people guiding others to become future navigators. The core of that training involves something called "The Principles for Opening the Mind", which is a way to focus, but also shows the way for tolerance to help others.

Now though, that aside, Skellan is inside the store, between the end-caps of a canned goods aisle peering through his face guard at the problem facing him just fifty feet away at a very technical array of wires mounted on what seemed to him paradoxically like a Claymore Mine! He releases his robot ("The Wheelbarrow") which is slowly creeping forward dual cameras clicking away. Up close it gives the EOD a clear picture of the top connections---a horrible jumble of wires!

As he feared the wires are crossed doubly, red over green, the black and yellow intermixed with those, buried deep in some form of gel or adhesive on the surface. Experience tells the EOD, release one entanglement and the other sets off the explosion!

Also, he could just barely see something that looked like a pressure cap, next a clock that showed 3 minutes with seconds disappearing! And, if the base is an explosive mine it most likely is touch sensitive. With this the sensors on the robot signal back to his receiver an explosive load, not C-4 apparently, but a huge mass of gun powder and Skellans little sniffer dog ("Chip"), standing behind also barks off a screaming shrill - high pitch warning!

So a decision is made backed from his vast experience. He calls into the police commander stationed outside behind a car barrier "se retirer', Pull Back, Pull Back, and Now!

He will use his concussion load to fire at the device, and the store and he will face what he remembers will be a good but fairly contained explosion. After he is sure contact is made with the police commander and the surrounding area is cleared, calmly as always with him, he decides to blow the thing up. Holding his breath and with good aim the load is fired straight at the device!

The result is, of course, not surprising. The deafening, fire colored, smoking blast - pulverizes the corrugated ceiling and explodes out to the side, front and back far enough to bring all the cans on shelves down and all over. What is surprising is that the large cans on the end-caps shoot out and ram into the Hawk with tremendous force pounding deep into his chest, knocking him through the store glass a full 10 feet behind. He lands onto his back with incredible deep bruising force even through his safety suit.

On the ground the EOD was---unconscious! The police commander logged the blast time as 3:22:34 p.m.

The picture Skellan had been getting at first was curiously like a Claymore mine with which he was, of course, very familiar. These anti-personnel devices were usually filled with C4 explosive and steel balls similar to the ammunition used in a shotgun. But this device was complicated with those multiple wires.

The mines, which were first developed around the time of Korean War, the Hawk knew, remain in use today. Normally they are armed for enemy infantry and detonated by remote or tripwire, but the wires on top made this one way too confusing to attempt a top disarming.

So the decision was made to back off the robot, and using a hand gun, explode the device, and take what damage had to be taken.

Obviously as Skellan well knew---nothing in his job, could ever be exactly planned or expected as such, and so the EOD was unconscious on a stretcher on the way to hospital, just about an hour after he answered the call from his old friend.

\`\`

While the EOD just started to face the weird claymore, back in the states the little drug investigation party were parking in front of the house where the baby was removed from the toilet (by a truly horribly horrified social worker).

The surrounding was a slum, but the house was absolutely the worst around. The picket fence was hanging down here and there, the yard was full of weeds and junk, even to include a couple of old refrigerators. There was nothing but peeling paint on the walls, and tiles from the roof seemed somehow to be stripped off, and hanging off the gutters, themselves rusted and almost it seemed … not attached.

The little party walked up to the door which was cracked open, dark interior peering out. Moving cautiously as would prevail the common sense of any rational being the police detective, a well-respected female officer (given the nature of the crime) rang and then without answer pounded the door, causing it to slowly but surely creak open.

On about the third pounding the sound of a shot gun blast exploded-shattering the corner window into shard of glass and buck-shot scattered what seemed like everywhere.

The officer ducked and looking back, saw the professor on his knees blood shooting from is left shoulder, all others were flat on ground and seemed uninjured.

Instinctively the officer spun around police issue Glock repeatedly firing into the window as she knelt preparing to lay on the ground off the porch. But, the return gun fire, one blast more, ceased and a youngish disheveled dirty man, was sloped over the broken glass, severely wounded. The officer glanced at her wrist watch, just as she saw the Professor turn writhing on the ground, punched the timer set to stop, the clock, read 9:22: 34 (a.m.).

This event ended with the Professor, passed out on stretcher as he was taken to hospital at the exact same time as the Hawk was being delivered across the Ocean, to hospital in France!

\`\`

The matter of the curious explosive coincidences wound up with the culprit on the New York end convicted. The terrible heart wrenching story of the discarded baby was indeed a result of a drug infused boyfriend of the saddest of young mothers, and the house turned out to be a supply house for local addicts.

The French event was attributed to radicals excusing their crowdedly action in defense of Islam, which of course Skellan experiencing that before knew it to be a sham and as his favorite columnist D. Brooks said, "For the religious person it's about God, but for the terrorist, it's about himself". The cowards, were in a short time discovered. There was a second explosion where DNA evidence made the connection. The Brooks comment was absolutely spot on. "Martyring themselves in the name of "Holiness', they were actually sad losers obliterating themselves for the sake of revenge."

Two months later the two friends were fully recovered and found the matter of the coincidence one for a good laugh and a great story for friends at the bar. What bothered them just a bit was that the times of both events were exactly the same. That is, 3:22 p.m. in France was 9:22 a.m. in New Port!

Still for these two worldly and intelligent friends, as the days moved on there lingered a wonder at the way and why this coincidence occurred. Both, of course sensible, knew coincidences happen, but then don't coincidences make one wonder, what is it all about, why was each one spared, for what, for a new purpose, what?

The days following recovery for Skellan were mostly steeped in loving his wife Angelei, and teaching son Alexander the means of becoming a most capable carpenter, a part of what he and wife believed was the way to raise a child. Concentrate on the skills needed to survive, and grow the child with knowledge, until at that self-actuating age, the child is adult enough to investigate and adopt such (non-proselytized) philosophies as appropriate for them. Such was the way they raised their older son Gabriel.

Even so, from time to time Skellan was called to a field somewhere in the world to locate and disarm those inhuman devices left festering in ground to destroy the lives of children.

Meanwhile, the following days for the Professor involved trying to focus on publications. That is In spite of all the full days at research creating and testing the BIOS+, Daniel managed to publish his second novel a sequel to one he had written called "Quest for Immortality" a book projecting the qualities of the "Ultimate Human'.

He was fully satisfied with it…after being with the Vistavien in Africa, and receiving those lessons from her on what she called "Future Speak". His new book followed on the theme and treated ways to make "Future Navigators "as he and friend Skellan had committed their years remaining.

Although the subject seems in a strange genre for his credentials.   He was a scientist but fully versed in the humanities also believing that the Ph.D. degree was grounded in an agenda of philosophical pronouncement!

Published and out there, when he reached home that night he found his wife Sue looking at an internet thing on the "Springs" that had his last name attached!

The Professor thought, *Those "Springs" are in Maryland. They must go way back, perhaps from early America! They must have a special meaning, we need to know about their history.*

And so it was he and Sue were off to Maryland to look at "Springs". Surely, there was something in the past that must be discovered.

The Professor was forced to contemplate, time's getting to be quite an item in my life!

TIMES "PAST INTERSECTING"

And connecting, some quite important things happened just about the time that the Professor finished his book. Aside from the bomb and shot gun coincidences and the "Springs" discovery he found himself interested, at Pi's suggestion, which was one in Astrophysics! She left on his desk (note "Check Prof") an article in which, though he found it a most curious proposal, it argued in favor of Einstein that all times past, present and future, persist in Space-time!

Always reflective of any striking proposal no matter the subject, his active brain, thought...although it really wasn't a parallel, if that is the case then the history of these Springs is in fact somehow traceable. I will just need to think through were to start.

For us, following this we would of course just jump in and go back to early American History. But suffice it to say that Daniel (at once a Professor and "Dr.Why") decided to dig way back into the 1500s! This was probably for him just barely good enough since he at first contemplated looking into the ice age! Even so, as it seemed logical, he decided just to look into the conflicts in Europe that led to Immigration into the continent where the Springs were located.

So it was - it all began to open up, that is more "Timing". In the New England, Maryland Historical Library he stumbled upon, the "Massacre of St. Bartholomew". Because of the religious faith of his father, he knew vaguely of this, and as is his way he found it absolutely captivating because of its historical ramifications. So he recorded a detailed description from the libraries' records as follows.

"This massacre constitutes one of the darkest blots on the history of France. The true story is as follows. Papal powers caused deluded and subservient European Catholics to strike this diabolical blow. The Papacy then never surrenders to a dissenter the right of conscience; hence, for the Protestants of those times, what cannot be accomplished by agreement must be done by assassination.

That came on Sunday morning, August 24. The signal was given by the tolling of the great bell, and the slaughter began. The massacre of St. Bartholomew was the most horrible tragedy of the Reformation period, and we may well say, with an illustrious statesman, "Let it be erased from the memory of man." The number of the slaughtered Huguenots has been variously estimated, but the best authorities agree in placing the aggregate at many thousands.

The news of the massacre was received at Rome with great joy, and the Pope had a medallion struck in commemoration of the event, while Protestants all over the world were steeped in mourning.

The Papists, however, utterly failed to stamp out the Protestant faith although regulations on marriage created scandalous situations for Protestants--in fact thousands awoke to the fact that they were not legally married. Children at the age of seven years were given the right of abjuration which resulted in wholesale transfers to Catholic charges and guardians, while their Protestant parents were compelled to support them.

No wonder the mind set of many Protestant Europeans was to escape. It is followed with 2 centuries of persecution of the Protestants (Huguenots'). And there was indeed a stampede of the Protestants to leave Europe. The most unheard of and astonishing methods of disguise in order to escape were needed.

The knowledge of secret pathways to the borders and the best methods of eluding the vigilance of the guards was communicated from one to another in a marvelous manner. Many fled to Alsace-Lorain near the German border, temporarily excused from the violence. They comprised all classes of people. The details of their sufferings are so sickening as to defy understanding in any true civilization, from breaking on the wheel to burning at the stake

This too is coupled in the 1530s by a priest from Italy, angry at the way slaves were tormented he traveled north to establish his church in Alsace. There was thus brought to a new home the family Jordyn.

In time, more northern yet, in Germany, a priest, (by name Leuder, i.e. Luther) came a long way in his life to another deep humane decision. He posted on the church a daring challenge. Every-thing was wrong, at least the way he saw it. He was a priest, within the cataclysm, but one torn between faith and a sense of reality.

Hence, this priest objected issue after issue, his books spoke far outside the allowed with critical comments about church practices! Then it came the excommunication, and the trouble. For a while they, these called protestants, tried to fight back, even to assemble an army, but so it was one with no military sense, and thousands were killed, mercilessly. Again, it spread across Europe, a catholic scourge in revenge, and killing of the new group the Brethren, otherwise known as the Dunkards."

Here with that name in front of him….Dunkard, and Brethren the Professor knew he had the connection, because some time back he devotedly researched his surname that is the "Jordyn" who were members of the Church of the Brethren.

In process of further exploration he came across a record, more a diary, once again in the Library. It was a very badly worn document, the longhand script just legible, all in a leather binder, held together with a lace of very fragile cloth. He was though from that humble diary able to piece together this story.

In the early 1700d a Jordyn…one young adult son named Peter and his two brothers were almost sacrificed. They were in the fields working to bring in the harvest, it was a successful endeavor, usually. But that day the field was on fire, and "The Cloaked" ones rushed from behind, hidden by the smoke, swords circling in the air. Those of clan Jordyn closest to Peter where hidden, but youngest brother John was struck and fell bleeding to death, head nearly severed.

They, remaining, hid well up next to the hills of Alsace. For Peter and Brother Aron there was no retuning to the fields, as they were well known.

The held for a little while. They knew Peter's youngest sister Magdalene would come, try to find them. They could only hope that the devastation all around would make them see the need to bring what they could, for Peter knew it was time to leave forever his home. In this the "Diary" has clear terms containing a prayer begging the Lord to guide them on their journey.

And as it became they were forced to the Ocean. These of tribe Jordyn had in conscience become Dunkards, members of the Church of the Brethren. Good people that family, farmers, merchants, even one once a mayor, but now their faith made them exiles. With the women and all packs of bare essentials on back they made the long dangerous, cold journey north to Holland.

There with every last bit of wealth they bargained for a place on Ship…to the "New World". Named the "Pearl of Ireland" It set sail, Oct. 1730, 80 emigrant passengers on board. Also there were among the European Protestants, poor Irish farmers.

The tales of their trip across the ocean, make it certain that those surviving were made of the sternest stuff.

Letter of Peter Jordyn July 25, 1735. *To the Very Reverend, Very Learned Mr.Dordoff!*

I, the most submissive servant of my very reverend, highly and very learned Mr.Dordoff, must forbear to report to your Reverence, how we are getting along.

After we had left Holland, behind us the cruelty of the church that killed our kin, and surrendered ourselves to the wild, tempestuous ocean, its waves and its changeable winds, we reached, through God's great goodness toward us, with good wind, England within 24 hours. After a lapse of two days we came to the island of Wicht [Wight] and there to a little town, called Caus [Cowes], where our captain supplied himself with provisions for the great ocean [trip] and we secured medicines for this wild sea. At that time boarded also some 30 Irish folk. Then we sailed, under God's goodness, with a good east wind away from there. When we had left the harbour and saw this dreaded ocean, we had a favorable wind only for the following day and the following night. Then we had to hear a terrible storm and the awful roaring and raging of the waves when we came into the Spanish and Portuguese ocean.

For twelve weeks we were subjected to this misery and had to suffer all kinds of bad and dangerous storms and terrors of death, which seemed to be even bitterer than death.

With these we were subject to all kinds of bad diseases. The food was bad, for we had to eat what they call "galley bread." We had to drink stinking, muddy water, full of worms. We had an evil tyrant and rascal for our captain and first mate, who regarded the sick as nothing else than dogs. If one said: "I have to cook something for a sick man," he replied: "Get away from here or I'll throw you overboard, what do I care for your sick devil." On one of these terrible days a mate on deck, began to accost our Magdalene. There then arose a terrible fight as an Irish man did attack the mate, severing then fingers of one hand. For that poor soul he stood some 30 lashes at the mast. In short, misfortune is everywhere upon the sea.

We never fared better across the whole sea. This has been the experience of all who have come to this new land and even if a king traveled across the sea, it would not change.

After having been in this misery sufficiently long, God, the Lord, brought us out and showed us the land, which caused great joy among us. But three days passed, the wind being contrary, before we could enter into the right river. Finally a good south wind came and brought us in one day through the glorious and beautiful, Telewa [Delaware], which is a little larger than the Rhine, but not by far as wild as the latter, because this country has no mountains, to the long expected and wished for city of Philadelphia. Here we have settled and we with the Irish have made progress in guiding kin to settlement. Our Magdalene in the months that followed, has become betrothed to that one Irishman who saved her from the fate she would have suffered at the hands of the Captain's Mate. They Magdalene and husband we are given to know from those about, we loosing contact, left Philadelphia and traversed to New York. Sadly so, she my sister is lost to me after all the purges we suffered.

Notwithstanding that, it please Mr. Dordoff, I with Mary Stoffen have too become betrothed, soon to expect one if son we will call after me Peter or her after her maiden name Mary. In full reverence, your servant Peter Jordyn.

So it was the Professor found his forefathers, and then he learned that they settled a town in Maryland and farmed a vast estate, which held those "Springs', still feeding the water supply of the surrounding area. While that completed the trip he and his wife were making the curious events over time continued.

The estate was in slave holding country where great-great grandfather Peter settled and the youngest son Samuel objected deeply to the plight of the enslaved workers on farms all around. As the civil war approached Samuel became a circuit minister and when the war broke out he was Chaplin in the Union Army.

To the Professors amazement this man was, indeed, his own great grandfather and he was one of those who gave a sermon when Lincoln was brought home after being murdered. What stood out was that the sermon's address. After noting the greatness of the president in the main of the full sermon, as recorded in a copy of the sermon the professor found in the Library of Congress, Pastor Samuel turned to focus his fullest attention. He offered ways of tolerance and understanding to help in recovery for his torn nation, hopeful thoughts to reach into the future, giving ways to heal. In a few words, he laid down ideas for future navigation in his troubled time!

The professor, amazed, stumbled upon that fact, the publication of his great grandfathers well after his own book "Quest"" had been published. Its message was also couched in ways to survive the future, wherein the mission of the "Future Navigator" is first described.

It was stimulated by a journey on research in Africa where he saw day by day in the cities then soaked in dollars of oil - the terrible contrasts. Some oil rich people were insensitive to everyone else, but most, vast hordes of people were in terrible poverty, and there was absolute horrible cruelty and tragedy for children evident almost everywhere, starving, so many lost wandering alone! Deeply depressed with all the tragic loss, repulsed, and seeking some insight - a way out-solutions, he traveled away from his base hospital there to leave the seeming unsolvable. He traveled well into the tribal villages where at last, he found among those who returned to the village vital compassionate ideas. Although he was a teacher He became the student and listened intently. Those lessons evolved into reforming the realities of life in ways that could give a deep, kinder future. These thoughts are best termed "The Future Dares"!

These were already expressed in the book "Quest" before he discovered his great grandfather's sermon and the title of the sequel was already set for his latest book to be "The Future Navigator".

While all of this the Professor saw at first as 'normal" the more he thought about it the more it troubled his inquiring mind. Was that connection, the mind of his grandfather and his essentially the same a type of reincarnation or does genetics go that far and that deep?

Nonetheless, it is fact that as Daniel was going through that personal family research it turned out to be of some considerable interest that his friend Skellan was also completing an ancestry search, wanting to know about his lineage!

Way across the City in his home near the docks, Hawk is looking at a document Angelei has handed him, sent from the genealogy library of LDS. On it is a Genealogy Chart, and beside it a historical account as follows.

"The Irish Famine of 1740–1741 (Irish: Bliain an Áir, meaning the Year of Slaughter) in the Kingdom of Ireland, was estimated to have killed at least 38% of the 1740 population of 2.4 million people. This is a proportionately a greater loss than during the worst years of the Great Famine of 1845–1852. The famine of 1740–41 was due to extremely cold and then rainy weather in successive years, resulting in food losses in three categories: a series of poor grain harvests, a shortage of milk, and frost damage to potatoes. At this time, grains, particularly oats, were more important than potatoes as staples in the diet of most workers.

Deaths from mass starvation in 1740–41 were compounded by an outbreak of fatal diseases. The cold and its effects extended across Europe, but mortality was higher in Ireland because both grain and potatoes failed."

Then following this historical fact there is the record from a Ship's log, that of the Ship "Pink Lady!

"The ship picked up these Irish passengers from the isles of Wright, and the then town of Cowes.

There are many entries in the log, but the following is noted, regarding this researched lineage. On deck June 10, year of our lord 1730 Shipmate O'connor accosted one O'Skellan who had rested away a lass Magdalene a sister of passenger Peter Jordyn."

The document now in Skellans usually controlled slightly shaking hands continues with the genealogy.

It shows a tracing from early Ireland. At the top is the name of a Clan Chief, and as one progress down one sees O'Schellan become Skellan.

And on the "Genealogy Tree" in the year 1728 he sees a side box, the name O'Skellan, and wife Magdalene Jordyn! Upon seeing this Skellan, stood up and wandered about the house in his way slowly coming under complete calm.

Then, the document shetails the New York Skellans and some he recognizes by first name, in stories heard about the Irish Mobs and one Jeremy who is listed there, but he knows from his father Jeremy was a bomber who terrorized the city.

This all, too much at first he crashes to his chair, the bomber -great grandfather is one reason why he devoted his life's skill to destroying such devices.

Even so, the most remarkable fact is the woman Magdalene Jordyn was wife of his great-great grandfather making him without question a cousin of Dr.Why, that is Daniel is a cousin! They are related, kin in DNA!

He dials his "friend now cousin' forthwith, to set up a meeting!

A "Forever Seeker" Panel is Conceived: In consequence of yet another coincidence, a meeting with an unusual but unexpected purpose was held in the back of the "Newport Tavern", where there was a small room with table and a curiously large number of chairs, and, yes, bar service was available for this almost speakeasy looking place. Skellan requested it having an idea that more meetings might be coming.

He started the conversations addressing the Professor in a rather casual tone. Dr. Jordyn, (taking the professor by surprise as the Hawk, never used Daniel's surname) last night I discovered that I am your 4th cousin! Clearly shocked by the statement all the Professor could utter was, What, How so?

Pulling the genealogy out of a red colored folder, he showed it to the Professor and siting next, pointed to the important notes. You see here, my great grandmother, was your great grandfather's sister! Surely not Hawk! Yes her name, recorded in ships log was Magdalene Jordyn, sister of Peter!

Well that takes the cake, finding this out just after we were both nearly killed at the same time.

The Doctor shakes his head and pauses, then extended the story. I just found out My great-great grandfather Peter settled in Maryland, a farm holder his son Abraham had 5 sons, one-Samuel was my civil war great grandfather who served in the Union Army and gave a sermon at Lincolns funeral. He wrote a sermon to help folks into the future. I found that out after my book Quest, the prequel to Future Navigator had been published, you know the one about us and our thinking and missions, that book tells much the same mission as he did for his time.

Where was your great grandfather about that time? Well he was a very skilled Irish Mob bomb maker…making me…as I discovered his history, know what I should do… what you know I have so devoted to the rest of my life!

The two, looked at each other with something of a truly perplexed look and sat quietly sipping their Guinness.

Then after a long pause and looking intensely at this friend, the Professor spoke up in a soft but stern voice. You know Hawk, these coincidences make one think don't they. Damn right Daniel! And this is one "Dr.Why" where I am right along with you.

Yes, they are most probably coincidences, or the transfer of DNA of the mind over time, perhaps, but it still makes one think deeply about time and change and events, doesn't it!

Right now for me as you know my Lab is about to complete our Bios+. Frankly, I worry that instead of helping the future, we could be creating something that would be of great harm!

Right, "cousin' and I have been thinking could I go back somehow and change things so bomb making disappeared. God that would be great, no-one could understand the pain of seeing the maimed children I have on my missions.

The Professor then said what was to become a burning question, not just for these two just discovered cousins.

In short Hawk we are both wanting to know about time and whether we are locked into it all- in some way. In fact can we return and do it all over again, but heading in a different way? Or can we head off some tragedy that we may set in motion in the future.

Hawk then gave that inquiry the name that would become a mission. Yes, we want to understand...what really is "Forever". We want to probe into it, to be "Forever Seekers"!

Let me emphasize. Do not most people believe they will live "Forever"? Is that not an abiding theme in the hopes and wishes of people just as soon as they began to think about their lives? Do we not in some way hold some suspicion, some hope that there is "Forever". Then what is it and is there is some way we can know about it, even enter it where we might want. And is there something about it, some twisting in it or some force that makes curious things happen?

Yes, my friend you have said it perfectly!

So, from his scientifically curious brain, the Professor said simply, why don't we find out?

It was from that encounter that a series of meetings was to get underway. At first it was merely social. It seemed a great topic to share with friends and family that in time (after many meetings) they would call "Forever Inquiries" or "Probes", and into each meeting each would bring along such papers on the subject as they could find, and friends and new company.

At first the Doctor would bring his staff, the Bean and Pi, and his technical secretary Jane, and the Hawk would bring his wife Angelei and invite the teacher Jehan at the School of Medicine.

Frankly, at first it did start out as just a great reason to have a party at the bar, but it very soon grew into something much more---a targeting and real inquiry.

And in time they were meeting quite frequently.

They found themselves becoming more of a "Panel of Forever Seekers". Then later there were many others, and they in turn began to motivate the original group, who became a sort of consulting panel to look deeper after the goal which simply put is "Forever" knowable, can it be entered, changed, are we a bit crazy for looking into this?

<u>A First Special Meeting:</u> So it was, shortly thereafter at eight in the evening on a Friday they gathered again back of the bar around that table with a focus in mind that developed logically.

What a diverse group was forming up! There was of course Daniel, and Skellan, but also Angelei, Pi and the Bean, and Dr. Jehan would be there, and all these were accompanied by Jane Caldwell. Jane was at first there to take notes, but it ended up that she too was also on a quest concerning the future. And Jane brought along her husband Chandler - a big brute of a man who was at first just curious.

Turns out, however, this was something of an ideal group. It consisted of three scientists, and shall we say working folks, one military, one medical, and two on the daily job. But these were a good deal more because Jane's husband Chandler, worked in construction, with architects and indeed, had become quite an expert in computers, software and the like. And Jane had become an expert in technical recording. And with Dr. Jehan (who was just entering the room) all eyes turned on that beautiful Pakistani knowing she gave the group a Medical Doctor but more as she was the lesson giver in methods for Future Navigation. Both Skellan and Daniel were more aware than all the others that this woman was the teacher bringing in the last of the "Future Navigator" ideas from the Vistavien "See-ela" before she passed away.

During several subsequent meetings each gave notice of their concerns, i.e. addressing what they would want about, or from digging into "Forever" as follows.

As was said, Daniel wanted to know if coincidence was controlled by the flow or conflicts in time and in what way, but he was most concerned as to whether his research would cause a dangerous future.

Skellan had the same concerns as Daniel on coincidence, but also wanted to know if a return somewhere in Forever could have prevented the killing and maiming of innocents from mines and bombs.

Pi wished to know where the future would lead in understanding the cosmos, and if her knowledge of it, already most confident, could be improved.

The Bean was troubled by the loss of the world's environment and what could have been done differently, or could change that and what the future would bring for humans and the earth's creatures…he thought in the next say 50 years.

Jane (surprising to all during the meeting) wished to see into what made the popes decide on celibacy for priests but no contraception for all the people, and said it out clearly…Where will we be with so many children, and so much disease for them, could we change that?

And Chandler- the practical sort- and in a surprise to all was curious as to where all the technology would take the working folks, and if it would cause harm… could that be avoided by some changes in the past or headed off for the future?

Jehan wished to know if See-ela's teachings could become more universal, and what mechanism might help that to secure the deep future for Human Kind.

What meetings these were, ranging up and down and back and forth. They all discovered how people worry about so many things in life, and that almost every day.

All kinds of questions were asked. Even some new thoughts arose in the serendipity.

If going back, could Daniel (after making them all aware of his family history) have changed the religious torment of his ancestors? Should he continue the BIOS+, which in effect would mean creating life, or perform a different research?

Jane wished to peek into the future for the support of her five kids. If it looked troublesome could she change that?

Could Skellan have prevented the bombs set by his diabolical nemesis, in the main though could his son Gabriel have been saved, kept from that last mission and was there some way he could head out into time and get his son back?

The answers involved the ability to move back and forth into what most had heard scientist, believers of Einstein's Space-time accepted as the persistent presence in space-time of past, present and future.

Pi, set a stage, a possible focus, although as usual, for some in the group she couldn't see (their worry) that they would not understand.

This was to be sure something that Daniel was concerned about and made a private vow to treat every subject with careful reviews, making sure all understood the topic at hand.

Nonetheless, as to her ideas on focus at this time, she went right on…."Remember this all is in your minds but that must also be an exercise of conscience coupled with an atomic place in what you will find is the arena of space time!

All were wondering just what she was aiming at as she went on…"The answers involve also the liberty in entropy and clear understanding of the uncertainty and duplicity of Quantum mechanics." Tim said here Pi, thanks, and I am sure we will want you to explain that.

At this Daniel, truly loving the company in this little club, the Forever Seekers… inserted a compromising and exciting idea. He had thought this through and in advance set in motion the path and the funding.

"All our concerns involve first a clear understanding of history, and second insight into the cosmos in which it all takes place. We need to get away, let our minds' be free. So I have an idea, one all will love, that is we need a retreat, a trip that is both a lesson and a holiday!

Let me first say, that there is National Institutes funding available through my research, as I am facing a matter of conscience, many fellow researches share. So, give Ideas on this my friends, where is our retreat, where would our extended inquiries take place?"

A Forever Seekers Plan: After it seemed all individual wishes had been aired, Skellan expressed his concerns about their forthcoming agenda. Addressing the "Study Group" with a serious tone, he asked are we on a path into the past to "redo", or are we concerned that…is there a way to see into the future, and to control outcomes? And so went the discussions for a bit, but it was clear, though, naively, that the group had needs to look into both possibilities.

Eventually, Pi, in her indomitable way, simply said out right, "We don't have this correct! We need to deal with reality seeing what is possible in Space-time and it must be done right coupling pasts theoretical or philosophical ideas to the present ones. Only then we will know the answer, our ability to see into "Forever" in totality. That is. We need much deeper inspection, a focus into proposals, scientific reviews, etc., rather than just assuming ahead we will be able to jump into past or future."

Daniel heard this and an idea came to him immediately. He proposed a "Retreat", in academic style, that is at a place all could enjoy, review proposals, meetings to archive consensus, and final recorded minutes and decisions.

My colleagues at Patel in India are very well qualified to help and there are some Post Docs available there, one each for you Pi and you Tim! So a trip to India should be a part of our retreat!

Then immediately seeing an excellent opportunity Skellan enthused... of course and on the way, let's visit Samyak the Jain Guru, Philosopher…His daughter knew my son Gabriel, I told you all he is missing in action. But it would be good to see them, his daughter was close to my son, and he is certainly one of the wisest persons I know when it comes to history, that is, he can be our expert on the "Past". As Pi says, that is a part of space-times persistence and for us to consider in Forever.

And I look at this group and I see all we need, scientist in Pi and Tim, technical recorder in Jane, a medical doctor in Jehan, in my wife Angelei an expert on faiths, and Chandler one with tools on computer, and please Chan… a man of strength to accompany me in defending the group from dangers we might face in less "policed" places. (See panel profile beginning next page)

So together they planned a trip to Delhi, vis. at first Jaisalmer India. Skellan, was happy with that decision, hoping to know more about his son Gabriel who was schooled by the mystic. That, and the discovery of Gabriel's relationship with Samyak's daughter Daya provided an awesome coincidence for him to get to know her. The others were wanting time with Samyak who they heard much about, though Pi said, if he claims to hypnotize, that is B.S.

Accordingly, they are off to visit SAMYAK! This man's full name is Samyak Darshon Jain. All in this belief are last name Jain. Samyak means right and true, Darshon means philosopher and visionary and he deserves his honorable names as many say he is wisest of all, he is so knowing of history that he can take you to each time and place as though you were there.

Forever Panel Guidelines: The Professor, recognizing that our group would be rather rare pursuing the idea of finding ways to enter "Forever", requested that the members of the panel be described, much as say a university committee's members would be regarding its academic evaluations or that a foundation's panel would be identified. That is, each of us should be in a relevant area in life, and stand exposure for any given bias, and of course have "credentials" relevant to the pursuit.

Once the objective was formalized it became clear that other experts would be required in addition. This was accomplished through detailed study by each member into scientific papers and consultations with experts in various Universities around the world.

It was intended as each Forever proposal was considered that the panel would work toward a consensus motion after which there would be a guiding summary.

The Professor felt it necessary that the Panel's decisions be available for future groups as a challenge as he believed that their work could be a focus for upcoming "Future Navigators".

The Forever Panel Members: At our retreat in India, there were to be 10 members of the Panel as cited on the following list.

1. Professor, Danial Jordyn. Name Italian sounding, as often pronounced Jordin-e' but descent is Germanic. Dr. Why as he is fondly known is Full Professor of Medicine, with specialty in Biomaterials as replacements for injuries to extend life. He is experienced in world travel, a Fulbright Scholar involved in humanitarian research in Africa. He is a widely published scientist but also the author of eight books in the area of "Objective Humanism" a conduct of life essay, which champions preserving through tolerance the distant future for the world's children. He was raised Methodist but has over the years become more Pantheist. His Panel Position was as agreed by the members to be ….Chairman.

2. Dr. Samyak (Darshon) Jain. The last name is indeed Jain as is carried by all so born. Samyak's names meaning philosopher and visionary rightly fit his life's accomplishments. Samyak is retired professor of world History. He is greatly respected for his wisdom and insight, justly known and honored as a Magi. Jainism has some similarity to the broader belief in Hinduism which he practices as totally nonviolent and benevolent. He together with his daughter Daya serve as hosts for the meetings of the Panel and as "Coordinator", selecting logic flow for the Panels discussions per request from Dr. Why.

3. Professor Ahab Singh. He is Middle Eastern Indian. However, he is of mixed ethnicity and is proudly Muslim. Dr. Singh is Full Professor of Astrophysics, Delhi University. He is a-political, devoted singularly to the pursuit of clarity regarding space-time a subject that Professor Jordyn recognizes the Panel will need cover. Dr. Singh is one of the many arising advocates of and devoted to understanding quantum mechanics as it relates to the infinite Universe. His Panel Position is "Space Technology Advisor".

4. Dr. Timothy J. Bean. Dr. Bean, holds a Ph.D. in Biochemistry with emphasis in Biophysics. He is a post-doctoral student in Dr. Jordyn's Laboratory in charge of the Biomaterials-BIO+ project, that is, synthetic cells being created to help fight severe injuries. He is a devout environmentalist and frequently joins in the gatherings of these groups who are objecting to all the thoughtless environmental damage, and believes in the threat of global warming. Tim's father is English. His mother is from Bosnia and was an expatriated Jew, although he was raised Jewish, his father is Church of England, and so he considers himself "Seeking". His Panel position… "Earth History and Future Advisor".

5. Dr. Pi Su chien Hsu. Dr. Hsu holds dual Ph.D.'s In Physics and Mathematics. She has taken the anglicized version of her name as Pillory. Her

doctorates concerned challenges to the Einstein's supposition of the constant speed of light in time's conjunction with space. Pi is the nick name she genuinely accepts it being of course the same as that famous one for the product of the ratio of the circumference of a circle divided by the diameter. Pi's family are followers of Confucius, though Pi holds no faith or dogmatic philosophy. She is rather certainly atheist and committed to seeking astrophysical truth. Her Panel position… 'Physics Proposals Advisor".

6. Master Chief, James V. Skellan. James is nicknamed the Hawk, because of a face injury suffered in his Navy Service as an EOD or explosive demolition expert. The Hawk is retired Navy Master Chief, with extensive experience disarming explosive devices almost everywhere in the world. He has made it his personal mission as he traveled to learn about the world's faiths, their successes and failures. Both he and the Professor have been schooled in the 50 principles for centering the mind, a fundamental schooling for persons who are devoting their lives to Future Navigation, i.e. as the Professor he is committed to doing what he can in his area of expertise to insuring the survival of the world's future children. Skellan is extraordinarily clear thinking. His Panel Position…"Investigator Critic".

7. Chandler N. Caldwell, M.S. Chandler is an Architectural Technologist, being educated, and holding an M.S degree in Mechanical Engineering. His wife is Jane Caldwell, the technical recorder in the Professors Laboratory. He joins the panel through deep interest in the future though he holds a critical ability as one who understands issues concerning structure and is also an expert in computing, electrical conductivity and related. His Panel Position…. "Adviser in Topological Matters".

8. Dr. Jehan Nirupuma. Dr. "Jehan' is a Professor of Medicine, who is responsible for life perspective teaching in her University. She is Pakistani by birth, but was raised in India as an orphan stemming from a terrorist attack during her student days. Dr. Jehan did a search in Africa for the "Teacher of Tolerance", where she was once again under terrorist threat as prisoner in a Wahhabi Enclave. She is Hindu. She wrote the "Declaration of Light"….And receiving the teachings of the visionary See-ela has in turn taught those to the Professor and Skellan, i.e. Dr. Jehan is a pivotal educator in Future Navigation….Role on Panel…"Future insight".

9. Jane L. Caldwell, M.S. This is myself, the recorder, the one who has written this Panel Profile. I am secretary in the Professors laboratory. I am mother of great children 3 who are now in teen-age. I am a catholic in faith. I

have a M.S in forensic science, though I have found my role in the laboratory as technical recorder one I truly love.

10. Angelei Skellan. Angelei as Skellan traveled became an expert, the most informed of all in panel on faiths and philosophies around the world. Her Panel role…."Faiths Advisor".

This panel to a member felt that it was time for someone to really look into that age old idea that we each have a "Forever".

They realize that their group is not one deep in experts for such a major matter, but they feel it is appropriate that a group-all who will learn as they go-might be the best, most unbiased to begin the process.

The panel recognized in advance that their inquiries and decisions would be subject to review and criticism, and to a member were of hope that the effort would stimulate other panels in future!

CHAPTER 2. TIME'S IMPRESSIONS

SEEKERS IN INDIA

Group identified, and united, the "Forever Panel' was off to India. The Professor himself classified "his panel" as diverse (eclectic) but that he thought that was indeed appropriate and they were of strong investigative ability, with a full range of faiths and ability to inquire deeply in matters scientific delving into "Forever".

The destination for the retreat was to be the city of Jaisalmer. Angelei prepared an overview of the retreat venue for the group.

"Jaisalmer is in the Jaisalmer District, a district of Rajasthan state in western India. The city is where a great many Jain have settled, in particular Samyak, to be the panels coordinator. He is certainly one of the most thorough world historians there are.

Jaisalmer boasts some of the oldest libraries in India which contain the rarest of the manuscripts and artifacts of history and of Jain tradition. The Jain themselves are among the most educated people in the world, in most areas of endeavor. They are of course completely vegan, and vow to take no life whatsoever.

There are many pilgrimage centers around Jaisalmer included among the many are Lodarva (Lodhruva), Amarsagar, Brahmsar and Pokharan.

The Jaisalmer District lies in the Thar Desert, which straddles the border of India and Pakistan.

It is bounded on the northeast by Bikaner District, on the east by Jodhpur District, on the south by Barmer District, and on north east and west by Pakistan and Iraq.

Jaisalmer is highly sandy, forming a part of the "Great Indian Desert". The general aspect of the area is that of an interminable sea of sand hills, of all shapes and sizes, some rising to a height of 150 ft.

Those in the west are covered with logs and bushes, those in the east with tufts of long grass. Water is scarce, and generally brackish; the average depth of the wells is said to be about 250 ft. There are no perennial streams, and only one small river, the Kakni, which, after flowing a distance of 28 miles spreads over a large surface of flat ground, and forms a lake Orjhil called the Bhuj-Jhil. The climate dry but healthy.

Throughout Jaisalmer only rain crops, such as bajra, joar, motif, til, etc., are grown; spring crops of wheat, barley, etc., are very rare. Owing to the scant rainfall, irrigation is almost unknown.

In June the average temperature is around 39 degrees Celsius.

The city is though between the desert and sea so there is a gentle breeze. However, because this is a desert formed place the humidity is low so the heat effect is not as uncomfortable as in hot humid places, for example like Kansas, U.S.A. in the summer.

Jaisalmer is the largest foreign tourist attraction district in the Rajasthan. Per year about 276,887 tourists visit the district, out of which about 100,000 tourist are foreigners.

It is a truly historic magic place, having and almost spiritual feel.

Every year there is a "Desert Festival" celebrated for tourists, which we will not see. Hospitality is widely extended a practice of the peace loving Jain people."

A major tourist attraction in Jaisalmer is Jaisalmer Fort and inside the fort are a number of beautiful Jain Temples and a Royal Palace.

Angelei's introduction extended well beyond this making the thought of the trip comfortable and exciting for all in the Panel.

The group now a cemented one, like a loving family set in very careful preparations quite compatible with their scientific objective.

Besides the necessaries, they included in their investigation packs, computers (mostly tablets), Secure Digital cards, mini printers, sets of books and pamphlets, fresh blank journals, medical supplies, and publications each assigned to the proper person as custodian, everything well selected for their needs being mortal to inquiries on philosophy to the various excerpts from text books toward understanding space time. And each was assigned to ask certain necessary questions, and each had assignments to review facts in relevant areas. All of this was agreed in several meetings before departure.

Although it was necessary that they traveled somewhat separated due to schedules and needs to secure this or that at home, they arrived in Jalalabad almost at the same time. Daniel flew in and used a rental car, having a long dusty confused trip, and the Hawk also flying in, hopped a train, and after leaving his jammed in new Indian friends, walked the last to the town. The others rode, that should say hopped along, jammed in a bus.

So, looking at each other with some surprise, they met on the road to Samyak's and walked along together or some in the Professors rental car, discussing again their purpose in being there. Hawk of course had the additional mission of seeing again Daya, Gabriel's loving friend and companion while he was staying with Samyak

After all gathered in the little Jain home, and introductions were made, they sat around on the incredibly bright colored carpet in the front larger room, as Daniel gave an overview of their purpose in the visit. This was over tea, served graciously by Daya.

We know of your wise perspectives Samyak, and hope you will join, perhaps guide us in our mission. As you know Skellan, and I and for that matter all here visiting consider our lives devoted to Future Navigation, that is where we can with what we have available, focus on the future, guiding so as to insure that the forth coming generations have a chance to mature into even wiser humans.

For each here though, curious events have made us reflect on that future. In part we are concerned that something we may do may alter it in such a way as to cause harm, and that harm would not have a chance to be removed, as life cannot be, as it were, recycled, there being no retune within "Forever "at least that is a possibility, that we hope to have rejected. And of course, we hope future humans will learn it all, but as Navigators we should like to be able to provide them with at least a rough map.

Pi then, without hesitation or even introduction to herself or topic, took up the discussion and reviewed some of her up front concerns. Shouldn't we know of Reincarnation and that "Reappearing Brain"? Shouldn't we know the impact of Einstein's Space-time on our concerns? Samyak, seemed not at all surprised with the magnanimous intentions of this group. However, he indicated that he could only be as each one would be in the group an equal adviser, and provided his natural perspective, based upon his Jain mantra which he thought he should address.

Here are some that the panel noted with great respect as they reflect a since of fairness; "purity of right faith, reverence, observance of vows without transgressions, ceaseless pursuit of knowledge, perpetual respect of the cycle of existence, giving gifts (charity), practicing austerities according to one's capacity, removal of obstacles that threaten the equanimity of ascetics, serving the meritorious by warding off evil or suffering, devotion to the scriptures, practice of the six essential daily duties, extending the teachings of the omniscient, and fervent affection for one's brethren".

After a detailed review of the Jain pursuit of wisdom, and the three right guides, his deep belief in harmlessness to all living things, he laid out what he considered to be what should be the essential first understandings. In this he began working in the role of "Coordinator".

Our search certainly must deal with history, that is the thinking on the subject from the past, and of course, the more modern views of Physicists and Thinkers searching for a "Unified Theory".

"Skellan" in anticipation of the visit you promised, I have put together an agenda, rather items that would be wise to consider.

I propose we discuss each and someone takes notes reviewed by all. Here is the list that should get you some answers in you quest.

This list was in copies for all and was handed out by Daya. It seemed very complete, the comment by Tim that it was well considered was agreed by all when Daniel canvassed the Panel.

Questions To Be Considered To View Forever
1.   What is Time?
2.   What is Infinity?
3.   What does monotheism propose?
4.   What do philosophical credence's propose?
5.   What do the proponents of reincarnation believe?
6.   What is Einstein's belief about afterlife?
7.   What is the Boltzmann Brain (Fractal Universe?)
8.   What is our realm, the Cosmos (Big Bang?)
9.   What is General Relativity and Space-time?
10. What are Einstein Mistakes?
11. What is Space Curvature?
12. What is this newer proposal, i.e., the Mobius Forever?
13. What are Dark Holes and their Importance?
14. What is Gravity?
15.   What is Boundedness?
16. What is the importance of Geometry?
17. What is the possible Topography?
18. What are Planks?
19. What is Quantum Control?
20. Do you (all) see a "Forever?"

The list was composed of some 20 items, taking the panel from existing faith ideas into Einstein's theories and on through the most modern thinking about "Forever" its existence, what people believe and how it may be impacted by uncertainty principles and so on.

So…I…believe you may first want to have an understanding of Time, what is it? And you also may need to investigate what is infinity.

Before he could proceed though, Pi the anxious physicist set in…Your holiness (not bothering to consider the appropriateness of the title) should not this have preface about Einstein's Theory? That is all, i.e. everything occurs in "a kind of locked time", i.e. Space-time.

Yes, child, perhaps that could be. A bit later, but please remember the matters first up in your concerns relate to time and infinity. And we do not want to bias the process ahead of careful consideration. If one wants to know about "Forever", then one must know that "Forever" (he put it in personal terms) has worries, things that need to be upfront. Two central concepts are "Time" and ""Infinity". That "locked" idea of time, you just described must be perplexing and in question, do all thinkers agree. So let's look first into "Time".

Skellan put in here, Oh, Yes! My son studied, the past and present part of that, looking for a continuous protective guardian for all of us, and found no such existed, either in government or religion, i.e. over all history there was or is not a trustworthy protector of humanity against "inhumanity" the killing of innocent people.

So, time is that backdrop, understanding time surely will help!

Before proceeding, the Professor enthused by the proposed pursuit, reminded Jane that it would be necessary with each discussion to do a full "Technical Record", distribute that for consensus and file that document under signature with the appropriate paper that was reviewed.

Each panel member was encouraged to organize and collate their papers and reports, then prepare to discuss the ones to be primary in the retreat. Each member was encouraged to rationalize their selection for discussion.

Jane of course was already taking notes against a recorder, and calmly agreed to do her best.

The Professor and Jane further agreed that in her typed out reports, she would put the comments of panel members in italic and those relating to or in substance the articles used in discussions put in regular type.

She agreed to put into the discussions the names of persons outside of the panel who were substantially those whose opinions were being considered.

The panel was advised that due to "Publish or Perish" in Universities there would be some "bleed over" on authorship, but to try to do their best in naming responsible parties.

So it was, before beginning the meetings, to insure protocol Jane passed an instructive note to all members of the panel.........

Dear Panel Members: "I will do my utmost to bring before you accurate minutes and final reports after your discussions. The following will be the format.

1.   All our own comments will be in italic.
2.   The words of the main authors of articles/sources after you have named them - will be in text, no italic.
3.   However, other persons cited within the main authors articles, will be noted by quote signs around their statements, but also in text.
4.   There will be associated with each report a list of the articles/sources you have collected filed in our computer system.
5.   Each formal session after it is completed will be labeled by date and time, signed off by me and filled a.) On my computer, b.) On thumb drive, and c.) Copied by e-mail to the lab and University computers. All these records will be given review by the Chairman.

While this will at first seem laborious, it is essential toward respecting the seriousness of the agenda, and all should soon adjust.

We plan for our meeting reports to eventually be published. The Professor would like them to be compiled in a book. Consequently, as we proceed and your discussions concerning the research in various areas are recorded in our reports, we will use the process known as "Documented Essay". Research papers of this type are writings in which there are incorporated the facts, opinions, and arguments which are reproduced exactly from the writings of authorities in a particular field. So as you proceed be sure to cite the author and such other reference information available as you read the papers in your presentations. In so far as possible we will follow the APA style for direct text inclusion in all our reports and publications generated from this "India Retreat".

Thank You, Jane Caldwell, Technical Recorder

FOREVER'S WORRIES (PANEL ANALYSIS BEGINS)

Forever Probe, Document 1,
June 5, a.m., first session

As planned, the discussion was to center on "Time", its meaning. It was presented by Samyak, against an article by one Dr. Tam Hunt.

What is Time? Samyak began...For this purpose, let us not ride on the "common train". Allow me to present comments from an article by Dr.Tam Hunt, in which he brought forward the thinking of the physicists Dr. Lee Smolin. I believe this has clarity and applies adequately.

And so Samyak does, handing out excerpts from the article as he sits cross legged on the plush carpet, pillow on each side, notes on a pillow in front of him, preparing to move forward.

Typical of all the probes to follow the presentation is recorded and I, Jane, will put it into report as a "Documented Essay"[1]. I am very practiced in doing this from my experience in getting such documents perfect and filed with their references.

Samyak then relayed to us as follows……."Here are Dr.Hunt's beginning comments... To us humans, time is like water to a fish. We're so immersed in it that it's extremely difficult to even think about except as the entirety of our lived experience. And yet there has been a concerted effort over the last few hundred years to demonstrate that the lived experience of time is ultimately an illusion!"

Hunt continues, when we get down to brass tacks there seem to be only two things we know with certainty.

1. That there is consciousness, here, now; and
2. That the contents of consciousness change.

We call this process of change "Time."

Everything other than these two basic features of reality, consciousness and change is, literally, inferred, by each of us as we go through our lives moment to moment.

So how can it be that the majority of physicists today believe that time is an illusion?

Samyak enters with...This will be of great concern to us, our agenda as our probe unfolds. And Hunt, says it is a good story and Dr. Smolin's book, Time Reborn, delves into this story in detail.

Smolin is a recognized American theoretical physicist, a researcher and founder at the "Perimeter Institute for Theoretical Physics", in Waterloo, Canada. So let me continue with Hunt's article, he says…

Smolin's book is certainly full of big ideas, expressed clearly and compassionately. Smolin truly wants to understand – and to help you, the interested reader, to also understand – the big questions in physics today. And, ultimately, physics is not just for physicists. Physics is, when we get down to it, about the nature of reality and our place in it.

Samyak comments…Dr. Hunt, it turns out had written previously, as a philosopher of science, about his concerns with the common view, to state it directly…that time is an illusion, and his objections to Einstein's relativity theory. He says, Smolin is politic about it in his book, but he's also suggesting that the prevailing views about the nature of time and relativity theory need some correction! Quoting Smolin…

"Why should we care about time anyway? Do different theories of time really impact our lives that much?"

"How we think about the future and the past determines everything about how we think about our situation as human beings

Are freedom, agency, will, discovery, invention, surprise, genuine? If time is an illusion so are they, and hence so are many of the human qualities we cherish."

Tim commented here and, yes, that does make up our real lives! Then, Skellan had a comment, my son Gabriel, spent months with you Samyak, trying to find the Guardian for people over time, and found none, but his review certainly made the reality of life and death due to inhumanity, perfectly clear.

And Daniel entered with…Our teacher, the Vistavien would be quite terse about this, noting the silliness of philosophies that purport illusion, when we in fact feel and made it clear that humans must leave such silliness as they alone can know the answers, but must survive the future to learn, i.e. as real living- feeling but ever mind matured creatures. Today worldwide, that is in our present, there is time and time again evidence that we have lost our sense of humanity, of the suffering of others!

Samyak being the 'Chair of the Day' held up hands nodding yes much appreciated and it gives us a sense of footing, well that is noted.

As we will discuss in detail this illusion idea stems from Einstein who famously stated that the distinction between past, present, and future is a "stubbornly persistent illusion." We of course, must step back and consider what he really meant by that.

But the article continues to argue on that, as Hunt says… This illusion idea is based on what Einstein called "Space-time". In that view it is just that, virtually all the time that matters.

Think in way that it overrides, overwhelms all the others which in effect are minute. So, why is it, do you think, that the idea of time being an illusion has such appeal among physicists and regular people alike?

Pi chimed in, is see, all other times are overwhelmed by the forces in space time! I do think that is the meaning of that statement…you know the man could easily have not used "illusion" - but said it as I just did. In fact that persistence is what is in our mind, that the past is past. But Einstein says it is there a part of the whole. To which Tim said, yes Pi I think you have it!

Yes, Samyak said, I think that was prominent in mind as Hunt continued to highlight.

Time is, as Dr. Smolin writes, one of the most real things we know. We can't, as conscious beings, exist except to exist in time, and everything about our existence suggests that time is real. And yet the idea that time is ultimately an illusion is pervasive.

It is a good question to which one part of the answer is the very common tendency to look down on what is changeable and temporary and admire those things we imagine are timeless!

To put it simply and directly, some of us have a great desire to transcend the time-bound realm, which we experience directly, for fantasies of eternal beauty and truth. *(I.e. Time said…we want time to be eternal, fixed, to be safe, that is for us to last forever.)*

So, how much should the human experience of time factor into our physics?

Smolin's argument is simply that the experience we have of time flowing from moment into moment is not an illusion but one of the deepest clues we have as to the nature of reality!

Many of our physical laws are said to be "time-reversible" because the equations work equally well when run forwards or backwards.

Unfortunately, Smolin points this out, "Many people consider these equations and believe something like: Look, time is reversible! Time is an illusion and there is no free will.

But, quite the contrary, this ignores of course that the universe we live in is by current thinking, entirely unidirectional. We proceed from the present into the future. We remember the past. There is nothing in our universe that proceeds from the present into the past, as far as we know!

So these equations, it seems, are wrong in their time-reversibility because they don't fully describe the world we live in.

Pi said here, what is that problem anyway, don't all equations have a right and left side. Seems that is function of mathematics, not time!

Samyak agreed…seems a telling point Dr. Pi. And Hunt notes further defense…

…Why do we so commonly mistake incomplete models of reality for reality itself?

Smolin proposes…"That the time-reversible laws whose action we observe are approximations and that there are more fundamental laws that are time-irreversible."

Smolin further notes…"That this seems a better explanation for the arrows of time than the standard one, which has to propose that the universe began in a highly improbable initial state."

"A key factor in the commonly held view of time today that time is an illusion, is the notion that the speed of light is absolute, a postulate of Einstein's special theory of relativity[1]."

"The previously held view was that space and time are absolute, but Einstein flipped these assumptions around, making the speed of light universal for all observers - no matter what their motion is in relation to the speed of light."
"This flipping of assumptions requires that[1] time and space become malleable because the speed of light is, of course, and by definition, distance (space) divided by time."

"However, setting aside any other debates about relativity theory for the moment, why would the speed of light be absolute? No other speeds are absolute, that is, all other speeds do indeed change in relation to the speed of the observer, so it's always seemed a rather strange notion to me."

"It is noted, however, that Einstein's [1] special relativity works extremely well and the postulate of the invariance or universality of the speed of light is extremely well-tested. It might be wrong in the end but it is an extremely good approximation to reality."

As a noteworthy related aspect Smolin's thoughts are full of delicious iconoclasm, argued sincerely and compassionately.

----

1. Einstein's theories on space-time, the theory of relativity, were proposed from his mind, not by experiment in the early 1900s. These are detailed in a later section of this book. They are among those several proposals that must be considered when probing into forever.

Samyak entered on this... by way of guiding us Hunt relayed Smolin's cautions on taking all physics postulates as law.

Smolin argues essentially, that much of modern physics has been waylaid by bad ideas and theories! I know that it's always hard to criticize relativity theory and to be simultaneously taken seriously as a physicist or a philosopher.

And yet, actually as discussion continues, he does tackle this sacred cow, and is taken very seriously as a physicist, sensing that colleagues are perhaps more ready now than in years past for new ideas...ones that go well beyond-even contradict special and general relativity!

Unquestionably his proposals and equations have had tremendous impact on human existence. His equations leading ultimately to the relation between mass and energy $E=mc^2$ is, of course, among the most important ones in physics, practical applications (nuclear fission as example), and understanding of our universe that exist.

 He offers regarding relativity theory several arguments embracing the experimental success of Einstein's special and general theories of relativity. He describe shape dynamics, which is a new way of reconciling the existence of a preferred time that is perceptible at the scale of the universe as a whole, with the validity of the principle of relativity on smaller scales.

Samyak noted, this idea of "Shape Dynamics" will become very important to you interested the "Forever", relativity or not.

Further is argued, the particular physical laws we know are likely to be a consequence of "cosmological natural selection," which results from black holes creating new universes, with slightly different laws than the laws in the universe that contains the progenitor black hole.

Pi entered here, yes, the mystery of "Black Holes" fascinates many in my field, and one cannot wonder if they serve as vacuum cleaners sucking in space and creating new Universes. What really dictates that ours, our universe is the only one... and of course that sets in motion new questions concerning Time!

Then Samyak continued to address the article at hand. ...The author continues to relate Smolin's words... This theory has a number of advantages, which you describe in your new book, particularly compared to alternative theories. However, at a basic level, why would new universes be formed through black holes?

Coordinator Samyak "General relativity predicts that time ends inside black holes because the gravitational collapse squeezes matter to infinite density chooses to have that addressed later in the meetings to clarify first certain basic ideas.

However, it has long been hypothesized that quantum effects[1] prevent this from happening, causing a "bounce" where the matter stops contracting and starts expanding."

"This creates a new expanding region of the universe that cannot be seen from outside the black hole. This can be called a new universe. This scenario has a lot of support from the study of mathematical models of quantum effects[1]in the interiors of black holes."

And why would each new universe's laws change a little, after being born from a black hole? "Because I can make that hypothesis without contradicting anything that is known and its implications are interesting."

Smolin argues that Leibniz's "principle of sufficient reason" should be a key criterion for good theories.

"This principle states that everything that is real must have some reason behind it, and thus some equivalent in our theories."

But isn't it rather hard to pin down what qualifies as a "reason"? To be a bit flip, we could argue that the moon is whitish gray because it's made of cottage cheese, and this is a reason - but it's just a really bad reason. How do we use this principle in a way that has teeth?

"Leibniz means reason in the sense of an explanation for why the universe has one feature when it might have had a different feature."

"The classic case is why the universe was not created ten meters to the right or ten minutes earlier. Since nothing in the actual universe would be changed in these scenarios Leibniz concludes there can be no meaning to absolute position or time!"

The panel all spoke favorably on this as it was more than a scientific matter, they felt one of common sense and related to us Humans.

"It was Hendrik Lorentz, a mentor to Einstein, who developed the "Lorentz transformations," the mathematics behind both Einstein's special relativity and Lorentz's own theory of relativity."

"Lorentz's theory---while it is considered to be empirically indistinguishable from special relativity, is not widely accepted because it relies on a version of absolute time and space." However, shape dynamics, a theory that you discuss

----

1. The use of "Quantum effects" appears a number of times as the Panel reviews various articles. This involves a chemistry and physics which developed just after Einstein's proposals, and it is one effecting them very substantially.

favorably, seems to reinterpret general relativity in a way that mirrors Lorentz's theory of relativity in that it takes time as fundamental. Can shape dynamics be viewed as a generalization of Lorentzian relativity?

"No, because the preferred time in shape dynamics is not absolute, it is determined dynamically as a result of the distribution of matter and fields in the universe."

"The general view in the philosophy of science is that new theories that gain acceptance do so not by replacing but by going beyond the old paradigm--- Einstein's general relativity (GR), for example, doesn't falsify Newtonian gravity, it goes beyond Newton by showing that Newton's gravitational theory is a limiting case of Einstein's GR."

"However, sometimes theories are simply replaced by new ones because there are, of course, an infinite number of possible theories for explaining any given set of data and sometimes new theories are simply better than old theories at explaining the data.
For example, Copernicus's heliocentric view of the solar system has entirely replaced Ptolemy's geocentric epicycle view because, even though Ptolemy's model was highly accurate in terms of explaining the data, it makes far more sense to suggest, as Copernicus did, that the Sun is in fact the center of the solar system, for a variety of reasons."

The Professor commented here, that there is a very sound practice of good science that with every hypothesis, one must seek alternated hypothesis, and exhaustively in order to ascertain the voracity of the original hypothesis.

*Samyak, indicated that we must of course honor that and the Panel will face such as we move on…however to return to the article the author says…*You criticize General Relativity in some ways in your book, but you also suggest that much of the theory has merit. Could it be, however, that it's in need of replacement whole cloth, even though it makes many correct predictions, like Ptolemy's view of the solar system?

I hate to pick on Einstein because he was in so many ways a great man: a great physicist, a great humanitarian, and all around a great human being.

But, I agree with one of your key points in your book – that Einstein's view that time is ultimately an illusion is not only wrong but very damagingly wrong, because of the consequences that flow necessarily from the view that time is an illusion: Free will is an illusion and, arguably, human consciousness becomes an illusion, because we seem to have no way to reconcile the view that time is an illusion with the obvious flow of time that is the foundation of human consciousness.

So let me pick a bit more on Einstein and ask you this: You write that Einstein showed that simultaneity is relative. But the conclusion of the relativity of simultaneity flows necessarily from Einstein's postulates (that the speed of light is absolute and that the laws of nature are relative). So he didn't really show that simultaneity was relative - he assumed it. What do I have wrong here?

"The relativity of simultaneity is a consequence of the two postulates that Einstein proposed and so it is deduced from the postulates. The postulates and their consequences are then checked experimentally and, so far, they hold remarkably well."

Chandler entered with…that needs to be checked, so far has anyone found that information? Pi said it's out there for sure, but we need to get into Einstein's relativity in more detail. But, Samyak are we getting too far out of Time consideration? Samyak replied, that is true, however, the "soundness" in a scientific investigation is always a matter to critique thoroughly in considerations such as yours. There is the need to always question, so let us look at the little bit left in the paper… Smolin is asked about "timeless perfect reality".

You argue against Platonism, the notion that our reality is a corrupted reflection of a timeless perfect reality, and I tend to agree. Yet you also state or imply frequently that laws "guide" physical outcomes. This seems to me to be reverting back to Platonism. Aren't laws better viewed as human creations based on observed behaviors in the universe around us? And behaviors are simply built in to the constituents of our universe.

*Smolin answered….*Please let's be careful here. When we human beings hypothesize that a law of nature holds – even temporarily or situationally–we are creating an idea, but we are also making a hypothesis about how nature behaves, whose truth or usefulness has nothing to do with what we know or believe.

And with this the Professor restated the requirements of scientific research. It is best to think of investigation as a black box, opening it provides another black box and so on, one is always reaching for a truth, better a more stable explanation.

Samyak then said and so in this article the two reach even father…and that does relate to us and Time.

*Thus, the inquiry continues with….*You (Hunt, talking to Smolin) venture far beyond physics in your Epilogue, including some musings on the nature of consciousness and Metalaw[1].

You discuss as I remember, David Chalmers favorably, a well-known panpsychist[1].This is the view that all matter has some associated mind/subjectivity and vice versa.

From Smolin there was… "The problem of consciousness is an aspect of the question of what the world really is. We don't know what a rock really is, or an atom, or an electron. We can only observe how they interact with other things and thereby describe their relational properties. Perhaps everything has external and internal aspects. The external properties are those that science can capture and describe---through interactions, in terms of relationships. The internal aspect is the intrinsic essence; it is the reality that is not expressible in the language of interactions and relations. Consciousness, whatever it is, is an aspect of the intrinsic essence of brains.

Last, you write that an entirely new approach to physics is needed, and that mathematics needs to be demoted a little in favor of more conceptual approaches to physics… *(This set Pi to a defensive, Oh-sure attack the means!)*

Yes, I do discuss alternative approaches to physics along the lines of the principles I propose. Because I am a scientist they are developed as explorations of models and hypotheses.

Those discussed in the book include cosmological natural selection, the principle of precedence, and the real ensemble interpretation of quantum theories, as well as the responses to the metalaws dilemma [1] describe, including the idea of the universality of those metalaws and the merging of the concept of state and law. All of these have been the subject of scientific papers which are referenced in the notes.

With that review, Samyak paused and looked over at us-his audience. Then with firm voice he said…"As we progress you may tend to feel lost in the postulations of physicists. But this review reminds us of two things, first all propositions we encounter, are not necessarily laws, but mostly hypotheses, and second Time is not necessarily owned only by space, but also that within it.

I propose that you add to that something we will call, with resolution, "Human Time"!

1.<u>Metalaw</u> is a concept of space law closely related to the scientific search for Extraterrestrial Intelligence and the categorical imperative: "Act only according to that maxim whereby you can at the same time will that it should become a universal law". This is a forerunner of the Metalaw, because if we wish to detect the intelligent signals from the Universe, we have to act in a similar manner, that is, we must also transmit intelligent signals into the Universe! <u>Panpsychism.</u> In philosophy, panpsychism is the view that consciousness, mind or soul (psyche) is a universal and primordial feature of all things. Panpsychist see themselves as minds in a world of minds. During the 19th century, panpsychism was the default theory in philosophy of mind, but it saw a decline during the middle years of the 20th century with the rise of logical positivism. The recent interest in the very hard problem of consciousness has once again made panpsychism a widespread theory.

That is a time of reality! It is a time of the many millions of years of evolution. It has a reference point as species have moved into more and more brain power, which is consciousness - that is Mind - whose reference in turn is the instantaneously awakened communication between DNA base pairs.

These are real atomic structures which bear the mass-energy equivalent that the physicists require. The chemicals therein are shared in places in space.

You seek answer to the question "Is there a Forever". That must, of course, be answered in reference to your Time's past, present and future. So it is essential that the matter of time forward... be resolved...but dare to recognize error in Einstein's theories! (Pi raised her arm in a fist pump-then apologized.)

`````````````````````````````````````````````````````````````````

*This first discourse was concluded by comments from Dr. Why...Samyak thank you for the presentation, and that to Drs. Hunt and Smolin, this being an article on time and physics relayed in April 2013.*

*It helps us to begin our inquiry. We must keep in front of us, that Einstein began his concern working with railroad clocks, then armed with the equations of physics he began to see (in his mind, no experiment but through thought) the functions of "Space-time").*

*That is— simply-- it was his Human Mind, so the Human Mind comes first, it is all in the end that matters in time, "Human Time" it is that mind that can if surviving, know in the end the reality of space-time!*

*Samyak then canvassed the group. Except for Pi there was agreement on the Professor's conclusion. Tim expressed "I have a whole new way of looking at time, now much more critical".*

*Pi said to conclude the experience, "We need to focus on that idea of persistence. I think of it now as he meant it as a function of our mentality, that is Human Time, of course exists in the vastness of space time, but it is not perhaps in past and present an after the fact isolatable entity. The future, however, is to me one time component that may be recoverable.*

*There was then a break invited by Daya. "Let's pause and contemplate, giving opportunity for each one here"... Then she provided the most delicious tea, a Jain one. During this Samyak called this meeting to a close, indicating he would think a summary of opinion on this should be coupled with the next topic.*

**Forever Probe, Document 1**
 **As recorded, and filed, June 5, a.m.**
**Respectfully,**
`````````````````````````````````````````````````````````````````

Jane Caldwell, Technical Recorder

NOTE: This, following, is a non-agenda record!

After the lengthy discourse on time and after tea---Samyak took our little party on a tour of the Jain's town. All were impressed with the many faith's houses of worship of various denominations, and the true unbiased attitude of the Jain citizens.

As the days of discussion and discovery moved on panel members, indeed, took frequent trips into town. The panel visitors discovered Jaisalmer streets are more than mere paths - they are public spaces too. They discovered, as I did, Jaisalmer is a compact network of streets each of just a right and comfortable length. The streets are filled with beautiful architecture (making Chandler often suck in his breath in awe.) Many of the buildings have ancient and have patterned curved walls, with ancient motifs. With fairly high buildings and width of streets rarely more than three meters, one can move around the town in cool shade. There is very little and limited vehicular traffic.

It will be wrong to call the growth of the city as organic as may be the case with many other Indian cities. Location of certain squares in very strategic places and a very well developed and definite order of streets and buildings make Jaisalmer a city well organized and planned.

Chandler was totally fascinated with the city and its residences. Here are his notes. "Platforms (otla) with entry steps are the key transition elements evoking the extension some houses hold for activities. Here, however, womenfolk are more restrained and these platforms are used more by the children and the older men. In tune with the need for privacy for women, facades are characterized by small openings often in the form of jharokhas, elements essentially generated by social customs of allowing women to peep out without being seen. Thus women are able to 'participate' in the outside activities and yet maintain their privacy. Besides, the streets are used by children to play and by adults to socialize. Jaisalmer being essentially a pedestrian town, people know one another and there is little evidence of social anonymity."

There are on buildings beautiful structures called Haveli's either built by rich merchants and trader's or people high up in the royal hierarchy of Jaisalmer. Random stone masonry is finished with mud plaster and major elements like doors and windows which are finished with a white border, typical of the surrounding rural areas. Even in the interior, the clay and the mirror work has a rural character. Yet there is a sense of design, continuity and resemblance in terms of the house form, and these houses are well integrated with the urban fabric of Jaisalmer."

"A reason for Jaisalmer's success in coping with the heat is the design of the havelis (palaces). The craftsmen who built the havelis used a system of modular construction, cutting the yellow sand stone into standardized columns, beams, wall panels and floor slabs that could be arranged in endless permutation and combinations to give each haveli both a unique character and kinship with its neighbors. However, like most stones, sand stone is a good insulator and a poor conductor. It reflects most of the sunlight, heats up slowly and allows little of that heat to pass through. At night, when the temperature drops the stone radiates the heat stored during the day. An important feature of the buildings in Jaisalmer is their porosity, a haveli is full of holes. The holes are different in size, from courtyards and shafts to slots and cavities to finely carved stone jalis, and all this allows passage for cross ventilation."

"The net effect is homes cool in day and warm at night with comfortable breezes" For me, Chandler said, "this was a lesson in how good human planning and history can be."

Returning to our new temporary "home", *Samyak said, we should pursue space alternatives, yes, but this is of course connected to the greatest concept of time, "Infinity". Is it directional, how could it be... does it exist...etc.? Then he said, as we go into it...keep track...what is said ....what seems to have proof, what is just proposed!*

Forever Probe, Document 2, June 6, a.m.

This meeting took place the day after the discussion on time. We rested the evening of June 5, Daya finding us all a place to sleep comfortably in her father's lovely little home, and all slept well with the peaceful desert breeze wafting us into deep dreamless sleep. Breakfast was Jain, delicious, and all surprised it took the life of no sentient creature to serve a healthy meal to twelve people. Then, shortly after breakfast, the discussion of infinity took place, which is the record following.
<u>What is Infinity?</u> *Samyak picked up on the discussion as follows....*

Well I hope Time is now in its "Balanced Place". Simply put from the viewpoint of reality, our reality, time is isolable within our consciousness? As it exists outside of that, or in some way enfolding it, involves postulates argued by theorist and physicists. Their current views we will shortly consider more thoroughly.

But, there is another concern for "Forever", which we will be 'worried about' in the challenges to come. I am speaking of the notion of Infinity. No matter the time reference we must think rationally about its ability to exist per definition. So my report today quotes from recent books by Timothy Gowers ET. Al. in The Princeton Companion to Mathematics with related input by Maddox and also Wallace in earlier years.

PI's eyes lit up commenting, oh yes, as a mathematics major I know of their writing. In mathematics, the infinity symbol is used more often to represent a potential infinity, rather than represent an actually infinite quantity. The infinity sign in equations is conventionally interpreted as meaning that the variable grows arbitrarily large (towards infinity), therefore recognizing its potential existence.

That is good Ms. Pi said Samyak complimenting her. So you will enter directly "If needed"!

To continue, In Western culture, Infinity means endless or immeasurable. To us, as we move toward the possibility of "Forever" it comes down to a question of Infinite versus limited or finite time! Is there a possible reality to the notion of Forever or is it just a magical, mysterious concept. Is it rather, simply a synonym for something truly existing? If so is there any evidence?

Here I will cite some wisdom from earlier philosophers. But to lead us out this is an excerpt from Wikipedia.... "To all of us, Infinity commonly inspires feelings of awe, futility and fear. The symbol for infinity-- ∞ -- is called the lemniscate... And the Greek word for infinite is apeiron meaning specifically unbounded.

To the Panel, that word unbounded is a must for us as there is to be seen the need to place space-time as bounded (meaning closed to filling) or unbounded (open, capable of total expansion).

Continuing with the handout. To the Greeks the original chaos from which the Universe formed was apeiron, or a crumpled handkerchief was apeiron. Thus, apeiron means not only infinitely large, but infinitely complex. *That will likely suffice as to Greek Philosophy, though we can site Plato's Ideas, those of Aristotle, and even progress through the number arguments in Galileo's Paradox.*

Nonetheless, Plotinus was the 1st thinker after Plato to adopt that at least God (or the One) is infinite. He states that `the One has never known measure and stands outside of number, and so is under no limit either in regard to anything external or internal; for any such determination would bring something of the dual into it. However, St. Augustine, who adapted Platonic philosophy to the Christian religion, believed not only that God was infinite, but also that God could think infinite thoughts. Nevertheless, later medieval thinkers did not go as far as Augustine and, although granting the unlimitedness of God were unwilling to grant that any of God's creatures could be infinite.

Samyak paused with this, asking if we would, indeed, consider monotheism and if so who would do that. The Professor indicated right away that it would be in the hands of Skellan's wife Angelei.

So answered, Samyak acknowledged Angelei with a tender bow and then continued…Nonetheless, to this comes the most important argument toward your inquiries. That is the notion of "Infinitesimals"! He underlined this with a sweep of his hands and continued to reference the handout…reading…

Thus, although the medieval proofs were for the most part self-contradictory, they did discover one paradox involving infinity.

Here is the exercise. Consider two circles, one twice the radius of the inner one. The circumference of the outer circle is twice as big as the inner one, then the outer circle should include a larger infinity of points than the inner circle. But, by drawing a radii we can see that each point P and Q on the inner circle correspond to exactly one point Q' and P' on the outer circle. Thus, we seem to have two infinites that are simultaneously different and paradoxically equal!

Thus, a different kind Shf arithmetic was needed. Its initial form was calculus used in the late 17th century. In order to understand motion, the space position of an object is a function of continuously changing time. But the variable, time, grows continuously (e.g. from zero to ten seconds) but is "apeiron" in the sense that it takes on arbitrary values (1, 2.5, 6, etc.) and also takes on infinitely many values in the interval.

In order to sort this all out, Calculus solves this problem through the use of "infinitesimals". *Samyak underlined this word, by repeating it several times.* For example, to calculate the velocity of an object at moment t, one measures the speed over an infinitely small time interval dt. So we realize, the quantity dt is an infinitesimal and obeys very strange rules. If dt is added to a regular number, then it can be ignored and treated like zero. On the other hand, dt is different enough from zero that it can be used in the denominator of a fraction. So is dt zero or not? Adding many infinitesimals together just gives another infinitesimal. But adding infinitely many of them gives an ordinary number.

Here, both I (Recorder) and Angelei interrupted - in effect saying this was well above our ability to understand.

This prompted Samyak to say, I apologize! Well, so was given the notion of something within infinity can still be "Infinite"! This turns out to be something called a "Transfinite"! He repeated this several times to lock it into our thinking, then proceeded to point to the handout, reading... To trace this, Georg Cantor, in the late 1800's, finally created a theory of the actual infinite which was consistent.

His point of entry to the infinite was to note it as being a mathematical problem. Cantor used trigonometric constructions to show that the set of points on a real line constitutes a higher infinity than the set of all natural numbers. One can see this intuitively when we consider the sequence of rational numbers between 0 and 1 (for example, 1/2, 1/3, 1/4, 1/101, 1/1,000,001). There are an infinite number of them, but always a gap between each value. For the real numbers on a line segment, though, from 0 to 1 there is a continuum with no gaps, i.e. a larger infinity than rational numbers.

So here is the crux of the matter Samyak pointed out as he read from the paper... In other words, by the use of mathematics, Cantor showed that there are "Degrees of Infinity"!

This fact runs counter to the naive concept of infinity---that there is only one infinity and this infinity is unattainable and not quite real. Cantor keeps this idea in this theory and calls it the "Absolute Infinity", but he allows for many intermediate levels between the finite and the Absolute Infinity. We call these stages Transfinite Numbers, numbers that are infinite, but none the less conceivable.

Hence, Samyak entered... There are various ways in which our physical world appears to be unbounded and, perhaps, infinite: sequential, spatial and endlessly subdivided i.e., microscopic.

As said, this notion of Infinity will be important to use as later the arguments on space-time as to bounded or unbounded arise. That, is infinity can be viewed logically as a sum of infinite parts, and anything within in any of those are still within infinity, 'transfinite", infinitesimal, if you will. Now back to "Human Time". Here I am quoting from the specified reference.

Human time is that time often expressed in terms of human generations, although certainly time existed before humankind and will exist even if we become extinct. If we escape extinction, then we have to admit that the number of generations of man is infinite!

So, Samyak emphasized, it is argued based on the forgoing thoughts, that Human Time can occupy its own transfinite place, since it is otherwise illogical to assume any time within "Absolute Infinity" is not itself infinite!   The paper continues with... While this goes against "common sense", it is in fact a rational idea, and not (it can be argued) incompatible with Einstein's theory of special relativity which has demonstrated that space and time are interlocked in something we now routinely call space-time.

It is space-time that is argued by Einstein and most astrophysists, that is fundamental and the passage of that time is for us an illusion.

That is, the concept vis. Einstein is past, present and future all exist together in space-time.

But, Samyak emphasized... our Human time, the point of my making the argument is an infinity of that within any "Absolute Infinity" that may be argued by anyone, upon Einstein's theory.

 In short recognize that there is possible all of your history within its own Infinity... I.e. "You're human forever". Even though qe exist in a microscopic slice of space-time we could ride throughout infinity. What is your opinion, Madam Pi? She answered forthwith, "I believe Cantor's mathematics is sound!"

The group then began discussion which was rather vigorous, but I have tried to summarize as follows.

Daniel said, *to treat the subject of Space-time, "Human Time" and their "infinity" are not addressed in the physics we see published and on the internet.*

Jehan said, *we have had "The Ancient Gods Time, God's Time, and now Space Time. These put humans subject to them, but we are the ones, probably the only ones who seek to know them, to interpret them all these "Times'. That is the notion and arguments regarding Time and Infinity, "in Forever" are too often focusing on the wrong realm.*

Angelei entered, *yes, if we survive, it will be us to control- to master. Focus should be placed on us, on our achieving our future, and we should focus on our home, our potential infinity within Space-time's, "Forever's", i.e. in reaching into it our existing past, present and future, those each perhaps a transfinite. That should be the emphasis, what the limits are and what the ways to succeed are. (There was consensus from all the group on this comment.)*

Tim said. And we should not forget that Human Time is a part of Earth Time and the incredible development of Life. Our Lab is investigating this, and whether we continue is at the crux of the matter of Forever, could we harm it for every one....So I am really concerned that we work our way to deeper understanding.

Tim continued then with his environmental worries. Jane reiterated her religious concerns, then with Pi, her physics understandings, and even Chandler, his concern about technology.

Pi then came in though---speaking rather emphatically. Let me enumerate. This she did as follows.

1. *Everything has and is taking part in Absolute Infinity.*
2. *Our Universe is part of that.*
3. *Our past is a transfinite of that in our Universe.*
4. *I argue that we can do nothing about that even if we could return, because return would give us the same result. (I am looking for mechanisms for return).*
5. *There are semantics that must be considered. Infinity includes the past and the future, thus is must be also equal to Forever.*
6. *The future is just that, i.e. ahead in infinity.*

The Professor stepped in on this. Pi thank you for that clear headed review, and Samyak for taking us down this necessary pathway. For the Panel, we have been offered clear hypothesis on time and infinity to take forward in the next part of our program.

With that the meeting ended. Adjourn was called by Samyak and that with an invitation to share a Jain pancake and tea.

Forever Probe, Document 2
Duly recorded and Filed, June 6, a.m.,
Jane Caldwell, Technical Recorder

Notes: *From Pi's comments I thought of this prompted by idea of Transfinites and passed it around, just a very crude line sketch as follows.* Infinity is Forever (holding massive cosmos Transfinites)

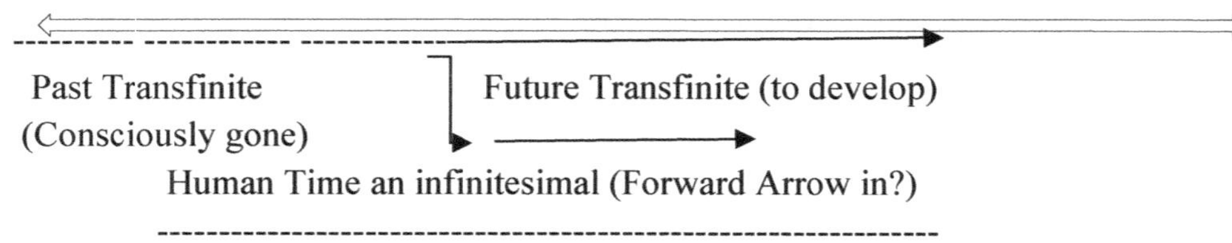

NOTE: I feel a bit weak about my little diagram, not being scientist, I know it is probably quite naive. Also, before the next meeting time (scheduled that evening) the Professor and Skellan went into town and reserved hotel rooms for everyone.

Although Samyak and Daya offered their home for the full meeting time that duration would be unknown and the two senior members of the panel felt it best to relieve their hosts of a constant crowd.

The hotel they reserved was Hotel Jeet Villa a 3-star hotel with both restaurant and business center.

It is located walking distance away and was within a 15-minute walk of Nathmalji-ki-Haveli, Bhatia Market, as well as Jaisalmer-Fort. Patwon-ki-Haveli and Gadi Sagar Tank are also within 2 mi. from the Hotel Other amenities include tour/ticket assistance.

PAST'S IDEAS

Forever Probe, Document 3, June 6, p.m.

Refreshed the group surrounded Samyak the Jain Guru---that afternoon, fresh teas in hand, and looked eagerly to him for the start.

Almost without introduction, he said, reincarnation should be considered do you not agree…as it seems a sort of being in "Forever" and of course also the worlds beliefs in the hereafter, the religious thoughts, should be brought up. I think that would be in order.

Knowing a pathway here Skellan interjected: "Angelei completed a diary record in this area. Handing out a set of papers, he continued… here in part are some extractions from that diary. Everyone reviewing these notes is put to a real challenge, agree or not agree with the beliefs.

Addressing the Chair…You know Daniel she wrote it all down and it sure sounds like it belongs next for consideration

Daniel agreed and said the matter of reincarnation… leads to ideas of hereafter I suppose. However, let's have Angelei lead it out with the Theisms, and then work toward that belief.

Skellan said, why so? Oh I see reincarnation would be more a philosophy, and that would preface the philosophies leading up to ideas about earthly "Forever".

Pi then set in, we should first treat the present major montheisisms as they are most of the world's believers, including many physicists and cosmologist and there is a point I wish to make. The group agreed and Angelei was given set up time for the next discussion!

The topic of montheisisms, then was to take place right after noon meal.

After the "lunch" again a simple Jain offering, Samyak began the meeting introducing the "Speaker". This afternoon Mrs. Skellan will review for us aspects of religious belief that we need to cover because they involve the notion of a Forever.

On that Skellan looked at Angelei with encouragement, and she immediately took the stage.

Yes, I agree, review of that is needed, but I guess I should proceed in a certain order. Skellan shared his travels with me and from his study of faiths over the years, and his relating those to me, I made a detailed study and a host of notes.

For every one of these he was close to the place of origin, and talked to those there or went to the faith church and obtained information from libraries. I also did an intensive library study. I will focus on "Monotheisms" as they, of course, relate most directly to a God and the thought of life after death, i.e. a Forever.

First is my entry on the older faiths. Skellan laid all out in an order that reflects travel through time, that is the years back in time that one is capable of seeing into. **<u>Theisms and Non-Theisms:</u>** *There are a large number of Monotheist groupings.*

The first of this is Zoroastrianism, beginning about 3000 years ago: This faith is among the first to argue for one God, to be honored and defended in the eternal battle of Good over Evil. "There is but one uncreated creator to whom all worship is ultimately to be directed."

The religion states that active participation in life through good thoughts, good words, and good deeds is necessary to ensure happiness and to keep chaos (evil) at bay.

The early history of this faith was in lands to become Islamic. The faith was once one of the world's most prominent with a Persian History, cementing the ideas of good versus evil as the operation of the world and indeed, many of the basic humanistic beliefs, and its monotheism were copied by those following. In time it faded somewhat in size because it encountered, extensively, and with cruelty, persecution by Islamic authorities.

Obviously, the foundational beliefs are good, but there is no real proposition that a forever is promised!

The next would be Judaism, beginning about 2650 years ago. This faith is also among the first believing in one God, though dating is argued. The faith is often cited as the "Abrahamic" impetus for Christianity and Islam. Judaism is associated, I believe almost everywhere, with the Ten Commandments. Within are the critical words, "Though Shalt not Murder." Massively persecuted over time, as for example the Holocaust, resulting in a reduced size of believers around the world, Judaism is even now locked in national conflict, killing on both sides, over "Holy Land Rights", versus the Islamic stance of false occupation in Israel. Joining God (that is assumed in a time forever) is one of the underlying ideas for most followers of this faith.

Following Judaism is Christianity beginning 2040 years ago. This is a monotheism that preceded Islam. The foundation is that Jesus is the son of God.

Catholics believe in the Holy Trinity; Father, Son and Holy Ghost. The notion is that God is in Heaven- a Forever.

(She said this looking at me, Jane. I simply smiled at her and signaled go on ahead dear. So she did.)

Through the gospels - as disciples communicated the activity of Jesus, there are ideas of brotherhood and kindness for humanity, reliant on the guidance of priests and pastors and as probable rewards to life after death which is to occur in heaven, guaranteed to all believers in the faith.

Christians hold that by praying and good behavior God will provide, i.e. that God is the primary recourse to problem solving. Unfortunately, the long term facts are that prelates, priests and pastors, have co-opted the faith into many sects and sometimes actions and practices contradictory, to the fundamental faith given by Jesus.

With a world-wide ministry the faith is among the world's largest and does some good through them although that is often of a nature as to secure converts.

Also, it is centrally important to bring forward that people adhering to the faith feel that they can be forgiven, have eternal life granted, and excused of abuses as "I am only human". Here though is the belief that there is an eternity, which of course comes from infinity, and that is in a place "Heaven", i.e. Forever!

Many feel that most Christians do not really practice what is preached. Child abuse happens with Catholic Priests. Christianity has found reason to do much killing, such as in the Crusades, and is in constant conflict with Islam. Right by divinity assumed - belonging to kings and lords did create terrible suffering and killing for centuries.

In democratic societies where there is by law to be separation of church and state, the faith still permeates and sometimes effects the way law is practiced.

The next is Islamism beginning about 1378 years ago: Prophet Mohamed's monotheistic core teachings respect humanity in many ways, and have many benevolent and sensible precepts and rules of life.

The principles-by oral tradition-and referenced in the Quran, dictate virtually every aspect of daily living. The young are proselytized into the faith from the beginning, and can be convinced into about all that the adults wish or command, based on a promised residence in the after-life, a great eternity.

Sadly, extremism using Islam as excuse has developed worldwide, in questionable interpretations of the faiths' principles, resulting in cowardly killing of innocent people!

The desire to return to the original teachings has produced backward philosophies that have created for the Muslim world vast populations in economic disaster, where once some of the world's great creative thinkers thrived. Honor murder of women has been an aberration of the faith, though it is nowhere in the primary teachings supported. Some Islamists are attempting to purge Islam of the extremism, though that needs to recognize inevitable resistance---as long as children are proselytized before they can see more holistically.

Pi said here, you are in a way with your report Angelei proselytizing about the limits in the faiths...we want to know about their Forever!

Angelei responded that she felt it necessary to provide some historical sense as the implant of faith in humans since the earliest times has involved faith conflicts and that would be one of the items that entry into forever would be of major concern. However, I will try not to show advocacy one way or another and apologize...

Next for consideration would be Sikhism. Proponents of Sikhism beginning about 500 years ago are Monotheists, who view themselves as "Soldiers" in defense of God and defend the rights of all who are wrongfully oppressed or persecuted irrespective of religion, color, caste or creed. Sikhs are of recent history gentle people. However, the early history of Sikhism, was fraught with wars over territory-Sikh versus Muslim, each trying for empire.

In recent history, there was politicizing of Sikhism, and some radicalism. That, however, has been largely reversed to allow the seekers of "Truth" to practice their faith. Belief in God is fundamental, but detailed descriptions of a herafter, a heaven is not common among these people.

Finally, but not comprehensivly among monotheist is Baha'ism beginning 138 years ago. This is a new monotheism that accepts all prophets without prejudice as the path leading to their beliefs. Therefore, all the good values are incorporated in their theology. That is, all the principles of the faith are benevolent. This faith has no war like attitudes, and no reason for killing, but it is severely persecuted in Islamic environments.

In some of their societies marriage with only Baha'i is recognized. Over time the core beliefs have undergone various changes but these are subtle and the main themes seem preserved. These believers as the others do look to an afterlife in a heaven.

I think that will be good enough on the topic of Monotheism! Angelei, then offered to address any questions comments.

I, Jane- indicated that there is much that is true in Angelei's report, but, I shall not ever give up my faith! To which Angelei expressed understanding. Of course, for a very great many people their faith is comforting. Our effort here is to see if there is an inroad, a deeper insight into Forever for us through these faiths, the living-now and in the future . It is not to impugn any belief.

Pi on the other hand put in a comment and criticism, straight forward. The great difficulty in this is that it all comes from "Prophet's divine messages received", and the ideas of afterlife (certainly a part of forever) leave us with no way of reaching into it without death. That is, its very foundation is foreclosed to us.

At this point, Daniel, sensing I think-arguments that would highly deflect from conclusions encouraged the group to listen to Angelei on the philosophical beliefs of groups that led into the notion of "Reincarnation".

So Angelei then continued, with yes thank you. I will go into this with as best and most succinct coverage as I can.

Looking somewhat shyly at her host she began. Well Jainism beginning about 2000 years ago prescribes a path of non-violence towards all living beings. Its philosophy and practices emphasize the necessity of self-effort to move the soul towards divine consciousness, this though not referencing a heaven, and liberation. Jainism encourages spiritual development through cultivation of one's own personal wisdom and reliance on self-control through vows. The triple gems of Jainism are right vision, right knowledge, and right conduct. The word "right" is simply meant to effect fairness and humanity. These provide the path for attaining liberation from the cycles of birth and death. That in a sense I believe is their notion of forever. So they deal with it in their minds, as it were, a matter of control to change directly in each new generation.

Jains believe that they stand for wisdom, and that is reflected in their contributions to Indian Society, but, in Jains history they have in country not been given the status as other religious group as the Hindu. Recent history shows the Jain faithful are among the most gentle and peace loving people, who accept others into their company with open arms.

Looking at Samyak she said, Jains though do suffer much bigotry, even killing and destruction of their places of worship. The men as the Sikhs wear turbans a religious requirement and are often mistaken as Arab- Islamic, which has led to their persecution.

Samyak nodded his head and simply said, yes child that is true. The matter though is what can be reached by this group for all people--- to control the past, present and future. We Jain's seek to live such as we avoid recycling birth and death rebirths. This reflects, of course, a kind of reincarnation, though not really in the same context.   And what about that subject, i.e., reincarnation, are there others that might have implanted that idea.

I do not believe there is Forever reachability for Confucianism, Taoism, Shintoism, and Taoism. These amount to "Behavioral Philosophy's". In the main I believe that possible precursors would be Buddhism and Hinduism.

Buddhism *was founded 2560 years ago. It can help some individuals discover a sense of "Nirvana" or ultra-restful peace. The "Nobel" truths developed by the Buddha hold foundational precepts that are of interest and could be helpful to humanity, such as not taking either things (stealing) or lives of other people or killing the world's creatures.*

While helpful toward making some individuals in developing peace of mind, the method is focused mainly on individuals per se with no clear worldwide objectives.

Further it has been captured by governments for their purposes of individual control such as the Japanese did together with Shintoism in WWII. However, the Buddha in his meditation, and that of his followers believe that reincarnation exists and the Buddha himself believed he had seen this many times.

Hinduism the oldest of all faith philosophies, believes what is fundamental to reincarnation, that is that one goes through rebirths representing advancement to ultimate state of existence. I believe then that these two practices represent fundamental acceptance of reincarnation, and this imbedded has supported and promulgated that idea.

With that sensing Angelei was finished, Samyak entered with a kind consideration. You have clearly covered much of the ground, but so we can understand you as one of our panel, would you care to tell us what you believe or hold important.

Angelei said, *I will just briefly, I think Humanism and "Mindism" are important for all to understand.*

<u>H</u>*umanism was founded in 1930s. It is a broad sociological terminology for populations that describes the secular ideal exposing reason, ethics, and justice, while specifically rejecting supernatural and religious ideas as a basis of morality and decision-making.*

It has, however, morphed by some into "Religious Humanism", which attempts to hold the original principles but has little choice other than to form group attitudes around the relevant faiths. Still, the rational foundation has some promise of helping the associated faiths to see the importance of non-polemics to achieve a future for humanity.

Pi commented, the basic seems rational but again, it gives us no way to deepen our inquiry, except that it would be encouraged by people practicing Humanism...

Angelei went on, Mindism, is newly formalizing, and would be in the same category that is people holding this way of behavior would encourage us to continue our search.   This is a viewpoint, not a faith per se. Skellan and I found it when we found Maslov"s Ideas.

The type of thinking has been around for generations, but has been more overt in the last century. It considers that geo-political, territorial prerogatives and faith entrenchment have and are setting the existing faiths into such a polemic that they are unable safely to secure the species.

The inevitable major conflicts will detract from that goal, preventing peaceful carriage of humanity forward. Mindism is in a way like Jainism's defense of Wisdom, but it is devoid of prophet worship and traditional fixings. It stresses the need for Mind freeing attitudes to help individuals make well founded choices on their own, toward openness and freedom of thought and actions.

Unlike the various faiths, she said as she looked at Jehan, the intention is to provide knowledge for "Navigator Mindfulness" in sufficient numbers of individuals so that a healthy mentality can guide humanity to a secure a realistic future, that is a knowledge grounded Forever.

In effect it could be considered a backdrop for our current pursuit. It might be mentioned that formal educational recognition of this view exists in some of psychologies' instructive.

There is though in what I have talked about a challenge to us. That is if we discover an entry into or rational understanding of Forever, should any of this be changed, or do we have such a right, does anyone? This is a massive undertaking. The statistics make it clear.

Skellan investigated all 12 "faiths", the ones most believed around the world. Adherents...com that estimates the proportion of the world's people who are more secular, non-religious, agnostics and atheists at about 14%. Among religions: Christianity has about 2 Billion followers, Islam 1.2 Billion, Hinduism 785 Million, Buddhism 360 Million, Judaism 17 Million, Sikhism 16 Million, Baha'ism 6 Million, Confucianism 5 Million, Jainism 4 Million, Shintoism 3 Million, Zoroastrianism 0.2 Million, and Taoism 0.1 Million.

They also have published the interesting statistic that there are 0.7 Million believers of Paganism. This includes Devil Worship, Modern Wicca, yand what they called "Other Spirits".

What I have thought about, working though this is that among the various interpretations of the word "faith" are assurance or confidence, but also, loyalty and devotion.

That is, there are two "ways" to view the word that persons steeped in religion might practice. The last way (loyalty and devotion) is simply "blind faith", as it has been applied through history.

From that has come what we must call "Religio-polimics" too often developing into "Spirit Wars". Persons of blind faith are at the mercy of those who would capitalize on their faithfulness.

This is found widely distributed, from prelates and religious "leaders" that abuse children and forgive unforgivable sins, in the devotion to one's god's image that is so entrenched as to kill others even children, and to the preachers who say one thing about morality and then practice exactly the opposite. In short can there be change? Both Daniel and Skellan commented on that, adding that the Panel is one obviously composed of "Future Navigators". Our search for Forever, may give people a new way to focus on responsibility.

The group did agree that the session was--aside from reachability into Forever, of value because it revealed that there was much that could be changed now. At the same time it revealed the challenges in helping future humanity.

Pi put in, people, we are in a naive stage, none of that can be an agenda now without an understanding of the mechanism of return or entry or change for the future.

It was thought, however, first noted by Jehan, that the future through rational guidance in the present would be a place to start.

Angelei, then thanked all for listening and Samyak, continued his "Temporary Chair-Ship" encouraging that this is the time to give more detailed consideration to Reincarnation.

That he said could begin tomorrow, and the group enjoyed company and discussions late into the night most sitting outside feeling the breeze and enjoying the incredible glow of starlight as it glistened off the golden sand not far from the Samyak home.

Forever Probe, Document 3
June 6, p.m.
Duly Recorded and Filed,
Jane Caldwell, Technical Recorder
SPECIAL ILLUSIONS

Forever Probe, Document 4, June 7, a.m.

<u>Reincarnations:</u> *The June 6 meeting was regarding Theisms and some devotions we referenced as "nontheisms" such as Buddhism. The June 7 meeting continued with Samyak leading the way, extending the nontheisms notion into reincarnation. He did this first by descripting Hinduism. He prefaced by noting that he was speaking from direct experience and familiarity. Here is his statement.*

Hinduism should take first standing in this, it was begun some 4000 years ago. It stands for absolute and complete freedom of belief and worship! It conceives the whole world as a single family that exalts one truth. Therefore, it accepts all forms of belief and dismisses labels of distinct religions, which would imply a division of identity.

Most important, well relevant to us, the philosophy holds truth in reincarnation! That is, human beings have the opportunity to raise in state from lower life form to advanced human form based on corporeal behavior. This belief does see "Avatars" and other God like models, as part of its history. As individuals reach the end of life, they gain freedom to seek their rest and such divinity as they may deserve. Yet, terrible conflicts have arisen between Hinduism and the Islamic faith. Unfortunately, Hindu radicalism has raised its head in killings! Secularism in some countries where the faith is practiced holds it back. The notion of and poverty state for many millions occurs as they are classified lower as "Untouchables".

Nonetheless there are arguments on the validity of the reincarnation idea...I will review to that end a paper presented in the 90s, at the 52nd Annual Sessions of the Sri Lanka Association for the Advancement of Science. The title of the paper is aptly "Reincarnation is Now a Scientifically Acceptable Phenomenon" The paper was presented by Dr. Granville Dharmawardenam University of Colombo. I am handing out excepts from the article.

*As the session progressed Samyak read the paper with only a few omissions. He stressed that the paper contained historical reference, and terminology that was important specifically on "general doctrines". (Paper is now on file.) He quoted the Dr. directly in his reading as follows...*In the seventeenth century when Rene Descartes divided everything in the universe into two realms as so called "Res Extensa" (matter) and "Res Cogitans" (mind), gathering knowledge within the realm of Res Extensa was called Science and the phenomenon of reincarnation got pushed into the other realm Res Cogitans which was condemned to be not respectable and not up to the dignity of Scientists to probe into. Science was considered the respectable realm to study.

All important and respectable knowledge of the universe was thus restricted to science which was restricted to the study of the aspects of the universe that are measurable. Scientists accepted that the universe consisted essentially of "objects" leading to the belief that the ultimate realities of the universe are things and not beings. Thus, it was believed that everything in nature could be explained in terms of interactions of matter particles.

Science developed in this framework is known as "Classical Science". Classical Science had great material success because it helped to develop technology which brought about wealth and material benefits to mankind. It helped the West to colonize the rest of the world and acquire economic dominance and political influence.

The framework of Classical Science was punctured by Henry Becquerel exactly a hundred years ago, in 1896, by the discovery of Radioactivity.

Albert Einstein "further cracked" it at the beginning of this century by proposing his theory of relativity. That in turn was "blasted" by the advent of Quantum Theory and the Uncertainty Principle.

Samyak at this point said to the Panel, we will of course eventually need to dig into this, to which Pi said, here-here! Samyak then continued his reading. "It is noteworthy that Einstein's discovery falls entirely within the realm of Res Cogitans as it did not involve any experiments or measurements!

In classical science scientists made idealized mental pictures of the phenomena to be understood. Imagined mechanisms were usually presented to make various phenomena and relationships between them understood. But as Modern Science boosted man's knowledge transcending the limitations imposed by the five senses took us to murky areas of nature, profound changes had to be introduced to procedures in science.

Our ability to understand everything by way of perceptible mental pictures diminished and it became necessary to imagine models with components which behaved in ways that had no counterparts at all in the world familiar to us.

Again Samyak stopped to put in a thought. He said yes, Einstein as we shall see forces us to picture four dimensions, which as 3D folks we cannot do without some tricks. Nonetheless to continue… The mechanisms involved in these models in most instances not only are invisible but also consist of elements that operate in ways never known in the world that we actually experience through our five senses.

Samyak noted, as you may be seeing Dr. Granville Dharmawardenam is coaxing us to see that the Mind is central to our perceptions! He continues…

For example a single electron can pass through two different holes on a screen at the same time and still remain a single particle on the other side. If we use some mechanism such as flashing a light on the electron to observe through which hole it passes, then it will pass only through one of the two holes. Mechanisms of such phenomena are beyond our imagination at least at present. Mathematical models devoid of pictorial content which are typical of modern science resulted from attempts to fit the concepts of atoms and waves to the discoveries made at the end of the 19th century which led to the quantum theory. Classical science usually stood for absolute precision whereas modern science stands for the impossibility of absolute precision! *Samyak said this is certainly worth noting, as we will observe is has some credibility.*

In short the Doctor is saying….Modern science joined up the two realms, Res Extensa and Res Cogitans and made us to understand that the universe cannot be broken up into two independent arbitrary realms as Res Extensa and Res Cogitans. They are not independent and cannot be studied completely independently.

Within the establishment of modern science some of the aspects of nature that did not strictly adhere to the realm of Res Extensa, which were therefore earlier condemned as unbecoming of scientists to talk about have become respectable!

He then notes… Reincarnation falls into this category. Therefore scientists now have the professional clearance to scientifically investigate reincarnation. *And he says as qualification…T*his paper, however, does not distinguish between subtle differences among reincarnation, rebirth and re-becoming.

If reincarnation is to be examined from an unbiased scientific point of view, it is necessary first of all to find a way of bypassing such unscientific barriers as religious bias.

This can be done by considering the standard procedure used at present for the acceptance of any modern scientific theory and testing reincarnation by following the same procedure.

Geremy Hayward has described how one ventures to deal with a new theory. He describes this procedure as a four step scientific process as follows;

a) Study the relevant phenomenon,

b) Formulate the new theory,

c) Use the theory to predict observations that we should be   able to make if the theory is correct, and

d) Look for these predicted observations.

The Professor entered here with a comment…this it should be noted, though not a deliberate omission, is not complete… Scientific method demands retesting of observations and seeking alternate hypothesis as to what seems to be before one... But continue Samyak.

Richard Feynman, Noble Laureate for Physics, describes this process in detail. He combines steps "a" and "b" and describes it as a three step process.

If the observations made in the last step do not agree with the predictions of the earlier step the proposed theory is not acceptable. If they agree the theory becomes acceptable. If more and more observations show agreement the theory receives stronger in scientific acceptance. Once a theory becomes scientifically accepted by this test it remains so unless someone finds reliable new data to prove its unacceptability.

This time Tim Bean entered...again this is only part of the process it is essential that full and true alternate hypotheses be explored, i.e. it must be put to the test of alternate Hypothesis!

However, Samyak, nodding his head at the protagonist continued. As the author doctor said...

Reincarnation is a very old belief and a large fraction of the world population believes it. For example Rene Descartes' statement "What I have said is sufficient to show clearly enough that the extinction of the mind does not follow from the corruption of the body and also to give men the hope of another life after death." This comment in 1641 confirms his belief in reincarnation!

*Pi noted that this he said is not necessarily referencing reincarnation, but go ahead. Yes, thank you Pi for the note, to continue...*About 20 percent of those in the Western World whose religions shun reincarnation nevertheless believe it. According to opinion polls this percentage is rising.

Pi seemed on the edge of her seat, saying "What is an "Open Poll", and where is the data? Samyak merely looked up at her and apologized, it is not with the article, never the less it continues...

Hence the phenomenon of reincarnation is already known and therefore the steps "a" and "b" are already there. In examining the scientific acceptability of reincarnation therefore one has only to go through the last two steps of the above scientific process. If this is done successfully the scientific acceptability of reincarnation is proved in the way any other theory in modern science is proved.

(This of course was met with some head shaking by the scientist on the panel, it being of the very weakest kind of acceptance as Pi related!).

Samyak said simply well let's hear this out... to continue the author said...

Reincarnation may be defined as the re-embodiment of an immaterial part of a person after a short or a long interval after death, in a new body whence it proceeds to lead a new life in the new body more or less unconscious of its past existences, but containing within itself the "essence" of the results of its past lives, which experience goes toward making up its new character or personality.

Thus, infancy brings to this earth not a blank scroll for the beginning of a new earthly record, but it is inscribed with ancestral histories, some like the present scene, most of them unlike it and stretching back into the remote past.

Angelei put in, you know this sounds a bit like that from the Scientology proposition, though in their case they see transfer of "Engrams". Nodding Samyak said, yes, that does fit doesn't it...never thought of that...Well the article continues with the issues, rather than with support.

Reincarnation is an issue of utmost importance, one that promises to touch the ordinary man, woman and child in a profound and far reaching way.

Crime statistics show that convictions are much lower among those who believe in reincarnation than among the others. If scientifically accepted, reincarnation will have a stake in defining human identity in the 21st century.

Jehan asked what crime statistics, those should be cited, yes? Samyak responded, they are not available this paper...but to go on....

There are two possible scenarios, No-Reincarnation scenario and Reincarnation scenario that can be considered.

The Human being is composed of the body and an immaterial part. The body which is the material part is well understood because it fell within the Classical Science realm of Res Extensa and was extensively studied by scientists. The immaterial part has not been studied by scientists because it fell within the Classical Science realm of Res Cogitans.

In the No-Reincarnation scenario death is something like the "Event Horizon" of a black hole.

Samyak noting here we will see more about those black holes, but I am sure most folks have seen depictions of these on T.V.

Crossing the event horizon is a one way journey and after crossing it nothing can come back, not even light. Here the body disintegrates after death and the immaterial part either annihilates or gets into a scientifically unknown state and remains there forever, i.e. each individual is borne, lives one life time and at the end of it passes the event horizon of death to a state of no return.

Angelei, not being scientific asks..."I wonder how that is known, it seems similar to "Devine Deliverance", yet it does relate a kind of Forever, specifying, however, that it is of no return, correct? But, what of behavior while here, so a way out is divined!"

*Well, sort of addressing your question, the Author continues with...*In the Reincarnation scenario death is not an event horizon because only the body, the material part, disintegrates and goes into a state of no return. The immaterial part enters into a scientifically unknown state and reappears, after a period.

Aha, from Angelei, here is the matter at hand, the immaterial. Do we wonder if that can be reached by anyone before return? Samyak said simply, that is not addressed, but we do have to classify it as a form of Forever, just as we do for the Monotheisms. Nonetheless the article continues…

The above given description of the phenomenon of reincarnation constitute steps "a" and "b" of the scientific process. *Are there alternated hypothesis, entered Pi? No said Samyak, the author does not suggest any, but continues…*

The next step of the scientific process is looking for observations that can be predicted assuming the existence of this phenomenon, observations that have a reasonable chance of being practically examined.

Abilities of individuals to carry memories of past events differ widely from individual to individual. Some people can remember events and experiences of long past whereas some easily forget things within a few years. Most people vividly remember special events such as tragic happenings for a very long time, even up to death.

Under hypnosis people recollect events which they had completely forgotten. Some people have the exceptional ability to recall knowledge and experiences gathered long ago and use them when necessary.

For example a friend of mine who had been discussing "Advanced Level Physics" with me when he was studying for the GCE ALL exam long time ago, but never did any science. There after he escaped injury in the Central bank bomb blast by instantaneously recalling his memories discussing AL Physics.

But others who had studied Physics more recently lost their eyes because that memory didn't flash back to their rescue at the time of impending disaster. As soon as my friend saw the flash of the bomb blast from his window, All Physics flashed back to his mind and prompted to him that the shock wave comes a little while after the flash. Instantaneously he threw himself back flat on the floor before the shock wave blasted the window glasses!

At this point all the panel, looked dubiously at each other but simply held critiques and allowed Samyak to continue with the article.

If reincarnation as defined earlier is true it should be possible to extend some of the above human capabilities, which result from immaterial aspects of the human being, beyond birth to the previous life and even beyond to earlier lives. Some people should be able to remember events in their past lives. Hypnosis must enhance this ability. Some must be able to make use of knowledge and experiences of past lives.

Skellan noted, more punctuated here, that the author seems to suggest that one's personal forever can be tapped and change their personal Forever. Yes though this all seems suggestion, we do need to keep this all in mind. It spells out a chain, creating Forever.

Well, that remains a very major issue, but the article continues… With these predictions we can move on to the last stage of the scientific process, to look for these predicted observations.

A large amount of data has been accumulated by research workers around the world on matters relating to reincarnation. There are three.

These are as follows.

- Spontaneous recall of past lives,
- Past life therapy,
- Child prodigies and others who can make use of knowledge and experience gathered in their past lives are some of the aspects that have been subjected too much research and investigation.

Tim asked at this point did the author give citations as to the articles showing the large amount of data, to which Samyak said. No that is not in his presentation but continued with allow please me to finish the presentation….

The observations made on the above areas agree with the predictions made in the third stage of the scientific process thereby successfully completing the four step test for scientific acceptability. No scientifically acceptable data that can go to prove the scientific unacceptability of reincarnation have appeared in scientific literature so far. *Samyak said, that seems to be the case, but to anticipate your critique, that no one has looked is not positive proof that it is valid.*

The Professor hastened to add, negative, rather non existing evidence is not evidence!

Well, the author stands on his premises, and says… On the basis of these tests it is concluded that the scientific acceptability of the phenomenon of reincarnation is proven at least on three counts in terms of the accepted principles of modern science.

A science minded person often finds it difficult to accept reincarnation because he/she had failed to perceive a reincarnation mechanism that is intelligible within the outdated Descartes' classical science frame work. But Modern Science, with thinking beyond Einstein has compelled us to accept unintelligible mechanisms of natural phenomena like the behavior of electrons and we do not hesitate to accept them. Likewise with the data available we are compelled to accept reincarnation as a reality.

The Austrian Scientist Rudolf Steiner says, "Just as an age was once ready to receive the Copernican theory of the universe, so is our age ready for the idea of reincarnation to be brought into the general consciousness of humanity".

At this point the Panel was opened for discussion. Samyak said it in such a way that it helped all to center.

As you know I am not a scientist but I have read a lot about this, considering the matter of my ancestors, my pursuit and for that matter Daniel's connection to his great-great grandfather.

I have found that in the last couple of years there has been a growing stream of debate and dueling papers, replete with references to such esoteric subjects as reincarnation, multiple universes and even the death of space-time, as cosmologists try to square the predictions of their cherished theories with their convictions that we and the universe are curious imaginations.

Even so, this idea is one that we really have no way to enter to check, it seems in evidence to be on an individual report basis. Other than hypnosis i.e. to make changes. While I personally have felt the force of reincarnation, I cannot, shall we say, globalize it as a means of understanding Forever based on scientific analysis.

However, in the same vein, I have read there is theory of "Floating Brains", recovered in space, should we not consider that?

Pi entered on that with a comment, more of a hope… I think we should consider that Samyak, but first shouldn't we know what Einstein thought of reincarnation and for that matter with the existence of God, all that would refer to our last two subjects.

Samyak entered with the comment, I have an article which I will share on that very subject once we have allowed Jane to catch up after a brief necessary break.

Thankful for that- the report on reincarnation was prepared and entered.

Document 4, June 7, a.m.
Respectfully Recorded
Jane Caldwell, Technical Recorder

`````````````````````````````````````````````````````````````

**Note:** After the break it was decided to allow all to have such discussions as they wished, and the meetings were not continued until the next day.
`````````````````````````````````````````````````````````````

I thought that the Panel must be suffering from "Jet Lag" or information overload, so that was a great idea. They all walked around town, talking to the residents, and then napped or slept as needed back at Samyak's home or at the Jeet Villa. All later (including me) retired for the night at the hotel. We noted Pi and Tim sitting together in the lobby, coffees in hand in what seemed a very deep discussion. Tim looked happier than I have ever seen.

Forever Probe, Document 5, June 8, a.m.

The group all gathered at about eight outside the Jain home for this discussion. The place was a kind of veranda or open porch. One could see the hills on the Tarr with its miscellaneous bushes, some stretches of golden sand, but there was a very nice gentle breeze, likely from the (really quite a distant) Ocean.

Jehan noted the way we are doing this with detailed review, reread and critique of important papers, really lets one focus. All agreed that the seminar format with critical review was right on.

Samyak, seeming very pleased with that, again chaired the meeting focusing on his promised article as center for discussion.

He led out…The subject is "Einstein on God" and such as reincarnation. The article is entitled "Einstein's Mystical Ideas about God, Death, Afterlife, And Reincarnation."

He goes on…and I believe that we all simply read or re-read the article then discuss it after all have done their reading. We then allowed an hour for all to look through the article, as we have been doing. After this Samyak got the meeting underway.

I have reproduced the article here in my report, I am citing that this is by Ron Rattner. Samyak then began the reading…

*It begins…*Albert Einstein was not only a great scientist but a wise philosopher but a pragmatic "true mystic"…of a deeply religious nature. He did not believe in a formal, dogmatic religion, but was religiously and reverently awed and humbled with a cosmic religious feeling by the immense beauty and eternal mystery of our Universe. *Pi, said he means. Religiously as dutifully?*

*Thank you, Dr.Pi, we don't really know, but here is the follow up…*He often commented publicly on religious and ethical subjects, and thereby he became widely respected for his moral integrity and mystical wisdom, as well as for his scientific genius.

In an essay entitled "The World as I See It", first published 1933, Einstein explained his reverence for God as "Eternal Universal Intelligence". But he rejected prevalent religious ideas of individual survival of physical death, reincarnation, or of reward or punishment in heaven or hell after physical death.

Angelei commented, think of that Universal Intelligence as God, I like that, god is that gift-our ability to be intelligent!

He said: "I am a deeply religious man. I cannot conceive of a God who rewards and punishes his creatures, or has a will of the type of which we are conscious in ourselves.

An individual who should survive his physical death is also beyond my comprehension, nor do I wish it otherwise; such notions are for the fears or absurd egoism of feeble souls. Enough for me the mystery of the eternity of life, and the inkling of the marvelous structure of reality, together with the single-hearted endeavor to comprehend a portion, be it ever so tiny, of the reason that manifests itself in nature. [This was in "The World as I See It"].

Jane commented on this briefly, drawing the panel's attention to the statement. My Goodness doesn't that seem rather prudish and from what data did he state that.

The Professor entered, *Jane I think we have to just pass that, he by this time had the world at his feet, and as so many believing they are genius… he must have felt above others… and note that he had a certain kind of reverence, and awe at the cosmos he entered with his theories. He put "overseer out", Mind in!*

Samyak noted, that does put some balance on it Doctor. But in the eyes of the religious members of our panel, surely they see Einstein as an Atheist. Nonetheless, let us all return to the article, picking up with the death of his friend.

On learning of the death of a lifelong friend, Einstein wrote in a March 1955 a letter to his friend's family: "Now he has departed from this strange world a little ahead of me. That means nothing. People like us, who believe in physics, know that the distinction between past, present, and future is only a stubbornly persistent illusion."

Samyak read that statement and clearly allowed interrupting the reading with his further input…That we are an illusion is prevalent with many in physics, as we have discussed. Thus, from Daniel came…we have noted qualifications! Our minds are the center as we know of no others in "space-time". And the meaning we as panel believe is our conscious view that there is a past, present and future, which by Einstein –restated more clearly- is simply time spent in space-time.

*Well to go on with Rattner…*Einstein's rejection of afterlife contradicted many religious teachings and credible experiential accounts of individual afterlife and reincarnation. But it was consistent with Einstein's revolutionary scientific paradigm and with highest "non-dualistic" Eastern religious teachings, the most ancient example of which is Hindu Advaita Vedanta philosophy.

Yes we must recognize that Einstein revolutionized Western science with his 1905 groundbreaking theory of relativity that "mass and energy are both but different manifestations of the same thing"; that there was an equivalence between all matter and energy in the universe, quantifiable by the simple and now famous equation $E = mc^2$.

And on his arrival in New York in 1919, Einstein summarized his theory of relativity in the single sentence: "Remove matter from the universe and you also remove space and time."(That is quoted from R.W. Clark, "Einstein: His Life and Times" (1973).

Still, though as Rattner points out this cold thinking was backed by a string of equations.

Yet, Pi said here, and by extension you would remove all memory, all past, present and future, I don't think he would really suggest that, and, well there is the dark matter, but we must come to that. And I see the article continues. By Samyak... The ancient Vedic Advaita teachings were first brought to large Western audiences by Swami Vivekananda – who came to the West as Indian delegate to the 1893 Parliament of World Religions.

And, it must be noted that Vedic Rishis or Seers had anticipated Einstein by millennia on a philosophical grounds[1], although their teachings were largely unknown in the West until shortly before Einstein revolutionized Western science. This thinking (Non-dualisim[1]) is---shall we say---closely parallel with Einstein's view on God and Reincarnation.

To that it is noteworthy the timing is- *well-* before Einstein made his postulations!

----

1.   From Wikipedia: "Nondualism, also called non-duality, means (as one suspects), "not two" or "one undivided without a second". It is a term and concept used to define various strands of religious and spiritual thought. It is found in a variety of Asian religious traditions and modern western spirituality, but with a variety of meanings and uses. The term may refer to such as: *Advaita,* which states that all of the universe is one essential reality, and that all facets and aspects of the universe are, indeed, ultimately an expression or appearance of that one reality.

This is an ontological approach to Nondualism, and asserts non-difference between Atman (soul) and Brahman (the Absolute). This idea is best known from Advaita Vedanta, but also found in other Hindu traditions."

At that Pi came in again. So, Einstein could, indeed, be "Polemicized"? For some reason Pi was acting very "critical" of Einstein, or was that just Pi? (Daniel said, Pi, we don't really know that, do we?)

Samyak said, Interesting position on Einstein Dr. Pi, though shall we continue with Dr. Rattner… Vivekananda, who was principle disciple of nineteenth century Indian Holy Man Sri Ramakrishna Paramahansa, eloquently explained that according to Advaita philosophy this impermanent and ever changing world is an unreal illusion called Maya or samsara; and, that "All that we see or seem is but a dream within a dream!

In an eloquent New York City lecture called "The Real and the Apparent Man", he equated Maya or Samsara with "time, space, and causation " and presciently predicted scientific confirmation of the ancient Vedic non-dual--- philosophy[1], that is to say "One Infinite Existence"…(*Samyak looking at the panel noted full attention!)*

…He said: "According to the Advaita philosophy, this Maya or ignorance–or name and form, or, as it has been called in Europe, time, space, and causality–is out of this one Infinite Existence showing us the manifoldness of the universe; in substance, this universe is one. *And we one with it said Jehan softly to not interfere, letting Samyak continue…*…So long as anyone thinks that there are two ultimate realities, he is mistaken.

When he has come to know that there is but one, he is right. This is what is being proved to us every day, on the physical plane, on the mental plane, and also on the spiritual plane.

"What then becomes of all this threefold eschatology of the dualist, that when a man dies he goes to heaven, or goes to this or that sphere, and that the wicked persons become ghosts, and become animals, and so forth? None "comes" and none "goes", says the non-dualist.

How can you come and go? You are infinite; where is the place for you to go? I.e. You Are Already Infinite!

"So it is with regard to the soul; the very question of birth and death in regard to it is utter nonsense. Who goes and who comes? Where are you not? Where is the heaven that you are not in already? Omnipresent is the Self of man.

Where is it to go? Where is it not to go? It is everywhere.

So all this childish dream and puerile illusion of birth and death, of heavens and higher heavens and lower worlds, all vanish immediately for the perfect. For the nearly perfect it vanishes after showing them the several scenes up to Brahmaloka. It continues for the ignorant."

"Time, space and causation are like the glass through which the Absolute is seen. In the Absolute there is neither time, space nor causation."

"Science and religion will meet and shake hands…When the scientific teacher asserts that all things are the manifestation of one force, does it not remind you of the God of whom you hear in the Upanishads? Do you not see whither science is tending?"

…"This separation between man and man, between nation and nation, between earth and moon, between moon and sun. Out of this idea of separation between atom and atom comes all misery. But the Vedanta says that this separation does not exist, it is not real."

"Your own will is all that answers prayer, only it appears under the guise of different religious conceptions to each mind. We may call it Buddha, Jesus, Krishna, but it is only the Self, the 'I'."

This was signed…~ Swami Vivekananda – Jnana Yoga

At this point the whole panel was silent, one could see in all the eyes a deep thinking, a kind of awe at the statements, because they were those that preceded Einstein and put in the Infinite!

The Panel all asked…were his equations generated believing at first that background…?

Well his expostulations as Tim said were certainly along those lines… that belief pattern was already there. And something we must contemplate in understanding Infinity is his statement "You Are Already Infinite!"

Chandler set in here, "I think I see that. We, you, and me we must be inside infinity, so already infinite. Or am I lost here?

Samyak said, well I don't think completely lost… but let us finish the article… and let that play out with you. Einstein's thinking we must examine, so this belief pattern is central to the pursuit of the panel… here is more.

Einstein's non-mechanistic science was very difficult for Western materialist minds to comprehend because his mystical view questioned the substantiality of matter and the ultimate reality of space, time and causality. Like Vivekananda, he said, "Reality is merely an illusion, albeit a very persistent one. Our separation of each other is an optical illusion of consciousness. Space and time are not conditions in which we live, they are modes in which we think. That which is impenetrable to us really exists. Behind the secrets of nature remains something subtle, intangible, and inexplicable. Veneration (Respect) for this force beyond anything that we can comprehend is my religion."

All noted on the text at hand that Samyak had underlined the very specific and shattering statement on space and time. However, there was much input, it seems most disagreed with the statement of "space and time not conditions in which we live".

But Samyak continued with the article… Thus, Einstein's rejection of prevalent religious ideas about God and individual survival of physical death and afterlife was consistent with his revolutionary science as well as with Eastern non-dualistic teachings explained by Vivekananda that apparent separation between subject and object is an unreal "optical illusion of consciousness."

Here the members of the panel could not help but put in qualification, remembering the discussions of time and infinity. It is human consciousness that sees it all and describes it all as best now possible. Jehan put in…our consciousness is in our time, human time. That indeed does---must exist in "Einstein's-Space-time". And, from Angelei came the comment---Einstein leaves open it seems to me the naming of a "Force", not daring to call it God. This because he seems afraid to make it even simpler in the face of his cold Space-time. That is, he hedges saying-there is just "It", the Cosmos, the Forever that is so hard for even him to accept?

Well Rattner bears on this, asks in the article… Did Einstein's psyche survive his death? Was he surprised on his demise?

Though Einstein didn't believe in a "God Plan" for individual survival of physical death, he may, indeed, have been surprised on his demise.

And here dear panel is why I have centered on this article. As Rattner continued a fundamental arises from the dust!

"Conservation of energy is basic to physics. So Einstein must have realized that his subtle energetic essence was indestructible and could only be transformed from one state to another! But we don't know how that knowledge may have influenced his opinion about what happens on individual death, or his experience thereafter.

The Professor had to interrupt here. In our training as Future Navigators we believe that the Mind DNA holds that energy, and that from transfer to generations as the Mind DNA by biological addition - expands so does that energy, and its signals are made more and more capable, so that the "Final, Ultimate Human" is an awesome creature who can understand it all.

Samyak said yes, and that is such a powerful view and in sympathy with the final thoughts of Rattner…

Except for very rare Buddha-like people who transcend all desires, it is probable that all humans survive physical death as psyches or mental bodies, irrespective of their beliefs. So the Dalai Lama has said: "[Physical qualities] cannot be carried over into the next life. The continuum of the mind, however, does carry on. Therefore, a quality based on the mind is more enduring. …So, through training the mind, qualities such as compassion, love, and the wisdom realizing emptiness can be developed."

Samyak said following that reading…this panel is from H.H. Dalai Lama, "Practicing wisdom: the perfection of Shantideva's Bodhisattva way."

Thus, to further the point… Buddhists say that Gautama Buddha experienced countless incarnations over eons of time before ultimately transcending the cycle of birth and death. And the Dalai Lama has said: "We are born and reborn countless number of times, and it is possible that each being has been our parent at one time or another. Therefore, it is likely that all beings in this universe have familial connections." *This is from* "H. H. Dalai Lama, from 'The Path to Tranquility: Daily Wisdom".*

`,,,,,,,,,,,,,,,,,,,,,,,,,,,,,,,,,,,,,,,,,,,,,,,,,,,,,,,,,,,,,`

So the article was presented, read thoroughly and the Panel discussion opened up…It touched each member of the panel in a deep way, so discussions, sometimes strongly expressed extended into the early afternoon.

These discussions ranged far and wide, but there was some agreement.

All recognized, though it was not at first so obvious, that it has been the record. The Hope of the 'Afterlife". Thus realizing the panel felt even more strongly that their rational pursuit was most worthwhile.

All perhaps except myself, believing there is a heaven with God, felt strongly that what has been covered offers no functional way to understand Forever. Pi said, why should it be a mystery?

And all certainly agreed with Ratner's final comment on Einstein which I paraphrase following… What would it be… if on demise of Einstein's physical body and extraordinary brain, his subtle mental body survived (with its unfulfilled desire to find a single simple "Unified Field" formula)? Nonetheless, we honor his immense evolutionary accomplishments and take inspiration from his compassionate social activism, and pragmatic wisdom.

The subject thus covered, the Professor guided us to adjournment. His final statement was as follows.

"In the main this last article forces us to focus outside of the ancient dogmas although reincarnation is an enticing path for mind transfer". We see that, certainly, within generations, but outside of that across decades, and without more evidence we are made to look deeper into the physical aspect of time always there past and all future.

Yes, said Pi, I agree with the need to look into this further and now from the perspective of scientific postulations. Well, maybe there is some kind of mind transfer as a function of space development...To that let me tell you about a discovery related and I believe we must put that on the Agenda...That is the idea of the "Floating Brain."

74

Forever Probe, Document
As Recorded and Filled, June 8, a.m.
Respectfully,
Jane Caldwell, Technical Recorder

FLOATING BRAINS

Document 6, June 8, p.m.

The group reconvened after a trip into town to see some most impressive ancient structures, with Buddha's positioned all around a beautiful planted pathway. Obviously not an appropriate observation for a technical report but I noticed that Pi and Tim sort of went off on their own! (Surely it involved a deep discussion of the last agenda!) Also, as the panel is human I do want to tell of them some.

Once all were back in the meeting area of the Jain home, it was indeed Pi who made the presentation. I have included the paper's text intersected with Pi's comments (making my job easier).

As she handed out copies, Pi noted that there were a fairly large number of people who created aspects of it. These are to include Holly Stevenson, Doctors Susskind of Stanford, Lisa Dyson, University of California, Berkeley, Matthew Kleban, at New York University, Alan Guth, MIT, and Andrei Linde, Stanford theorist. She said this is a pretty august group of contributors. The formal idea is generally referred to as the Boltzmann Brain.

I have divided up the report into 3 sections (my labeling), The Idea, The Proponents and the Non-Proponents. I hasten to add that although there is an absurdity in this, there are also observations that will relate to our foray into space-time which is inevitable.

The Idea: As these authors point out "It could be the weirdest and most embarrassing prediction in the history of cosmology, if not science."

Skellan interjected...if that is so why we are thinking about it." Pi with no apology simply enumerated. 1. Because it relates a kind of space-time path for reincarnation, and 2. - It starts us on the way to get into potentials, i.e. things that could happen within the cosmos! The article continues remarking about the absurdity....

Nonetheless, if true, it would mean that you yourself reading this article are more likely to be some momentary fluctuation in a field of matter and energy out in space than a person with a real past born through billions of years of evolution in an orderly star-spangled cosmos.

By this theory your memories and the world you think you see around you are illusions!

This bizarre picture is for sure the outcome of a recent series of calculations that take many of the bedrock theories and discoveries of modern cosmology to the limit.

And so in the last couple of years there has been a growing stream of debate and dueling papers, replete with references to such esoteric subjects as reincarnation, multiple universes and even the death of space-time, as cosmologists try to square the predictions of their cherished theories with their convictions that we and the universe are real.

Jehan raised her hand and said as she did that, so once again we look at ideas that will challenge i.e., tend to ignore, time and infinities meanings, the fact there is our consciousness and that within Human Time.

Well, Pi said, not exactly. Note next they say…

The basic problem is that across the eons of time, the standard theories suggest, the universe can recur over and over again in an endless cycle of big bangs.

But by this theory, it's hard for nature to make a whole universe. That is the crux of the matter! It's much easier to make fragments of one, like planets, yourself maybe in a spacesuit or even — in the most absurd and troubling example — a naked brain floating in space.

Jehan noted the obvious for us all, the cosmologist has no sense of life needs, naked functioning brains are of course impossible, I guess they are just sketching abstracts for example, Pi responded, I guess that is the case, anyway…

<u>*The Proponents Say:*</u> Nature tends to do what is easiest, from the standpoint of energy and probability. And so these fragments ---in particular the brains---would appear far more frequently than real full-fledged universes, or than us. Or they might *be* us!

Alan Guth, who is a cosmologist at the Massachusetts Institute of Technology (who agrees this overabundance is absurd), pointed out that some calculations result in an infinite number of free-floating brains for every normal brain, making it "infinitely unlikely for us to be normal brains."

So Panel, welcome to what physicists call the Boltzmann brain problem, named after the 19th-century Austrian physicist Ludwig Boltzmann. It was he who suggested the mechanism by which such fluctuations could happen in a gas or in the universe. Cosmologists also refer to them as "freaky observers," in contrast to regular or "ordered" observers of the cosmos like ourselves.

Cosmologists are desperate to eliminate these freaks from their theories, but so far they can't even agree on how or even on whether they are making any progress.

If you are inclined to skepticism this debate might seem like further evidence that cosmologists, who give us dark matter, dark energy and speak with apparent aplomb about gazillions of parallel universes, have finally lost their minds! (*Pi noted for us that the 'dark ideas' and parallels are indeed important and will be detailed after we have visited Einstein.*)

Continuing with Proponents: Some cosmologists say the brain problem serves as a valuable reality check as they contemplate the far, far future and zillions of bubble universes popping off from one another in an ever-increasing rush through eternity.

What, for example is a "typical" observer in such a setup? If some atoms in another universe stick together briefly to look, talk and think exactly like you, is it really you?

"It is part of a much bigger set of questions about how to think about probabilities in an infinite universe in which everything that can occur, does occur, infinitely many times," said Leonard Susskind of Stanford, a co-author of a paper in 2002 that helped set off the debate.

Or as Andrei Linde, another Stanford theorist given to colorful language, loosely characterized the possibility of a replica of your own brain forming out in space sometime, "How do you compute the probability to be reincarnated to the probability of being born?"

The Boltzmann brain problem arises from a string of logical conclusions that all spring from another deep and old question, namely why time seems to go in only one direction!

This set the group into commenting, which in summary is-we believe it does, Pi interjecting...with question as to which direction at what time! Pi then said further on the matter......Well, perhaps that needs more insight, but here from theorists, are expressed some limitations on Times "pliability".

*These theorists comment...*Why can't you unscramble an egg? The fundamental laws governing the atoms bouncing off one another in the egg look the same whether time goes forward or backward. In this universe, at least, the future and the past are different.

"When you break an egg and scramble it you are doing cosmology," said Sean Carroll, a cosmologist at the California Institute of Technology.

Boltzmann ascribed this so-called arrow of time to the tendency of any collection of particles to spread out into the most random and useless configuration, in accordance with the second law of thermodynamics (sometimes paraphrased as "things get worse"), which says that entropy, which is a measure of disorder or wasted energy, can never decrease in a closed system like the universe.

Which said Tim, begs the question is ours a closed universe?

Pi did not let that deflect....their argument is ...If the universe was running down and entropy was increasing now, that was because the universe must have been highly ordered in the past.

This then leads to a discussion on Bubbles in universes which I classify as "Fractals", and we have already named "infinitesimals". Pi said remember that term Fractals, as well as dark energy, and parallel universes!

In Boltzmann's time the universe was presumed to have been around forever, in which case it would long ago have stabilized at a lukewarm temperature and died a "heat death." It would already have maximum entropy, and so with no way to become more disorderly there would be no arrow of time. No life would be possible but that would be all right because life would be excruciatingly boring.

So what gets us into this…Is that Boltzmann said that entropy (randomness) was all about odds, however, and if we waited long enough the random bumping of atoms would occasionally produce the cosmic equivalent of an egg unscrambling. A rare fluctuation would decrease the entropy in some place and eventually start the arrow of time pointing and history flowing again.

Or, as Pi said…lets don't lose this, a change in entropy is a reason that time might reverse (egg unscrambling). That is a point that we need to hold onto. Our sought Forever, would have the necessary property of constantly being there for past and future. Anyway to continue…

<u>*The Doubters or Alternate Theorists Say*</u>: That is not what happened, though. Astronomers now know the universe has not lasted forever. It was born in the Big Bang, which somehow set the arrow of time, 14 billion years ago. *Pi again entered, I am not convinced that it is, was the only "Big Bang". However…That there was the Big Bang… a thing going forward does support that our local living time in space time is felt forward, future moving.*

….The linchpin of the Big Bang is thought to be an explosive moment *(Pi notes here we will cover this)* known as inflation, during which space became suffused with energy that had an anti-gravitational effect and ballooned violently outward, ironing the kinks and irregularities out of what is now the observable universe and endowing primordial chaos with order.

Pi, the teacher in this section, wanted us to remember dark designs, parallels and inflation. She said… and one more term, bubble or "pocket universes" which you see in this article next…

…Inflation *(again something we will cover again)* is a veritable cosmological fertility principle. Fluctuations in the field driving inflation also would have seeded the universe with the lumps that eventually grew to be galaxies, stars and people.

However, according to the more extended version, called eternal inflation, an endless array of bubble or "pocket" universes are branching off from one another at a dizzying and exponentially increasing rate. They could have different properties and perhaps even different laws of physics, so the story goes.

I noted that the panel now was sitting silently, looks of various kinds, from doubt to humor, to frowns. Pi continued though, even so as said in the paper… A different, but perhaps related, form of antigravity, glibly dubbed dark energy, seems to be running the universe now, and that is the culprit responsible for the Boltzmann brains.

Further to this, the expansion of the universe seems to be accelerating, making galaxies fly away from one another faster and faster. If the leading dark-energy suspect, a universal repulsion Einstein called the cosmological constant, is true, this runaway process will last forever, and distant galaxies will eventually be moving apart so quickly that they cannot communicate with one another. Being in such a space would be like being surrounded by a "Black Hole".

Now, said Pi "remember that paragraph and the authors give us a simple example"…

Rather than simply going to black the cosmic horizon would glow, emitting a feeble spray of elementary particles and radiation, with a temperature of a fraction of a billionth of a degree, (this is courtesy of something that will certainly look into, i.e. "quantum uncertainty").

That radiation bath will be subject to random fluctuations just like the so called Boltzmann's eternal universe, however, and every once in a very long, long time, one of those fluctuations would be big enough to recreate the Big Bang! *(Yes said Pi, which would be my suspicion!)*

In the fullness of time this process could lead to the endless series of recurring universes. Our present universe could be part of that chain!

In such a recurrent setup, however, Dr. Susskind and colleagues pointed out that Boltzmann's idea might work too well, filling the mega-verse with more "Boltzmann Brains" than universes or real people.

And, said Pi, the "Brain" people come back in with this… In the same way the odds of a real word showing up when you shake a box of Scrabble letters are greater than a whole sentence or paragraph forming, these "regular" universes would be vastly outnumbered by weird ones, including flawed variations on our own all the way down to naked brains, a result foreshadowed by Martin Rees, a cosmologist at the University of Cambridge, in his 1997 book, "Before the Beginning."

At this point, Pi was smiling at us, unusual, but this was with a very sarcastic look. Then she followed with, you can only go so far with outlandish analogies, but do remember what we learned…i.e. possible multi-universes, and as already known, the Black Holes. So next we take up the opposites….

<u>*Non-Boltzmann Proponents Say*</u>: The conclusions of Dr. Dyson and her colleagues were quickly challenged by Andreas Albrecht and Lorenzo Sorbo of the

University of California, Davis, who used an alternate approach. They found that the Big Bang was actually more likely than Boltzmann's brain.

"In the end, inflation saves us from Boltzmann's brain," Dr. Albrecht said, while admitting that the calculations were contentious. Indeed, the "Invasion of Boltzmann brains," as Dr. Linde once referred to it, was just beginning.

In an interview Dr. Linde described these brains as a form of reincarnation! Over the course of eternity, he said, anything is possible. After some Big Bang in the far future, he said, "it's possible that you yourself will re-emerge. Eventually you will appear with your table and your computer."

Several of the group put in ....Well that does bring us back to reincarnation...or is that really correct here as this could take place anywhere else than in our own human time.

Pi grabbed the stage with that by saying well, hold on---he followed up, perhaps kidding, and finally capping the matter with logic. But it's more likely, that you would be reincarnated as an isolated brain, without the baggage of stars and galaxies. In terms of probability, he said, "It's cheaper."

You might wonder what's wrong with a few brains — or even a preponderance of them — floating around in space. For one thing, as observers these brains would see a freaky chaotic universe, unlike our own, which seems to persist in its promise and disappointment. (Pi, said, note the emphasis here.)

*Then as lead in to a kind of rebuttal...he goes on...*Another point involves one of the central orthodoxies of cosmology that humans don't occupy a special place in the cosmos, that we and our experiences are typical of cosmic beings. If the odds of us being real instead of Boltzmann brains are one in a million, say, waking up every day would be like walking out on the street and finding everyone in the city standing on their heads. You would expect there to be some reason why you were the only one left right side up. *And here, Pi noted, in that discussion, the idea that Humans are Important was at least to be raised! This brought all the panel to attention! And so Pi continued with her noting from the article in hand...*

Some cosmologists, James Hartle and Mark Srednicki, of the University of California, Santa Barbara, have questioned that assumption *(that we are just unimportant things hanging around)*. "For example," Dr. Hartle wrote "on Earth humans are not typical animals; insects are far more numerous. No one is surprised by this."

In an e-mail response to Dr. Hartle's view, Don Page of the University of Alberta, who has been a prominent voice in the Boltzmann debate, argued that what counted cosmologically was not sheer numbers, but consciousness, which we have in abundance over the insects! *Yes, came a chorus from the Panel!*

"I would say that we have no strong evidence against the working hypothesis that we are typical and that our observations are typical," he explained, "which is very fruitful in science for helping us believe that our observations are not just flukes but do tell us something about the universe."

Dr. Dyson and her colleagues suggested that the solution to the Boltzmann paradox was in denying the presumption that the universe would accelerate eternally. In other words, they said, that the cosmological constant was perhaps not really constant. If the cosmological constant eventually faded away, the universe would revert to normal expansion and what was left would eventually fade to black. With no more acceleration there would be no horizon with its snap, crackle and pop, and thus no material for fluctuations and Boltzmann brains.

String theory *(yes, another idea we will look into)* calculations have suggested that dark energy is indeed metastable and will decay, Dr. Susskind pointed out. "The success of ordinary cosmology," Dr. Susskind said, "speaks against the idea that the universe was created in a random fluctuation."

But nobody knows whether dark energy — if it dies — will die soon enough to save the universe from a surplus of Boltzmann brains. In 2006, Dr. Page calculated that the dark energy would have to decay in about 20 billion years in order to prevent it from being overrun by Boltzmann brains.

The decay, if and when it comes, would rejigger the laws of physics and so would be fatal and total, spreading at almost the speed of light and destroying all matter without warning.

There would be no time for pain, Dr. Page wrote: "And no grieving survivors will be left behind. So in this way it would be the most humanely possible execution." But the object of his work, he said, was not to predict the end of the universe but to draw attention to the fact that the Boltzmann brain problem remains.

People have their own favorite measures of probability in the multiverse, said Raphael Bousso of the University of California, Berkeley. "So Boltzmann brains are just one example of how measures can predict nonsense; anytime your measure predicts that something we see has extremely small probability, you can throw it out," he wrote in an e-mail message.

Another contentious issue is whether the cosmologists in their calculations could consider only the observable universe, which is all we can ever see or be influenced by, or whether they should take into account the vast and ever-growing assemblage of other bubbles forever out of our view predicted by eternal inflation. In the latter case, as Alex Vilenkin of Tufts University pointed out, "The numbers of regular and freak observers are both infinite." Which kind predominate depends on how you do the counting, he said...

Pi then entered with, in other words the discoveries are to be challenged with mathematics. Even so, after all this back and forth, which outlines a possibility that we might consider Dr. Lind capped, rather chops it off like this and I quote.

"In eternal inflation, the number of new bubbles being hatched at any given moment is always growing, Dr. Linde said, explaining one such counting scheme he likes.

So the evolution of people in new bubbles far outstrips the creation of Boltzmann brains in old ones. The main way life emerges, he said, is not by reincarnation but by the creation of new parts of the universe. "So maybe we don't need to care too much" about the Boltzmann brains," he said. "If you are reincarnated, why do you care about where you are reincarnated?" he asked. "It sounds crazy because here we are touching issues we are not supposed to be touching in ordinary science.

In response to all of this the panel spent several hours in discussion and yes, I would say, argument. Pi began the discussion, by stating firmly that we shall see evidence that our universe is expanding... hence the scientists in this article so noting the existence of infinity, have reason for that.

The net- net was finally issued as the following. "Boltzmann or the concept of floating brains arising from bubbles formed in space provide a way for a kind of reincarnation, but that is not a proper terminology as the "new humanoid" would not be at all the same.

It appears that the ideas back and forth are those of physicist reaching for deeper explanations as to what may occur in space time. But the effort is not without yield, as we are made more aware of the possibilities that our universe is not the only and that ours was generated with room for inflation.

Again, what we see here is an example of cosmologists reaching, trying to explain observations that range on the other side of fixed Einstein, but that is a trend since the 1920s.

It seems unlikely that these ideas represent a Human Time that we could somehow control after the fact we are though learning of the great complexity, and potential contradictions in the matter of "Space-time". The possibility of multiverses, one of which is ours, however, is clearly not one to be discarded!

Forever Probe, Document 6, p.m.
 As recorded and Filled, June 8,
Jane Caldwell, Technical Recorder

CHAPTER 3: SPACE'S TIME

THE COSMOS AND WHAT WE KNOW (FROM EVIDENCE!)

Forever Probe, Document 7, June 9, a.m.

After the lengthily discussions on the curious floating brains, the panel agreed to retire and enjoyed rest and an evening dinner.

The panel was aware that the Jains observe strict rules regarding what and when they eat. In general, ingredients including root vegetables are totally avoided by Jains as that kills the continuation of life. This often makes people think that their cuisine is uninteresting, which is not so. As the panel discovered in their time with Samyak and Daya most dishes, ranging from traditional to modern they prepared are very tasty without using these ingredients but that is by knowing the proper substitutes and intelligent methods of preparing the dishes.

At this sitting the hosts served "Badam ka Sheera" a meal containing of blanched almonds (badam) milk, ghee, sugar, cardamom (elaichi) powder and saffron strands garnished with almond silvers. This was served with Chocolate Cinnamon Coffee. Pi recorded in her diary another serving she loved called "Amritsari Gobi Mutter", containing cubes of peeled gourd, oil, chopped cabbage, curds, peas, cauliflower florets, cashew nut paste, cornflower, milk and cream. She also put in her diary the recipe for Jain Chop Suey they were served one day, having all but meat sauce-yet all substitutions created a truly delicious serving.

As the recorder of all this it was pleasing to see how much they all have become a family-joking and interrelating with much camaraderie. PI and Tim seem to have become "an Item"! And as things have progressed, there is no doubt that this Panel realized that they were working on something very precious.

The next morning, arising later than usual, Daniel brought the panel before Samyak and then he led off with the following question, which all had been asking.

We have had several explorations into Forever, from faith and philosophy, to reincarnation, to some proposals of what could happen in space. Part of that was quite curious, but as Pi said we have come across the dark holes (known), and the idea of multiple Universes, which are possible from the data record. Even so, more to our concern, what do we know from actual experiments, not just theories about the milieu in which we exist? That is what do we know about the cosmos around us, and then is there a hint of Forever in that?

More to the point we should look at what is known about the formation of our Universe and issues pertinent to that. He then pulled out a sizable file and began to teach morphing back into his Professorship, prefacing his comments **with**---*for the most part---I will take you into the thoughts of the American National Aeronautics and Space Administration. The articles are via the scientists of the Advisory Committee. The current members and their biographical sketches are available on the members' page of NASA (on line access is available). They are all very statured scientists.*

In these handouts we will follow various excerpts from the on-line articles as relate to central concerns. First up is The Big Bang! And within this is discussed the idea of "Inflation" that we heard of yesterday. This is an idea that clarifies certain problems on the form of our universe.

The notes following are a combination of the Professor's lecture and NASA's issue on that topic. Non-italic are directly from the NASA pages. He began as follows...Current belief is that our Universe began---as popularly described---a "Big Bang" from exploding concentrated atomic material....

The Big Bang Model citing directly from the source is based on.... "Cosmological Principle" which assumes that matter in the universe is uniformly distributed on all scales - large and small. This is a very useful approximation that allows one to develop the basic Big Bang scenario, but a more complete understanding of our universe requires going beyond the Cosmological Principle." *Samyak noted, indeed I see in the notes this brings in the inflation idea we saw back with the Boltzmann Brains.*

Yes, many cosmologists suspect that inflation theory, an extension of the Big Bang theory, may provide the framework for explaining the large-scale uniformity of our universe and the origin of structure within it. They think (The Professor was reading carefully and clearly from the articles)...Inflation was both rapid, and strong. It increased the linear size of the universe by more than 60 "e-folds", or a factor of ~1026 in only a small fraction of a second! So inflation is now considered an extension of the Big Bang theory since it explains the puzzles that have developed so well, while retaining the basic paradigm of a homogeneous expanding universe. Moreover, Inflation Theory links important ideas in modern physics, such as symmetry breaking and phase transitions, to cosmology.

Well, how does Inflation solve these problems? Here are three that the NASA scientist address. The first of these begins to get us ready for later discussion on the shape of space. The other two are ideas that one finds touched on later. And there is a bonus that will directly relate to the quest of this panel.

1. The Flatness Problem: The geometry of the universe is assumed flat as argument we shall soon see. However, imagine living on the surface of a soccer ball... It might be obvious to you that this surface was curved and that you were living in a "closed universe". However, if that ball expanded to the size of the Earth, it would appear flat to you, even though it is still a sphere on larger scales.

Now imagine increasing the size of that ball to astronomical scales. To you, it would appear to be flat as far as you could see, even though it might have been much curved to start with. Inflation stretches any initial curvature of the 3-dimensional universe to near flatness!

2. A Horizon Problem: Since Inflation supposes a burst of exponential expansion in the early universe, it follows that distant regions were actually much closer together prior to Inflation than they would have been with only "Standard Big Bang expansion". Thus, such regions could have been in causal contact prior to Inflation and could have attained a uniform temperature.

3. The Monopole Problem: Inflation allows for magnetic monopoles to exist as long as they were produced prior to the period of inflation. During inflation, the density of monopoles drops exponentially, so their abundance drops to undetectable levels[1].

As a bonus, Inflation also explains the origin of structure within the universe. Prior to inflation, the portion of the universe we can observe today was microscopic, and quantum fluctuation in the density of matter on these microscopic scales expanded to astronomical scales during Inflation. Over the next several hundred million years, the higher density regions condensed into stars, galaxies, and clusters of galaxies.

So now, panel members, we arrive at the question for Human Time above the simple descriptions of the Big Bang and the link between space and time soon to be discussed. "Human Time" might occur within some shape, and that shape could govern our ability to reach (best perhaps, look into) past and/or forward time.

On this rather highly suppositional proposition I prefer to relate to the findings of the U.S. National Aeronautics and Space Administration Scientists to follow the needed here. They are hooked into various analytical surveys that seek clarification on 'Shapes of Universe".

1.A magnetic monopole is a hypothetical elementary particle in particle physics which is specifically an isolated magnet with only one magnetic pole (a north pole without a south pole or vice versa). In more technical terms, a magnetic monopole would have a net "magnetic charge", as opposed to one centrally neutral when there are two poles. These hypothetically should be formed in Big Bang but where are they Inflated away?

Slices through the "Survey" which is a 3-dimensional map of the distribution of galaxies with the Earth at the center, is one example of an experimental attempt to catalog the observable universe. "There are two aspects to consider:
1. Its *LOCAL* GEOMETRY, which predominantly concerns the curvature of the universe, particularly the observable universe, and
2. Its *GLOBAL* GEOMETRY, which concerns details in the topology of the universe as a whole."

Here are thoughts from the source for this discussion. The observable universe can be thought of as a sphere that extends outwards from any observation point for 93 billion light years, that is going farther back in time and more "redshifted" the more distant away one looks.

Ideally, one can continue to look back all the way to the Big Bang. However, in practice, the farthest away one can look is something referred to as the cosmic microwave background (CMB) as anything past that was opaque.

Well here is what is said about that "Space", if you will.

"Experimental investigations show that the observable universe is very close to isotropic and homogeneous."

Samyak recognized that some definition would be helpful, on that pronouncement. Let me help, i.e. define…isotropic for an object or substance means it has a physical property which is the same value when measured in different directions…not varying in magnitude according to the direction of measurement.

Jehan said, I think, the comments so far mean we are within a sphere? Still if it is isotropic then all within or on the surface must behave in what we must eventually treat is a "Torus way". The notion of Torus in space will therefore need to be amplified, later.

The panel all agreed complimenting Jehan on that description, which all but I knew about. So the general notion was explained by the Professor who took a strip of paper and made a "Mobius" as example of a Torus. Then he continued to quote from the NASA reports…

…If the observable universe encompasses the entire universe, we may be able to determine the global structure of the entire universe by observation.

However, if the observable universe is smaller than the entire universe, our observations will be limited to only a part of the whole, and we may not be able to determine its global geometry through measurement.

From our experiments, it has been possible to construct different mathematical models of the global geometry of the entire universe but it is currently unknown whether the observable universe is identical to the global universe or it is instead many orders of magnitude smaller than it. The universe may be small in some dimensions and not in others. This would be analogous to the way a cuboid is longer in the dimension of length than it is in the dimensions of width and depth.

To test whether a given mathematical model describes the universe accurately, scientists look for the model's novel implications—what are some phenomena in the universe that we have not yet observed, but that must exist if the model is correct—and they devise experiments to test whether those phenomena occur or not.

For example, if the universe is a small closed loop, one would expect to see multiple images of an object in the sky, although not necessarily images of the same age."

Skellan, listening intently, added to that, it makes sense as traveling forward in the loop, would eventually bring us back but by that time what we see should be older, right?

Yes, that seems right, well, to go on…Cosmologists normally work with a given space-like slice that is called the commoving coordinates, the existence of a preferred set of which is possible and widely accepted in present-day physical cosmology. They are working at the level most correctly in "Space-time", Einstein's discovery which I believe Pi will cover next. We want first to see what NASA's real time experiments show.

Pi said, yes, that is the decision advised by our Astrophysicist Consultant, though it makes for a challenging order for discussion. I agree Pi, but to go on focusing on NASA…

…The section of space (yes, Space-time, said Pi) that can be observed is the backward light cone. That is all points within the cosmic light horizon, given time to reach a given observer, while the related term "Hubble Volume" can be used to describe either the past light cone or commoving space up to the surface of last scattering."

Pi said this seems for a great many folks confusing, almost "garbeldegook" but is Ok if you think deeply on it. Anyway the cosmologist do hasten to youte that shape cannot be described just as one point in time. They say as in the handout….To speak of "the shape of the universe at a point in time" is "Ontologically-Naïve". This is due to the outcomes of Einstein's theory, the so called relativity "of simultaneity". We cannot speak of different points in space as being "at the same point in time" nor, therefore, of "the shape of the universe at a point in time".

The Professor clarified...As we shall see from Einstein, Space-time is four coordinate or four dimensions, not observable by us three dimensional creatures. Further, shape implies topography, i.e. the establishment of multitude points in time. That, i.e. topography will be central to our later discussions.... The cosmologist point out, however ...We can define the geometry of Space-time. That is done by using a simple coordinate system.

So following is a "geometry" discussion dealing with the matter of the global universe and that is allowed within general relativity theory. That is In terms of geometry we can appreciate the overall "Curvature of Universe"

Before getting to that Pi interjected saying... some may not really know what that term Ontology means. It is the philosophical study of the nature of being, of becoming, of existence, or reality, as well as the basic categories of being and their relations.

She continued really seeming to enjoy bringing back her philosophy class notes, waiting in her exceptional brain. Traditionally it is listed as a part of the major branch of philosophy known as metaphysics. Ontology often deals with questions concerning what entities exist or may be said to exist and how such entities may be grouped... i.e. you see why the cosmologist would have said that regarding a point referencing space.

Samyak his eyes lighting up and a great smile forming looked at the young Ph.D. and simply said great addition and thank you child. Pi's facial reaction to that was almost comical as in no way did she think of herself as "Child".

*At that the Professor brought us back to the matter at hand introducing a number of questions written into the NASA articles, first...*What if our universe had only lasted for a second, or a year, or even one million years? The age of the universe is controlled by the basic rules that govern matter, energy, and time.

We needed almost 13.8 billion years to evolve and come to recognize this fact. How long the universe lasts and how it evolves depends on its total energy and matter content.

A universe with enormously more matter than ours would rapidly collapse back under its own gravity well before life could form. And, a very long lived universe might not have enough mass for stars to ever form.

In addition, our experiments (called "WMAP") have confirmed the existence of something we have begun to call, dark energy! (*Pi had to say, yes!*) This acts like an anti-gravity, driving the universe to accelerate its expansion. Had the dark energy dominated earlier, the universe would have expanded too rapidly to support the development of life.

Now we all know our universe seems to have Goldilocks properties: not too much and not too little -- just enough mass and energy to support the development of life.

But be that as it may, the circumstance demands that we master its dynamics. And those do clearly relate to shape and content. *Pi again said, "Yes! We do have to go in that direction, no question!"*

\`\`

That ended the review of the Big Bang! Various members of the panel helped to a consensus. The point was learned, our universe is probably inflationary, and quite central and importantly, although impacted by Einstein's theories, post the Big Bang and because of its subsequent formations, cosmologists are highly interested in the geometry and topography of it and that subject-geometry and topology would have a great deal to do with the quest of the panel. The reason is that it must be a part of Forever.

Samyak added...also to this is a "Human Time Compass". If we live in a shape, is there other intelligent life in the universe? I ask this because if we find them, they might tell us about that shape, since they would have traveled into ours.

Daniel, our Dr.Why, held up his hand on that and directed the subsequent discussion. He said, the point Samyak is well taken and clearly relates to our mission. It is simply a matter of life's persistence within Forever. We should think a bit about that, if it is not possible, then pursuit of Forever by us Thinking creatures seems redundant.

Tim's time had come, he definitely had some thoughts on this, so indicating. And the Professor stressed to all, we should extend this meeting for Dr. Bean's comments.

So it was, Tim put in the following. It reflected his concerns about life in general, but also helped us to understand its and our potential.

He said he was as Dr.Why borrowing from comments by NASA scientists and handed out a document with excerpts he felt were most important. They stimulated much discussion and are as follows, with Tim reading.

*As some here know....*The recipe for life requires a delicate balance of cosmic ingredients. The differences in the early soup of universe particles were very small, so large scale changes take time to manifest themselves. In point of fact, we don't know whether or not there is other intelligent life in the universe. There is no reason there shouldn't be. We know by our own existence that the universe is conducive to life. But there are many hurdles to overcome for intelligent life to form, and many threats to its continued existence once it does form.

Life constantly faces the prospect of extinction. Life requires as is well known, energy, water, and carbon; an environmental disaster that will remove water, dooms life. Other environment disasters threaten all life.

Here are some more points on matter, once again from NASA scientist. On Earth we have had huge meteor impacts that are believed to have caused mass extinctions. The harsh radiation of space is blocked only by Earth's atmosphere and magnetic field. Environmental instabilities cause ice ages. One day, billions of years from now, our Sun will burn out. Other, heavier stars end their lives in explosions called supernovae; the blast and radiation from a nearby supernova could destroy all life on Earth."

Tim said, and here again is a reference to that "Dark Energy" that we are having highlighted. "The dark energy will inexorably stretch the universe into an icy cold end. Since we don't know what the dark energy is, this might be wrong, but no less deadly depending on how the nature of the dark energy changes.

Threatening as that is, and as most know… Many people are engaged in efforts to detect life in the universe outside of our world. There are two strategies: we look for it, or it finds us. Perhaps a middle ground would be if we detected signals for life. Nevertheless, someday, we may know for sure whether we are alone in the universe. In the meantime the search goes on, as we also try to understand the universe and how it may be conducive to life.

By detecting and measuring the density fluctuations in the cosmic microwave background using the WMAP space mission *(As just brought up that will detect dark energy)* we are learning about the early universe and we begin to understand the basic ingredients that make life possible."

Tim then said, In the future, it is the intention of these scientists to enhance these life seeking efforts with other missions, such as NASA's "Einstein Inflation Probe", which would strive to detect the gravity disturbances from the era when the universe originally inflated. This passionate search for knowledge is characteristic of human life.

Tim then continued with the following… But life did happen, in space time. We know for certain because we are it, and so it the most important of all considerations, to know and understand is "Human Time"! That time required Space within Space-time…past, present and future connected.

What could that space look like? Answers to that require we deal with Einstein and that which followed his theories.

However, no one has yet succeeded in synthesizing a "protocell" using basic components which would have the necessary properties of life. Tim noted here, although recent work, such as that of our laboratory and that of Jack Szostak at Massachusetts General Hospital and the Howard Hughes Medical Institute, may be about to change that.

Some commentators argue that…The spontaneous development of life runs counter to stipulation in the Second law of Thermodynamics that entropy and disorder inexorably increases over time and that order and organization always declines.

However… The work of the Russian-born Belgian chemist Ilya Prigogine in the 1960s and 1970s, showed that many systems spontaneously organize themselves if they are forced away from thermodynamic equilibrium (such as by radiation or other unknown influences). Besides, the law specifically applies to isolated systems, whereas living systems are necessarily open and interactive systems.

And, there are many other examples of apparent spontaneous increases in order (such as the growth of crystals from featureless liquids, the development of large scale structures in the universe, etc.), but the growth of order in one place is always at the price of entropy generated elsewhere (such as the production of heat or other types of radiation).

A recent experiment, led by Jason Dworkin, subjected a frozen mixture of water, methanol, ammonia and carbon monoxide to ultraviolet radiation, attempting to mimic conditions found in an extraterrestrial environment. This combination yielded large amounts of organic material that appeared to self-organize, and to form cell membrane-like bubbles when immersed in water. The bubbles were also found to actually seemed to glow or fluoresce when exposed to test system ultraviolet light (perhaps precursor to primitive photosynthesis?), as well as providing a protective layer to diffuse any damage that might otherwise be inflicted by the ultraviolet radiation, which would have been vital in an early world without an ozone layer.

Tim was, after reading this on life genesis, asked what all this has to do with the quest of the Panel. He simply said, our objective, on the outside of expectations, is to see if there is a way to see the past and the future, and then enter and change as needed. Obviously, this involves the very beginning of Human Time, and that the genesis of life on earth! Further, as Dr.Why said if there is no potential for life as intelligent then the quest for Forever is redundant.

This quieted the panel, all nodding their heads and they listened intently as Tim finished his report.

So such evidence seems to suggest that all life on Earth has developed from a single organism back in the mists of time, and perhaps even from one single common ancestral cell.

*Current thinking suggest that…*The "last universal common ancestor" (the hypothetical latest living organism from which all organisms now living on Earth descend, or, in other words, the most recent common ancestor of all current life on Earth) is estimated to have lived some 3.5 to 3.8 billion years ago. However, the actual mechanism for its origination is still far from clear! *Would it not be incredible to be able to see that? Think how much we could learn about saving the future!*

While the circumstances that led to life on Earth are no doubt special, there is no reason to suspect that they are peculiar to Earth. As Richard Dawkins points out, if the universe contains a billion planets (which some scientists consider a conservative estimate), then the chances that life will arise on one of them is not really so remarkable.

*If, as we shall see into, and I have found in my search… some physicists claim…*Our universe is just one of many in a multiverse, each of which contains a billion planets, then the chances that life will arise on at least one of them is almost a certainty. Indeed, many scientists believe that it is entirely possible that different forms of life may have appeared approximately simultaneously in the early history of Earth. Some of these may now be extinct, or they may survive as extremophiles (an organism that thrives in extreme conditions that are detrimental to the majority of life on Earth), or they may simply have gone unnoticed. Obviously, it is important to our agenda that we be aware of such possibility. It is only in quite recent years that living things have been discovered in conditions as unlikely as hot volcanic vents deep beneath the sea and in totally dark and Dr. Why lava tubes in the desert.

As science progresses, there is even the possibility - or the specter, depending on your outlook - of one day creating man-made life. Harvard scientist George Church for example is hot on the trail to building a completely man-made living cell. He has identified a total of 151 essential components which he believes represent the minimum for the creation of life - a sort of blueprint for life itself - and has been making rapid progress in synthesizing them in the laboratory.

Think deeply about this my friends, is that an advantage or is that a tragedy to happen in the near future. Our agenda, would possibly let us look into that - praise or warn as need be. This remains an area of intense debate and speculation in both scientific and religious circles-while new discoveries are made almost every year (which may, or may not, throw some light on the subject), no definitive solutions have yet been yielded!

But, to close my report, in answer to Dr.Why's invitation, Yes Forever would seem to contain the possibility of forward production of life, that would of course we hope include more Human Time.

After Tim's report (all saying an excellent summary of scientific thinking) the group held a two hour discussion on the possibilities.

Skellan, noted (indicating that it was hard for him to let loose of the notion) if we were to go back in time, how we would know where to "Land". Still others as Jehan and Angelei thought it would be wonderful to know how it all began, and from that perhaps change the outcome giving an end to cruelty for Human Beings!

Forever Probe, Document 7,
As Recorded and Filled, June 9, a.m.
Respectfully Submitted,
Jane Caldwell, Technical Recorder

EINSTEIN'S THINKING ABOUT SPACE

Forever Probe, Document 8, June 9, p.m.

The presentation and discussion to follow Document 7, June 9, a.m. was taken up after an extended break, most of the party traveling into town to the "Parliamentary as Angelei put it" to meet on behalf of Samyak many officials who he knew well.

During the last discussion, and review of the Cosmos-i.e. what is known, the importance of something called dark matter and dark energy arose again and then came an inquiry from Daniel. Doesn't much of this that has come up, you know---the questions on the Cosmos and our agenda have most centrally the need to understand Einstein's Theory... as we all know at least it proposed "Space-time", and "Time" are at the root of our concerns?

So it was that Samyak our Coordinator decided that we should at last look into "Space-time' in detail, although he stood by the progression so far. He commented that before pushing into equations we needed to understand the basic components, time, infinity and evidence on the Cosmos. It also was a naturally targeted matter for after that, as he said, it was related to questions concerning the curvature of space, dark matter, dark holes, quantum effects and others that would affect our thinking about Einstein's Theory and our mission. There would be serious questions on those matters and how well they fit in Einstein's theories!

Tim and Angelei noted for this that any technical matters would be reviewed and presented by Dr.Pi their physics-mathematician and they had on hand an astrophysicist who would be a reviewer and consultant for the group. It was however, agreed to keep the topic "in scale" as much as possible for the more general reader.

So the panel came together directly after breakfast. They gathered in the Jane home the doors nearly shut as there was a great dust storm forming.

All, indeed, agreed it was time to look into Albert Einstein's Theories. Samyak seemed satisfied as he had lead the group to understand the importance of various matters that impinge upon the details of the theory and its voracity.

Space Time--Einstein's Relativity. *Samyak introduced the topic ...Well the ideas of time and infinity, the older beliefs and the basics of the universe explored, I think we are now ready to deal with Dr. Einstein's Space-time. There will be the geometry and topology we brushed on involved which will I am sure be at the center of your concerns about "Forever'.*

Ms. Pi would you like to begin this discussion.

Pi entered right away...

The theory involved is deceptively simple, yet it is considered by in large correct and it certainly is dictating massive effort in fitting it into recent thinking toward a "Unified Theory of Space and Time".

First there is no "absolute" frame of reference! The laws of physics are correct, alternate perceptions as earlier proposed do not apply. Thus, every time you measure an object's velocity, or its momentum, or how it experiences time, it's always in relation to something else (I think of this as chosen in its own realm.)

Second, and here is the - shall we say fixing proposition - the speed of light is the same no matter who measures it or how fast the person measuring it is going. Third, nothing can go faster than light!

So it was that Einstein's theory of special relativity created a fundamental link between space and time.

This he did without experiment, in his head as we have said, marking to us all at least that his was human time and the human brain in effect controlled our vision of time. Well that is a deflection from his pure theoretical stance.

In his view, the universe can be viewed as having three space dimensions — up/down, left/right, forward/backward — and one time dimension.

This four-dimensional space is widely referred to in a specific way as the Space-time continuum!

So it is, if you move fast enough through space, the observations that you make about space and time differ somewhat from the observations of other people, who are moving at different speeds.

Furthermore, the theory does not contain any fixed geometric background structures, that is, it is background independent. It thus satisfies a more stringent general principle of "relativity", namely that the laws of physics are the same for all observers in their own place and Space-time frame!

Pi, surprisingly, tried to help us (like me), warning "There are terms and references that may confuse the average reader, but not to worry these are merely descriptive. So to continue...

Locally, as expressed in something called the "equivalence principle", space-time is "Minkowskian", and certain laws of physics exhibit "Local Lorentz Invariance".

That is, to put it more simply but directly---in special relativity, the Minkowskian space-time is what is commonly called "a four-dimensional manifold", created by one Hermann Minkowski.

Hermann Minkowski introduced a certain method for graphing coordinate systems in Minkowski space-time.

At this point Pi handed out a page with equations and a diagram (which I have included in the dictation record next) and then she continued...different coordinate systems will disagree with an objects spatial orientation and/or position in time. As you can see from the diagram, there is only one spatial axis (the x-axis) and one time axis (the ct-axis). If need be, one can introduce an extra spatial dimension (say x'-axis); unfortunately, this is the limit to the number of dimensions in that graphing in four dimensions is impossible!

So the accepted means for graphing follows a special rule. The rule for graphing in Minkowski space-time goes as follows:

1)　The angle (α) between the x-axis and the x'-axis is given by ...
*　　...tan Ø = v/c*

2)　Where v is the velocity of the object.
*　　(The speed of light, i.e. c through space-time always makes an angle of 45 degrees with either axis.)*

Simply, as I have said, the theory describes space having four dimensions: three dimensions of space (x, y, and z) and one dimension of time.

In mathematical-geometric terms...Minkowski space-time has what is called a metric signature of (-+++) and is always flat! That idea, that it always flat, though hard to come into most of us is nonetheless the fixed principle! Pi showed us displays from various articles, to help see the planes, then continued...

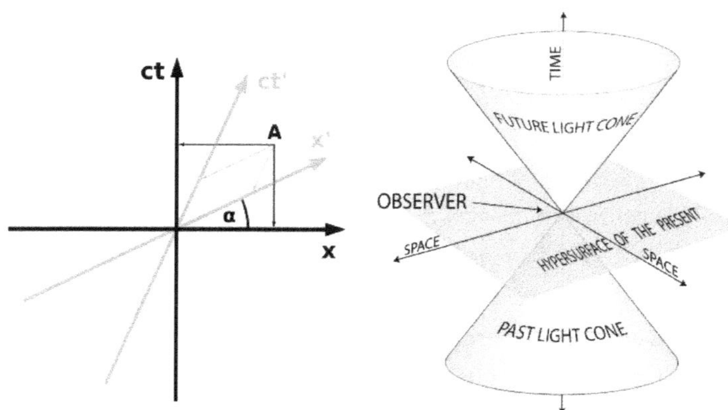

Angelei came in with a concern. Pi.. I can't see, understand--what the label is on the cones plan on this side. Pi cleared this for us a bit. Well that says "Hyperspace of the Present". The notion of Hyperspace is a topological description and will be covered, don't know by me or the "Astrophysics Adviser". But it will be amplified later!

Although, the convention often is to call Minkowski space-time (simply space-time). It must be noted, however, that Minkowski space-time is only applicable in special relativity. This is the case for objects not moving relative to each other. So it is, by long practiced description, space-time can be thought of as a four-dimensional coordinate system in which the axes may be expressed as shown in this diagram I passed out.

More precisely to Einstein, however, space-time in the general relativity theory (following after special relativity) uses the well-known and so called field equation or the "Einstein Field Equation" (EFE). Pi wrote these out on a paper hand out for all.

She noted though, unusual for her, that this is just to see our report complete, but she understood that the equations were not immediately understandable to most folks.

Here in the report for completeness are the EFE. *The Einstein field equations (EFE) may be written in the form…*

$$R_{\mu\nu} - 1/2\ R_{g\mu\nu} + \Lambda_{g\mu\nu} = 8\pi\ G/c^4\ T_{\mu\nu}$$

…where $R_{\mu\nu}$ is the "Ricci curvature tensor", the R (with no subterm) is the scalar curvature. To continue $g_{\mu\nu}$ is the metric tensor, Λ is the cosmological constant and G is Newton's gravitational constant. The c, of course, is the speed of light in vacuum, and lastly $T\mu\nu$ is the stress–energy tensor.

The EFE is what may be called a tensor equation-relating a set of symmetric 4×4 tensors. Each tensor has 10 independent components.

Now please pardon the following…we are just making sure of the record…There are four "Bianchi" identities that in effect reduce the number of independent equations from 10 to 6, leaving the metric with four gauge fixing degrees of freedom, which correspond to the freedom to choose a coordinate system!

OK, obtuse to many, but what to us is most noteworthy is that <u>the equation contains a curvature factor</u>, in the Ricci tensor. Pi emphasized this twice.

Although the Einstein field equations were initially formulated in the context of a four-dimensional theory, some theorists have experimented, exploring their consequences in "n" dimensions.

The equations in contexts outside of general relativity are still referred to as the Einstein field equations. The vacuum field equations (obtained when T is identically zero) define Einstein manifolds.

Despite the simple appearance of the equations they are actually quite complicated (Causing quite a laugh from the panel!).

Given a specified distribution of matter and energy in the form of a stress–energy tensor, the EFE are understood to be equations for the metric tensor $g_{\mu\nu}$, as both the Ricci tensor and scalar curvature depend on the metric in a complicated nonlinear manner. In fact, when fully written out, the EFE are a system of 10 coupled and nonlinear---hyperbolic-elliptic partial differential equations!

At this point the panel was looking totally lost and frankly exhausted, So Pi, most unusually sympathetic, said, OK, sorry, but bear with me…Why is this a construction of his equations?

Well, Einstein believed Space-time is curved! This he thought must be because space contains mass, planets, and so on. To allow for space-time to actually curve; the resulting effects must be those of gravity (g). Note in the equation that important term! Gravity, Light, Time, yes.

For the panel, however, and most importantly, introducing something like shape, tensors and gravity, opened the door to questions on special searching, which is travel within this space's "Forever". To these comments, Pi brought the Panel back to a kind of more simplistic ground zero.

Pi, said, "in spite of this complexity, it is clear that Space-time can be in Einstein's "Minds-Eye" thought of as the "Arena" in which all of the events in the universe take place!

Whatever the whole is there---even within little events, each is referenced to something within itself, wherein the speed of light is the same, constant and the fastest there is.

All that one needs to specify in space-time "lingo" is a certain time frame and a typical spatial orientation!

In Space-time light speed never changes for any given time and all times, but for "outside observers" moving near light speed aging is slower as they are catching up with the Arena's Overall Time. Pi said, that is always a hard one, but think deep.

A basic question then is, where are we in that "Arena", what forms does our space-in space time take, and in what format could we be? Well it is certain that we exist in a Universe, we have explored that, i.e. is time and references are there!"

And PI said with some emphasis, like she was mounting a war horse "We must first put in the question if the Master Einstein was perfect!"

I submit that he was not! Samyak entered here. "Thank you madam Pi. On your suggestion I believe we do have to consider that matter! I have here a paper by a Karen Wright presented in 2004.

It is copied and appears in your folder as document #51. I will read and paraphrase as necessary in the way we have been doing…

...While Einstein's theory set physics on fire, he was often wrong the author says, something most people do not know, but panel keep in mind please, as she says even his errors led to deep truths. However, further quoting her we have the following"...

"Albert Einstein got it wrong. Not once, not twice, but, well, countless times. He made subtle blunders, he made outright goofs, and his oversights were glaring. Error infiltrated every aspect of his thinking.

He was wrong about the universe, wrong about its contents, wrong about the workings of atoms.

Yet Einstein's mistakes could be compelling and instructive, and some were even essential to the progress of modern physics.

"Most scientists would give their eyeteeth to make even one of Einstein's mistakes," says theoretical physicist Fred Goldhaber of the State University of New York at Stony Brook.

But they were still mistakes!

And Samyak put in here, "Yes, and that makes a great deal of difference to us in pursuit of "Forever", in understanding it's, i.e. Forever's role in relation to "Space-time" or for that matter vice a versa!

Let us take a rest and then continue this "Einstein's Theory and His Mistakes" after the break.

Meanwhile we will impose on Ms. Pi to work the equations over for those of you who feel you can grasp the math, though I don't believe that is really an essential since we are not likely to change it!"

THE MASTER'S MISTAKES

Forever Probe, Document 8, June 9, p.m.
The "Einstein Meeting" Continued

Samyak brought the group back together after the break and began immediately saying, *this is all from an article as said by Karen Wright. I will just read it, and you can question or comment as you wish as we go along...*

In 1911 Einstein predicted how much the sun's gravity would deflect nearby starlight and got it wrong by half.

He rigged the equations of general relativity to explain why the cosmos was standing still when it wasn't.

Pi, set in, yes that has always worried me!

Beginning in the mid-1920s, he churned out faulty unified field theories at a prodigious rate. American physicist Wolfgang Pauli complained that Einstein's "tenacious energy guarantee[s] us on the average one theory per annum," each of which "is usually considered by its author to be [the] 'definitive solution." And, while other physicists built careers describing the random antics within atoms, Einstein never even allowed that God *might* play dice with the universe.

However, Einstein's blunders reveal the unique mind behind his winning thoughts. Einstein's mistakes get upstaged by a few of his good ideas. Still, his reported errors deserve scrutiny, and not just for the schadenfreude. "There is no logical path to these laws; only intuition... can reach them," Einstein said. In retrospect, however, his discoveries seem eminently logical.

Only his errors preserve the doubts, quirks, and prejudices that fed his intuition. If his triumphs describe how the universe works, then his mistakes describe how he worked.

In 1916 Einstein found what he considered a glitch in his new theory of general relativity. His equations showed that the contents of the universe should be moving— either expanding or contracting. But at the time, the universe seemed the very definition of stasis. All the data, facts, and phenomena known in the early 1900s said that the Milky Way was the cosmos itself and that its stars moved slowly, if at all.

Einstein had presented the definitive version of the general theory of relativity to the Prussian Academy of Sciences the previous year, and he was not inclined to retract it. So he invented a fudge factor, called lambda that could function mathematically to hold the universe at a standstill. The term implied that space itself had energy that resisted the contraction caused by gravity or the expansion from the stretching of space.

Lambda "was not justified by our actual knowledge of gravitation," Einstein said. But he stood by the ideal of the unchanging heavens until the moment, in 1929, when American astronomer Edwin Hubble discovered that the universe is expanding! Einstein later called lambda his greatest blunder. But a greater embarrassment—with the benefit of hindsight—was his failure to predict universal expansion.

Pi said just a note here panel it is fact that "our" universe is expanding!

He should have questioned the plausibility of a paralyzed universe, says emeritus physicist James Peebles of Princeton University: "A static universe isn't physically self-consistent. The sun can't shine forever. He didn't recognize that, and I've always found that startling."

Here Pi stood up proudly and wrote on a little blackboard Daya had obtained the following equation to be passed around. Here is the equation of focus...

$$G_{\mu v} - \lambda g = - \kappa (T_{\mu v} - 1/2 g_{\mu v} T)$$

*Then she said, pointing to it (λ) this is a "fudge" factor that would allow the equation to describe a static universe. Note how that value can affect the value of Guv and g or gravity... Well, sorry Samyak you were reading...Yes Doctor to go on......*Some of Einstein's peers recognized it in the master's own equations. When Dutch astronomer Willem de Sitter pointed out that one interpretation of general relativity looked awfully like an expanding universe, Einstein sought a flaw in his reasoning.

Russian mathematician Alexander Friedmann showed that general relativity explicitly posits a cosmos in motion; Einstein responded by publishing a short note claiming that the analysis was downright wrong. In a second paper, he conceded that the model was mathematically correct but dismissed it as physically absurd.

Why was Einstein so set on an immobile universe? Part of his insistence may have been fatigue. He had just completed the last mile of a decade long intellectual marathon that made his earlier breakthroughs—special relativity, say, or the discovery of light quanta—look like a sprint.

Yet, General Relativity was the first, and remains the only, theory (*I suppose that has been checked, Samyak said*) capable of uniting space, time, mass, energy, motion, and light in a grand vision of the nature and the fate of the cosmos.

Its formulation had cost Einstein so much effort that it quite literally made him ill—he collapsed with stomach pains and lost more than 50 pounds in the winter and spring of 1917.

"You have to remember, he started the game. He did all the heavy lifting," says Goldhaber. "He said, "Let's make a model of the universe." Nobody else even had the tools to begin that. He couldn't be expected to get it all right."

Einstein never questioned the longstanding evidence for a static universe, even when new observations gave the first hints of expansion. When de Sitter showed him data from the Lowell Observatory in Arizona that suggested distant nebulas were speeding away in all directions, Einstein balked: OK, quasi-stationary then, he said.

Einstein was as much an aesthete *(a connoisseur I believe this is implied)* as a scientist, and he seemed to have a fundamentally aesthetic reason for preferring a stable cosmos.

Pi raises her hand, and was issued a go ahead from Samyak who stopped reading… *she said, "but we see that instability often don't we in simple things like comets, and the suns wave"s...*

*"Yes, Pi...reading on"...*Although he never fully articulated it, this instinct for beauty would surface again and again in his very particular sense of how a proper law of physics worked, what proper math looked like, and the way nature should operate.

Samyak interjected before the next comment … *This author did note what we have, that our minds are outlining all of this, it is occurring in our Human Time....She said...*

He gave primacy to "free inventions of the mind," as he called them, which were aloof from facts and phenomena. The German mathematician Felix Klein accused Einstein of working "under the influence of obscure physical-philosophical impulses."

Those impulses drove his imagination beyond common sense and ordinary insight to radical and fundamental truths. But he sometimes turned against the daring implications of his ideas—especially when such implications were presented by someone else.

General relativity provoked a welter of secondhand analyses, and it seemed to gall Einstein to watch other theoreticians spin webs of sticky perplexities from the silk of his great achievement. He was often disapproving of the claims colleagues made based on his equations. "In my personal experiences I have rarely learned better to know the shadiness of people than in connection with this theory," he wrote to a friend.

Einstein objected when one colleague dared use general relativity—a geometric description of pliant Space-time—to predict a cosmic phenomenon in which space, time, and the laws of relativity cease to exist. The phenomenon is now known as a black hole.

Yes, now the subject of the Black Hole, said Pi, and a danger to all scientists is to think one an absolute genius so as to not respect opinion of others. A good point said Samyak, and the author does go on with…

…The German astrophysicist Karl Schwarzschild spent the early years of World War I on the eastern front, calculating ballistics trajectories for artillery units. He used his spare time to vet old astronomical problems with the new metric of general relativity.

One exercise considered was what would happen if a star were radically compressed into an infinitesimal volume.

Schwarzschild's results showed that, at some critical density, the star's gravity would become so strong that it would swallow everything—matter, light, even space and time—within a specific radius. Schwarzschild thus developed a mathematical description of black holes decades before they were observed or understood.

Einstein never took the idea seriously. "He thought they were an artifact, a sloppy application of the equations," says Peebles.

Samyak then emphasized that it is important to us this notion…mathematically, a black hole is a so-called a singularity—a place where space and time become so distorted that the equations of general relativity yield infinities, rather than rational numbers, as solutions. We all need to mark such observations in our notes!

*Nonetheless to continue…*To Einstein, infinity was no answer at all—it was a failure. He could believe in gravity waves and other unlikely predictions of general relativity because math supported them. Black holes defied math. He called Schwarzschild's results "a true disaster."

General relativity was Einstein's favorite "free invention." He was confident it could describe the behavior of every object in the universe. Thus he claimed, somewhat tautologically, that any instance in which his equations failed could not actually represent nature. "Einstein didn't think that [Schwarzschild's] solution corresponded to anything real," says theoretical physicist Frank Wilczek of MIT.

Samyak outlined for us though once again… we have considered infinity, and rationally and it is out and within… But to continue with the article…

Einstein had merely to step into another viewpoint to reconcile the apparent singularity with his philosophical beliefs, says Wilczek. Yet the man who knew the most about relativity failed to regard Schwarzschild's solutions from a different vantage point. To an observer trapped within a black hole, the laws of general relativity still obtain. In fact, all the laws of physics would appear to function as usual. "We could be in a black hole right now and not know it," Wilczek says!

That would be an idea worthy of Einstein, were he not "distracted".

"The most beautiful experience we can have is the mysterious," Einstein once wrote. Yet when his thinking revealed one of the most notorious paradoxes of the physical world, he ultimately shunned it.

The mystery has to do with the nature of light. *Daniel said, oh, yes, my (very tough) assignment into the uncertainty principal, but we have an astrophysicist to detail that later, that is we must and will consider this much deeper later. And, Samyak said Doctor you have been given a heady assignment, but repeating can reinforce, so to continue…*

…Experiments conducted at the start of the century had shown that light shining on a metal plate produced showers of electrons whose speed, or energy, was the same no matter how bright the light. Einstein explained the so-called photoelectric effect by asserting that light, which was known to flow in continuous waves, could also be regarded as sputtering along in discrete particles, or quanta. Each of these particles—every quantum of light at a given wavelength—carried the same amount of energy, he argued, and so dispatched a single electron with the same energetic kick. Thus, did Einstein discover the photon. However, he lived to regret it.

The wave-particle duality was unsettling enough. But when Danish physicist Niels Bohr showed that the electrons in atoms, too, must behave as quanta to account for observations, Einstein made a conceptual leap that troubled him even more. In pondering the quantum interactions between matter and light, Einstein found he could calculate neither the timing nor the direction of the photons spontaneously emitted from atoms. The emissions were fundamentally random!

Chance seemed to be an ineluctable *(panel this meaning is unable to be resisted or avoided; inescapable)* element of the quantum world! *And Samyak outlined for us, this "Quantum" idea is one that we too must know about, how it may impact our agenda. Well that we will have on the "do it" list, but to continue with the article…The author notes…*

In fact, "Quantum Theory" suggests that random events are rampant at the subatomic level. There is no way to predict cause and effect on a case-by-case basis. The best that physicists can do is calculate probabilities, which do or do not prove out for a large number of events. *(And that may mark the case for us, Pi said here, we await the review by our astrophysicist.)*

To Einstein, a statistical probability was even less acceptable than the infinities of a singularity.

A physics that could not predict individual events was no physics at all, he said. It was, at best, guesswork. And it certainly did not correspond to reality, which, like the universe, Einstein preferred to see as stable, orderly, and knowable to the most intimate detail. Apparently, he regarded mysteries as beautiful only if they offered some hope of solution.

"That he would choose to play dice with the world," Einstein wrote of God, "is something that I cannot believe for a single moment." Bohr supposedly replied, "Stop telling God what to do!" But the aesthete in Einstein turned his back on quantum theory.

A new generation of physicists rushed to embrace it. In the 1920s quantum mechanics became the rage, and it advanced by leaps and bounds, thanks in large part to Einstein's persistent efforts to discredit it. At the famous Solvay conferences in 1927 and 1930, Einstein challenged his friend Bohr, the chief proponent of quantum mechanics, with thought experiments meant to reveal logical contradictions in the theory. At first Bohr would be devastated, but he always managed to produce an answer to Einstein's critique.

By the 1930s quantum mechanics had become intellectually unassailable. The vast majority of physicists today believe that the subatomic realm really is, in some sense, unknowable! *Pi said to this again there are consequences our astrophysicist will undoubtedly review. Sorry Samyak…continue…*

…Einstein eventually relaxed his vigilance, but he never accepted quantum mechanics as truth. "The more successes the quantum theory enjoys, the sillier it looks," he said. With its wave-particle paradox, the theory offended his aesthetic sensibilities; with its irreducible randomness, it impugned his scientific potency; with its popularity among the younger crowd, it may have triggered some very human aversion in an aging icon! "He had dominated fundamental physics from 1905 to 1915, with an extraordinary series of insights," Wilczek says. "And then he continued to dominate for 10 years more. To be competing with young whippersnappers would not be a very appealing prospect for a scientist of his stature."

Einstein seemed to agree. "Truly new things one finds only in one's youth," he once opined. "Later one becomes more experienced, more famous, and dumber." (*The panel clearly found the humor and possible truth in this!*)

In the last decades of his life, Einstein chose to work far from the madding crowd of quantum enthusiasts. He followed the mathematics of general relativity toward what he hoped would be a theory subsuming *(including)* the laws of gravity and subatomic particles. He would recognize this unified theory, he said, by its beauty or self-evident rightness. He never came close to finding it, but he never doubted that someone would. "I cannot base this conviction on logical reasons," he said. "My only witness is the pricking of my little finger."

Some might call his last, fruitless quest a mistake too. But it's a mistake other physicists are more than willing to emulate.

The "Theory of Everything", the deeper truth that unites all the forces of nature, that pulls cosmology and quantum theory together, remains the most important quest of physics.

No one has pursued Einstein's peculiar approach, but before his efforts are dismissed, it may be instructive to consider the eventual fate of Einstein's self-proclaimed greatest blunder, lambda (λ). Lambda, also known as the cosmological constant, has come in handy of late. In the last decade astronomers discovered the expanding universe is also accelerating—expanding faster and faster! *This was clearly noted by the panel, pens working. Each could readily see the implication in their Quest.*

That seeming confounding scenario can be represented mathematically if general relativity includes a term, just like the cosmological constant, that imbues empty space with an unidentified force. "Making use of the cosmological constant is by now a venerable aspect of contemporary cosmology," says Fred Goldhaber. The day may come when all of Einstein's blunders seem equally prescient!

Our Coordinator then noted, I think we all observe that as a great and truthful paper. However, it is important that we respect the man, and those that would dare challenge, It is important that as we reach our conclusions that we stand recognizing that no matter the seeming greatness of a scientist, science means we always continue with alternated hypothesis. Even so, though that is the case from our look into the Cosmos, we do need to move into shape and the matter of curvature, which is one that we must understand, in so far as it leads us eventually into or out of "Forever".

I have a publisher to see in town today, for my book on the evils of time. So let us reconvene tomorrow morning.

Jehan mentioned, *In addition to the matter of curvature we should not forget that there are other items on our list to know. On the review of Einstein's equation gravity seems to be something we need to have a look at as well as the matter of Black Holes, and Uncertainty Effects.*

Samyak insured the Panel that all this would be covered as each has papers that will get us there. He then took up a manuscript in a binder and wished us all well as he departed after a graceful bow...

Given the time, the panel members took the opportunity to wander about town and to 'eat out". Following is a note I typed out on that later after their report. I know this was personal but it did contain some nice information.

'Daya walked with Pi and Tim. As they walked along Tim reached for Pi's hand, Daya said. She at first looked at him with a curious grin, then with Daya smiling she took up the extended hand giving Tim a softly warm look, and smiled somewhat embarrassed at Daya. The three knew all was well.

So the walk turned into a visit, the two always holding hands to the main attractions in Jaisalmer Fort & Fort Palace as well as the local market, Gadisisar Lake and the Sand Dunes, where they witnessed the glowing yellow sand from whence the city gets the name of one surrounded by gold. After a casual tour they stopped at what had become the favorite restaurant of some, who are the non-vegetarians in the Panel...The Trio Jaislmer.

I found this on Wikipedia before we left...”Jain objections to the eating of meat, and fish are based on the principle of non-violence (ahimsa, figuratively "non-injuring"). Every act by which a person directly or indirectly supports killing or injury is seen as act of violence (*himsa*), which creates harmful reaction karma. The aim of ahimsa is to prevent the accumulation of such karma. The extent to which this intention is put into effect varies greatly among Hindus, Buddhists and Jains. Jains believe nonviolence is the most essential religious duty for everyone (*ahinsā paramo dharmaḥ*, a statement often inscribed on Jain temples). It is an indispensable condition if there is to be liberation from the cycle of reincarnation, which is the ultimate goal of all Jain activities. Jains share this goal with Hindus and Buddhists, but their approach is particularly rigorous.”

However, I was told, at the Trio, where the three went, there is for visitors a bit of a respite, thereby attracting some members of the Panel from time to time. Tim let me read the entries in his diary on this. There is in the diary the comment...”Jaisalmer per se is not a ”very non-vegetarian food kind of a place” so we didn't really have much choice but to try this small restaurant almost shack in appearance but offering one of the most delectable mutton dishes you would have tasted. Their “laal maans” and “mutton nagori” are just so amazing one who is not vegetarian must try those dishes!”

“As one need know Mutton, the meat from adult sheep, provides a more gamey alternative to standard beef or pork. You can use mutton as you would use pork or beef, and some options are mutton stew and roast mutton. The meat is rich in a variety of minerals and vitamins, but it contains more fat than very lean cuts of beef. In moderation, mutton can be a beneficial component in an overall healthy diet.”

"In the Muslim world the eating of mutton foods is permitted if the animal is raised and slaughtered under certain prescribed methods… Tim was content being one seeking his faith between father and mother, Pi was not particular being atheist, though Daya staid, of course with her vegetarian fare. "(End of special note.)

After that time of tourism and discovery wherever they chose to visit, they all arrived promptly back with Samyak's for the evening.

There was before that next meeting a good deal of discussion and much review as the concepts were very challenging for many in the party. Still, having our variety Panel helped all.

Forever Probe, Document 8, June 9, p.m.,
Einstein and Mistakes,
Duly Recorded and Filed, Jane Caldwell,
Technical Recorder

SHAPES IN SPACE!

Forever Probe, Document 9, June 10, a.m.

It was Chandler who was to start the meeting after breakfast. The panel gathered once again in the little Jain front room[1]. Pi was to help on this subject.

<u>Curvature:</u> *Chandler entered with…So blunders or not it is clear that we need what is known about space curvature since it was so needed by Einstein!*

Chandler then handed out several papers on the subject commenting…As you see we have used several papers to put this together, particularly clarifying is one will use as focus by Maria Temming. So to the reading from her paper… As to the curvature of space assuming the Pythagorean Theorem is valid for spatial coordinates describing the curvature, there are three possible curvatures the universe can have.

1. Flat (A drawn triangle's angles add up to 180°)
2. Positively curved (A drawn triangle's angles add up to more than 180°)
3. Negatively curved (A drawn triangle's angles add up to less than 180°)

General relativity explains that mass and energy in effect bend the curvature of space-time and is used to determine what curvature the universe actually has by using a value called the density parameter, represented with Omega (Ω). The density parameter is the "Average Density" of the universe divided by the "Critical Energy Density", that is, the mass-energy needed for a universe to be flat!

Pi, said that means needed to hold it all flat. Then she passed out a figure and symbols of the three options. The symbols are as follows, the figure is after that.

If $\Omega = 1$, the universe is flat

If $\Omega > 1$, there is positive curvature

If $\Omega < 1$ there is negative curvature

----

1. Here is a required definition for the forthcoming presentation the panel asked me to insert in the notes: In mathematics, the Pythagorean Theorem is a fundamental relation in Euclidean geometry among the three sides of a right triangle.

It states that the square of the hypotenuse (the side opposite the right angle) is equal to the sum of the squares of the other two sides. Most of us may remember this from school.

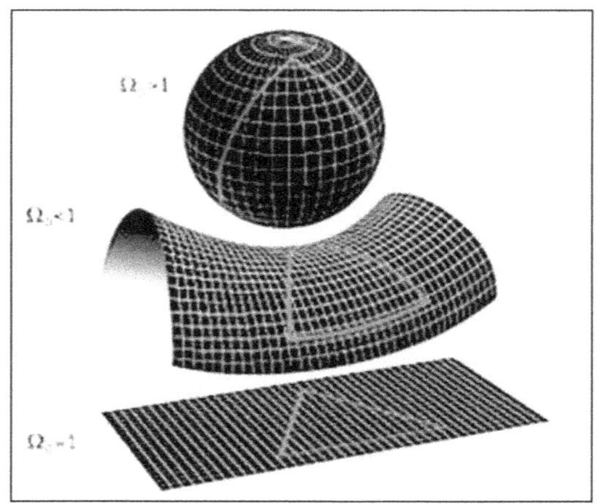

She stated the figure was from NASA's Big Bang Report, and seems rather widely available on the internet. Then the reading continued..........

An example of a "flat curvature" would be any Euclidean geometry, e.g., for example, a triangle drawn on a flat piece of paper *(lowest depiction on the figure)*.

Curved geometries are in the domain of Non-Euclidean geometry. An example of a positively curved surface would be the surface of a sphere such as the Earth. A triangle drawn from the equator to a pole will result in at least two angles being 90°, making the sum of the 3 angles greater than 180°. *(Top of Figure)*

An example of a negative curved surface would be the shape of a saddle or mountain pass as one cosmologist put it. A triangle drawn on a saddle shape will result in the sum of the angles adding up to less than 180° due to the curving away as the triangle moves away from the center. *(Middle of Figure)*

So in short, what we will call the local geometry of the universe is determined by whether the density parameter Ω is greater than, less than, or equal to 1.

Chandler with a note of pride in his voice referred to the figure, from top to bottom: a spherical universe with $\Omega > 1$...a hyperbolic universe with $\Omega < 1$, and a flat with $\Omega = 1$. And remember this is about the "local and that is geometry"

Pi noted that these depictions of two-dimensional surfaces are merely easily visualized analogs to the 3-dimensional structure of (local) space.

*She also said, there is a possible difficulty too, as we might wonder if it is correct to say, "The Curvature of Space-Time" rather than just space, as how does time curve?... Well that is a major point said Chandler, but, let's continue with the reading...*The geometry of the universe is usually represented as we discovered earlier in the system of co-moving coordinates, according to which the expansion of the universe can be ignored. Co-moving coordinates form a single frame of reference according to which the universe has a static geometry of three spatial dimensions.

One can experimentally calculate this Ω to determine the curvature in several ways. By the first way, one is to count up all the mass-energy in the universe and take its average density then divide that average by the critical energy density.

Pi said, we must trust that the mass-energies are correct, but continue Chandler....Yes the author indicates the data source...

...Data read out from the Wilkinson-Microwave-Anisotropy Probe (WMAP) as well as the Planck spacecraft (NASA allied information) give values for the three constituents of all the mass-energy in the universe – normal-mass (that is baryonic matter and dark matter), relativistic particles (these are-photon and neutrinos)...and dark-energy or the so called cosmological constant.

By this view we have, Chandler assertively says as you see on the paper, the values as follows ...

$$\Omega_{mass} \approx 0.315 \pm 0.018$$
$$\Omega_{relativistic} \approx 9.24 \times 10^{-5}$$
$$\Omega_\Lambda \approx 0.6817 \pm 0.0018 \text{ or-}$$
$$\Omega_{total} = \Omega_{mass} + \Omega_{relativistic} + \Omega_\Lambda = 1.00 \pm 0.02$$

...Thus, giving the result, as seen from these values, within experimental error, (and note -0.02, the universe seems to be flat!)

The second way of measuring Ω is to do so geometrically by measuring an angle across the observable universe. We can do this through measuring what cosmetologist called the power spectrum and temperature anisotropy.

Using the method similar to this, the so called BOOMERANG experiment has determined that the sum of the angles to 180° within experimental error, correspond to a $\Omega_{total} \approx 1.00 \pm 0.12$.

That is again, the Local geometry is flat.

Even further to this, there is the so called Friedmann–Lemaître–Robertson–Walker (FLRW) model that uses "Friedmann equations". This is commonly used to model the universe. The FLRW model provides a curvature of the universe based on the mathematics of fluid dynamics, which is, modeling the matter within the universe as a perfect fluid. Although stars and structures of mass can be introduced into an "almost FLRW" model, a strictly FLRW model is used to approximate the local geometry of the observable universe.

Pi entered with another way of saying all this is that if all forms of dark energy are ignored, then the curvature of the universe can be determined by measuring the average density of matter within it, that is, assuming that all matter is evenly distributed (rather than the distortions caused by 'dense' objects such as galaxies).

This assumption is justified by the observations that, while the universe is probably weakly inhomogeneous and anisotropic it is on average homogeneous and if you will, isotropic.

Also under the assumption that the universe is homogeneous and isotropic, the curvature of the observable universe, or the local geometry, can be described by one of the three "primitive" geometries (in mathematics these are generally called the model geometries).

These and other astronomical measurements have constrained the spatial curvature to be very, very close to but not zero, although they do not constrain its sign.

This means that although the local geometries of space-time are generated by the theory of relativity based on space-time intervals, we with cautious assurance can approximate, yes, something we will see called 3-space by the familiar Euclidean geometry. This 3-dimensional Flat Euclidean geometry, is most usually notated as E3.

(Alternatively there would be a 3-dimensional spherical geometry with a small curvature, often notated as S3 and a 3-dimensional hyperbolic geometry with a small curvature can indeed be generated.)

*So, Chandler entered the article goes on...*Although within general relativity... space time is flat, we can model the global universe structure based upon FLRW or Euclidian references. *That last bit, based on "Euclidian References" is important to our quest. Chandler says that is a case in point and the article continues...*Global structure covers the geometry and importantly the topology of the whole universe—both the observable universe and beyond. While the local geometry does not clearly determine the global geometry completely, it does limit the possibilities, particularly a geometry of a constant curvature.

Given this the universe is often taken to be something called a geodesic manifold, free of topological defects. However, it is to be realized that relaxing these complicates the "shapes" analysis and interpretation considerably. *Pi came in, there is challenging math involved but for our purposes geodesics refer to the properties of curves.*

Then as Pi said net-net to questions of a confused panel. So, let's put it in a nutshell...Calculations show the local geometry of Pi said it as space-time (though hesitating on the "time") to be flat with small curvature. It is believed that there are developing techniques to appreciate the global geometry and topology, and some cosmologist are postulating the global is "A Geodesic Manifold"! That is evidence leads us to the possibility of "Shapes in Space".

Thus, it seems that Einstein postulated curvature as existing has some credibility.

However, as noted dark matter has been put forward as important in calculations. And remember the forgoing comment about free of complexities. One at this point is forced to ask--- how does this change things.

Chandler asked, yes, why is that important. Well, gravity at any locus in space-time could have effect on shape was Pi's answer. That is, simple curvature is not the only issue. The question is what gravity has to do with this and the connection to dark matter is also important. Pi said, to all I hope to cover this as it is most important to our goal.

She then made it clear that she would read and highlight an article presented by Le T Dieu, concerning alternative views on Gravity.

<u>Gravity in Close up view:</u> *This paper was distributed to the panel and she proceeded to read it forth with brief comment. This Author called his paper "Gravity - A physically correct definition". I will proceed with our practice of the paper in your hands, then reading and or paraphrasing as needed. This is just to provide a proper base line that relates to larger questions.*

First, for Einstein's Theory--- Clearing up gravity is very important to ideas about the shape of space, and this to Forever!

T Dieu does say curvature is "A Definition Full of Nothing" but it relates to the "Einstein Gravity Theory".

The author goes on... This is an astonishing discovery that reflects its author's super intelligence and his genius in physics. It completes Newton's theory by answering the hard question that before him, nobody, including Newton, could answer: Why Gravity happens in the universe?

Einstein's theory supposes to guide scientists and physicists to quickly understand the structure and the operation of the universe, revealing many secrets, busting many myths. But, instead, it has provided few positive results, and inspired numerous absurd theories. The reason for this is its "definition" is misleading, to say the least.

In an article titled "Why Einstein will never be wrong" (Universe Today) Brian Koberlein cites the definition of Einstein's Theory of Gravity as follows: "Gravity is due to the curvature of space and time by masses"!

Dr. Koberlein is not alone. Scientists all over the world have been using the same statement for a great many years.

Here has been all along this two-dimensional analogy of space-time distortion generated by the mass of an object. Simply put, matter changes the geometry of space-time, this curved geometry being interpreted as the result of gravity directly.

The essay "Newton vs. Einstein vs. the Next Wave" from the American Museum of Natural History- provides some important details in the history that led to establishment of Einstein's observations and conclusions.

"He *(Einstein)* theorized that a mass can prod space plenty. It can warp it, bend it, push it, or pull it. Gravity was just a natural outcome of a mass's existence in space", the essay described.

So, Einstein, at first, concluded that an object's gravity is a result of the curvature of space.

To help us understand the core logic of his theory, Einstein used the physical example of the behavior and reaction of a trampoline while being pressed on. Here is the analogy usually put forth.

"You can visualize Einstein's gravity warp by stepping on a trampoline. Your mass causes a depression in the stretchy fabric of space. Roll a ball past the warp at your feet and it'll curve toward your mass. The heavier you are, the more you bend space. Look at the edges of the trampoline—the warp lessens farther away from your mass"

At the end of this essay, the author added: Being the creator of the theory of Special Relativity that theorizes that the speed of an object can slow down the speed of time (or dilate it); Einstein believed that the process of creating Gravity should include time!

So, not only space, but time would also be curved wherever Gravity occurs! *Pi says here there seems a logic fault to many including me, which he pursues....*

Assuming then that the phenomenon in which the curvature of time-space produces Gravity really exists, we will break down and examine each step of the physical occurrence although, they actually happen at once.

Step 1: A mass, the earth for example, constantly orbits the Sun, spinning around itself.

Step 2: With these movements, the earth is continuously pressing itself on space and time - exactly as a foot stepping on the stretchy fabric of the trampoline – creating the gravity that pulls everything toward the earth.

Step 3: The area where gravity happens is sandwiched between earth and time-space. Since the earth is a round mass, it presses on Space-time creating a curved area that wraps around it, distributing gravity evenly everywhere. But a part of it, if pictured, indeed, would be a curvature.

Therefore, the curvature of Space-time is part of a chain of activities and events. It's the last phase, the result of several preceding actions and reactions. Even so, this alone cannot serve as the complete definition. It is vague, lacks details and lacks sense.

It is merely a snapshot at the end of a long day. Like a photo taken at the scene of an accident in the police report, it plays a supporting role, but does not hold all the clues to the entire investigation. A police officer has the duty to provide as much detail of the event that led to the accident.

Einstein, the author of this theory, had the responsibility of providing a definition that contained every contribution, activity, and element that created gravity. We want to know the "making", not only the picture showing how it finally looks.

And overall, this short, one sentence definition is worded with the vocabulary showing that the whole structure of this theory was based on emptiness, literally!

The final figure is always a curvature? Not really!

Even if we are still assuming that when a mass presses on Space-time, creating gravity, the area where gravity is born is not always in the shape of a curve.

Maybe Einstein only thought of stars' and planets' gravities when establishing his theory, and did not go further. Planets and stars, being round, would indeed leave curved spaces when pressing on time-space.

But they are not the only objects that produce gravity. Any object massive enough with any shape and size could generate gravity while moving and pressing on space.

Only recognizing curved objects, and not considering the many different shapes of objects existing in the universe, leads to misjudgment, limited logical thinking, and failure to see the whole picture.

In the definition of a theory that covers a phenomenon occurring all over the universe, the existence of such a poor, narrow statement, is unacceptable*!*

Pi notes, to put it bluntly the author says here...there is absurdity in the meaning of "curvature of time!" Was Einstein really the author of those peculiar words?

At first, I thought: No. From the beginning, the definition had only space to be curved. Then the curvature of time was added later.

Einstein was an articulate scientist. To prove that his Special Theory of Relativity was correct, he used mathematics, detailed charts, drawings, physical logic, and convincing arguments. It's hard to believe that the same person would throw the curvature of time into a new important theory without explanation.

I first suspected that his disciples and fans were the culprits. They added "curved time" into the picture of gravity as a decorative feature, making it sound more prestigious, and more Einstein-ish.

But on second thought, I couldn't believe that anyone would dare speak for the Grandmaster that way. Einstein was the one and only genius who proclaimed that time could be dilated, and then successfully convinced almost the entire world to adopt that belief. No one else but him would have the ability to theorize that time could be curved by a mass!

But no matter who the real author is, the wording of the definition is flawed! It transformed Einstein's amazing thinking, observations, and conclusions into an absurd statement that makes no physical sense.

Obsessed by his own theory that concluded time is as flexible as a rubber band; Einstein confidently announced that time can be pulled, pushed, and warped. Philosophers, poets, and artists can also share the same fanciful vision since the nature of their works also ignores the realm of physical possibility.

But physicists and scientists should have recognized that time has no role in the process of creating Gravity!

As of today, I admit that picturing a "curvature of time" still escapes my wildest imagination.

And even if the phenomenon of time being curved by mass really happens, the encounter of mass with an absolute no substance entity - a nothing - such as time, would produce no significant physical effects, let alone Gravity.

Pi noted, that "no substance entity", comment is really telling to me, but excuse…And now to this "The anti-physics meaning of the words: "The curvature of space." They are anti-physics and absurd no less than "The curvature of time." Space is where everything, including the entire universe, resides. However, in its definition, it is a vacuum, an absolute emptiness.

Masses moving around in a vacuum do not press (or curve) anything, would generate no gravity, because they were encountering no resistant or opposite force which is the most important element of gravity.

*So, no need to look farther than the trampoline's reaction and behavior to find correct and useful information.

At this point Pi noted, the author decided to challenge through attacking the time honored "trampoline example of Einstein's. He does this as follows.

When stepping on a trampoline, pressing and stretching its fabric, you immediately meet a resistant/opposite force that pushes you upward. The force is strong enough to help you jump much higher than you normally could.

Gravity occurs---in the area being sandwiched between the trampoline surface and the soles of your feet. Whatever exists under your feet at that moment will be stuck to their soles.

Without the trampoline, your foot presses on nothing except air, encountering no resistant force, generating no gravity.

Unlike time the trampoline is indeed an object with physical existence!

Thus note the definition of Einstein's gravity is full of nothing! The trampoline test's interpretation of the process and result--- is only partly correct, and misleading, too.

"Stepping on the trampoline creates gravity" is correct, but the following interpretation stating that "Look at the edges of the trampoline—the warp lessens farther away from your mass… and … roll a ball past the warp at your feet and it'll curve toward your mass"… is wrong!

The ball rolled toward the warp surrounding your feet simply because it was pulled by the gravity of the earth!

It had nothing to do with the gravity you just created by stepping on the trampoline.

Just put the trampoline up vertically like a wall, you'll see how erroneous those observations and conclusion would be.

Pressing your feet as forceful as possible on a vertical standing trampoline, creating a deep curved - or warped - area, then trying to roll a ball past the warp, you'll see that it immediately falls to the ground.

Furthermore, only the fabric of the trampoline is curved in this situation. In short, Water, air, and space do not. They were immediately wrapped around your feet if you step on or penetrate into them.

A fast moving object as a bullet can create an insignificant curved area surrounding it. But this occurrence has no contribution to the gravity.

Actually, only objects that are stuck between two opposite forces your feet and the surface of the trampoline) will enjoy the new born gravity to the fullest. The ball, in the same sandwiched position, will not fall. So, while analyzing what really happens, I found two more types of gravity based on the process of creating them!

Pi helped us with a brief statement. At this point the author lays out the types of gravity likely to apply, taking in new thinking and I emphasize these must be relevant, that is effect shape of our Universe. These are listed as you see in the article-the types of gravity- follow along with my reading...

GRAVITY # 1. Stars, planets, and masses in general are constantly moving and pressing – collapsing may be the right word – on space, a vacuum, cannot produce gravity. But gravity exists. So, they should've pressed on something residing in the space that generates resistant/opposite force exactly as the fabric of the trampoline.

A scientist of Einstein's generation quickly recognized "the true trampoline of the universe." Upon hearing about Einstein's new theory, he observed that this theory of gravity proves the existence of what is called Dark Matter!

Pi entered, so now we begin to see the role of this "Substance'. It is a shape-gravity facilitator in the vacuum of space.

Apparently, he, although having no genius to detect the original source of gravity himself, had understood the process, vital elements, and contributors that practically make gravity occur. He got a clearer view of the mechanical details inside gravity than Einstein's.

In actuality it takes Dark Matter, which fills up space playing the role of the trampoline, constantly generating the resistant-opposite force against stars, planets, masses etc. creating gravity. It's Gravity type #1.

GRAVITY # 2. So, does that mean there is no gravity in a vacuum, an absolutely empty area? Fortunately, another kind of gravity exists, also thanks to Dark Matter. It's Gravity type # 2, created by a different process.

Let's say a star explodes. The explosion suddenly creates an area almost absolutely empty where it was before. Dark Mater from a different source –a black whole-creates another type of gravity.

Matter immediately moves in to fill up the vacuum. The sucking power of this type of gravity is located at the center of the explosion, usually, the center of the exploded star. If the mass is huge and the explosion is extremely forceful, this event will create a giant empty space and Dark Matter - like streams of water of numerous falls – will be pouring in, heading toward the same spot with full force. This phenomenon may give us a little Black Hole.

The author then goes on to give examples using released balloons under water and reservoirs, with released vacuums, which I do not include as it seemed intuitive. Nonetheless, he continues with a third type of real contributing gravity.

GRAVITY # 3. *So, to review for the author, dark matter, as the resistant-opposite forces of planets, stars, and massive objects, generates the Gravity type 1. Creating pressure, such as explosions in space, matter always quickly moving in to fill up the vacuum or where there is less pressure and density, dark matter then offers type 2 Gravity. He goes on...*

...But, dark matter also creates an extremely forceful type of additional Gravity – let's call it type 3 – the strongest one in this universe. Here is a description.

Two gigantic condensed masses of Dark Matter moving towards each other with high velocity - being resistant/ opposite forces – would generate a gravity when they collide that would be unbelievably violent (as violent and destructive as we feel a tornado seems to us on earth but many times more).

In the atmosphere surrounding the earth, the movement of air produces hurricanes, storms, and tornadoes.

In space, the same phenomenon (without water) is the product of Dark Matter's behavior.

Take a look at the photo of a galaxy with a Black Hole in it. If we're not paying enough attention, we may confuse it with a photo of a storm.

The "eye" of a galaxy looks like that of the eye of a storm. The gathering and movement of stars, planets, gas and dust... are taking shape similar to the stormy clouds hovering above the area being hit on earth. Air's movement creates tornadoes on earth; Dark Matter produces tornadoes in the universe. The Black Hole is the cosmic tornado. With gigantic size and force, it sucks in and destroys everything it touches.

Stephen Hawking believes that Black Holes disappear by evaporating.

I totally agree. That is how tornadoes dissipate on this planet of ours.

With those arguments, Pi said the author makes a final definition of gravity, one not relying on bending time!

Therefore, a correct and complete definition of Gravity should include all the important details. That is, there is a physically correct definition of gravity

Here are my suggestions:

"The pressure and movement of Dark Matter, when becoming into resistant/opposite forces of masses, generates Gravity type 1.

The vacuum or the area where the density and pressure of Dark Matter is lower than surrounding's creates Gravity type 2.

The head-on collision of two gigantic volumes of dense Dark Matter moving with high velocity will create a Black Hole or Gravity type 3."

We should revise Einstein's definition and get rid of the "curvature of space-time" nonsense. (I.e. the curvature of time.)

Then focus on the real Gravity caused by Dark Matter!

That Gravity provides essential information about the movement, nature, and characteristic of its cause…Dark Matter which is filling up and inflating the universe. Telling us a detailed story of the structure, operation and even the life of the universe from the first nanosecond.

Pi said, *interesting isn't it, that does, however, conclude the article!*

And Samyak entered saying thanks Ms. Pi, excuse me, I mean Doctor Pi, and Panel the time is now open for discussion!

The panel went into a great deal of argument about this, because of the inference of time being changed within the notion of space-time, and the curvature of space.

However, this article and its inferences all the Panel felt must be kept in mind, not lost within further reports and discoveries.

At this point, Daniel indicated that the group retire to prepare a summary.

It took a good 6 hours to come to agreement. Here though is a brief summary from that report.

Report Summary. *Our search for a way to look into "Forever" has covered a number of topics.*

The faith in hereafter ideas we accept that people will pursue, and wish them well, in so far as these do not cause harm to others of different belief.

We do not, however, see a path road to our quest with those or the notions of Reincarnation as these come via personal revelation, and thus have no way of confirmation. However, we do not want it lost that within those is basis is a sense of respect for the feelings of others, i.e. love.

Our Existence considering that in the Cosmos and indeed its own existence we believe is the path that we should continue to pursue.

Thus far we have gained an understanding of it as our reality, the understanding derived from physical-chemical evidence by physicists and cosmologist. The theoretical aspect, from Einstein's postulations suggest that at least our universe is an Arena in which the time and infinity aspects of our concerns may be pursued. The notion of time warp (i.e. effect) based purely on curvature of space seems not correct as there are reasons for the curvature of space per se from gravity caused by dark energy and holes.

Yet the idea of some curvature as a geometry for local space-time seems proven, and suggestions for shape, in form of various manifolds applied to global space has some evidence and is promising, that is if there is that in space, perhaps one can find their way around in it, to locate events, though we recognize we are reaching into the future with that notion.

Einstein's Theory's require space-time to capture past, present and future, i.e. they would be continuous (separation an illusion) one to the next, but his definition of time change with curvature causes some conflict to his own theories in that regard. These matters are of great concern to us as the ability to dig into the events of forever seem to require a shape to follow at least see, otherwise we have no way to enter.

There remains an overriding feeling of the panel that it is our "Human Time" that is the major operator, as no notion, no theories on Space, the past, present, or future can occur without us. That places on our knowledge of space-time in relation to Forever, an extraordinary value. Hence we are most anxious to continue to explore.

Forever Probe, Document 9, June 10, a.m.
Duly Recorded and Filed,
Jane Caldwell, Technical Recorder

Note: I (Jane) think some kind of table or diagram or figure needs to be made to help clarify this to most of us. That would be designed to relate time, infinity, space-time, transfinite, human time, dark matter-gravity, our universe's shape, and the usable interrelation to "Forever". Of course, that would be a real challenge However, it would sure help.

Forever Probe, Document 10, June 11, a.m.

The Mobius Entry Idea: *The a.m. session, Document 9, June 10, with its focus on summarizing curvature and gravity lasted well into the afternoon so that the panel decided to move to the next day to consider the next topic.*

That topic is the main content of this report, though it had to start with some 'mopping up'. Once that was complete the Panel decided to then dig into the ideas of shape in the cosmos, as some observational astronomist and particle physicist, i.e. cosmologist propose could be.

There was first further discussion on curvature relative to dark energy and matter. The Professor waded into this feeling articles he possessed needed to be covered. Here is his report, which he delivered mostly reading.

By Einstein mass effects curvature. Hence, "Dark Matter/ Energy" becomes important in one aspect we have already seen. There is some data that will give us a fixed point that I found in recent papers. The main issue is one though that we will have to have clarified, that is, although the thinking is an infinite universe the manner in which this infinity exists will require clarification that is in something called its boundedness. I appreciate that we may wish to consider that later when we look into 'Shapes", but let's all record the following.

The current observations and estimates of dark matter is that 20% of dark matter is probably in the form of massive neutrinos, even though that mass is uncertain. The other 5% to 10% is in the form of stellar remnants and low mass, brown dwarfs. The rest of dark matter is called CDM (cold dark matter) of unknown origin, but probably cold and heavy. The combination of all these mixtures only makes 20 to 30% of the amount of mass necessary to close the Universe, i.e. make it Finite.

Thus, on this basis and with detailed calculations concerning this mass, the Universe appears to be open with flat curvature.

This is sometimes referred to as the Benchmark Model which gives an age of 'Our' Universe of 12.5 billion years. And we have a model of the universe in which the universe expands forever because there is not enough mass to counteract the expansion by means of gravitational attraction!

Further to this discussion is the impact of density. This is the convers of effect on expansion.

If the density of the universe is greater than a so called "critical density", then gravity will eventually win and the universe will collapse back on itself, the so called "Big Crunch".

However, the results of the WMAP mission and observations of distant supernova have suggested that the expansion of the universe is actually accelerating, which implies the existence of a form of matter with a strong negative pressure, such as the cosmological constant. This strange form of matter is now referred to as we have seen as the "Dark Energy". If dark energy in fact plays a significant role in the evolution of the universe, then in all likelihood the universe will continue to expand "forever" and as discussed that the universe is flat with only a 0.4% margin of error.

This suggests that the Universe is infinite in extent; however, since our Universe might have a finite age, we can only observe a finite volume of the Universe.

To this Pi and Tim both brought in papers and articles they had researched on the matters of time, infinity, gravity and curvature, prompted by Daniel as these could possibly relate to an eventual presentation on "Boundedness and the Topography" that Samyak recommended we cover.

Then the discussions returned to Einstein, his theory of special and general relativity and of his great but sometimes faulted genius. This simply consumed a good deal of this morning's discussions and well into the afternoon.

All in the group were able to grasp the notion of a "Great Arena" where all occurs, has, is, and will in this specific Universe. They also realized this was within an infinity, some noting that ours was rather possibly an infinitive fractal of that Absolute Infinity.

Still they were concerned that there seemed no way to enter or view that fractal by any practical method. And the ideas of closed vs open and bounded and unbounded confused the panel.

So to help Samyak entered with the following, a means he felt for the panel to focus saying…Within the mathematical and experimental realm, within the actual cosmos, from all the forgoing it may be proposed that topographies (or shapes) should be allowed, i.e. exist. And perhaps we might exist in such a realm.

Well, we can envision all kinds of shapes, ones that have interesting properties that give in their structure a "Forever's Gate". So let us turn to that matter.

Then at the request of Samyak, Pi agreeing, the following article, was discussed by Jehan, an article that deals with the potential of that notion. She was assigned to know and discuss an article by Janna Levin. Because Chandler was a builder, one who has a mentality of shape and construction to the end of final products - he was assigned to assist Jehan.

<u>Return to Home (Mobius and Torus Ideas)</u>: *Jehan first said…The article treats the idea of the Mobius as a space topology, and through it the argument is offered we might be able to return home, i.e. to the start of "one's" time. The return of course would be highly arguable and fraught with contradictions, but does offer- in laying out the design- useful knowledge about our Universe.*

Janna Levin begins the article this way… Imagine you walk down a strange street and pass a gate in a wall. You keep walking in a straight line only to pass another gate in a wall. You keep walking and pass yet another gate, yet another wall. You might begin to suspect it is the same gate, the same wall. Even though you walk in as straight a line as possible, never turning back, you come upon the two landmarks again and again.

Well, this, of course, could actually happen on the surface of the Earth, although on a much larger scale.

Think of it Jehan noted to us… continuing the article… If you started in London and walked in as straight a line as possible for a very long time, you would eventually come back to London. This is because the Earth is curved and finite, and has a surface with the overall geometry of a sphere!

Jehan noted: *That, due to the spherical earth is a reality in our place in space time! On the statement though I think she meant Topology…But to continue…*Over the past few hundred years we have made ourselves quite familiar with the Earth's compact surface, charting oceans and flying around the globe.

*Now Jehan began to separate the authors thoughts in short paragraphs to let the panel take notes in the form of definitions and descriptions. That was her promised real agenda. So further in the article…*Here I'm using the word "Compact" to mean that the surface has no edge, but rather is smoothly *connected* to itself.

With this definition, the surface of a sphere is compact, and so is the surface of a bubble or a doughnut.

The surface of a square would not be compact, because it has edges. However, a compact surface can be made from a square by smoothly gluing the edges of the square together.

Chandler entered, yes, that deals with fascinating ideas of construction which we will look into later. Correct, said Jehan, and this is led into the following.

A remarkable possibility is that the entire universe is compact (no edges) and connected (to its self). In other words, if we were to launch a spaceship from Earth and fly in as straight a line as possible, we could find ourselves returning home!

A question was raised by Tim here… Wouldn't that mean though that we are on top of the Universe? This is very confusing!

Well, she doesn't address that but goes on.... As we see the Earth receding in the distance behind us, we might also see it growing nearer in front of us.

Of course, a compact universe would be far more dramatic than a compact planet.

From Einstein we have learned that the universe has three spatial dimensions and one time dimension. According to his theory of relativity, we all move along the natural curves in that space. Even light follows these curves.

If that strange street lived in a short, compact universe, the world would get even stranger. Light from the street lamps would wrap around the compact space, following the natural curves. If you were to stand there you would see ahead of you the light reflected off the street which had traveled all the way around the space!

Pi said here, what about time, it can't as we have seen, warp with space....hum! To which Jehan said, that is not addressed.

And, so does that mean we are somehow just within the compacted-space, Tim said, scratching his head?

Jehan answered, "You know that really isn't clear to me also.

Any way she goes on"....Further in the distance, you could see the same scene again: yourself standing in the middle of the more distant but otherwise identical copy of the street. Like a hall of mirrors, the pattern would go on infinitely and in all directions.

Though we know from personal experience that the universe is not this small, it could be finite and compact on a much huger scale: thousands of times the size of a galaxy, but finite nonetheless. *Pi said here, latter I will address the real meaning of finite, but do continue...*

Then Jehan said, I will look forward to that and here Tim is maybe some clarification for your concern....

To visualize how this is possible we can utilize the theory on geometry of surfaces. *That is more correctly, we can consider the "Topology". Note in the article...*

...The geometry of surfaces can be classified according to two properties. These are as follows...

1.   The local curvature of the surface, and

2.   The global topology of the surface.

Jehan followed on in the article. This is something we have, indeed, seen before i.e. the words local and global. These two references I believe, right Samyak, are essential understandings for us. To treat and understand this we need to look into 'Topology", so I read from the author to continue into that realm...

...Topology is the branch of mathematics that describes properties which remain unchanged under smooth deformations.

If we will imagine surfaces to be made of clay, a smooth deformation is any bending, mushing and shaping which does not require the discontinuous action of a tear or a punching of holes.

A favorite example is a clay doughnut which can be smoothly manipulated into the shape of, for example, a coffee mug. The doughnut hole becomes the coffee cup handle so that the number of holes is preserved. The doughnut and the coffee mug therefore have the same topology!

That is that a given mass may take different shapes in conditions wherein the same surface is involved.

So our universe can be shaped differently as long as the same material is not broken up... I think that would make it a matter of topology. This is noted as she goes on and to extend the idea, in the author's words... We can make topologically connected surfaces with handles and holes by starting with a flat rectangular sheet of paper! You can glue the left edge to the right edge to make a cylinder. This will result in what mathematicians call a torus. *So in effect a donut is a torus! Am I saying this correctly Pi? The answer was simply, yes!*

...The surface of a torus is topological space found in most video games, where a spaceship goes off the right-hand side of the screen only to reappear on the left, or off the top to reappear on the bottom.

To illustrate life on the surface of a torus one takes a simple square with only one pair of edges glued with no flipping top to bottom.

Jehan said...I will do this following the hand-out diagram from the article... Which she did so we all were able to be convinced of her authors end argument. (And, I tried it, OK.)

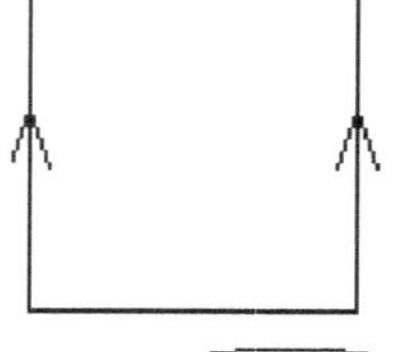

This is always the surface!!! (The outside on the reverse), Then, the square can be rolled so that the two marked edges meet. The resulting shape would be...like the following. That is a cylinder.

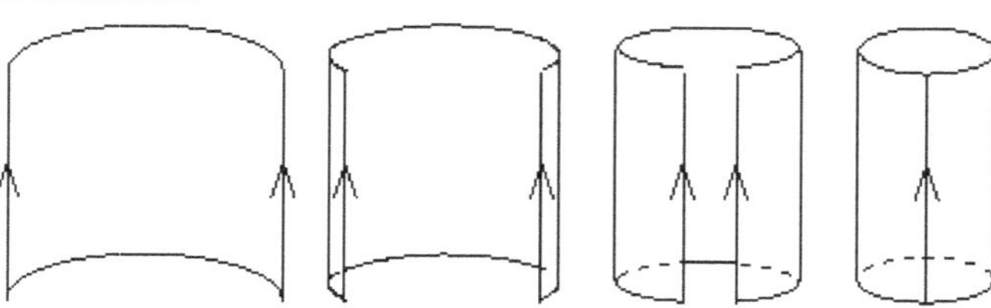

If the top and bottom edges of the cylinder were also pulled together and glued, then the shape in three dimensions would be a torus!

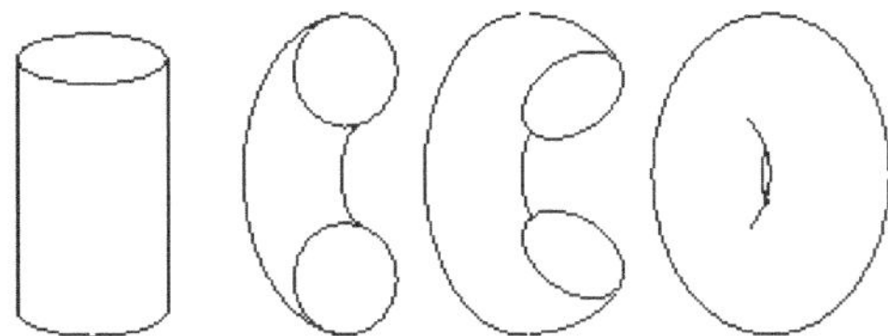

....Or to put it directly there results the topological equivalent to the doughnut and the coffee cup. *So you see, and the author goes on continuing with surfaces*...Now for another kind of surface.

If you glued the left to the right after twisting a sheet of paper by 180 degrees, you would build a Mobius strip!

Oh, I see said Tim, now no matter, you are always on the edge, or surface and there is no formal inside or outside, right Jehan.... Yes!

Jehan said, this is an exercise that is taught in many schools around the world. Chandler interrupted this, saying yes, I do remember in high school we had a great deal of fun with this. I'll bet you did Chandler, because as my author says...If you walked around the Mobius strip starting on one side, you would find yourself on the other side after one full trip and on the starting side again only after two full trips.

This is a property that we usually don't know about. It is known as "non-orient-ability"!

...Gluing the top of the Mobius band to the bottom would give another kind of topology which is called a compact Kline bottle after the scientist who conceived it. This complicated shape is impossible to draw properly in three dimensions.

Both these surfaces, however, are constructed from a flat rectangle! And, Tim said, I bet no matter where you start and walk you can always come back to where you began, even though you think you are "inside" at the beginning.

The panel then began discussing the obvious... Einstein's Space-time is proposed to be flat, right? That is the geometry, not the topology that is possible, right?

Yes, well, I am sure we will get back to that, but notice that we started with a flat sheet of paper and then built a torus.

Pi observed regarding her companions that--- the notion is building in you all, in which a flat space could become by some forces twisting into a torus, so we would be at once inside and outside. She noted to them, though, it would be more complicated and there was more to come as Jehan continued...

The article goes on and in the interest of not confusing every one, (my demonstrating the authors figure complete) I will simply read and if you want, I will let you enter with questions that we will try to clarify. The author continues...

…However, the torus I depicted, in the end is not flat. It is curved in a way that is not constant across its surface. This is an artifact of living in 3-dimensions and bending the 2-dimensional sheet of paper into 3 to help our 3-dimensional selves visualize the compactness and topology of the surface.

Nonetheless, strictly speaking, a two-dimensional flat space can exist which has the fundamental shape of a rectangle with its edges glued together in pairs, but which doesn't bend up into three dimensions.

This truly flat torus has the same topology as the torus we built of paper. However, it is not curved and does not even require the existence of three dimensions! *(We just saw it on the paper.)*

A video game works this way, as does the strange recurrent street I mentioned. Old-fashioned cartoons worked like this too. If you've ever seen the Flintstone you've seen Fred running through his house and passing the same window and lamp over and over again. *(The screen was of course, flat.)*

(So)…We can get rid of the third dimension entirely and visualize a compact surface using a tiling picture. Consider flat creatures living on a flat torus that has the fundamental shape of a rectangle. A flat explorer can mark their starting point and then walk straight from left to right. After traveling a distance, they will come back to where they started.

We can represent this within one fundamental cell by following simple rules each time we cross an edge. If we exit the right edge, we reenter from the left edge. If we exit the top, we reenter from the bottom edge and so on.

Alternatively, we can visualize the compact space by gluing together identical copies of the fundamental cell edge-to-edge according to our simple rules. We take an identical copy of the original tile and glue the left edge of the copy to right edge of the original. We then glue the lower edge of another copy to the top of the original and so on until all the edges of the original are tiled against copies. We then take more identical tiles and glue them to the edges of the copies. We follow these rules until an entire infinite plane is tiled.

We could have started with a hexagonal flat cell instead of a rectangular cell. The edges of the hexagon can also be glued together in pairs to make another torus, so the fully identified hexagon has the same topology as the fully identified rectangle. We can also represent the flat hexagonal torus as a tiling of flat space. While the interior angles of a triangle add up to 180 degrees in flat space, the angles sum up to less than 180 when drawn on a negatively curved space, and more than 180 when drawn on a positively curved space. *(Remember figures discussing Omega.)*

For this reason, if we draw the octagon just the right size on a negatively curved space, we can fit just the right number snugly around a vertex and fully tile what is known as the hyperbolic plane! *Pi said that would be in the saddle shape, I think. Continue…*

And Jehan did, reading… For this reason, if we draw the octagon just the right size on a negatively curved space, we can fit just the right number snugly around a vertex and fully tile what is known as the hyperbolic plane.

The group contemplated this as Tim said, are we saying that the geometry is constrained to be planar, we can still depending upon the curve fit in some selected shapes such as octagons. Then when we do that we have something "Hyperbolic" Yes, said Pi. Here is a definition... She handed out a sheet[1] with the hyperbolic concept fully described, saying also I know this is difficult, but not necessary to memorize, it's just for completeness sake.

Jehan pausing with that so all could read... then continued the article with...

These two-dimensional examples give us an idea of how to build the more difficult three-dimensional, topologically compact spaces.

We cannot actually visualize these as bent into four spatial dimensions since we only have three at our disposal. But we can begin first with a volume of fixed curvature, select a fundamental tile, and apply the rules for gluing the edges.

I (Jane) said at this point, you know I will never understand this because I can't get the visualizations. To which Chandler said in warm voice, when we get more time I will help you, but I'm thinking in the end it will all work itself out.

So let's continue with the paper… Up till now, we have only considered what are called "two-manifolds", but naturally there are non-orientable three-manifolds

----

1.Hyperbolic Geometry – In mathematics a non-Euclidean geometry in which the parallel axiom is replaced by the assumption that through any point in a plane there are two or more lines that do not intersect a given line in the plane; "Karl Gauss pioneered hyperbolic geometry. "Generally in math it is a science or group of related sciences) dealing with the logic of quantity and shape and arrangement. That is a non-Euclidean geometry – mathematics based on axioms different from Euclid's; "non-Euclidean geometries which discard or replace one or more of the Euclidean axioms". (We are talking about a function of an angle expressed as a relationship between the distances from a point on a hyperbola to the origin and to the coordinate axes, as hyperbolic sine or hyperbolic cosine: expressed as combinations of exponential functions.)

also. Mathematicians would call the rectangle the fundamental domain for that space. Likewise, we will use the cube as a fundamental domain when we consider most of the three-manifolds! Note in the remaining article she illustrates.

Consider a solid cube. (It is important to stress that the cube is solid or that we are **talking about the space inside of the cube and not just the cubical surface.** *Tim interjected…"At last we are talking about a real inside i.e. beyond my last observation!"*

…The cube itself is a three-manifold with a boundary on all sides. Now, what if we connected the right wall to the left wall? Then when you walked through the right wall, you would return to the cube through that residing left wall. Better yet, you could play catch with yourself. Just throw a ball towards the right wall, turn around, and catch it as it comes through the left wall. We could also connect the front wall to the back wall and the top wall to the bottom wall. This new "manifold, as topologists say" is called a three-torus!

The three-torus has no boundary and therefore if you lived in a three-torus it would seem to be an infinite space! In theory our universe could be a three-torus.

Samyak and Jehan together asked the Panel to special mark that thought as it could relate to a Forever entry, should we rationalize that. Then we were brought back to the article…

… If this were the case, if you looked out in any direction far enough you would see yourself (ignoring the fact that light travels at a finite speed).

Of course, we cannot build a three-torus in three-space, just as we can't build a regular folded torus in the plane.

More generally, a manifold without boundary, which is not infinite, cannot be built in the same dimension of which its local topology consists!

So now the author asks…What if we wanted to create a non-orientable three-manifold. How would we do it? In two dimensions we connected the edges of a rectangle with a flip. We can do the same in three dimensions.

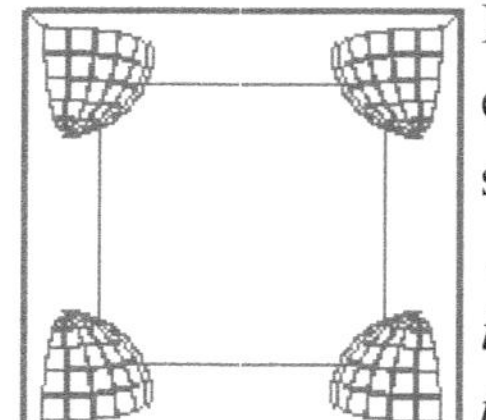

A sphere in a 3-torus.

In fact there are two ways to cause a mirror reversing effect. We could connect opposite faces of the cube with a side-to-side flip or an upside-down flip.

Jehan showed a figure, in which a sphere in parts was placed inside of a box, back and side walls showing, then continued to read… Let's say we connected the front and back walls of our cube with a side-to-side flip. Now, when you walked out the right side of the back wall, you would return on the left side of the front wall. You would also be mirror-reversed.

What if we connected the front and back walls with an upside-down flip? Then, if you left the back wall standing on the floor, you would return through the front wall hanging from the ceiling (this, of course, ignores gravity).

Well to put this in a nutshell, for instance, we can begin with a flat 3-dimensional space and select a cube as the fundamental cell. *That said Jehan is what is shown in the figure.*

We can then glue the faces of that cell in pairs and use those gluing rules to lay down these three-D cells to fill the 3-volume with identical cubes. *Jehan notes the author said…* Our own universe may be such a vast cube! *(Yet, caution, not certain this, said Pi!)*

Cosmologists and mathematicians have pooled their efforts over the past few years to try to observe the global topology of the cosmos. The observations rely on an imprint of the geometry in intricate patterns in the sky and we await the data from future satellite missions to answer our questions.

Even if the universe is compact, it may well be too huge for us to see all the way around. In the meantime, we can't be sure if those are all new galaxies on the horizon, or if it really is ourselves we see at the observable edge of the universe.

Well that is pretty much where the author was going… here though are some concluding thoughts. The two-dimensional examples give us an idea of how to build the more difficult three-dimensional, topologically compact spaces. We cannot visualize these as bent into four spatial dimensions since we only have three at our disposal.

But we can begin first with a volume of fixed curvature, select a fundamental tile, and apply the rules for gluing the edges. That is what the author wants us to learn. And further here we, Chandler and me are using pieces of various references.

Chandler has picked from them some examples…So what do 4D objects look like anyway? We haven't seen a 4D object yet.

There are only assumptions. However, to give a small example, let's look at the case of something called a tesseract that is indeed a hypercube!

At this Chandler handed out a figure, remarking…Here is the generation of that tesseract, so we can all see how, at least, a 4D object might "look" in 2D.

We form it as in this depiction… So to follow the figure.

Wrapping a line around 4 points gives us a square, that is [1D -> 2D]. A square pattern (cross) when folded in space, gives a cube [2D -> 3D]. Similarly, a cross formed by cubes when folded, gives us a 4D object called a Tesseract, or the hypercube! Of course we are only showing it in the plane of the paper.

131

Although, this is not really easy to depict---this, however, leads us to an idea of Hyper-space!

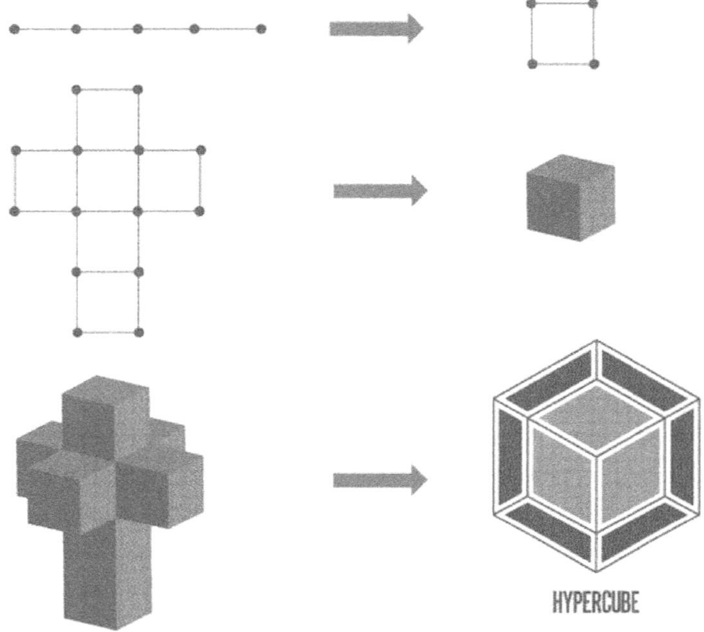

Let's take up some further clarifications and examples, which one hopes are helpful. Space is normally considered unbounded, meaning that if you travel outward with a spaceship you never encounter a barrier. However, there is a technicality, things can be unbounded and finite. Jehan showed a drawing illustrating just that.

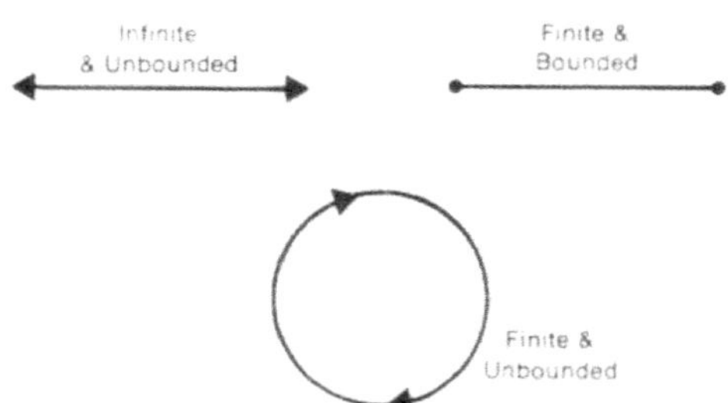

HOW FINITE CAN BE UNBOUNDED

As said, a circle is a one dimensional example. A 2D example is the surface of a sphere, such as the Earth's surface. You can travel forever on the Earth in what seems like a straight line, even though you only cover a finite distance. The reason the surface of a sphere is finite and unbounded is because it is bent in three dimensional space. In the same way, it is possible to imagine the three dimensional space of our Universe bent in four dimensional space, into that HYPERSPHERE, an example of an infinite, yet bounded, space. In that spirit let me continue, with an illustration that may help a bit with that four dimensional aspect.

An astute enthusiast by name Sahaj Ramachandr comments on this and provides a "cartoon description".

In this he depicts lower spaces moving through higher, to help in visualization! What a great idea! I (Jane) breathed a sigh of relief!

His article then begins as follows… The concept of hyperspace is Amazing! Even "supernatural" phenomenon could possibly be explained with Higher Dimensional physics. For example, God, if he would ever exist, would do so in the 4rth Dimension.

Even "Ghosts", if real, would have the ability to walk through walls just because they would have access to a higher dimension. We humans live in the third dimension. However, there is a way to visualize objects in 4D.

Chandler then passed around for Jehan-drawings he did of Ramachandr's Cartoon and read from the article…

This display helps us visualize objects in 4D! As 3-Dimensional beings, we cannot visualize 4-Dimensional space, let alone an object say a being that is present in it, at least, not directly.

We can, however, see their cross-sections! In the following are depictions of that, higher orders of dimension moving into lower, and what 'someone living at that level" would see.

So let's begin with the lower levels of dimension. For example to set up the idea we can depict a 2 dimensional object passing through a linear world. Consider a 2 Dimensional object, say a circle that is going to pass through a linear space. As it passes through this space, it will appear as a point that gradually increases in length, then decreases and finally vanishes.

With that Chandler emphasized the drawings…..

The author describes…The lines are the intersection of the circle as it passes through the 1 Dimensional space, the heavier being the circle.

Next, take the case of A 3 Dimensional object passing through a 2 Dimensional space. For example, consider a Pyramid that would pass through a plane (3D vs. 2D)... How would this look like to folks living in 2 D space --- consider the following depiction?

As it passes through what is seen on the plane as it passes through is a small point that gradually grows into a square that increases in size. If there are beings on this 2D world, they would witness that meeting of spaces as in this drawing above.

What we are seeing is just the cross-section of the four dimensional object.

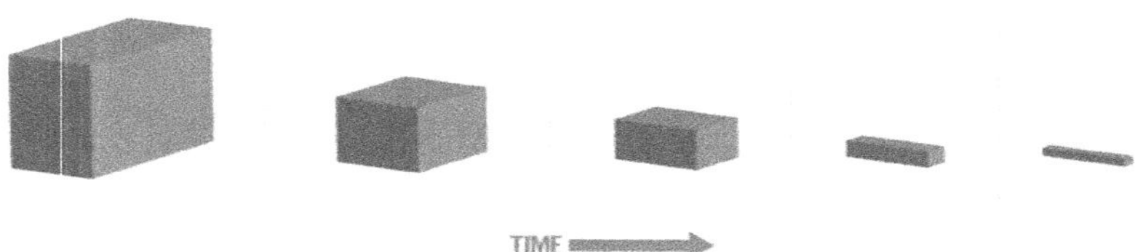

It could be a blob, or anything that constantly changes size.

So it was Jehan and Chandlers report on the fundamentals of Topography were presented. (All agreed a good job with a big subject.)

Tim put in a rather strong notion if you think about almost (any life form, you can see it is a variant of the Mobius and fractal dynamics, i.e., holarchies (fractals) of many lower. Hence, the earth being spherical, is it possible that our Universe mirrors that spherical local topography, reflecting in turn the shape of Forever.

Then after sitting around and thinking about the presentation the group drew up a consensus report. It was quite short and follows.

On the matter of "Return to Start": *The presentation designed to help us see the possibility of topology in space, was "successful" although those of us do not see structure as well as Chandler had trouble conceptualizing the outcomes.*

Even so, not proven it seems --- our Universe could have an infinite hyper-cubical shape. Still how we would enter it, move around in it is highly challenging. Moreover, we still remain curious as to whether it is bounded or unbounded, finite or infinite or if that specific matters as to seeing into Forever. That is of course an essential understanding which is unwinding in our quest seeking the nature of Forever, a most critical concern. Indeed, our universe, we are now beginning to see is "Forever's" child. Yes, that is what we are beginning to realize, Forever is something physical real where the processes or decisions about us begin. Even so, to put this topology thing in the authors terms... "Really "Can all Roads Lead Back to Home?

Forever Probe, Document 10, June 11, a.m.
Duly Recorded and Filed
Respectfully Submitted,
Jane Caldwell, Technical Recorder.

SHAPING TIME'S EDGES

Forever Probe, Document 11, June 11, p.m.

This meeting was again held at the house of Samyak and his daughter. The group spent casual time together, talking about most everything including their personal lives and there were many questions of the Jain family, no holds barred, such as if the vegetarian diet made them happy, if the diet increased life span, etc. (Statistics are at minimum, but life span may increase when lived in the Jain way.)

Boundedness: *Arriving at 1: 30 p.m. was Dr. Raga Singh. He is a Professor from Deli, Patel Institute, who was invited to join the group by the Professor.*

He did this knowing that expertise at the highest level of physicist-cosmology would be necessary. This proved to be a wonderful addition in many ways as Dr.Singh was to be Pi's and Tim's Post-Doctoral Professor!

Pi was, indeed, to everyone's surprise outwardly joyful in the opportunity to meet the Patel Professor, but also she was just given the assignment by Samyak to address the matter of space infinity *(and questions of boundedness).*

She began by reviewing the panels past experience with the Cosmos, Big Bang and thinking from NASA. It was clear that the Professor was pleased with the prospect of his new Post Doc!

Pi then entered the subject of concern for the panel, indicating that they wished to get an idea of Forever, and path by which they could deal with its mechanisms if that were possible. (Recent discussions focused on Future!)

She continued, although they have looked at such as topology, and more. The matter of the "Boundedness" of space-the panel did not feel was resolved.

They were given the notion of 3-manifold, but, it was presented as though that could be closed or open.

At this point she shared a picture in the hands of the panel of that 3-manifold as the generation of a hypercube. This was a bit of a repeat but the alternate help depiction.

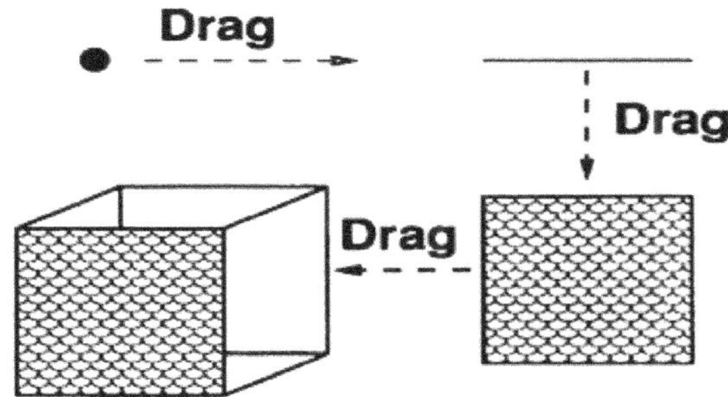

Lower dimensional figures trace out higher dimensional figures when the lower dimensional figures are moved.

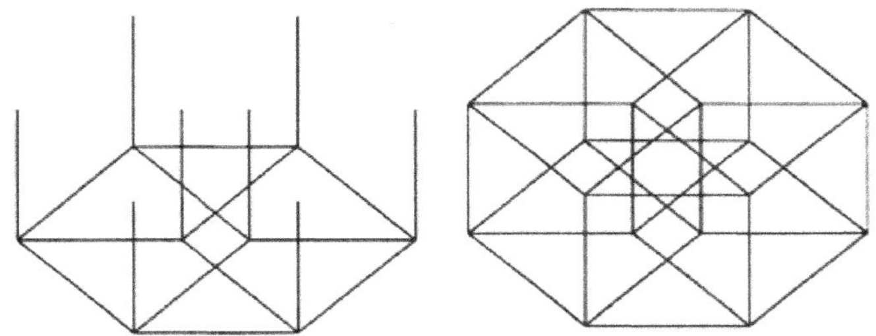

A hypercube is produced by moving a cube along the fourth dimension.

Figure Pi handed out
Yet another Depiction of Generating a Hyper Cube.

She then looked into a file with a rather large pack of papers which she referred to indicating her job would be to summarize them, hopefully giving a conclusion, wiping brow symbolically!

She said, actually with a proud and assured look on her face…"*our subject is Space Boundedness, is it infinite or finite?*

I would like before shifting through all of this to start with a concern expressed by many that shows the extent of the questioning, this is from one J. Day.

He beings with a maxim as most folks accept"…Space is definitely curved, the question is whether it is open.

As Day says, "Part of the problem is terminology. Frankly, cosmologists and topologists should be banned from writing until they've been forced to listen to their papers read as poetry!

The whole panel laughed at this nodding heads. Jane came in "Oh My" do I wish that. As I said we need a glossary or tables or something, anyway…sorry continue Pi. Which she does…

…Suffice to say…There are so many arrangements for the universe, here are just six that he brings to the front. These are as follows.

1. <u>Bounded, finite in space, closed in time</u>, <u>finite in expansion</u>: A rubber sheet universe that stretches only so far and eventually vanishes.

One possible model. After heat-death, there's no time and no expansion. But it can only be bounded if gravity is insufficient to make our universe a hypersphere. I dislike this model, it creates absolute space and that's a bad thing.

Pi enters here with comment, well we know space is not absolute as we are sitting on a changeable mass that is in it! I am sure this prompted the author to continue to number two.

2. <u>Bounded, finite in space, closed in time</u>, <u>infinite in expansion</u>: A fractal rubber sheet.

You can't otherwise have infinite expansion in finite time. Not ours, as nothing can be smaller than one Planck unit of space, nor exist for less than one Planck unit of time.

Pi defines here the "Plank Unit". Sorry for digressing, but I believe the panel may not be familiar with this important term. So (She is showing off to her future adviser, I think) here is a useful description of the Plank Unit.

In the late 1890s, physicist Max Planck proposed a set of units to simplify the expression of physics laws.

Using just five constants in nature (including the speed of light and the gravitational constant), you, me and even aliens from Alpha Centauri could arrive at these same Planck units.

The basic Planck units are length, mass, temperature, time and charge.

Let's consider the unit of Planck length for a moment. The proton in an atom is about 100 million trillion times larger than the Planck length!

To put this into perspective, if we scaled the proton up to the size of the observable universe, the Planck length would be a mere trip from Tokyo to Chicago. The 14-hour flight may seem long to you, but to the universe, it would go completely unnoticed.

The Planck scale was invented as a set of universal units, so it was a shock when those limits also turned out to be the limits where the known laws of physics applied.

For example, a distance smaller than the Planck length just doesn't make sense—the physics breaks down.

Physicists don't know what actually goes on at the Planck scale, but they can speculate.

Some theoretical particle physicists predict all four fundamental forces, that is, gravity, the weak force, electromagnetism and the strong force—finally merge into one force at this energy level. Other proposed physics descriptions such "Quantum gravity and Superstrings" are also possible phenomena that might dominate at the Planck energy scale. In a nutshell, the Planck scale is the universal limit, beyond which the currently known laws of physics break! In order to comprehend anything beyond it, we need new, unbreakable physics.

Here the panel paused PI and asked many questions. The outcome from the panel's perspective was a very strong idea that the laws of physics may not be as fixed as drove Einstein to his proposals!

After this definition, Pi made a statement that made all in the panel look almost unanimously at each other.

She said…"*It is this i.e. unbreakable physics which limits us, we are on this edge, one whose size we must grow in mind to know!*"

Samyak entered to comment, "Grow to surround the idea that all were surely beginning to feel. Yes, Pi …your word "Edge" may be a critical one to us. Thank you though for defining Plank for us, please continue with Dr. Day's article on Boundedness."

"Yes, well to go on, he explained his view of a third space description."

3. <u>Bounded, finite in space, open in time,</u> <u>finite in expansion:</u> This requires no heat-death.

To work, matter must enter the universe no faster than the rate it decays and must either enter at an identical rate (provided gravity reduces expansion to precisely zero) or be capable of entering in "dead space" (space where there is no matter, energy is uniform and entropy has ceased).

Problematic but workable. Unlikely, though.

So to go on he describes a fourth…

4. <u>Bounded, finite in space, open in time,</u> <u>infinite in expansion</u>: As above but doesn't need expansion to stop. This is Problematic, but more likely.

An example of a bounded, infinite shape (expansion) is a ball. You can go in a straight line round it as long as you want, but it has a defined boundary. Not in any direction you can go in, if you're living on the surface, but it has one.

That's the preferred shape for a universe, since you preserve relative space and you don't have to worry why part of the early universe fell off. These things don't come with warranties, so you want a universe that doesn't fall apart after the inflationary phase.

5. <u>Bounded, infinite shapes,</u> <u>cannot have infinite expansion</u> unless matter is being added. I reference Fred Hoyle's article i.e., "Continuous Creation" model.

The reason for that is much the same as the reason the upper bands of the atmosphere do not behave like liquids.

The particles are just too far apart, the influence (including gravity) falls below the Planck limits, the particles become distinct universes. Instantly, you get false vacuums springing up, which is where this model joins up with the "Foam Multiverse".

Pi noted here, "all this may be confusing, but we have seen multiverse ideas before, for example when we dealt with the Boltzmann."

By implication, you do NOT have infinite expansion of a universe or its interior, you have an infinite foam in which bubbles expand, pop and become other bubbles.

This was popular for a while, not so much now, but if that's what is happening then that's the only way it can happen.

"And finally he addresses unbounded shapes, but in effect, no criticism intended, gives up."

6. <u>Unbounded shapes require the universe to expand into something.</u>
Popular with the movie …Doctor Who in the 80s, but it just doesn't work.

Pi notes should we deny a 'something'? And should we let movies dictate our judgement of such scientific matters?

We ask on that having an education on infinity, why not continue to expand assuming an infinity? That is the universe is in space-time, if it is expanding there is time for this, i.e. an infinite time ahead!

The Professor, was most pleased with this, saying so and all could tell he was quite proud with his Post Doc. She gave him a pleased look and continued…

Well that gives you all some more or less argumentative views, many that are "out there" and shows the difficulty of the problem.

I will now turn to the technical side, and will draw from here and there for my report.

As she gave this we could all tell that Pi was simply shining, the stage was hers and she would show she was mounting the top of the field. These arguments appear in a great many paper.

The papers I have reviewed indicate that a topology alone does not give a global geometry: for instance, Euclidean 3-space and hyperbolic 3-space may have the same topology but different global geometries!

As we have seen before - investigations of the global structure of the universe include this threesome:

1. Whether the universe is infinite or finite in extent,
2. Whether the geometry of the global universe is flat[1], positively curved, or negatively curved,
3. Whether the topology is simply connected like a sphere or multiply connected, like a torus.

For intuition, it can be understood that a finite universe has a finite volume that, for example, could it be in theory filled up with a finite amount of material.

In contrast an infinite universe is unbounded and no numerical volume could possibly fill it. (That is the word infinite = unbounded in cosmology)

PI said…In other words whether the space is finite or infinite, does not deal with the infinity we have studied, rather the amount of stuff that can fill it!

I spoke up here because I was totally confused. I asked for some kind of table on terms. Pi immediately said "yes, oversight, I will provided after break or with the written report."

However, purely mathematically speaking the question of whether the universe is infinite or finite is referred to formally as "boundedness".

An infinite universe (unbounded metric space) means that there are points arbitrarily far apart: for any distance d, there are points that are of a distance at least d apart. ("The universe does not have a well-defined volume.")

Assuming a finite universe, the universe can either have an edge or no edge. Many finite mathematical spaces, e.g., a disc, have an edge or boundary. Spaces that have an edge are difficult to treat, both conceptually and mathematically. Namely, it is very difficult to state what would happen at the edge of such a universe. For this reason, spaces that have an edge are typically excluded from consideration.

----

1. *Joseph Silk reminds us that "Flat" is just a two-dimensional analogy. What we mean is that the Universe is 'Euclidean', meaning that parallel lines always run parallel, and that the angles of a triangle add up to 180°. Now, the two-dimensional equivalent to that is a plane, an infinite sheet of paper. On the surface of that plane you can draw parallel lines that will never meet. In distinction …..A well curved geometry would be a sphere. If you draw parallel lines on a sphere, these lines will meet at a certain point, and if you draw a triangle its angles add up more than 180°. So the surface of the sphere is s finite space but it's not flat, while the surface of a torus is a flat space.*

A finite universe is a bounded metric space, where there is some distance d such that all points are within distance d of each other. The smallest such d is called the diameter of the universe, in which case the universe has a well-defined "volume" or "scale."

However, there exist many finite spaces, i.e., such as the 3-sphere and 3-torus, which have no edges.

Mathematically, these spaces are referred to as being compact without boundary. The term compact basically means that it is finite in extent ("bounded") and is a closed set.

The term "without boundary" means that the space has no edges. Moreover, so that calculus can be applied, the universe is typically assumed to be a differentiable manifold. That is, a mathematical object that possess all these properties, compact without boundary and differentiable, is termed a closed manifold. The 3-sphere and 3-torus are both closed manifolds! That is they are compact but without boundary!

An infinite universe (again an unbounded metric space, or infinite in a specific spatial direction must be unbounded in that direction. To look into, i.e. to understand that aspect it is necessary to treat again the curvature of the Universe (remembering the arguments on gravity that we covered, from... Dr. Le T Dieu.)

(2.) Whether the geometry of the global universe is flat, positively curved, or negatively curved.

*In a universe with **zero curvature,** the local geometry is flat. The most obvious global structure is that of Euclidean space, which is infinite in extent! Flat universes that are finite in extent include the simple torus and Klein bottle. Moreover, in three dimensions, there are 10 finite closed flat 3-manifolds*

Cosmologists have suggested various 'wrap-around' shapes for the Universe: it might be shaped like a football or even a weird 'doughnut'.

In each case, the Universe would appear to be infinite, because you would never physically reach its edge *- if you travelled far enough in any direction you would end up back where you started, just as if you were circumnavigating the globe.*

Undeterred, Steiner and his colleagues have re-analyzed the 2003 data from NASA's Wilkinson Microwave Anisotropy Probe, looking for different shapes, including the so-called '3-torus', also dubbed the 'doughnut universe'. Here is a statement on that...

...Despite its catchy nickname, this shape is tough to visualize, says Steiner. The 3-torus is an extension of the familiar doughnut shape and can be formed from a rectangular piece of paper. *Pi indicated to Dr. Singh that, of course, the panel*

had been through that exercise, but I will allow the author to repeat, repetition always the best for memory.

You can imagine gluing together first one set of opposite edges to make a cylinder, and then the second set of opposing edges to make a doughnut shape, *explains Steiner.* The 3-torus is formed in a similar way, but you begin with a cube and glue together each of the opposite faces. So if you were to attempt to exit one of the cube's faces, you would immediately find yourself entering again through the opposite one.

Very important here, in effect this defines "edge" as within the notion of infinite, but existing!"

In the absence of dark energy, a flat universe expands forever but that is at a continually decelerating rate, with expansion asymptotically approaching zero. With dark energy, the expansion rate of the universe initially slows down, due to the effect of gravity, but eventually increases. The ultimate fate of the universe is the same as that of an open universe!

Now the status when a Universe has positive curvature. A positively curved universe is described by spherical geometry, and can be thought of as a three-dimensional hypersphere, even some other spherical 3-manifold (like the Poincare dodecahedral space), all of which are quotients of the 3-sphere.

Poincare dodecahedral space, is a positively curved space, colloquially described as "soccer ball-shaped", as it is the quotient of the 3-sphere by the binary icosahedral group, which is very close to icosahedral symmetry, the symmetry of a soccer ball. This was proposed by Jean-Pierre Luminet and colleagues in 2003 and an optimal orientation on the sky for the model was estimated in 2008!

And lastly a Universe with negative curvature. A hyperbolic universe, one of a negative spatial curvature, is described by hyperbolic geometry, and can be thought of locally as a three-dimensional analog of an infinitely extended saddle shape.

There are a great variety of hyperbolic 3-manifolds, and their classification is not completely understood. Those of finite volume can be understood via the Mostow rigidity theorem. For hyperbolic local geometry, many of the possible three-dimensional spaces are informally called horn topologies, so called because of the shape of the pseudo sphere, a canonical model of hyperbolic geometry. An example is the Picard horn, a negatively curved space, colloquially described as "funnel-shaped". *PI said in mercy I know this seems overwhelming...However, the net-net, if you will, mathematically speaking in my opinion, whether the geometry of the global universe, i.e. its curvature is flat, positive or negative,* **hyperbolic**

structures can be found that "represent" the " infinite" or unbounded space! *So, Pi went on next regarding curvature…*

Open or closed, i.e. what is proposed in the next item is…

*… (3) When cosmologists speak of the universe as being "open" or "closed", they most commonly are referring to whether the curvature is negative or positive. She emphasized…***These meanings of open and closed are different from the mathematical meaning of open and closed used for sets in topological spaces and for the mathematical meaning of open and closed manifolds, which gives rise to ambiguity and confusion!**

We must note that in mathematics, there are definitions for a closed manifold (i.e., compact without boundary) and open manifold (i.e., one that is not compact and without boundary).

*A "closed universe" is necessarily a closed manifold. But **to state it directly an "open universe" can be either a closed or open manifold!** For a specific example, in the Friedmann–Lemaître–Robertson–Walker (FLRW) model the universe is considered to be without boundaries, in which case "compact universe" could describe a universe that is a closed manifold!*

<div style="text-align:center">```</div>

At this point although Dr. Singh was truly impressed with his future student's knowledge, the rest of the panel were showing signs of wanting to give up. So Pi usually not one of sympathy, did move on directly toward conclusion.

Well, to complete this there are two other offerings. One is the so called Milne model or "spherical" expanding model".

If one applies Minkowski space-based Special Relativity to expansion of the universe, without resorting to the concept of a curved space-time, then one obtains the Milne model. Any spatial section of the universe of a constant age (the proper time elapsed from the Big Bang) will have a negative curvature; this is merely a pseudo-Euclidean geometric fact analogous to one that concentric spheres in the flat Euclidean space are nevertheless curved. Spatial geometry of this model is thus an unbounded hyperbolic space (exaggerated). The entire universe is contained within a light cone, namely the future cone of that "Big Bang". For any given moment $t > 0$ of coordinate time (assuming the Big Bang has $t = 0$), the entire universe is bounded by a sphere of radius exactly $c\,t$. The apparent paradox of an infinite universe contained within a sphere is explained with length contraction: the galaxies farther away, which are travelling away from the observer the fastest, will appear thinner.

144

*This model is essentially a degenerate FLRW for $\Omega = 0$. It is incompatible with observations that definitely rule out such a large negative spatial curvature. However, as a background in which gravitational fields (or gravitons) can operate, due to diffeomorphism invariance, **the space on the macroscopic scale, is equivalent to any other (open) solution of Einstein's field equations. After my study, I am inclined to accept this model, i.e. our universe may "bounded" by a sphere, but one that can still be rationalized as infinite and exists with edges zero in thickness.***

Dr.Why entered on this saying Pi we appreciate your effort, but I am sure most of us are lost in some of the terminology. Before the consensus meeting I would appreciate if you would give us a glossary, say in table form. That follows up on Jane's request.

To which Pi agreed with no apology, however, she went on with a comment on dark energy which she said would round off and conclude her presentation.

Since mass effects curvature via Einstein, Dark Energy becomes very important, to this business of shape. The Professor has covered dark matter, and showed on that basis that the Universe is "open", which in practical terms is my zero in thickness thought.

And to continue briefly, if the density of the universe is greater than the "critical density", then gravity will eventually win and the universe will collapse back on itself, the so called "Big Crunch".

However, the results of the WMAP mission and observations of distant supernova have suggested that the expansion of the universe is actually accelerating, which implies the existence of a form of matter with a strong negative pressure, such as the cosmological constant.

At this point Dr.Why interjected in strong voice… If the universe is accelerating- it is expanding! Then the question is into what! That is something this panel is thinking on actively, very actively!

That is we are returned to Forever, to Infinity. While we are concerned about our Universe, is it now important to give regard to understanding that outer edge, what is it going into!

At that statement the whole Forever panel said an almost simultaneous "Yes, of Course, we continually ask that!"

And Pi, agreed, that should be in someone's attention for sure! However, I will return to the question at hand.

In....conclusion...within the available mathematical and topological analysis I have presented, topologies should be allowed, i.e. occur-functioning for our universe!

Hence, it is possible that our Universe, within the spherical local topography, could be 3-Möbius like. It is infinite with, shall we say--- boundaries of or near zero thickness.

Dr. Singh truly impressed with his future post-doctoral student complimented her and stated for the panel, knowing that Pi would agree based on scientific caution that....We of course must truly be able to conclude that the Universe is much larger than the volume we can directly observe. However, the volume we observe has flat, slightly curved geometry, with a possible 3-manifold and seeming cyclic, i.e.in itself infinite topology.

The group's discussion on this were of course extremely important and it helped to have Dr. Singh present.

Tim spoke first..."It seems the central question is ... Is there an edge within our Universe, now we see that within it, one might ride on to reincarnate? I am thinking that it is there, but we have much more to learn! But, excuse, I am commenting, perhaps ahead of facts...

Dr. Singh helped with the simple statement," alternately what does edge mean? Can it mean Advantage? Perhaps that is more the crux of the matter?" he Professor entered with...At this point I find myself agreeing...But, whether we hope for a true edge or simply an advantage (I see as better understanding)... is that not so far in future we can only use it through massively advanced minds! The time-distances within space time are very likely so vast that we cannot achieve the 'times frames" to rejoin.

Moreover, although space-time sees all connected, i.e. past, present and future, we are not hesitating at all to say it. We are already able to control the future, by the way we behave! And I add that can be implanted not just in our Universes' space but in that in which the Universe is existing...Forever, in Infinity. To state it frankly, and this does not at all denigrate our study, there is Forever, in it is our future, and it will be fixed with each day as we live...Forever means, in my mind that for each of us -what we make ourselves to be we are always, because we are a part, a record of infinity.

Yes, Jehan added...It is important now that we throw off the violence that consumes us daily, in that way we can already control the future. "

After much more discussion, Pi suggested that we have not seen the whole picture. "Reaching toward Forever means that we must consider the more modern theoretical impact on our agenda!"

On that announcement and with complete agreement from the panel, it was moved to take that up next day and rest the remainder of this one.

That would give Dr.Singh opportunity to meet and get acquainted with the Potential Post Docs.

He was pleased that his astrophysics group would have the new input of a skilled mathematician, and also the input of a biologist to put a balance on the wanderings of those fixated on space-time.

Following, the discussions in the report above, there appeared my promised table from Pi on boundedness.

It is presented following -attached to the last page in this report.

To all, it has been a challenge in many ways and this area was one truly hard for me. So a special thanks to Pi for the table.

(Attachment, Table on Boundedness of the Universe)

Forever Probe, Document 11, June 11, p.m.
Duly Recorded and Filed
Respectfully Submitted,
Jane Caldwell, Technical Recorder

UNIVERSE BOUNDEDNESS-MATHMATICAL SPEAKING	
'Finite',i.e.,meaning bounded metric space	**"Infinite",i.e.,meaning unbounded metric space**
Volume can fill up	No well-defined volume
distances d-d available	no d-d distance to points
The smallestd d is universe diameter	Infinite d's, i.e., (unbounded) in extent
If such a d - has fixed volume	Has no fixed volume
Edge math is outlawed	Edge math "allowed"
Finite in extent	Infinite in extent
Closed (that is without an Edge)	Open-has not got a formal boundary
being Closed is in a sense-bounded	Boundaries are so to speak zero in thickness
Called compact	Infinite
Flat Universe (finite extent)	Flat Universe (infinite in extent)
Appears infinite (can't reach an Edge)	Is infinite
Closed manifold necessary	Closed or open manifolds are possible.

Pi's comment

I think it is consistent that our universe is within a spherical geometry (Milne model "probably") with radius ct. It is known to be expanding and is unfilled, as dark matter is "optimal'.

Expanding suggests probable infinite availability!

CHAPTER 4: WITHIN FOREVER'S ARENA

DEEP REFLECTION

Forever Probe, Document 12, June 12, a.m.

The panel met with ad hoc discussions all last evening. Then after a quite night and good rest they reconvened at 7 a.m. on June 12 in a conference room in their hotel.

Their consensus report was one accepting that hyperspace topological models might possibly form the basis of entry into the space-time axes holding "Forever". Yet they felt that "Resistive".

On Pi and Dr. Singhs encouragement they agreed that the next day should look at what alterations or limitations operating within Forever might be suggested by the modern theories in so called Quantum Theory or Mechanics.

Dr. Singh was accepted as the editor and presenter of the discussions this day...

...Well, I am a University Lecturer and so I think it is necessary for this panel to have the backdrop and main issuances from the subject. He handed out a paper that was an excerpt from "Universe Review" (http://universe-review.ca/F13-atom.htm).

I will comment on the document you have from time to time, although the words themselves tell the story for your files. I know you have touched on this before, but as has been said review is reinforcement. So, here begins the article, and I read...

To use a well said line "The frame work of Classical Science was punctured by Henry Becquerel exactly a hundred years ago, in 1896, by the discovery of Radioactivity. Albert Einstein cracked it at the beginning of this century by discovering the theory of relativity."

That was, however, totally blasted by the advent of something called Quantum Theory and the Uncertainty Principle.

One can begin to tell of the importance of this with the following....It was found that the cosmic horizon would glow, emitting a feeble spray of elementary particles and radiation, with a temperature of a fraction of a billionth of a degree.

From this observation there was proposed what became referred to as "Quantum Uncertainty". That radiation bath would be subject to random fluctuations like Boltzmann's universe, however, and every once in a very long, long time, one of those fluctuations would be big enough to recreate the Big Bang!

In the fullness of time this process could lead to the endless series of recurring universes. Our present universe could be part of that chain!

As another example, Einstein's General Relativity predicts that time ends inside black holes because the gravitational collapse squeezes matter to infinite density.

However, it has since been hypothesized that quantum uncertainty effects prevent this from happening, causing a "bounce" where the matter stops contracting and starts expanding. This creates a new expanding region of the universe that cannot be seen from outside the black hole. This can be called a new universe. This scenario has a lot of support from the study of mathematical models of quantum effects in the interiors of black holes.

So what exactly is this Quantum Effect? …This mystery has to do in first discoveries with the nature of light. Experiments conducted at the start of the century had shown that light shining on a metal plate produced showers of electrons whose speed, or energy, was the same no matter how bright the light. Einstein explained the so-called photoelectric effect by asserting that light, which was known to flow in continuous waves, could also be regarded as sputtering along in discrete particles, or quanta.

Each of these particles—every quantum of light at a given wavelength—carried the same amount of energy, he argued, and so dispatched a single electron with the same energetic kick. Thus did Einstein discover the photon? He lived (*as Pi noted earlier in your study of papers*) to regret it.

The wave-particle duality was unsettling enough. But when Danish physicist Niels Bohr showed that the electrons in atoms, too, must behave as quanta to account for observations, Einstein made a conceptual leap that troubled him even more. In pondering the quantum interactions between matter and light, Einstein found he could calculate neither the timing nor the direction of the photons spontaneously emitted from atoms. The emissions were fundamentally random. Chance seemed to be an ineluctable element of the quantum world!

In fact, Quantum Theory suggests that random events are rampant at the subatomic level. There is no way to predict cause and effect on a case-by-case basis. *I understand that you touched on this when you talked about mistakes by the Master…Well…*

…The best that physicists can do is calculate probabilities, which do or do not prove out for a large number of events. To Einstein, a statistical probability was even less acceptable than the infinities of a singularity.

A physics that could not predict individual events was no physics at all, he said. It was, at best, guesswork. And it certainly did not correspond to reality, which, like the universe, Einstein preferred to see as stable, orderly, and knowable to the most intimate detail. Apparently, he regarded mysteries as beautiful only if they offered some hope of solution.

"That he would choose to play dice with the world," Einstein wrote [of God], "is something that I cannot believe for a single moment." In that famous retort, Bohr supposedly replied, "Stop telling God what to do." But the aesthetician in Einstein turned his back on quantum theory.

A new generation of physicists rushed to embrace it. In the 1920s quantum mechanics became the rage, and it advanced by leaps and bounds, thanks in large part to Einstein's persistent efforts to discredit it. By the 1930s quantum mechanics had become intellectually unassailable. The vast majority of physicists today believe that the subatomic realm really is, in some sense, unknowable."

Nowadays scientists are working to achieve Einstein's dream that is "The Theory of Everything, the deeper truth that unites all the forces of nature, which pulls cosmology and quantum theory together, remains the most important quest of physics!

However, Einstein's Lambda, also known as the cosmological constant, has come in handy of late.

In the last decade astronomers discovered the expanding universe is also accelerating—expanding faster and faster. That confounding scenario can be represented mathematically a point you have touched upon, if general relativity includes a term, just like the cosmological constant, that imbues empty space with an unidentified force. "Making use of the cosmological constant is by now a venerable aspect of contemporary cosmology," says Fred Goldhaber.

The day may come when all of Einstein's blunders seem equally prescient.

Inflation allows for magnetic monopoles to exist as long as they were produced prior to the period of inflation. During inflation, the density of monopoles drops exponentially, so their abundance drops to undetectable levels.

As a bonus, Inflation also explains the origin of structure in the universe. *This is something for the Panel to note again and keep in mind said Pi*!

Prior to inflation, the portion of the universe we can observe today was microscopic, and quantum fluctuation in the density of matter on these microscopic scales expanded to astronomical scales during Inflation. Over the next several hundred million years, the higher density regions condensed into stars, galaxies, and clusters of galaxies. That covered …the doctor entered…So, next…we will trace…

…The Development of Quantum Mechanics: *Well you are all wondering a bit I am sure about how did this critical theory develop. So let me now review the development of Quantum Mechanics. My information is largely from "the Universe Review".*

The earliest steps in the development of quantum physics arose from the investigation into something as mundane as why metal glows red when hot. The great German physicist Max Planck had been studying the problem of black body radiation in the late 1890s. The "problem "Planck was dealing with was the observation that the greatest amount of energy being radiated from a black body (or any perfect absorber) actually falls near the middle of the electromagnetic spectrum, rather than in the ultraviolet region as classical theory suggested.

While Planck's initial black body radiation law described the experimentally observed black body spectrum quite well, it was not perfect, and it was Planck's genius to realize that the only way the law could work perfectly was to incorporate the supposition that electromagnetic energy could be emitted only in "quantized" form (i.e. restricted to discrete values rather than to a continuous set of values).

In 1900, he proposed that light and other electromagnetic waves were emitted in discrete packets of energy, which he called "quanta", which can only take on certain discrete values (multiples of a certain constant, which now bears the name the "Planck constant"). He concluded that the energy radiated from a black body could only be a multiple of an elementary unit, E, where $E = hv$ (where h is the Planck constant, and v is the frequency of the radiation).5

In effect, Planck showed that the very structure of nature is discontinuous, in the same way as the population of a city, for example, can only change in discrete increments (i.e. whole number of people). Although, quantization was a purely formal assumption in Planck's work at this time, and he never fully understood its radical implications (that had to await Albert Einstein's interpretations in 1905), it has come to be regarded as the first essential stepping stone in the development of quantum theory, and the greatest intellectual accomplishment of Planck's career, for which he was awarded the Nobel Prize in Physics in 1918.

Building on this earlier research by Planck and by Philippe Lenard, Einstein became, in 1905, the first person to clearly realize that light was made up of photons. He saw it as the only way to make sense of the so-called "photoelectric effect" (the phenomenon whereby certain metals, when exposed to light, eject electrons).

Einstein found that, no matter how bright the light shone on the metal, only light above a certain frequency caused electrons to be given off. Above that point, as the frequency of the light is increased, the energy of the electrons given off also increased. Furthermore, he noted that all the electrons were emitted instantaneously, with no delay whatsoever, which could not happen if the light was a wave sweeping over the metal, but only if the electron emissions were caused by individual particles of light.

Einstein, therefore, extended Planck's discovery by theorizing that energy itself (not just the process of energy absorption and emission) is quantized. Light, he concluded, must consist of tiny bullet-like particles, now known as photons. In fact, it was for this work on the photoelectric effect in 1905 that Einstein was awarded the 1921 Nobel Prize in Physics, not for his better known work (in the same year) on the Special Theory of Relativity.

Then most notably, in 1913, the Danish physicist Niels Bohr further built on Planck's insights and on the recent discoveries of J. J. Thomson and Ernest Rutherford about the structure of atoms.

Bohr introduced the idea that electrons can only orbit an atom's nucleus at certain discrete distances (or "shells"), orbits that are different for different elements. This happens because electrons are also waves of specific frequencies, and the waves only fit (without interfering with themselves or cancelling each other out) on orbits of certain sizes. Electrons closer to the nucleus have lower energy than those further away (even though they are traveling faster).

However, although an electron can only exist in certain discrete energy levels (or "quantum states"), it can move from one energy level to another. For example, if an atom is heated or forced to collide, the energy imparted can cause an electron to move to a higher energy level (we say that the electron is "excited").

Bohr noted that it did not gradually pass through a continuum of energy levels in between, but rather there was a "quantum leap" or "quantum jump", and the electron instantly leaped from one energy level to the next. A useful analogy is that of climbing a set of stairs, where it is possible to stand on any given step, but not somewhere in between two steps.

He also discovered that when an electron drops from a higher energy orbit to a lower one - which it will do whenever there is a lower energy state available for it to occupy - it emits in the process a photon (an individual quantum, or packet, of electromagnetic radiation) with energy exactly equal to the difference between the energy levels of the two orbits. Conversely, if light with the right energy strikes an atom, then its electrons will be excited and rise to a higher energy state, and the light will be absorbed.

This phenomenon is essentially why a heated object glows: the heat causes electrons to jump into excited states; then, when they drop back down to the "ground" state, the atom gives off photons of light. It is also the basis for the invention of the laser: in a nutshell, energy is pumped into atoms, thereby exciting them, and then, when the electrons drop down in energy, the photons emitted are collected and focused.

Bohr's revelation that an electron jumps from one distinct state to another neatly explained why the light was emitted in distinct bands of color, as electrons with specific energy levels within different elements changed their quantum states. For example, an electron moving from the third orbit of an atom to the second orbit emits red light, from fourth to second creates blue-green light, from fifth to second violet light, etc., all corroborated by Bohr's model.

This arrangement of the electrons within atoms also has some very useful practical applications. Because of the very structured and regular arrangement of atoms in solids, the energy levels of electrons within constituent atoms combine to form continuous energy bands (known as valence bands) separated by band gaps. The band structure of a material determines several characteristics, in particular the material's electronic and optical properties (e.g. some materials have very close, or even overlapping, bands so that electrons can easily move between them, which makes them good conductors of electricity; other materials have very large band gaps which makes them good insulators; etc.).

So, the early stepping stones towards a fundamentally new type of physics *(which was to become known as quantum theory or quantum mechanics)* were gradually falling into place, and *it was becoming clear that an essential element of it was the conception of light (and indeed all radiation and all matter) as composed of discrete quanta or particles.*

But there was more to come. In 1923, Arthur Compton's famous "Compton scattering" experiment showed how x-rays (generally understood as waves of electromagnetic radiation) can be observed to bounce off electrons, thus exhibiting particle-like properties, just like billiard balls impacting with other billiard balls. He also showed how this particle-like characteristic of electromagnetic radiation could be measured by its frequencies, previously considered a characteristic property only of waves.

Furthermore, in 1924, the French physicist Louis de Broglie showed that *wave-particle duality was not merely an aberrant behavior of light, but rather was a fundamental principle exhibited by both radiation and ALL particles of matter.*

According to de Broglie's findings, then, at least in theory, everything (a baseball, a car, even a person) has a wavelength, although their wavelengths are so small as to be not noticeable. Just as Planck and Einstein had shown that waves can have particle-like characteristics, de Broglie showed that particles can have wave-like characteristics.

Thus, it became clear that a particle like an electron (or even an atom) could in some way interfere with itself, and was in some sense "spread out", or at least was able to be in many places at once. It should be noted, though, that this is not to say that an atom can spread itself out in a broad beam of some sort: the wave we are talking about is a wave of information, of what can be known about the atom, a probability wave. Essentially, the wave is not the particle itself but a measure of the probability attached to its particle nature.

Well to go on with this introduction, there are two aspects that I should certainly point out. The first is Probability Waves and Complementarity and the second is Nonlocality and Entanglement.

…The Probability Waves and Complementarity: The acceptance of light as composed of particles (or photons) led to another shocking realization. For example, if light shines on an imperfectly transparent sheet of glass, it may happen that 95% of the light transmits through the glass while 5% is reflected back. This makes perfect sense if light is a wave (the wave simply splits and a smaller wave is reflected back). But if light is considered as a stream of identical particles, then all we can say is that each and every photon arriving at the glass has a 95% chance of being transmitted and a 5% chance of being reflected.

The actual behavior of any individual photon is therefore totally random and unpredictable, not just in practice but even in principle. Although the tossing of a coin, for example, is random in practice, if we knew precisely everything about the force, angle, shape, air currents, etc., we could, in principle, predict the outcome accurately. The behavior of a sub-atomic particle, however, is random on a whole different level, and can never be predicted.

Thus, it is not possible to predict a single definite result for an observation, only a number of different possible outcomes, each with a particular likelihood or probability. Physics had therefore changed overnight from a study of absolute certainty, to one of merely predicting the odds!

The reason we do not see the effects of this on a more macro scale is that everyday objects are composed of billions or trillions of sub-atomic particles. Although the position of each individual particle may be highly uncertain, because there are so many of them acting in unison in an everyday object, the combined probabilities add up to what is, to all intents and purposes, a certainty. This is an important note for the Panel, as you are by in large wanting to deal with the Macro that is physical lives and events.

*To continue through the paper though…*In order to reconcile the wave-like and particle-like behavior of light, its wave-like aspect needs to be able to "inform" its particle-like aspect about how to behave, and vice versa. It was the Austrian physicist Erwin Schrödinger, along with the German Max Born, who first realized this and worked out the mechanism for this information transference in the 1920s, by imagining an abstract mathematical wave called a probability wave (or wave function) which could inform a particle of what to do in different situations. Erwin Schrödinger proposed a ground-breaking wave equation, analogous to the known equations for other wave motions in nature, to describe such a wave. Born further demonstrated that the probability of finding a particle at any point (its "probability density") was related to the square of the height of the probability wave at that point.

Schrödinger worked out the exact solutions of the wave equation for the hydrogen atom, and the results perfectly agreed with the known energy levels of these atoms.

It was soon found that the equation could also be applied to more complicated atoms, and even to particles not bound in atoms at all. In fact, in theory it applies to ALL matter, although massive objects exhibit very small wavelengths, so small that it is rather pointless to think of them in a wave fashion. But for small objects like elementary particles, the wavelength can be observable and significant.

Like light, then, particles are also subject to wave-particle duality: a particle is also a wave, and a wave is also a particle. *Using Schrödinger's wave equation, therefore, it became possible to determine the probability of finding a particle at any location in space at any time. This ability to describe reality in the form of waves is at the heart of quantum mechanics.* In 1926, Schrödinger published a proof showing that Heisenberg's matrix mechanics and his own wave mechanics were in fact equivalent, and merely represented different versions of the same theory.

The Danish physicist Niels Bohr, who, along with Heisenberg and Schrödinger, was integrally involved in the early development of quantum mechanics, tried to come to grips with some of the philosophical implications of quantum theory in the early 1920s. He felt that the classical and quantum mechanical models were two complementary ways of dealing with physics, both of which were necessary, an idea he called "complementarity". This idea of complementarity formed the basis of what became known as the "Copenhagen interpretation" of quantum physics, a deeply divisive idea in the world of physics at the time.

Bohr felt that an experimental observation "collapsed" or "ruptured" the wave function to make its future evolution consistent with what we observe experimentally (an idea that will become very important in our subsequent explanations of quantum effects such as decoherence, entanglement and the uncertainty principle). As soon as a photon, for example, is observed or detected in a particular place, then the probability of its being detected in any other place suddenly becomes zero. Up until that point, the particle's position is inherently uncertain and unpredictable, an uncertainty that only disappears when it is observed and measured. This immediate transition from a multi-faceted potentiality to a single actuality (or, alternatively, from a multi-dimensional reality to a 3-dimensional reality compatible with our own everyday experience) is sometimes referred to as a "Quantum Jump".

However, Bohr also believed that there was no precise way to define the exact point at which such a collapse occurred, and it was therefore necessary to discard the laws governing individual events in favor of a direct statement of the laws governing aggregations.

Here then is another observation that might affect your agenda ...According to this model, there is no deep quantum reality, no actual world of electrons and photons, only a description of the world in these terms, and quantum mechanics merely affords us a formalism that we can use to predict and manipulate events and the properties of matter.

The Copenhagen interpretation, then is it not essentially a pragmatic view, effectively saying that it really does not matter exactly what quantum mechanics is all about, the important thing being that it "works" (in the sense that it correlates with reality) in all possible experimental situations, and that no other theory can explain sub-atomic particles in any more detail.

And so it remained until the experimental work of the American physicist John Clauser and others in the early 1970s, as we will see in the next section on Nonlocality and Entanglement.

...Nonlocality and Entanglement: Another of the remarkable features of the microscopic world prescribed by quantum theory is the idea of nonlocality, what Albert Einstein rather dismissively called "spooky actions at a distance". This was first described in the "EPR papers" of Einstein, Boris Podolsky and Nathan Rosen in 1935, and it is sometimes referred to as the EPR (Einstein-Podolsky-Rosen) paradox. It was even more starkly illustrated by Bell's Theorem, published by John Bell in 1964, and the subsequent practical experiments by John Clauser and Stuart Freedman in 1972 and by Alain Aspect in 1982.

Nonlocality describes the apparent ability of objects to instantaneously know about each other's state, even when separated by large distances (potentially even billions of light years), almost as if the universe at large instantaneously arranges its particles in anticipation of future events. *Again Panel, here is an aspect of*

Quantum Theory, that in some way, perhaps in the distant future that Navigators might employ...

Thus, in the quantum world, despite what Einstein had established about the speed of light being the maximum speed for anything in the universe, instantaneous action or transfer of information does appear to be possible. This is in direct contravention of the "principle of locality" (or what Einstein called the "principle of local action"), the idea that distant objects cannot have direct influence on one another, and that an object is directly influenced only by its immediate surroundings, an idea on which almost all of physics is predicated.

Nonlocality suggests that universe is in fact profoundly different from our habitual understanding of it, and that the "separate" parts of the universe are actually potentially connected in an intimate and immediate way. In fact, Einstein was so upset by the conclusions on nonlocality at one point that he declared that the whole of quantum theory must be wrong, and he never accepted the idea of nonlocality up till his dying day.

Nonlocality occurs due to the phenomenon of entanglement, whereby particles that interact with each other become permanently correlated, or dependent on each other's states and properties, to the extent that they effectively lose their individuality and in many ways behave as a single entity. The two concepts of nonlocality and entanglement go very much hand in hand, and, peculiar though they may be, they are facts of quantum systems which have been repeatedly demonstrated in laboratory experiments. For example, if a pair of electrons are created together, one will have clockwise spin and the other will have anticlockwise spin (spin is a particular property of particles whose details need not concern us here, the salient point being that there are two possible states and that the total spin of a quantum system must always cancel out to zero).

However, under quantum theory, a superposition is also possible, so that the two electrons can be considered to simultaneously have spins of clockwise-anticlockwise and anticlockwise-clockwise respectively. If the pair are then separated by any distance (without observing and thereby deciphering them) and then later checked, the second particle can be seen to instantaneously take the opposite spin to the first, so that the pair maintains its zero total spin, no matter how far apart they may be, and in total violation of the speed of light law. *Pi said, so can a message take the opposite? She was answered, there is no proof in the macro world of that, nonetheless...*Despite Einstein's misgivings about entanglement and nonlocality and the practical difficulties of obtaining proof one way or the other, Irish physicist John Bell attempted to force the issue by making it experimental rather than just theoretical.

Bell's Theorem, published in 1964, and referred to by some as one of the most profound discoveries in all of physics, effectively showed that the results predicted by quantum mechanics (for example, in an experiment like that described by Einstein, Podolsky and Rosen) could not be explained by any theory which preserved locality. The subsequent practical experiments by John Clauser and Stuart Freedman in 1972 seem (despite Clauser's initial espousal of Einstein's position) to definitively show that the effects of nonlocality are real, and that "spooky actions at a distance" are indeed possible.

It was now time for Pi to return, and she did saying…so it is to be grasped panel, from Quantum Mechanics there are two observations that may play into the operation of Forever, i.e. Complementarity and Nonlocality.

These ideas, of course, will affect the way one tries to enter, to view forever, and that is, of course, a matter for far greater understanding. If it were a goal to seize an event, these propositions show avenues. Where one event may have a distant opposite the opposite might be one that the interloper may want to take the dominant path.

Of course as said this insight is one clearly for the far future. As we now see it the mechanisms for entry are suggestive but technology has not yet given full descriptions of the Topology to ride. The matter, frankly is not yet fully tested. We have an edge there if that were to be the case for some future humans, but is just an edge.

And the Professor said very simply, "Why not just work on this present to make the better future!"

Dr. Shingh at this point indicated with a hand out... I have one last matter to show, here is a very remarkable and level impression from one Dr. Stenger. That is Victor J. Stenger from his book "Timeless Reality: Symmetry, Simplicity, and Multiple Universes.

He shows how time symmetry at the quantum level makes it possible to draw a model of underlying reality that is simpler and more symmetric than the conventional view!

This reality is timeless, with no beginning, no end, and no arrow of time…..

….Time is indeed reversible. And in this "timeless reality," nothing rules out the existence of other universes besides our own; in fact, such a multiverse is strongly suggested by modern theories of cosmology.

But whether or not reality has one universe or many, it had no beginning and was not created. It neither was nor will be. "It" just is!"

Tim our biologist commented on this being moved by the message. He feels so strongly the love of precious earth his comment mirrored that love and we all simply sat in awe as he said...

"All this is in our human time-that we-our remarkable minds had ability to see 'it', have that power, and can know of it as much as we do. "It" is awesome and in its majestic way beautiful in design. I know of this, our existence is made of fractals, here on earth even...we see that clearly, everywhere in everything. The leaves of the trees show in their microscopic design the same shape, as the pattern in the bark. Each mirrors that above!

The view we now have of Jupiter and its moons circling in the way the very atoms with protons have electrons do, shows the incredible homology of all within which we exist. Yes, I think he is right, our universe is one among many, one among parallels in an infinite cosmos, that is within in a Forever, an awesome infinity!"

And we in ours as we have discovered, may have the form through which we can know Forever if in patience we can just insure survival of Human Time there will be a deep sufficient understanding in the full workings of Forever".

At this point it was clear Samyak so saying that the study of Forever, was nearing the end of all that could be had for our Panel.

Dr. Singh indicated that he hoped his contribution on Quantum theory helped the Panel, to become up to date for their Quest. He said it is clear that quantum effects give possibilities never before seen.

That is, bubbles in the cosmos, new universes, even parallel universes, and life beyond Dark Holes. However, in his opinion the path the group has taken is by no means void, certainly not complete and he knows the panel or someone so stimulated will continue its search. Every day we have gained insight. We are in our wisest understanding when we listen to the Poet Riainer Rilke's words.

"Be patient toward all that is unsolved in your heart and try to love the questions themselves."

With this, the meeting was adjourned and the Panel retired for consensus seeking.

This took almost 5 hours, with the following report on the last meeting (Excerpts, read out by Daniel).

Here in summary is our joint opinion. "There are and will be ramifications from Quantum Theory. It is one more step in a unifying theory that eluded Einstein.

Ramifications include a degree of uncertainty, and it is clearly possible there are as fractals, bubbles throughout space, one of which we may indeed occupy, that is the one that is our arena. That is the one where our Human Time takes place.

It is clear from all we have reviewed that space-time, that arena---holds all past, present and future. But, and importantly in our view, it also clear that is within another Arena, Infinity, a physical/chemical one which is "Forever"!

What we have learned, tells us it is possible someday to look into those worries we expressed, for their answers - we are just on the edge of resolving, just on the edge of Forever!

With that we are certain that it does exist, there is a Forever, and Infinity! Our conclusion must be, however, after our detailed study, for anyone who has followed our quest. "Forever means, all that you make of yourself to be, you will always be', and that is for everyone--for everyone else.

Not just joking...It does occur through this investigation that each of us should make well of ourselves, because some day, someone may navigate to you and if you are doing wrong for everyone else you will be made to know it!"

As the report was filled, Daniel said to the panel, you know Friedrich Schiller said it well.

"He who has done his best for his own time has lived for all time."

Forever Probe, Document 12, June 12, a.m.
Duly Recorded and Filed
Respectfully Submitted,
Jane Caldwell, Technical Recorder

SECURING TIME

Concluding the Visit:

Awaiting (me) to set up arrangements for the panel members' return home they visited town again and had a number of off-the-cuff meetings. One such when gathered around in a park involved this most interesting discussion. (It seemed at first it was outside of the agenda, so this is just regular typeface.)

The first comment by Tim was, "I think we should never trivialize the coincidences that brought us into this most curious quest. There is the pull of curiosity, of coincidence that demands seeking knowledge, a look into "Forever's Real life" seems a rational mission. Jehan entered right away, "And you know there is so much more to look into when we understand Forever better."

Angelei said also right away, "And, Oh My! There are so many unbelievable coincidences and challenges, so often thoughts haunting, for sure millions of curiosities that would if answered satisfy our human inquisitive souls, give us a more secure footing.

She pulled out a piece of paper with a list and read off just a few, saying I have been keeping tabs after Skellan's explosion time conjoint with the Professor's shot-gun injury! You can find so many of these examples.

I discovered that Robert Todd Lincoln, the son of Abraham Lincoln was present at Ford's Theater in Washington in1865, when his father was assassinated. He was nearby in 1881 when President James Garfield was shot at the B&P Railroad in Washington, and in 1901 he just happened to be a few feet away when President William McKinley was shot at the Pan-American Exposition in Buffalo, New York. Well if you can justify this here is another of many.

In December, 5, 1664 a boat sank while crossing the Menai Strait in the Irish Sea. Just one of the 81 passengers survived, a man named Hugh Williams. On December 5, 1785, a boat sank in the Irish Sea. The only survivor was a man named Hugh Williams. And on August 5, 1820 - 24 passengers drowned in a stricken vessel at sea. One man was saved. His name was Hugh Williams.

Now on a roll, Angelei said, "well sure those are perhaps just interesting but did you know…Motorists driving along Croy Brae in Strathclyde, Scotland, sooner or later usually slow down or stop completely in utter confusion. For Croy Brae is one of the most disorienting places on earth. Approaching the Brae or hill from the north is an uncanny experience. The road appears to slope downward, and drivers assume that the slope will accelerate the vehicle. Yet if they slow down, they are really likely to grind to a completed halt. Despite every appearance to the contrary, the road clearly runs uphill. Unable to believe what has happened, many motorists stop—only to find that their cars begin to slide backward, "uphill"…(They are on a hill)!

Investigations have been unable to sort this out, everything from variations in the earth's magnetic field to simple errors in visual perspective have failed to explain the "reality". And to top it off there are several other places on earth having similar problems. However, having the education we had do we not wonder if these places could be start and finish spots on the earths winding within an inclusion of a torus located within our "universe transfinite." (The group broke into laughing at this.)

"And we have been living with the fourth dimension each day but some scientists are proposing that there are more than four dimensions. This is from efforts to explain the existence of the known forces in the universe, aside from gravity such as electromagnetism, strong nuclear force, holding nuclei of atoms together, and a force which repels subatomic particles.

It turns out if one looks deeply into an object in our four dimensions of space-time, one can get an idea of how other dimensions may be contained in the world we know.

For example, the surface of a wing is two dimensions and we can give an exact reference position of the wing tip in our time in space-time, i.e. we can cite time, date, latitude, longitude, and height above sea level. However looking at the same wing through an electron microscope that wing tip is not smooth, it has towering peaks and huge valleys, with massive boulders and debris. To add a point in that world, say on a massive electron boulder it is necessary to add two more figures to the two we have- the latitude and longitude of the point we are seeking on the spherical surface of the boulder. Added to the four in space-time this is two more for a total of six dimensions. And to this add the new knowledge in particle physics, worlds even smaller than the electron microscope can see, actually exist. What we might see in those, clearly suggests even more dimensions on an unimaginable small scale. Would it not be nice to know what that says about Forever?" (I should have italicized!)

So it was they enjoyed each other's company, but the time came to depart. They resided with Samyak for a full additional week until arrangements were fixed for travel, and then parted just the same as they came---in three ways.

To a person though - involved in a most complicated mission they carried away a deep feeling of respect for each other.

They each knew it was true "It is not just where you go, or what you do, but it is who is beside you that counts!" Deeply within each was the recognition that every day is a gift and that they are fortunate to exist in space-time within the incredible Forever.

As the Technical Recorder I have by their instructions filed the final report which consists of one hundred thirty five pages of detailed discussion. Here, however, on the following page is a summary.

Summary from the Final Report of the Forever Panel
June, 5-June 12, the India Retreat

"We achieved our mission, that is, in so far as we could. There were extensive complications involved which have led us to appreciate firmly that a great deal is yet to be determined!

Even within our own solar system there are great puzzles from the paradoxes regarding space as we discovered. In one of our references, the red spot on Jupiter makes no sense, is yet to be explained, and the topology of that same universe is nowhere fully understood let alone confirmed. Even so, we have great respect for the insight astrophysicists have given us in the last one hundred years regarding our cosmos.

In spite of the many limitations in current knowledge it is absolutely clear whether we accept the revelations of faith arguing for a here-after for all, or more directly and concretely the massive body of scientific evidence--is that we exist in an unbounded infinity. Forever is real!

Our search for "Forever" began with the notion as proposed by religious groups and proffered by Einstein that Space-time holds the past, present and future.

Thus, the panel wanted to find out if there might be a way to, shall we say, intercept that triad with ability to change the past or work on the future to the benefit of Mankind. Coupled to the space-time argument there is also, however, the notion that existence is simply an illusion no matter how persistent is our idea of time.

While none of our personal coincidences or circumstance could be resolved, as we are as yet unable to look into Einstein's Arena of space-time's past, present and future, we did find avenues wherein Humans should see, understand and adjust the future for a far better distant one, as our vision of its role clarified---it belongs to us, our fate, we have now time to control Human Time's lasting existence into Forever.

Nevertheless, the curious vision, the means of changing the past is not yet with us. There is in that though a central idea that far in that future some derivation of us will be able to do that and for all those involved in evil actions, they may stand a final trial!

Still each in the panel felt deeply rewarded by the effort, it showing clearly that humanity must recognize there is a real Forever and within that what each makes of self is what they will always be for all of us.

Our panel after examining original precepts, and present concepts agreed on a number of concerns with these propositions. These we hope a future panel, more data available, will pursue.

First it need be said that time is the property of Humans, i.e. it is Human-Time that matters. It is from humans that the concept of Space-time and Quantum effects relative to Space-time have developed. In effect we own those ideas and have full right to question.

The next concern relates to Einstein's space-time. This hinges on the "constant velocity of light". We agree with the astute observation that it is extraordinarily curious that light should be the only speed that is fixed. We also are concerned that Einstein's proposal was made first to hold then existing "laws" of physics proposed in a time when his focus was on our own observable universe, without knowledge of the cosmos and its potential for alternate universes and alternate laws of physics. Thus, while the "Master' proposed ideas that set many further inquiries, and we honor his tenacity, we feel the future will bring ideas that radically change the fixation on space-time!

Pertinent to this are our expanding ideas of uncertainty that have led to rather reasonable propositions of an infinity, an unbounded cosmos, in which other universes, (called bubble, for example) are existing and there is even the possibility that on the other side of black holes there are others that once existed in our universe---have been through the vortex creating new universes.

Proposals have been made, riding on Einstein's proposal of curvature dictated by planetary mass, that there is a local topography, possibly a 3-manifold that would allow following, i.e. an eternal loop, back to start!

Although this is an attractive proposal (hopeful idea) that could allow humans to "light upon", the past, or present or future (assuming a fractal infinity in space-times infinity) it is unclear by what mechanism one would enter at the appropriate time, and further to move back to a start with the distances so vast as to require warp speed, not accessible to today's humans. Further, it would be essential that the universe under the influence of dark matter would be proven energetically armed to such intense and specific special organization.

Even so, the inquiry by our panel has been most informative, and we are truly impressed by the efforts of past and present scientists to provide an understanding of the vast realm in which we exist.

In the end we find our general agreement is with Victor J. Stenger's notion of "Timeless Reality: that is Symmetry, Simplicity, and Multiple Universes." He shows how time symmetry at the quantum level makes it possible to draw a model of underlying reality that is simpler and more symmetric than the conventional view. This reality is timeless, with no beginning, no end, and no constrained arrow of time. Directly put, it simply exists, and there it is the Forever!

Although there is that and various other ideas our Chairman the Professor spent some time with us as we together suggested our opinions, and from that he drew a more directed summary depiction.

We realized, after all, that our central question was indeed about Forever, and that the matter of the structure of the universe was in the end ancillary or perhaps more correctly subservient to that. That is, the universe must fit into "Forever". It is the master of time! The universe with its space-time requirement is expanding and that tells the tale, there is a Forever as there must be time for that expansion.

That brings up a broader much more important question, how Forever functions! One can argue that is merely a rhetorical question or one for the theisms, but Forever is infinity so it is to be addressed! Here everything is open for interpretation. However there are certain basics that arise.

In our later meeting we discussed this and the following became clear. Obviously Forever's vastness is unbounded, like the Universes within it, it can have no limits. It contains Universes of course, and we accept that there must be more than ours, as it, Forever---is so vast and powerful that a limit to one universe would not be statistical and by quantum theory a contradiction.

The stuff in the universes, the atoms that make up substance in the Universes must be in its "Future's Hold", so we see it as having spread throughout atomic organizations', and within that fissionable groupings that could explode into new universal structures.

That there are black holes and dark matter is not surprising as both suggest the outcomes that must arise from an atomic containing Forever.

What also became clear, as we focused on the issue, was that Forever would have a mechanism allowing it to hold both past and future, that is it would be capable of touching always, from the start of any universe to the deep future of that Universe, from Big Bangs to Big Crunches. It should in face of its vastness behave as a manifold with full return to home capability that attracted us in our original naivety.

In the end the question of mounting, i.e. landing on or before some given event based on ability to access the universes structure, became a side issue, rather a matter for the distant representations of us. Why, now a side issue? Because Forever is infinite, and we are a part of that and therefore as Swami Vivekanada said infinite! Our existences demand that our representation in that infinity should be the best that we can muster now, for we will be held in that forever.

Time's existence in such an infinity might be reversible. Nonetheless, we reiterate, in this "timeless reality," nothing rules out the existence of other universes besides our own; in fact, such a multiverse is strongly suggested by modern theories of cosmology.

Even so, whether or not reality has one universe or many, it had no beginning and was not created. It neither was nor will be. It just is! And that if one opens one's mind can be seen as beautiful and indeed, loving to us Humans.

And to this we find an awesome beauty, that we would exist, our Human Time being within it and from such knowledge recognize there is Forever, and we can relate to all the others of our species that in our best advice Forever means what you make of yourself you will always be, and that for all the rest!

And our Forever in its design gifts us the ability to make of ourselves, the best we can be.

To our future kin, we hope from this knowledge you will believe in a new compassionate humanity, and with that you will achieve the best to always be!

It was Jane who asked several times to have our thinking on Forever depicted and hence we have a Figure. It is attached to this report as "Forever's Probable Mechanism Relating to Us".

Summary from the Final Report of the Forever Panel
June, 5-June 12, the India Retreat.
Duly Recorded and Filed,
Jane Caldwell, Technical Recorder

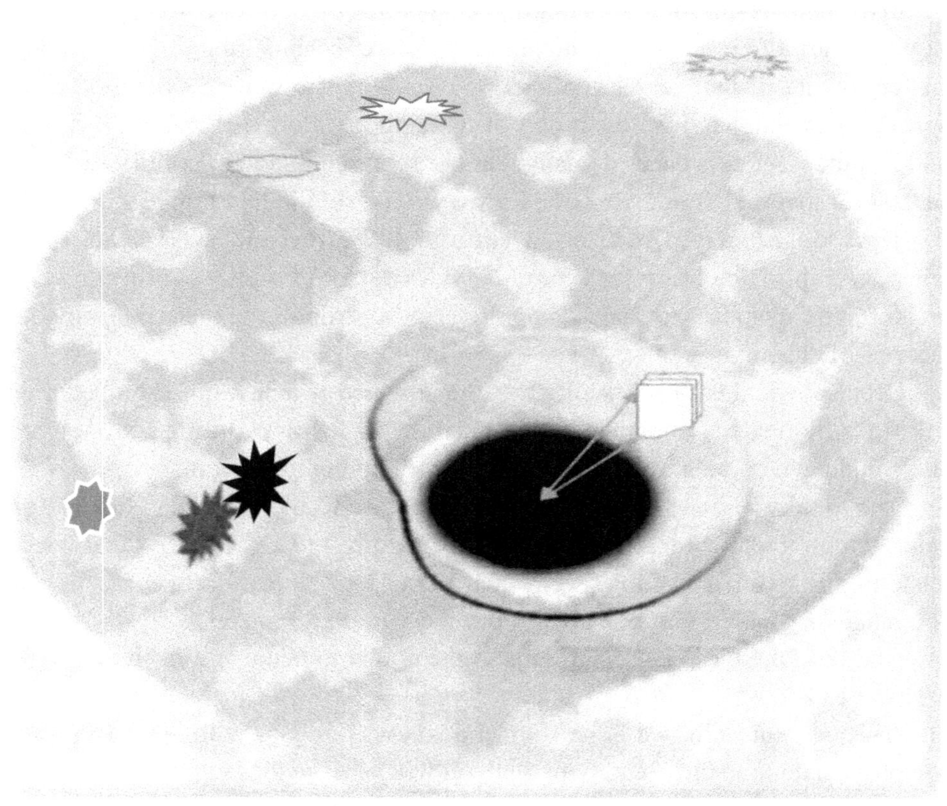

FOREVER'S PROBABLE "MECHANISM"RELATING TO US

This figure depicts the panel's overall idea of Forever. We have styled it as "Real", an "Eternal, Infinite, and Boundless - Expanse". The limitlessness, of course, cannot be depicted here.

Our vision is based upon a simple standard. First, we see our universe as a "child" of Forever! That is, ours is based upon an atomic structure, which certainly came from somewhere. Our universe is expanding into somewhere, substantiating a vast Forever. If it advances into another universe, then that is stronger support for an infinity. Therefore, we feel Forever equals infinity!

Moreover, *to emphasize we move out of the assumption box to say it is a real physical/chemical entity!* Our Universe a child of this real entity is one of incredible ability, to make, planets, and plants and organisms and allow fabrication into all sorts of things. So we see Forever holding all the ingredients necessary to explode into Universes, and when they begin to form - to have a wide variety of existences.

Second we see it boundless, it is just that, "It" is extended everywhere, holding all past and all to be. That it must be capable of "recycling" to accomplish total control of time as it does, we propose that forever has Hyper-Mobius like capability, i.e., having that return ability within its structure. That is though perhaps even in dimensions higher than prescribed in Einstein's Space-Time.

Third, it would by natural chemical equilibrium inject parts of its constitution, for example dark matter, into its children, to accomplish the incredible it does or there would not be the awesome capability in our Universe. We see it as a beautiful infinity, one capable of both creating and holding all in file. Within it is the record of all sentient creations.

And, to all believers this is particularly important. No matter how one wishes to describe it, as a "Singularity", a "God" or serendipitous "Mind giving Atomic Substance", that substance of Forever loves us truly in the rewards that happen, it gives us the super DNA to know our feelings, to see ourselves, to make of ourselves what we can and then it preserves us in an eternal library. In short we are considered by it as children of its child, our Universe-all together in this vast everlasting!

Forever is, of course, something extraordinary to grasp. And so it was important to have a statement from each member of the panel on her/his conception of and feelings about this finding. These are as follows. This includes couples who are in agreement, but of note a variety of belief philosophies!

<u>Daniel</u>: I am pantheist and scientist. It strikes me that the proposal of the panel is well considered, of course, not complete. It also strikes me that Forever is so awesomely beautiful that it defies words. How at once it is magnificently capable, yet in its design it has an element of mercy, by holding the record of each piece in the past, present and future, as a library, a record of creation. It is merciful in that change to better is allowed during consciousness.

<u>Jane (me) and my husband Chandler</u>: We wanted to be upfront in this because I am religious, a Christian. *As I look at the proposal I find it entirely within my notion of God. That is it seems to be a place of eternal love, in a magnificent design that gives almost every option for sentient creatures.* And if you will, that heaven is there in its library, where, indeed, because of its atomic structure, we will perhaps not understand until there! As to our own Universe within this…that is expanding and accelerating so we see that as great evidence there is Forever, as it must have the outward "room" in which to move, something that most everyone is, or has been reluctant to mention. As to the figure the legend and drawing are close to what I wanted. (Universe expanding into another space and so on...still infinite.) It is designed to relate infinity, allow space-time, transfinite, human time, dark matter-

gravity, our universe's shape, and to envision the interrelation to "Forever". Thanks panel for daring to depict this!

<u>Jehan.</u>   I am speaking also for Samyak, who agrees with me after our discussion. To me, too, this conception is beautiful and we feel very lucky indeed. But, first, I would direct a deep feeling. We must stop killing our children for reasons of faith. Forever would be unforgiving in that, a human time terminating agenda! As Daniel says Forever means that whatever you make yourself to be you will be always, and that is for everyone. There can be no long term future recorded within Forever, without recognizing that and all behaving so to avoid that fate. As to other matters, i*t is clear, although we passed over reincarnation because of lack of documentation, the description of Forever would permit that as to the multiplicity of creations via universes, and the very quantum character possible would allow for sporadic re-implantations, because Forever is cycling over all time.*

<u>Tim and Pi:</u> We wrote this together. I, Pi am atheist and Tim is seeking a way to believe. We both, however, are scientist and feel strongly that the proposition is good and for now the best available. Further, *we too find this beautiful, it describes a totally awesome, thoughtful idea of atomic-molecular potentials, leading to awesome creations.*

<u>Dr. Singh</u>:   My comment should be brief, but that is impossible.   The observation that Forever exists as an eternal vast chemical pool is rational, giving all needed potentials and room for all universes, their parallels, and alternates. It encompasses the full Quantum Chemical possibilities. Further, being raised in Islam, *I feel as mentioned by Jane that the postulations of our prophets as to an overseer-a god, are fully possible in this awesome molecular environment that may operate just as an all knowing entity...This is evidenced by the fact that the molecular structure has, indeed, created us, sentient beings, and creatures with breathtaking constructive possibility, i.e. emulating itself!...* We think it must exist as a "Mobius" but in an open way, so it is non-directional, always cycling-yet holding beginnings (in the past) and, of course, always forwarding's (in the future). Because matter exists, we believe Forever is filled with atomic substance (shown in grey) containing organizations' of fissionable foci, capable of exploding into new Universes. Between grey spaces is glue, dark energy, pushed into its Universes.

<u>Skellan and Angelei:</u> To us this design of Forever is not only logical but a priori the way it must be. This is first because a large body of scientist see our universe and its existence as time dependent, and dependent on organizations of matter, the basic organization in our Universe, i.e. the presence of Dark Matter and

Energy, is surely a reflection of substance in Forever that is carried along from it on the Big Bang. Further *as in discussions with our panel members we see that Forever as absolutely beautiful, with which we cannot provide a more perfect design. As the Guru we associated with Einstein said It is the one, the infinite the one no other can surmount. It holds within the answer--- to all beliefs!*

In short for the whole panel Forever exist, it is found and as we feel it must be. We do note that this is a provocation, prompting all to care deeply for each other and to look further into the edges of our magnificent Forever.

Finally some comments about our Universe (largest black in the depiction). We assume it is really a Transfinite- one of probable infinite numbers, perhaps exiting from a black hole. It is shown having a spherical topology depicted boundless, which we accept as most likely, expanding into Infinity' (it's "ct" potentially might be from the center to a boundless although invisible edge). Inflation versus dark matter/energy may have created internal structures within and over the universe-a geodesic manifold of unknown type perhaps even surrounding our own galaxy. Because the universe is expanding again we think documents infinity as real, as the universe must have time-room to expand.

Human time is idealized here as a file system ("It's a manifold of illustrative convenience") whose real shape is assumed held by dark matter's induced gravity. Past time is the lowest-closest record. Forward records (top of file system) are dependent upon human behavior. Future Navigators focus from the center records knowing past mistakes in effort to preview the most forward or future time (the top file record) with aim of making it optimal. Perhaps, (with many questions contingent) in some distant time they might look into the future through a special topographical method created by space aware generations of humans. The file system is shown of fixed size as that may be the eventual case without changes in our current world wide behavior.

And, highly important to grasp...the overwhelming chemical/physical vastness, the inherent control in Forever reflective of an overriding awesome consciousness, tells an important underlying message. No amount of guesswork as to creation or creator justifies killing on behalf of faiths and philosophies! It is the creator whose mechanisms and outcomes we do not currently have the ability to philosophically describe in unsubstantiated beliefs.

Of course, our universe seems to behave as Einstein's space-time proposes but always - since it began (Big Bang)—is expanding - thus time is naturally perceived forward. And as per Einstein's "Own Guru"....Humans within this are obviously a part of infinity. That is, they are Infinite, since their record, in whatever form they make it, is implanted in infinity!

~~~~~~

Post Script to The Final Report: With Samyak's blessing Daya and her child---Gabriel's son, left with Skellan ultimately for Virginia to be with Angelei and Alexander. It was to be a blessed visit and Alexander although just a boy discovered he was an uncle. Angelei was so happy, the joy simply overflowed!

Following on a very positive invitation Daniel had set up at Patel institute Tim and Pi left for Delhi and a program of six months Post-Doctoral research. They would later return to the Lab, to help Jean follow up on instructions that the Professor forwarded.

Tim and Pi's relationship grew even with Pi's seemingly reticent nature. Both recognized that their Forever Panel pursuit was something most special.

 That was framed one day when Tim read Pi's Horoscope to her. It said…"Is almost ever enough? Well "nearly" isn't of course right there, but it is not nowhere either. Stand where you landed for a while, and consider your options. This valiant but only partially achieved effort isn't the last step you will take." To which in her way of punctuation, she said, "Yes, how true, the future is still ours to create".

The Professor resolved to return to Africa, and Lagos and look up the Dean School of Pharmacy a friend and colleague since his Fulbright journey on the Lagos teaching hospital campus.

His return flight two weeks later took him to Zurich and a visit with Peter Sech-valde at the Swiss Institute of Technology (Einstein's School) who was on contract with the Biosimulaters Research Group involving viability analysis of the finalized cells.

The Professor left about a week after to Nice and from there he took an Egypt Air flight headed toward Libya and a visit with another colleague.

 The flight never reached its destination!   All radar tracing led to the conclusion it seemed to disappear over the Mediterranean near Libya. An exhaustive search over the many subsequent months up to this report has turned up nothing.

Just before that flight a letter arrived at his lab, addressed to Jane.

It had been mailed from Zurich. It was usual for him to advance instructions, and was a reflection of his ultra-caution, part of his always thinking personality. Here are its contents.
~~~~~~

Dear Jane:

In event I am unable to return to Lab due to contingency, first please make copy of this letter for Skellan, Samyak, Peter, Pi and Tim, and of course my wonderful wife, Sue.

As is known we designed a mission because of a remarkable set of coincidences, and my own desire to understand if we completed creating the living cells---would that matter in some as yet inconceivable tragic impact on the future. So we delved into the possibility that for us humans there was a controllable, evidentiary physical forever. As you know our inquiry's led to the meeting with Samyak the Jain in India.

There we touched on the topic from ancient ideas of reincarnation through it all to the most recent and modern perspective, that is Space-time and Quantum Theory.

We are now aware, educated of it, if you will, that Infinity, i.e., Forever exist as real physical-chemical entities. Further we became aware that depending on serendipitous topographies of space-time and its ultra-micro components, paths to the past and future might be visible, but specific knowledge of that must await a formidable ability of humans to conquer the vast distances of space, and a much deeper understanding of how the entry into Forever would work, if indeed, it would be allowed.

That is, in short, we are on the edge of forever, awaiting the continuation of the species and its mind development.

*In my last book "The Future Navigator', the message of the African Teacher, the Vistavien See-ela was carried forward. **As can be seen now, the words of that "Vistavien" ring true, the continuity of the species depends on Future Navigators, who work to insure the survival of our children's-children and theirs, who will be those to create the deepest understanding of the cosmos that is necessary.** I have mailed to you the completed manuscript that connects that work to our current inquiries and would hope that you and Pi and Ted could have it published. The title would be appropriately "Future Navigators--On the Edge of Forever".*

Please see after the story of our Forever Panel is told, that the text of the Declaration and Mind Principles are included in the work (as we did with the "Future Navigator"). See that it finally rests in the form of an Agenda, for Human Kind. This is because one does not know which book may be read and of course these are two documents that may help set the compass for future generations. Also, there is a moral guide to life involved which must be preserved in our reports even if repeated. We do not know at what point Forever will be captured by humans, at what time in Human Time. Each person is thereby constrained by the following life guide. ***Forever is, and it means all you make yourself to be you are always and that for everyone.***

To my colleagues on the bio-simulating project, I would encourage you to proceed with creation of those life helping cells, though at every step focus on the problems you may create and solutions to those as well as the healing aspects that would be possible. And, to all the Panel…Securing time now, depends on the behavior of those in Human Time…Please promulgate the Declaration of Light and the Principles of the Mind [1]that through See-ela and Jehan we were all taught……. With Admiration and Love to All…..Daniel.

Note: Actions for Securing Human Time

Actions for securing the best of humanities embedded persona are detailed at the end of Part 2, but involve The "Declaration of Light" which was first written in Jehan's short hand when she was imprisoned in a terrorist enclave.

This was carefully translated into English, based upon the observation that it is the official language in more countries than any other. It is a document in just a few pages composed of straight-forward text and can be transferred to other major languages with some editing being cautious of idiom and inflection.

Reproduced in Part 2 it is one of the foundations making rational Navigation possible!

After that is a description of the "Principles for Opening the Mind", taught by Jehan to the members of the "Forever Panel". She received the instructions in this document from the African Visionary, See-ela, who is correctly referred to as one of the first "Vistaviens', people who exist to help Homo sapiens reach into the future sufficiently long enough to know the Cosmos completely and live forever in peace and harmony. That is to know as they have earned it, Heaven, Shangri-La, Darul as-Salam.

The Principles provide a pathway, a guide, a way for Navigators to secure the Declaration. These documents, these ideologies are a realistic path in living long term in Eternity's child that is of course, our Space-time Arena.

IN A TRANSFINITE…

…In a humble Jain home, in a scene reminiscent of an East Indian Plain, all sitting about on a warm beautiful carpet, is an old sailor of Irish lineage, his wife, a wise Jain man, his daughter, her son, and a young Irish looking boy named Alexander.

The boy is so named as his parents wished him to know growing up that he is named after a "Leader of All" and he could be a new kind of Navigator for others, should he choose.

The Children are comfortably sitting looking up intensely but with a peaceful aura in their eyes at the old sailor. To him, the boy askes just one question "Pa- Pa can I live forever?

So it is, with the Jain looking on a clear eyed stare and a soft smile on his face the Sailor gives his response.

"I am very certain Alex." And in a firm voice to that short answer he said. "Yes, Alex you will in a special way. But do learn how you will be within Forever as you grow!"

The boy glancing at his sister, gave her a warm hug and gentle kiss, just as the open door of the little home revealed a most handsome young man in navy blue dress-uniform standing there tears in his eyes.

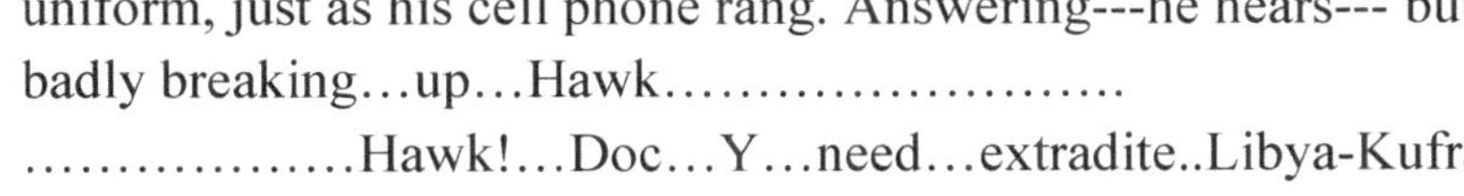

The old sailor, joyously fulfilled in the vision, did note, though briefly, the insignia on the left shoulder of the navy blue uniform, just as his cell phone rang. Answering---he hears--- but badly breaking…up…Hawk………………………
………………Hawk!…Doc…Y…need…extradite..Libya-Kufra ………………….23… 15.. 00.. E……24 10

PART II
THE OMEGA SHIELD

Great minds must be
ready not only to earn
opportunities
but to make them work
for everyone
with
the real end in mind!

INTRODUCTION

The following carries forward "Eternity and the Omega Shield". While the first part relays what Forever--our Eternity is, this part gives recognition to the fact that humans are evolving, which means they will (likely and hopefully) be reaching into the deep future. So it does involve a need to address new terms. The reader thus made aware, can if preferred first use the glossary and then turn to the story.

The story is built upon the remarkable insight of a handful of visionary thinkers who lived in the times of awesome discovery, the times of Einstein's proposals and of the beginning of much of the incredible communication devices developed for today's world.

These thinkers proposed the futuristic agenda that allows us to focus on the most important challenges leading to a successful outcome for human kind.

The work is therefore dedicated to them - whose names will unfold as the story is progressing.

~~~~~~~~~~~~~~~~~~~~~~

The Empires of the Future
Must Become the Empires Of The Mind!
From
Winston Leonard Spencer-Churchill
~~~~~~~~~~~~~~~~~~~~~~

FORWARD

Most of us experience but do not really "see" the dominant influence of world-wide-communication. Of course, our communicating to each other-interlinking the globe began sometime back. But, now its vastness, its deep influence on our minds is growing day by day, indeed minute by minute!

This leads to the proposal, quite realistic, that we humans if not now, will soon be functioning under one network, a Global Brain! Thus, as a species we will be heading somewhere gradually growing better or worse toward a fully unified cyberspace existence. Our world will then be reaching toward a "Vistavia" a final "Homo definitivien" existence one which some scholars have chosen to call Omega, i.e. the "Omega Point". Their vision sees that as an awesome, beautiful out bursting into eternity!

In the story to follow the realistic expectations and needed solutions address Omega with hope of developing a shield for everyone so that eternity will, indeed, be reached in safety and wonder.

Human Kind has a destiny in Forever, which we cannot fully envision. It could be tragic or with hope truly magnificent. That destiny, however, no matter how we may see it in our personal beliefs is now controlled by the ever increasing massiveness of cyberspace. What is it that may shield within that influence-our humanity and take us along safely with the developing Global Brain, such that our final destiny is indeed stellar?

CHAPTER 5: AN EVOLUTION AGENDA

(Leading to a Most Thoughtful New Focus!)

The boat cruised in, incredible powerful sounds clapping the waves as it headed straight toward the sand beach between two islands near the southern tip of Somalia.

They were waiting there almost in awe as the MkVIPB the Navy's next generation Patrol Boat (a part of the Navy's Expeditionary Combat Command's fleet) came toward them. The mission was appropriate although this rescue was on the edge of the usual!

The MkVI Patrol Boat provides operational commanders capability to patrol shallow areas beyond sheltered harbors and bays, and into less sheltered open water for the purpose of protection of friendly and coalition forces and critical infrastructure. The Patrol Boats two powerful diesel engines mated to water-jet drives allowed the joystick controlled patrol boat to hit speeds over 35 knots as it headed in. The site is awesome, she is bristling with weaponry, including a pair of remotely operated and stabilized 25mm chain guns and six crewed 50 caliber machine guns in her configuration. All this, however, mattered little for the current job!

Three, haggard, turbaned figures were waiting there, one with white skin, he hobbling aid of a cane. This was many months after he was thought to be burned to death in the crash of a disappearing commercial air-liner!

Later, rescued onto that PT boat, remarkably back at home he called a get together of his special research group!

The man with the cane was Dr. Daniel Jordyn. The Doctor's Laboratory was on the frontier working to develop living cells to replace those needed in injury and other very difficult healing circumstances. This was not an economic pursuit or for him a drive to the Nobel Prize. His personal mission was to help extend life aiding humanity itself into the distant future! Daniel was as we see not a timid thinker.   That is, he was skirting the very wild idea of creating ever-lasting life!

His research group shared his vision and the mission. They considered themselves "Future Navigators". And, incredulous as it seems they had been on retreat in India sharing with others an inquiry into what really is "Forever"! They were attempting to clarify the related idea, one most everyone believes exists, i.e. if there is a Forever. What really is it? And although (again) that seems rather absurd, the aim was to determine accessibility, i.e. a view into the Future, by inquiring into the governing principles of Space-Time.

This pursuit was not an amateur exercise. It was through an academic meeting of experts called "The Forever Panel". Nonetheless, how near insane that appears, at least they learned from their inquiries that "Forever", is indeed! And, specifically it is an "Infinite Physical-Chemical Mobius Reality". That is one, fixed and working in ways that knowing the future is way beyond our current ability.

Suffice it to say, having returned home, the Doctor called a meeting of his "Research Family". From this group there were ten members all once in the Future Panel. We recall among them are, the following

The Professor himself is Daniel Jordyn, head of a laboratory in advance biology, Dr. Samyak (Darshon) Jain, retired Professor of History, Professor Ahab Singh, Professor of Astrophysics, and Dr. Timothy J. Bean, Ph.D. is in the Biological Sciences, Dr. Pi Su chien Hsu, holding dual Ph.Ds. in Physics and Mathematics. Also there is Master Chief, James V. Skellan. James is nicknamed the Hawk, because of a face injury suffered in his Navy Service as an EOD or explosive demolition expert. The Hawk is retired Navy Master Chief, with extensive experience disarming explosive devices almost everywhere in the world. He has made it his personal mission as he traveled to learn about the world's faiths, their successes and failures. Both he and the Professor have been schooled in the 50 "Principles for Centering the Mind", a fundamental schooling for persons who are devoting their lives to Future Navigation, i.e. as the Professor he is committed to doing what he can in his area of expertise to insuring the survival of the world's future children. Skellan is, indeed, a prized member of the group because of his extraordinary clear thinking (a certain necessity of the job as EOD and his centered clear mind).

Continuing with the group, one of extraordinary credentials in combination there is Chandler Nowell Caldwell, M.S. Chandler is an Architectural Technologist holding an M.S degree in Mechanical Engineering. His wife is Jane Caldwell, the Technical Recorder in the Professors Laboratory. He joins the panel through deep interest in the future although he holds a critical ability as one who understands issues concerning structure and is also an expert in computing, internet, electrical conductivity and related. Critical to the group's broader philosophy there is Dr. Jehan Nirupuma. Dr. "Jehan' is a Professor of Medicine, who is responsible for "Life Perspective" teaching in her University. She is Pakistani by birth, but was raised in India as an orphan stemming from a terrorist attack during her student days. Dr. Jehan did a search in Africa for the "Teacher of Tolerance", where she was once again under terrorist threat as prisoner in a Wahhabi Enclave. She is

Hindu. She wrote a document in defense of children the "Declaration of Light"…and receiving the teachings of the visionary See-ela (called a "Vistavien") has in turn taught those to the Professor and Skellan, i.e. Dr. Jehan is a pivotal educator in "Future Navigation" for all the group.

Jane L. Caldwell, M.S. is most important to group functions. Jane is the technical recorder for the group, the one who has written this "Panel Profile". She is also ongoing secretary in the Professors laboratory. Jane is mother of three who are now in teen-age, a catholic in faith. She holds the M.S in forensic science, though she truly loves her recorder role in the laboratory. Last but certainly not least, is Angelei Skellan. Angelei following her husband Skellan's travels became an expert, the most informed of all in panel on faiths and philosophies around the world. She is of such depth in the subject that she consults for the group on all matters pertaining to faith or philosophy needing unbiased input.

This panel to a member felt that it was time for someone to really look into that age old idea that we each have a "Forever" an Eternity. They are united in discovering ways to insure that there will be a future for all the world's children.

Being called together once again by Dr.Why was most precious as these all had become not just co-workers but emotionally much a family!

So the meeting, the reunion called by the chief was to take place and it was as always when in the U.S. In the "old digs", that is, the back room of the "Newport" a most popular bar (and Grill).

When Daniel came in, leaning heavily on his cane, they all stood up cheering and applauding having lived through a time when they believed he had died in that crash. So-to at first avoid putting him on the spot, possibly making him uncomfortable each member of the group told of their own stories when returning to the U.S.

For most it was the usual, long crammed in–flights, working through customs and in the case of most as Jane, spouse Chandler and Jehan warm return to families.

Doctors Tim and Pi were in Delhi for Post Docs at Patel Institute, so were not able to return for several months. Pi told a troubling account because she was assumed from her oriental appearance, one to be ultra-questioned and was held for a while, under a tighter (and new) immigration protocol. Her trip in rerouting, led her to a stop in northern Africa and some very uncomfortable nights in what was basically a ghetto hotel. She in fact was accosted near a store an event that did not last long as Pi as in everything she does had mastered Taekwondo. Shortly after she was able to return, there appeared on the streets three Arabic men with considerable face bruising!

Tim made it back all the way home but had the unshakable memory of his grandfather's grave being vandalized with Nazi Swastika when he took his Jewish mother to the cemetery for her monthly respects. That as it seemed was happening around the country, a largess many assumed to be a creeping standard in his beloved U.S. (where the just elected President seemed to forget he was a mixed people's servant, and the internet abounded with bigotry).

These tragedies born by the two were held even more in mind as they were also, in their life's' work goals---looking toward ways to reach the long term future for mankind. They knew more so than most, understanding forever, that it means whatever we make of ourselves, we will be forever for everyone. The center of attention of that trip back though was to be focused on the Professor's tale of his remarkable return.

"Well it is all due to Skellan and a kindly Arab", he said as he started out. "And, if my old friend hadn't stepped in for the rescue, I wouldn't be here. The crash was in southern Libya and all were killed except me and a lovely young woman, the two of us laying there amongst the horror of burning and bodies. She managed to pull me free, and we lay in a ravine for at least two days, no one coming, the plane not located."

"Finally, a group of Arabs, found us and we were hauled off to a hut, belonging to an eastern Libya tribal group. The young woman, most tragically passed about a week later her injuries must have been deeply internal. The people we wound up with were thankfully peaceful, though they might have held us thinking of the potential for ransom. I believe these were "Bani Zoghba" who originally, after settling in Tripolitania and Gabes, were expelled by Banu Salim to the eastern parts of Algeria, and currently they are found between Bjaya and Telmsan (place easily found on the maps, but then unknown to me). In the end though, these people couldn't decide what to do with me!

Turned out that they brought along with me what I was wearing, the belt was still there with my little pouch and miraculously my cell phone, and some little battery still there worked just enough to give approximate coordinates to Skellan.

Don't know much of the rest of the stay in Libya, spending time in and out of consciousness. But Skellan somehow reached out to someone he knew there from his EOD bomb-diffusing Navy time and I found myself on a truck full of food stores, rice they were calling Bariis, traveling further through Libya, then across Ethiopia heading deeper south east and winding up near Hudur, a military complex located in southwestern Somalia. There in a rather happenstance village I was put in the care of a non-Somali ethnic minority group made up primarily of the Bravanese, Bantus and Bajuni. The Bantus are the largest ethnic minority group in Somalia. They are the descendants of slaves who were brought in from southeastern Africa by Arab and Somali traders.

Well, I won't go on and on about that except to say, they spoke Swahili so most fortunately my Fulbright experience came into play and I was very lucky indeed. I think these folk were thinking about ransoming me! However, one of them had a terrible sore running down his back into his rear. I had of all things some lip balm, and a piece of candy with cinnamon. With some water and then some of the local peanut oil I made a creamy slave, knowing the cinnamon would be anti-infective (crossing my fingers). The long and short of it was (probably crazy luck) after about a week the man's sore cleared up and I won a deep new friend! This man was then able to take me to the Hudur base where I contacted Skellan again. He would be unable to pick me up in Hudur, but a pick up from the Bajuni Islands[1] off the coast of Somalia would be possible, as the Navy was patrolling that area in hopes of holding off Somali Pirates.

The Hudur coordinate, I will never forget them is sitting at 4°7′12″N 43°53′16″E. These were corrected to a pick up site just on the coast of one of the islands where the pickup could occur. Then it was that I was able to have my new friend struggle me there, various transport, and await a boat. This all must have been a trip of a couple thousand miles, so I am so very thankful for that Arab (name Absamea) who supported me the journey. When I was in Africa earlier in my life I learned quickly how most people have an inborn sense of humanity, which of course holds for many although surrounded by horrible poverty and killing!

Even so, I have to tell you all it was one of the highlights of my life when we saw that boat swing around the reef and head straight to us.

I knew Patrol Boats as a sailor-corpsman years back when in the Navy, but when the sound of those engines on that awesome modern version, the Mk VI PB resounded in our ears, my eyes just dripped tears of joy.

---

1. The Bajuni Islands, also known as the Bajun Islands or Baajun Islands are an archipelago in the Indian Ocean, situated on the southern coast of Somalia, from Kismayo to Ras Kiyamboni. They lie at the northern end of a string of reefs that continues south to Zanzibar and Pemba. It is of note that the president's travel ban meant, Sudan, Somalia and Libya remain banned, for people to enter the U.S. from there. Navy ships fitted with heavy weapons are reported to have arrived in the Somalia territorial waters and set up base around Bajuni Islands of Kudai, Ndoa, Chuvaye, Koyama, Fuma Iyu na Tini and Nchoni Islands, during the Islamist insurgency of 2000 and fortunately for the Professor, they still held presence there as the Somali Pirate scourge continued.

The boat of course took me to a U.S. Hospital Ship harboring near Australia, some healing and ultimately home to you all, and that my friends is all thanks to Skellan and a very noble Arab man!

The doctor hobbled over to where that old sailor was sitting, hugging him as the whole group cheered and applauded so loud the Newport bartender opened the door and gave the please quite sound.

The meeting that then proceed was to say the least deeply welcoming and warm, all sharing their most recent experiences.

Jane and Chandler had us laughing at the funny things the kids did. Jehan shared her experience with the new rather green med students, and Pi and Tim shared the news of their forthcoming marriage…the ceremony, they said would be one to attend, a cross between the traditional Jewish and some oriental admix.

There had to be, of course, this first discussion of all that is happening around them, and what occurred to get back. However, this group live and breathe proposal, questioning, and intellectual pursuit!

So it was very soon that things turned academic as one might suspect from such and egg-headed clan. It was at this first meeting that they decided to continue their "Future Navigator" gatherings and continue meeting at the Newport Bar, the place where their Forever Panel[1] was conceived and that pursuit now was published[1].

So, as though it was born in inertia, the subject turned immediately to their shared objective the long term future of humanity, which they know (now) cannot be predicted, but there is deep concern. They know humans are special, unique as they may be alone in understanding the secrets of life.

Dr. Bean said, framing the question for the whole group, "Dr. Why is right--- we have an embedded sense of empathy, a sense of humanity. We know Forever will not let us see into it, that is what will happen in the coming millennia." But how much of that can be understood and they worried about that, as it is indeed, in their fiber. Jane said, OK we can't predict tomorrow, but perhaps we can imagine what can be done to insure the best long outcome!

Chandler looking around the room, pausing then asked. "Ok, but do they, these Homo sapiens, deserve such consideration. I mean are we really unique?"

So first is that question of uniqueness, which was addressed by Jehan, who certainly knew of human potential!

---

1. The beginnings and further history of the "Forever Panel" can be found in Part One of this book and in the book "Future Navigators on the Edge of Forever" with ISBN: 978-0-692-77138-9 (2016).

"Understanding Forever, we know that its chemistry will explode again and again, unknown number of big bangs, so what is our importance, our likely uniqueness? If you permit let me review for us briefly, and I mean rationally."

And she gave a bit of a review as follows. "The Fermi paradox or Fermi's paradox, named after physicist Vicente Fermi is the apparent contradiction between the lack of evidence and high probability estimates, e.g., those given by the Drake equation, for the existence of extraterrestrial civilizations. The basic points of the argument, made by physicists Vicente Fermi (1901–1954) and Michael H. Hart (born 1932), are as follows.

There are billions of stars in the galaxy that are similar to the Sun, many of which are billions of years older than Earth.

With high probability, some of these stars will have Earth-like planets (as astronomers are currently seeking, some discovering) and if the Earth is typical, some might develop intelligent life. Indeed, some of these civilizations might develop interstellar travel, which is as we know a step our Earth's scientists are investigating now.

Even at the slow pace of currently envisioned interstellar travel, our Milky Way Galaxy could be completely traversed in a few million years, a short span in space-time.

According to this line of reasoning, th*e Earth should have already been visited by extraterrestrial aliens*!

In an informal conversation, Fermi noted no convincing evidence of this, leading him to ask, "Where is everybody?" There have been many attempts to explain the Fermi paradox, primarily either suggesting that intelligent extraterrestrial life is extremely rare or proposing reasons that such civilizations have not contacted or visited Earth.

In short we are unique creatures-at least, and with our abilities deserve to last, but with inability to see into the future, how do we do that, what influences us most?"

Tim, very excited about the question, puts in a worthwhile comment. "I will stand on my comment about uniqueness and it is more. *Our success so far has been due to our sense of benevolence-our humanity.* If not that we would not have survived. Just think of that, over history, time and time again, against the scourges of cruelty, from the Nazis and on and on, that has kept us going. And we are now trying to see the goodness of our democratic ways against the ongoing Religio-polimics, the "Spirit Wars" as Dr. Why calls them." *So to get into the far future, we must understand our direction better, what else has and will influence us?*

Well our history is a kind of covering that is influencing our future evolution. In short and in a nutshell, in the main and to focus…*What we are talking about, i.e. all that matters as to our ability to deal with the future is the question of the greatest influence on our EVOLVING HUMANITY!*

OK, then that is right, subject is "Evolution" Pi set in, "what was, what is and from that what is likely to be. Perhaps what counts here, first is what we know here on earth actually came about, us eventually being a part of that!"

And Tim was quick to seize on that…"So, let me set a kind of backdrop. Having my Post Doc experience on biogenetics, I should spend a moment on our own earth history its "Biogeochemistry" and its relation to us from that! What do you think? I mean, hey you all, really, I won't make this technical…just an overview."

The Professor seeing, perhaps a too technical "deflection" but also sensing agreement from the group on the subject of "Future Evolution" indicted…"Good idea Tim! That could clearly lead us to an important understanding. What is human influence on their home, and the converse… it on our future, what could be our own long term existence, all factors, given the various realms into which we humans inquire… if you will." And I think we should look deeper also, for example into what kind of existence we are really experiencing. For example, perhaps we should look at the importance of our communications, its impacts on our past and future, as in our communication to each other--- it has been and will be central to our future, our evolution!"

"So, let me suggest a way of approaching this. Both you and Pi have completed related post-doctorals to cover the necessary basics for us in shall we say three weekly seminars. And, the Doctor then said looking encouragingly his way and pointing at him, "Mr. Vicente Costa our new student (and Lab Tech) could be working toward a dissertation on, well if I may propose a title "Future Human Evolution", Yes!"

"Vicente, to center this, could you consider posturing your dissertation, on that subject we just exposed, i.e. "Communication"! That is, how has past communication between us humans likely effected our future environment and how is our new global communication going to impact the ultimate fate of Humanity! This will fit I think because of your ability to cross the world-shall we say- as you come to us-with a major and masters in computer networking."

Since the mission of the Lab is to find ways to help mankind toward the future, all carrying the flag of "Future Navigators" this laid down very well with everyone in the group and the new Ph.D. student clearly was excited about the possibly of a focus for his dissertation that fit well with his background!

The Professor encouraged Vicente, looking at him directly. "Yes, it could be, that is, it is justifiably a dissertation! I gather that is, indeed, compatible with your background? Certainly the lab would support that. And the faculty are likely available for a committee here at the University-in our history and computer sciences departments. So, as you focus your research your opinions and findings would define the ultimate subject, which of course you will stand to defend, an experience there you know having done so with your master's thesis.

Vicente now fully synchronizing with the whole idea, said "I will be honored for the opportunity!" (He was told as a boy his name sake was "Vicente" Blasco Ibáñez the highly admired Spanish writer. Consequently, he carried that name identity always within himself feeling he was destined to be a fluid writer and advocate.)

So, the boss said, "let us get this underway. Next week, we will have the first report, a mini-seminar first by Tim, then one by Pi following on Dr. Tim's report. Dr. Pi what do you think?" Pi in her way, of course, had no difficulty, always cutting just the briefest size response simply replied, "My Pleasure! The direction, must of course, lead us into "Long Term Future Human Evolution", that is the subject of central importance if we can presuppose there will be a distant future given all the insane things people with no sense of history get us into!"

So it was the Future's objective for the Panel was re-kindled and after warm good wishes for the evening the members of the team, new ideas exciting their very deeply inquiring minds, left for home.

Regarding that, here is a look into the home life for a sampling of what we now should call the "Future Evolution Panel Members". This look into home life…is observing the Skellans, sons Gabriel and Andrew.

On this evening they have a guest in Vicente, who is temporarily rooming in their home, until he can establish rooms for himself.

Skellan and Anjelei are watching their son Gabriel teaching his younger brother Alexander how to make bread! Alexander it needs be said is just a very little boy. Vicente knows Gabriel as a navy hero and one to be greatly admired. One would assume from his courageous accomplishments that he might be, shall we say "macho", and not really interested in house-hold chores. Vicente is fascinated with the scene though because of its seeming domesticity, far outside of what he would expect from Gabriel, who is in an apron.

Skellan seeing Vicente's curious viewing of the event, comments. "Vicente, believe it or not this is in the way that made Gabriel strong. Of course not just making bread, but learning all the basic skills of survival at a very young age, that is the means to take care of oneself. Before he was nine, he could do great carpentry, had a full garden, and was reading into the classics. We raised him toward having an independent mind, making his own way, free from superstation. That he gained knowing---the "Principles for an Open Mind" as passed on from the original teacher, we in the "Future Navigator Team" knew as "The Vistavien", and to that we used our insight into the ideas in Maslow's "Hierarchy of Needs" a theory in human development and psychology proposed by Abraham Maslow in his 1943 paper "A Theory of Human Motivation". You are welcome to a copy of his book if you like.

Vicente---as he asked "What kind of bread Alex"---responded, "yes, I would love to borrow that book!" (And Alex answered, "It's my version of potato bread, darn good if I do say so myself, I will give you some.")

CHAPTER 6: THE HUMAN OVERSEER'S FATE

So as planned, about five p.m. a week next, in the evening, lab work complete, the panel gathered at their familiar haunt, once again the back room in the Newport Bar (and Grill). After drinks were obtained and each found their favorite place in the room and around the table, Tim got a "Seminar" underway. "Ok, team, let's go! In process I will do a good deal of definition, and use terms some may not be familiar with, but the concepts are really straight forward, really!"

As he began, you could tell Dr. Bean was totally excited and into his topic, this clearly from his "teacher posture". "Biogeochemistry is our first subject, as agreed. This is the scientific discipline that involves studying the chemical, physical, geological, and biological processes and reactions that govern the actual composition of our natural environment here on precious earth!"

"These concepts to be more specific in terminology are the biosphere and the cryosphere, the hydrosphere, the pedosphere, the atmosphere, and the lithosphere.

I am being deliberate, the "sphere" language here is a form of linguistic mimetics but in these cases does amount to real spheres of influence!"

"In particular, biogeochemistry is the study of the cycles of chemical elements, such as carbon and nitrogen, and their interactions with and incorporation into living things transported through earth scale biological systems, of course, in space through time. And that we on the panel understand is a part of an infinity of our physical-chemical Forever."

"The biogeochemical field of study focuses on chemical cycles which are either driven by or influence biological activity on our planet. Specific emphasis is placed on the study of carbon, nitrogen, sulfur, and phosphorus cycles. Biogeochemistry is, thus, a systems science closely related to Systems Ecology. Sorry, definition may help, recall that Ecology is the branch of biology that deals with the *relations* of organisms to one another and to their physical surrounding.

The founder of Biogeochemistry, and from whose work I report was the Ukrainian scientist Vladimir Vernadsky a Russian geochemist, whose 1926 book "The Biosphere" (in the tradition of Mendeleev) formulated a *physics of the earth as a living whole, that is, the earth as a whole living being!*

That I am sure as we go forward must be constantly in mind! *We will need to view our planet and what goes on with it, including us, as an organism, a living whole!*

We now of course, most of us, do appreciate that reality with the onset of global warming." (There was from this informed group a good deal of comment at this point, mostly as to how so may humans ignore this, heads in the sand so to speak.)

Staying on course though, Dr. Bean continues "Vernadsky distinguished three spheres, where a sphere was a concept similar to the concept of a phase-space[1].

He observed that each sphere had its own laws of evolution, and that the higher spheres modified and dominated the lower! They are as follows…

1. A phase-space is a multidimensional space in which each axis corresponds to one of the coordinates required to specify the state of a physical system, all the coordinates being thus represented so that a point in the space corresponds to a state of the system.

1. The Abiotic sphere - all the "non-living" energy and material processes.

2. The Biosphere - the life processes that live within the abiotic sphere, and…

3. The Nöesis or Nösphere - the sphere of the cognitive process of man! This is one of the results of our existence! That is, human activities (e.g., agriculture and industry) modify the Biosphere and Abiotic sphere."

In the contemporary environment, the amount of influence humans have on the other two spheres is comparable to a geological force! This comprises a new field of insight! "

"Well to continue. The American limnologist and geochemist G. Evelyn Hutchinson is credited with outlining the broad scope and principles of this new field. More recently, the basic elements of the discipline of biogeochemistry were restated and popularized by the British scientist and writer, James Lovelock, under the label of the "Gaia Hypothesis". (Note all, Gaia is via Greek mythology-personification of the earth)."

"Lovelock emphasizes a concept that life processes regulate the Earth through feedback mechanisms to keep it habitable!

Given the importance Sf the topic, there are biogeochemistry research groups in many universities around the world. Since this is a highly inter-disciplinary field, these are situated in a wide range of host disciplines including: atmospheric sciences, that is, biology, the ecology, geo-microbiology, environmental chemistry, geology, and oceanography and soil science. These are often bracketed at Universities into larger disciplines such as "Earth Science" and "Environmental

Science". I think it is a mark of our fundamental humanity, an Engram, if you will, that this caring area of study has found many homes. And, this research has obvious applications in the exploration for ore deposits and oil, and in remediation of environmental pollution!"

"However, that aside…Now, though… the reason for going on about this… a very important aspect on this, which clearly relates to the distant future of humans is something called the "Anthroposphere". Which Pi, I believe is your pursuit, as we agreed, yes!"

Dr.Why, indicated "great introduction Tim, and yes Pi, where are we going from here?"

She began…"Well dear colleagues, following on my assignment and providing the backdrop for Vicente, yes, I will say a bit about the "Anthroposphere".

This in a manner of speaking lays right on top of Tim's "Biogeo" discussion (group chuckles). That is, clearly, a subject of total contribution to our long term future, i.e. we are in effect, that is for simple survival we are by default, and must be more so, the "Overseer's" of our very precious home! There is though, a terminology that applies!

The Anthroposphere (sometimes also referred as the Technosphere) is that part of the environment that is made or modified by humans for use in human activities and human habitats. It is rightly classified, if we think deeply of it, really as one of the Earth's Spheres, that earth a living whole! And Humans in effect are, as said, this Earth's Overseer!

This continues the terminology that Tim relayed…i.e. *"Spheres"*, since they encompass the earth that is a really easy to grasp notion. We encompass the earth's fate that is up to us, how we function in our Anthroposphere.

As human technology becomes more evolved, such as the greater ability of technology to cause deforestation, the impact of human activities on the environment potentially increases. This leads us into a type of anthropogenic metabolism, and its output, the "Novel Ecosystem".

These "Novel Ecosystems" are human-built, modified, or engineered niches of the Anthropocene.

These ecosystems exist in places that have been altered in their structure and function by human agency. Novel Ecosystems are part of the human environment and niche (including urban, suburban, and rural), they lack natural analogs, *and they have extended an influence that has converted more than three-quarters of wild Earth!"*

"A Novel Ecosystem is aptly described as one that has been heavily influenced by humans but is not under human management. A working tree plantation doesn't qualify under this particular terminology. However, one that was abandoned decades ago would."

Well, to further define, the anthropogenic has "Biomes". These include technoecosystems that are fueled by powerful energy sources, fossil and nuclear- including ecosystems populated with technodiversity, such as roads and unique combinations of soils called technosols. Vegetation on old buildings or along field boundary stone walls in old agricultural landscapes are examples of sites where research into novel ecosystem ecology is developing."

"In fact, Human society has transformed the planet to such an extent that we may have ushered in a new epoch that should justifiably carry an expansion of the title I just gave, that is we are in the "Anthropocene Epoch" as coined by serious scientists. That is certainly a part of "Human Evolution", now and in the future! "

"Again, this is all surrounding our spherical earth, and so justifies labeling the influences we talk about as "Spheres".

And, again, the ecological niche of the anthropocene contains entirely novel ecosystems that include technosols, technodiversity, anthromes, and the something thence aptly called and I am sure will become extraordinarily important in our discussions.. The "Technosphere".

These terms are deliberate as they describe the human ecological phenomena marking this unique turn in the evolution of Earth's history! "

"The total human ecosystem (or Anthrome) describes the relationship of the industrial technosphere to the ecosphere. Let me define them, these terms, briefly.

Technoecosystems interface with natural life-supporting ecosystems in competitive and parasitic ways.

Current urban-industrial society not only impacts natural life-support ecosystems, but also has created entirely new arrangements that we can, indeed, call techno-ecosystems. These new systems involve new, powerful energy sources (fossil and atomic fuels), technology, money, and cities that have little or no parallels in nature. *At the root of both our future survival and our potential demise is the matter of energy source and utilization.*

Yes, even though Novel ecosystems are creating many different kinds of dilemmas for conservation biologists to this we must now consider something called Anthropogenic Biomes i.e. in other terms *"The Total Human Ecosystem".*

The Anthropogenic Biomes tell a completely different story, one of "human systems, with natural ecosystems embedded within them"! This is no minor change in the story we tell our children and each other. Yet it is necessary for sustainable management of the biosphere in the 21st century.

The researcher Ellis identifies twenty-one different kinds of anthropogenic biomes that sort into the following groups: 1) dense settlements, 2) villages, 3) croplands, 4) rangeland, 5) forested, and 6) wildlands.

These anthropogenic biomes (or anthromes for short) create the technosphere that surrounds us and are populated with diverse technologies (or technodiversity for short)."

"And here is a very telling fact…within these anthromes the human species (one species out of billions of earth creatures) appropriates 23.8% of the global net primary production. Hence, there is a vast energy expenditure!

"This is a remarkable impact on the biosphere caused by just one species." And it has arisen through the last several centuries from ever increasing technology, ever increasing interconnection between the people of the earth."

"Here are terms applied to various aspects of the anthropogenic biomes system.

The technosphere is the part of the environment on Earth where technodiversity extends its influence into the biosphere.

Virtually every aspect of analysis into the Anthorpocene biomes reveals an increasing time dependent alteration of the human world."

Thus, for example, Technosols are a new form of soil group in the World Reference Base for Soil Resources (WRB). Technosols are "mainly characterized by anthropogenic parent material of organic and mineral nature and which origin can be either natural or technogenic."

There is precision in terminology needed of course, for the development of suitable restoration strategies."

"Suffice it to say, with most careful analysis, ecologists stipulate that the weight of Earth's technosphere is calculated as 30 trillion tons, a mass greater than 50 kilos for every square meter of the planet's surface."

"Such Technoecosystems interface with and are competitive toward natural systems.

Such is reality, Technodiversity, is creating an ever increasing time accelerating impact on the future of human life here on earth! This is becoming ever more relevant with our power in communicating what we observe so that we can increase or if appropriately carefully reduce the effects!"

Then Pi, looking intensely at her audience says, *"It is all now and will be here and in the future in the hands of our ability to communicate with wisdom!"* After which, she stops and listens because…

…Here Vicente, taking courage in hand before the very learned group, interrupts… "Yes, if I may, I can contribute here a bit, as in my masters I studied something called…The Wayback Machine. The Wayback Machine is giving us awesome insight into whatever we may wish to influence. All information is becoming available to go either way for our future, good or bad."

"The Wayback Machine is a digital archive of the World Wide Web and other information on the Internet created by the "Internet Archive", a nonprofit organization, based in San Francisco, California, United States."

"This Internet Archive launched the Wayback Machine in October 2001. It was set up by Brewster Kahle and Bruce Gilliat, and is maintained with content from Alexa Internet. The service enables users to see archived versions of web pages across time, which the archive calls a "Three Dimensional Index". The Wayback Machine has been continually archiving cached pages of websites onto its large cluster of Linux Operating System Nodes. It revisits sites every few weeks and archives a new version. Sites can also be captured on the fly by visitors who enter the site's URL into a search box. The intent is to capture and archive content that otherwise would be lost whenever a site is changed or closed down."

"The overall vision of the machine's creators is to archive the entire Internet! Thus if you will --- no effect on us will be lost, the preservation of history is there i.e., our global memory, which is so important to preventing mistakes, if interpreted wisely."

"The name Wayback Machine was chosen as a reference to the "WABAC machine" (pronounced way-back), a time-traveling device used by the characters Mr. Peabody and Sherman in The Rocky and Bullwinkle Show, an animated cartoon. In one of the animated cartoon's component segments, "Peabody's Improbable History", the characters routinely used the machine to witness, participate in, and, more often than not, alter famous events in history."

"To show how powerful this machine is already, let me refer to its' computer termination, i.e. as an Internet Archive called "The Petabox".

"Here are a few highlights about the Petabox storage system. There are 1.4 PetaBytes/computer rack that is 100 plus Terabytes/rack, 4 data centers, 550 nodes, and 20,000 spinning. Total used storage, as of time my thesis was written, was--50 PetaBytes! In the development is Tech-Target whose own site offers a useful point of departure for thinking about how big a Petabyte is. "A petabyte is a measure of memory or storage capacity and is 2 to the power of 50 bytes or, in decimals, approximately a thousand terabytes! (The memory in my new laptop is listed as one terabyte.) Currently there are on board this Way-Back millions of books/music/video and various collections: amounting to 9.8 PetaBytes. Contained in the system are unique data of thousands of different kinds and types of information…amounting to 18.5 PetaBytes!"

The successful deployment of this kind of data to list just a few, gives Internet Archive's replication ability for major academic institutions, digital preservationists, government agencies, Major research sites of all kinds to include agronomy, medical imaging providers, digital image repositories, storage outsourcing sites, and many-many other enterprises around the globe".

"And, there is no doubt what-so-ever the PetaBox storage technology is expanding steadily!"

"That must remind us of an awesome power we humans have and what is involved within us…. Does it not? Therein lies a complete record of all that everyone does and most importantly could share, and, there is potential that it is entrench-able into their thoughts."

"It marks a very special interrelation we have with the earth, and ourselves a complete perspective into ourselves and everything in and on our planet.

I know, sometimes I kind of think randomly, but to this comes my recollection of the "Kardashev Scale", which, not incidentally, I researched via the Way-Back Machine!"

"The Kardashev scale is a method of measuring a civilization's level of technological advancement, based on the amount of energy that an advanced civilization is able to use for communication.

The scale originally proposed had three designated categories and people now suggest seven-the later which take us way into what many would consider science fiction. Nonetheless, I present this as our concern is "Human Evolution Coming", and it relates to that over long terms assuming survival. So here is a sampling of the Kardashev scale (somewhat updated)." Vicente shows preparedness as he hands out the following list which he reads…

"Type 0 civilization – also called planetary civilization – can use and store energy which reaches its planet from the neighboring star.

Type 1: civilization can harness the total energy of its planet's parent star (the most popular hypothetical concept being the Dyson sphere that is a device which would encompass the entire star and transfer its energy to the planet.

Type II civilization can control energy on the scale of its entire host galaxy."

"The scale is of course hypothetical, and regards energy consumption needed on a cosmic scale. Various extensions of the scale have since been proposed, including a wider range of power levels (Types 0, IV and V) and the use of metrics other than pure power!

Nonetheless, this is a reflection on evolution, is cognizant of our intense need for energy to survive and has some worthy considerations in terms of time frames. The expanded set with example (anticipated) time frames is as follows:

Type 0; a civilization that harnesses the energy of its home planet, but not to its full potential just yet. As you might have guessed, that's our present humanity. We're currently, according to some experts are at about 0.73 on the Kardashev Scale. It is presumed we'll reach the next, i.e. type 1 in about 100 years, plus or minus, depending on how fast our technology advances and how diligently we procreate. Michio Kaku suggests that humans may attain Type I status in 100–200 years, Type II status in a few thousand years, and Type III status in 100,000 to a million years.

Type I: This references a civilization that is capable of harnessing the total energy of its home planet. This is where we're heading, whether we want it or not! Thus, it expresses an aspect of our future evolution. The good part would be that we'd achieve an ultimate peak, the bad part is that we'd then soon have more energy demand than supply, because evolution can't be so easily halted. We would have to leave Earth and start pumping other planets for their worth, or even milk our own star directly for its power. Regardless, becoming a type I civilization is considered by some as an overall a good thing.

As a type I civilization, we would, it is proposed, be capable of controlling Earth entirely, maybe even influence the weather, control volcanic eruptions and earthquakes, influence global flora and fauna, geological makeup, plate tectonics, etc. That seems awesome! But there is a flipside, we'd have to recycle everything to get by! And of course this all depends on how we behave, which must come from inside us, our inner motivations and sympathies, our sense of humanity, caring for others. Present behavior, well--- trouble!

Type II: These people must be an interstellar civilization, capable of harnessing the total energy output of a star. This is the next stage in the evolution of a civilization, and presumes a level of technological development that allows for gigantic constructions and utmost efficiency. Dyson structures would be proposed here, i.e. hypothetical megastructures that completely encompasses a star capturing most or all of its energy, thus power. A type II civilization would not just build these megastructures, but also inhabit them and completely control what goes on inside them. It would control the orbit of all planets in that system, harvest asteroids and comets at its leisure, and basically consume the entire solar system. An intimidating power to behold! Of course, from our current perspective we see such as fictional dreams! But do recall that 100 years ago we would never imagine, Neil Armstrong's appearance on our moon. Well to go on….

Type III: This would necessarily be a galactic civilization, capable of inhabiting and harnessing the energy of an entire galaxy. Here, of course, we start to venture into truly extraordinarily wild science-fiction territory. And, yes, I am smiling at this, but keep in mind we are focusing on the next human Evolution. Thus, a type III civilization would span the entire galaxy, colonizing and controlling numerous systems. It would be able to harness, store and use the energy output of all stars within that galaxy. Such a civilization would use planets just like building blocks, being able to move planets from one solar system to other, merge solar systems, merge stars, absorb supernovae, and even create stars. The galaxy as one writer put it, is their playground, and everything in it becomes a toy!"

I have read the account of Forever composed by the folks of this lab, and your premise that it is an eternal physical-chemical infinite pool suggests that there would be ways that such could be manipulated, but would we last long enough to have the tools? That is very much in question. Nevertheless after that, then the vision takes us to Type IV and beyond.

Type IV: is a universal civilization, capable of harnessing the energy of the whole universe. This civilization would be super galactic, able to travel throughout the entire universe and consume the energy output of several—possibly all—galaxies.

It would also be capable of projects of gargantuan proportions, such as manipulating space-time and tinkering with entropy, thus reaching immortality on a grand scale. It would be an essentially indestructible and highly utopian civilization."

Here, Pi set in. "Vicente, we of this panel have studied Forever, and we know it to be, everywhere as you reiterated a chemical-physical recycling entity.

So let us not be too uncertain that humans won't achieve these states. It all depends on how we work our way up to our most advanced stage, that which the Vistavien calls the Ultimate Humans. *It all depends on whether we can get along with each other, and that surely has to do with what is inside us, how our genetics drives our humanity from the ape-state."*

"Yes that is surely the case, although I am happy that I opened this up." And, said Pi "We are too, it is that long term future that we will focus on, and you have laid out an important staging. "

"Thanks Dr. Pi, that is enough, though…I hope I have adequately sketched in the idea… Humans could progress way into the future, given many variables and the capture of sufficient energy, no questions as we see some of that. This covered says if we continue to exist we have rather awesome possibilities…I will not go on with 5-7, but those are proposed out there."

"Of course we do not really use yet use all of "Type I" civilization methods, although we do use nuclear power, and we use electrical flow to communicate and this, to me seems critically important to Human Evolution and is growing very fast! Moore's law reflects this!

It refers to an observation made by Intel co-founder Gordon Moore in 1965. He noticed that the number of transistors per square inch on integrated circuits had doubled every year since their invention. Moore's law predicts that this trend will continue into the foreseeable future."

Here Chandler, another computer oriented one of the panel enters.

"Now if we think of that PentaBox-Way-Back machine Vicente told of, with its power---we are forced to wonder about the overall evolutionary effect on us in growing cyberspace as it is clearly here! And so, it is important to remember that is our real and probable controlling evolution that is our computers and cyberspace. Is it not?

I mean it is needed in the energy computation context, and seems to be everywhere and into everything else."

Pi entered with, "Yes, Chandler and Vicente, I see what is important here in a way, deeper. Perhaps we are coming, i.e., raising up the importance of the "Law of Complexity", or as it is sometimes called "Complex-Consciousness"!

Specifically, the Law-of Complex Consciousness is the postulated tendency of matter to become more complex over time and at the same time to become more conscious, more controlling. Shall we continue with that Professor?"

At this Dr. Why held up his hand (though there was a very pleased look on his face)! "My goodness, this is getting interesting, and it seems it is heading toward a rational point, don't you think Vicente?

"Yes sir, I can see a focus, and I am very excited to delve into researching the subject fully."

"Great, as I would expect, unfortunately, it is getting good and late. Jane, Angelei, I know have some worries about kids. So I propose we take this up at the next Friday evening session. Remember crew it is a big day in the lab tomorrow, and that into next week…let's get some rest and back to the lab."

Here Dr. Why paused, and sort of wiping his brow commented. "But, working it out of this evening revealed the path on which to focus I know all agree…we have much to chew on don't we? Exciting inquiries are on the horizon!"

CHAPTER 7.THE ENCOMPASING HUMAN MIND

It was actually three weeks later that the group could get together. There was much work in the lab on their man-made-living cells (BIOS+), because the membranes were being re-assayed as to amino acid content, and there were some family complications that arose. However, everyone was most anxious to meet and once again the panel paraded into the back room of the Newport Bar (and Grill) chatting with enthusiasm.

Tim and Pi, beer in hand, the rest with, well you know less alcoholic fare, a tomato juice here, and a ginger ale there…etc. Everyone seated…Pi started in.

"Remember team… we ended last meeting with the leading thought, the Law of "Complex-Consciousness".

This is really, really an important idea when it comes to Future Human Evolution!"

"And, it was put forward by thinkers in the very same times that Einstein was pushing his agenda. We should honor those thinkers, of course, again and again as they give perspectives on our lives and the future."

"Well the "The Law" was first formulated by the Jesuit priest and paleontologist Pierre Teilhard de Chardin in his 1955 work "The Phenomenon of Man"! Some of us remember Teilhard's thinking as having parallels with our mentors "Future Speak", that is, the teacher and Vistavien See-ela, as revealed to the Professor in his Fulbright in Africa.

So to put it in an easy to see flow…Teilhard held that… in all time and everywhere, matter is actually endeavoring to complexify upon itself, as is clearly observable in the evolutionary history of the Earth."

"Matter complexified from inanimate matter, to plant life, to animal life, to human life. Or, from the geosphere, to the biosphere, to what he and several other thinkers of this time referred to as the "Noosphere" (of which humans are centrally represented, because of their reality, possession of a consciousness which reflects upon themselves). That as most here know is "Dasein"!

As evolution rises through the geosphere, biosphere, and Noosphere, matter continues to rise in a continual increase of both complexity, consciousness, and adaptability!"

"The rates of this are in fact documentable"… Here, Pi passes around a display from the internet.

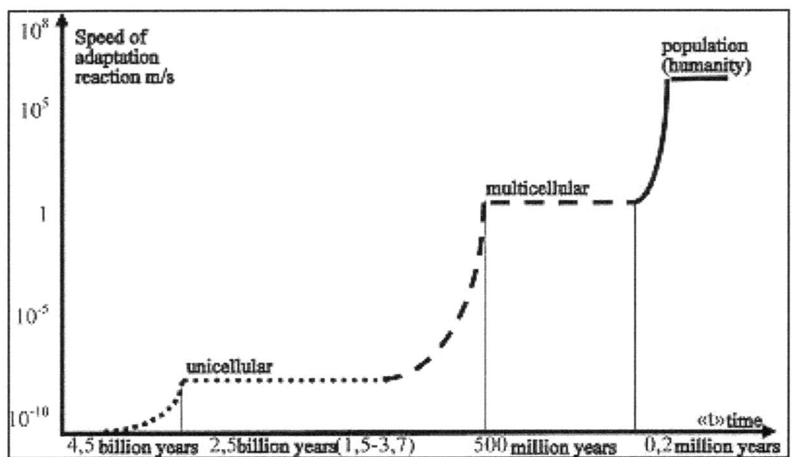

Then Pi relates. "This displays the evolution of the reaction rates (speed in adapting to situations) in (and for) living systems from the unicellular organism (ions through membranes), to multicellular (e.g. blood through vessels, momentum along nerve fibers) and in human populations, i.e. communications: sound (voice and audio, the speed of radio-electromagnetic waves, electric current, light, optical, tele-communications[1.])"

"To help here as we go along, the Anthrosphere has to do with what physically humans do to earth. This "Noosphere" which will be a most important subject for Vicente has to do with their united thoughts! In the terms of many 'The Global Brain". In my terms, if you will, it is the "Encompassing Human Mind"!

For the priest Teilhard, more explicitly, the Law of "Complexity-Consciousness" continues to run on today in the form of the socialization of mankind!"

"Now, so as to emphasize an important relationship. The closed and circular surface of the Earth contributes to the increased compression (socialization) of mankind!"

"As human beings continue to come into closer contact with one another, their methods of interaction continue to complexify in the form of better (maybe higher is a more fitting word) organized social networks, which contributes to an overall increase in consciousness, or the "Noosphere".

What is most critical to us, we who focus on the future, is the healthy saving of humankind as this complexifies."

---

1. The display is simplified from Wikipedia in an extensive, well documented section on the subject of the "Noosphere".

"Teilhard imagines a critical threshold, the so-called "Omega Point", in which mankind will have reached its highest point of complexification (socialization) and thus its highest point of consciousness."

"At this point in Teilhard's view, consciousness will rupture through time and space and assert itself on a higher plane of existence (a stellar one) from which, in Teilhard's thinking, it cannot come back."

"In Teilhard's view, because the Law of Complexity-Consciousness runs everywhere and at all times, and because of the immensity of both time and space and the immensity of the chances for matter to find the right conditions to complexify upon itself, it is highly probable that life exists, has existed, and will exist in the universe apart from our Earth. (This met with firm objections from his church.)"

"This of course is within the finding of our Forever Panel. The physical chemical makeup of Forever, necessarily leaving the possibilities of "Life" as nearly infinite and not including only us, though we may have come from "Such Other", i.e. following Fermi's paradox."

"However, to continue and clarify that unusual term…Noosphere (sometimes Noosphere') is the "Sphere of human thought". The word is derived from the Greek νοῦς (nous "mind") + σφαῖρα (sphaira "sphere"), in lexical analogy to "atmosphere" and "biosphere". This term was "first' introduced by Pierre Teilhard de Chardin as early as 1922 in his "Cosmogenesis".

It is important at the same time to note that there are others who thinking along the same line deserve attention and credit here.   Thus, the first use of the term, may have come by Édouard Le Roy, who together with Chardin was listening to lectures of Vladimir Vernadsky at Sorbonne (We have discussed this thinker)."

"In 1936 Vernadsky presented the idea of the Noosphere in a letter to Boris Leonidovich Lichkov (though, he states that the concept derives from Le Roy). Citing the work of Teilhard's biographer Rene Cuenot. Even so, Sampson and Pitt stated that although the concept was jointly developed by all three men (Vernadsky, LeRoy, and Teilhard), Teilhard believed that he actually invented the word. He said, "I believe, so far as one can ever tell, that the word 'Noosphere' was my invention: but it was he [Le Roy] who launched it."

"Well, anyway, I suggest we reference mostly or at least always "Teilhard' to simplify our discussions, and so back to the theme and if you will in reference to the handout figure. …It gives a succinct view of our Universal evolution. Remember Tim gave us a backdrop with his BioGeo report."

"Having seen the ways in which the earth is affected by us, we may now consider in more detail, the idea of Universal Evolution involving the theory formulated by Pierre Teilhard de Chardin and Julian Huxley that describes the gradual development of the Universe from subatomic particles to human society, considered by Teilhard as the last stage!"

"Including Vernadsky's these thinkers' formulated very similar theories describing the gradual development of the universe from subatomic particles to human society and beyond. Teilhard's theories are better known in the West (and have also been commented on by Julian Huxley), and integrate Darwinian evolution and Christianity, whilst Vernadsky wrote more purely from a scientific perspective."

"Three classic levels are described. They are Cosmogenesis (Teilhard) or the formation of inanimate matter (the Physio sphere of Wilber), culminating in the Lithosphere, Atmosphere, Hydrosphere, etc. (Teilhard), or collectively, the Geosphere (Vernadsky). Here progress is ruled by structure and mechanical laws, and matter is primarily of the nature of non-consciousness (Teilhard - the "Without")."

"This is followed by Biogenesis (Teilhard) and the origin of life or the Biosphere (Vernadsky, Teilhard), where there is a greater degree of complexity and consciousness (Teilhard - the "Within"), Ecology (Vernadsky) comes into play, and progress and development is the result of Darwinian mechanisms of evolution."   At this point Pi draws a breath, examines her audience, smiles pleasantly and continues…

….."Finally, a main point, there is human evolution and the rise of thought or cognition (Vernadsky, Teilhard), and a further leap in complexity and the interior life or consciousness (Teilhard), resulting in the birth of the Noosphere (Vernadsky, Teilhard). "

"Just as the biosphere transformed the geosphere, so the Noosphere (human intervention) transformed the biosphere (Vernadsky). Here the evolution of human society (socialization) is ruled by active psychological, economic, informational and essential Communicative Processes."

"For Teilhard there is a further stage, one of spiritual evolution, the Christing of the collective Noosphere, in which humanity converges in a single divinization as mentioned that he calls the Omega Point!"

Great Pi! Dr.Why interjects, "That surely sets for us an important stage. That is the earth's spherical structure, delimits humans to increasing interrelation via our communication, into as you put it, "Encompassing Human Mind" or in Teilhard's words the Noosphere.

Vicente the Professor asks... Could you at the next meeting amplify Pi's introduction. And, of course, carry us into some theory as to how this all may impact the forward evolution of Mankind, with a bit of our evolutionary history.

For now group let's all see to those various home matters that must be taken care of, as I know in the end---well we are just "present humans".

Present humans, yes! But, it must be said they have challenged themselves to consider the far distant future for your forthcoming children, something that few, soaked in the collective insanities of the present are not considering at all!"

....

Gathered next Friday night, all minds cleared from the pressures of daily needs, the pursuit into Future Human Evolution was on again. On the Doctor's previous instruction... Vicente chooses to start with the topic of our "Evolutionary Stages".

He begins with "I will get us underway, a bit will be a repeat of some that Pi introduced, i.e. we will return to the "Noosphere"." There are actually nine levels described in the literature for "Universal Evolution". The "classical" biological stages conclude with levels 6, 7 & 8 within complete universal evolution. Stages 1 to 5 are grouped into the Lithosphere, also called Geosphere or Physiosphere, where the structure of organisms is ruled by mechanical laws and coincidence. Stages 6 to 8 are grouped into the Biosphere, where the structure of the organisms is ruled by genetical mechanisms. Then stage 9, the one called *"Noosphere"*, where the structure of human society (socialization) is ruled by the three processes psychological, informational and communicative!

For the *Noosphere* the prime reference is Teilhard's Book "The Phenomenon of Man". The Noosphere (/ˈnoʊ.əsfɪər/; sometimes noösphere) is in my estimation easiest to "think of 'as the *"Sphere of Human Thought"*.

The word to be specific derives from the Greek νοῦς (nous "mind") and σφαῖρα (sphaira "sphere"), in lexical analogy to "atmosphere" and "biosphere".

As said, it was introduced by Pierre Teilhard de Chardin in 1922 in his Cosmogenesis. Another possibility as has been covered is that the first use of the term was by Édouard Le Roy (1870–1954), who together with Teilhard was listening to lectures of at the Sorbonne. In 1936, Vernadsky accepted the idea of the Noosphere in a letter to Boris Leonidovich Lichkov (though he states that the concept derives from Le Roy).

Just as this was said the Professor received a phone call from one of the lab technicians, Johan. "Well, sorry Vicente-Folks, looks like we will have to discontinue, seems the power was out at the School of Medicine, and our lab is without power in the incubators, we will all have to rush there and put the generator into action to save the incubations."

~~~~~~

The rescue mission for the BioSims+ was partially successful, such that near late stage cells were saved in sufficient numbers to continue experiments. The lab, however, was not fully up to power so most of the staff was given leave for personal time.

Vicente took advantage to deepen his studies and to find rooming. There was not much available so he settled for an efficiency apartment in a rather rundown neighborhood, but at a price he could afford.

Pi and Tim on this 'leave' were able to work on something magic for themselves, that is, their wedding! This was to all in the group sometimes thought to be a bit of a flight of fancy that they would really get married, though a union was suspected from those 'close encounters' in the lab. One reason for the surprise was that Pi is oriental, and Tim is a Jewish man (yet still hunting for foundation). So the ceremony was in the end, as promised, to be one very unusual, Jewish in basic vows but, with oriental décor!

Chandler and Jane, took the time to communicate with the kids teachers, as it was near term end. And they were pleased that their offspring were doing well, except for young James who seemed to visit the principal's office a good deal. The pair was also dealing with the lingering intestinal illness that Chandler acquired on the India "Forever Retreat".

Jehan took the opportunity to return to Pakistan to visit with her adopted father who had saved her after the terrorist attack at the Institute in India where she had attended school.

The Professor had this time to consider his potential retirement, and a probable new replacement.

And Skellan, Angelei and Gabriel took the time to tour the Princeton Campus, showing Alexander, yes even so young, the various facilities, and they were sure to take him to the home where Albert Einstein lived. Skellan filled in for the boy as they looked at the rather traditional house. Herr Doctor Professor Einstein lived from 1879 to 1955. He first visited Princeton in 1921, the year before he received the Nobel Prize. He was here at Princeton to deliver five "Stafford Little" lectures on the theory of relativity and to accept an honorary degree. He returned again in 1933 as a life member of the newly founded "Institute for Advanced Study" and
~~~~~~

lived here for the remaining twenty-two years of his life.   One of my favorite quotes by this genius is "We cannot solve our problems by the same thinking that created them". To which the boy said, "You would think most people would realize that" which prompted his brother Gabriel to lift the boy with a hug---expostulating… Oh how much we wished they did!

CHAPTER 8: A STUDENT'S LEGACY

In their next meetings, Vicente expanded extensively on the concept of and factors effecting the Future Evolution of Humans, at first stressing theory, such as the following…

…"In the theory of Vernadsky, the Noosphere is the third in a succession of phases of development of the Earth, after the geosphere (inanimate matter) and the biosphere (biological life). Just as the emergence of life fundamentally transformed the geosphere, he argued that the emergence of human cognition is that which is fundamentally responsible for transforming the biosphere.

In contrast to the conceptions of the Gaia theorists and the promoters of cyberspace, Vernadsky's Noosphere emerges at the point where humankind, through the mastery of nuclear processes, begins to create its necessary resources through the transmutation of elements. This thinking is as so many subjects concerning the Noosphere currently being researched as part of the "Princeton Global Consciousness Project".

In contrast to that line of thinking, Teilhard perceived a directionality in evolution along an axis of increasing Complexity/Consciousness. For Teilhard, the *Noosphere is the sphere of thought encircling the earth that has emerged through evolution as a consequence of this growth in complexity in consciousness.*"

"The Noosphere is therefore as much part of nature as the barysphere, lithosphere, hydrosphere, atmosphere, and biosphere. As a result, Teilhard sees the "social phenomenon as the culmination of and not the lessening of the biological phenomenon." These social phenomena are part of the Noosphere and include, for example, legal, educational, religious, research, industrial and technological systems."

"In this sense, the Noosphere emerges through and is constituted by the interaction of human minds! The Noosphere thus grows in step with the organization of the human mass in relation to itself as it populates the earth."

Here Jane a catholic contributed. "I learned that Teilhard argued the Noosphere evolves towards ever greater personalization, individuation and unification of its elements. And deep in his understanding he saw the Christian notion of love as being the principal driver of oogenesis."

To this Vicente contributed. "Although a Catholic he remarks that this sees love as the driver, i.e. the human sense of benevolence and caring essential as Omega is approached, and it is the primary workings inside the Noosphere to achieve the most beautiful ascent into eternity. Although he may have as priest, by a kind of default, imply Christianity as the driver, he certainly recognized that there are a great many philosophies, and faiths that center on love for each other."

"With love as the driver the theory is that evolution would culminate in that time called the Omega Point---an apex of thought/consciousness which he as a Christian representative identified with the eschatological return of Christ." *Yet, this same apex of thought/consciousness could be applied to all faiths if they are in union of accepting each other and solidly standing on their benevolent beginnings. Further, it must be commented that without that basic operation of humanity for all peoples, whatever their faith, there can be no Stellar end at the Omega Point.* "

Also, Vernadsky's clear minded idea, nuclear conversion to substantiate the species could be categorized the same. That is, in short, our long term evolution could head toward a magnificent culmination, if correctly matured through collaboration of all human communities!"

"I like to think of this as the complete human soul coalescing into the stars, belonging to Forever!"

"But all of this has a "Catch Twenty-Two', if you will allow me to use that well-worn phrase. We need to keep in mind that there will be an end, why should it be a disaster?"

The Future Navigator Panel at this, of course, nodded agreement one to the next. They understood through research what the character of Forever is and how important our record in that must become. After some discussion on that, Vicente continued…

…"Well, one of the original aspects concerning the Noosphere does indeed deal with evolution."

"Henri Bergson, with his L'évolution créatrice (1907), was one of the first to propose evolution is "creative" and cannot necessarily be explained solely by Darwinian natural selection. L'évolution créatrice is upheld, according to Bergson, by a constant vital force which animates life and fundamentally connects mind and body, an idea opposing the dualism of René Descartes."

"In 1923, C. Lloyd Morgan took this work further, elaborating on an "emergent evolution". This could explain increasing complexity including the evolution of mind, which I would submit is now in our more complete understanding, right before us, in our knowledge of the evolutionary steps from Homo habilis to sapiens."

"Morgan found many of the most interesting changes in living things have been in some cases largely discontinuous with past evolution. Therefore, these living things did not necessarily evolve only through a gradual process of natural selection. Rather, he posited, the process of evolution experiences (experiential) jumps in complexity (such as the emergence of a self-reflective universe, or Noosphere). "

"So one can say complexification of human cultures, particularly language, facilitated a quickening or jump in evolution in which cultural evolution occurs more rapidly than biological evolution."

"Consequently, recent understanding of the human impact on the biosphere have led to a link between the notions of critical co-evolution---that is a forced harmonization of biological and cultural evolution."   And of course, cultural evolution today is heavily steeped in the rapid evolution of our communication. (Accelerated communication, could lead to accelerated biological changes in our future and to our behavior.)

"So there is clear rational in my thinking regards dissertation content. I wish to emphasize, that subject i.e. the increasing volume of communication in cyberspace, which in effect is the allowance for humans to place (uninhibited, perhaps counter humanitarian) thoughts into computer language!"

So it was this aspect-computer driven communication-its effect on Human Evolution that Vicente proposed to bear on in our future meetings.

And this evolved, his development of it, over the semester. He spent most of his seminar time explaining the way the internet is designed and how it reaches virtually everyone on the planet. His thoroughness left no stone in electronic communication unturned, the panel without the advantage of a degree could still have been awarded one if tested - the teaching was so complete!

~~~~~~

Even so, reaching home one evening near the end of the semester Vicente noticed down the street under a street lamp four or five people holding baseball bats! Then the next night he saw the crowd had grown. He felt the hair on the nape of his next stand on end, because he had seen that before! In his childhood in a similar neighborhood, the youths in gangs, often came to seedy and deadly ends after such night time confrontations!

And, indeed there was an unbelievable and horrible, tragic event and unbelievable loss. Vicente is killed, an innocent bystander - in that gang- related situation! This kind and brilliant man was killed while getting out of his car. He lay in the street shot twice, for hours before someone called for help, and although transported to the hospital by the EMTs, he passed away well before reaching the Emergency Room!
~~~~~~

When the trouble was brewing, being a proactive man, he was concerned about his safety and he hurried to complete the writing and get his "dissertation proposal" to Pi and Tim, whom he rightfully viewed as his "Personal Teaching Assistants'.

The afternoon of the incident, He met them in the lab, described his concerns and with a courage that Tim and Pi greatly admired, exclaimed it was just a caution.

Yet, when he returned home that evening, just at his front door, getting out of his car, he was gunned down. Although the crowds he worried about had formed, he was killed in a drive by shooting. And this was the fate also of three of those under the lamp post.

The death of Vicente was beyond understanding for the lab staff. For Gabriel who knew this man once in the Navy as fellow Navy Corpsman and friend, it was deeply disturbing, leading him (with Pi in support) to investigate the killing and find restitution, which he accomplishes, working with the police and tracing the shooters.

There are no words to describe the distress and atmosphere, the overwhelming deep angry feelings at the funeral. For all those in the group it was truly crushing this loss of such an intelligent and gentle man, and this from a group who investigated and understood life and death deeper than most. Knowing the pain himself, the Professor gave his administrative staff and the group a week off. Most, though continued to work although they consulted the University Grief Counselor.

In time, that is in the new academic year a new student was accepted to replace Vicente. She entered the group as a laboratory assistant with prospects to pursue a doctorate. This is Chivonn Washington who has as Vicente a Master of Science Degree in Computer Science. After all get to know her, and find her most dependable, indeed she is especially intelligent, she is given Vicente's files and assigned to continue his series of reports. To help her synchronize with the group's overall mission, Jehan also gives her some insight into the "Vistaviens" teaching and provides a copy of the group's books, including "The Edge of Forever. From her interest, daily obvious---in questions and comments, it is suspected that she will most likely assume Vicente's line of research and take on a similar dissertation.

So it is that Vicente's inquiry into our Evolutionary Future, is not lost. The following account will present the essence of Vicente's assessment but as reported by Chivonn.

Being one of her first assignments it is noted that Chivonn will quote directly from the document, but selecting as she sees most needed.

She is in fact well qualified to step into Vicente's place as she was a fellow M.S. student with him, and the group could not help but hear the quiver in her voice, the first time she began to report his work, tears in her eyes. Here, following, is the way she prefaces and continues to report the work.

"As I found it, the total construction of his work is already formed as a valid dissertation! That is, the expected dissertation design is present. It contains an abstract, an introductory chapter with statement of the problem that begins the work containing hypothesis and delimitations.

There is a literature review chapter, there is a chapter on research design and methodology, a chapter detailing analysis and findings follows that, and his last chapter is appropriately a summary, giving conclusions, with discussions and recommendations. The final references section is massive and comprehensive!

In net, the work, the core of Vicente's dissertation reviews causation for and potential solutions to problems regarding reaching Omega that carry Teilhard's proposal to its consideration limits. It seems to me that Vicente provided us all the words which are appropriate to include background, history, objectives, research line for any dissertation using the Teilhard propositions.

Although he centers on Teilhard, he does give credence to other notions of our developing Noosphere, or as used much in the work "Our Global Brain." I probably do sound biased but to me it is a truly scholarly work. Here is the critical introductory statement.

"The notion of the Noosphere must now- in post Teilhard days be subdivided and expanded and those aspects be set into the expectations and solutions for the future." He continues…

…. *"We must realize he spoke a great truth, and take the basic idea of our Noosphere to its logical-course of consideration and describe the necessary to insure its successful final outcome!*

His document then proceeds in traditional, yes, the expected dissertation form.

However, I am handing out an introductory outline in summary language but using dissertation components.

That is, I have compiled his information much as one would for a Journal Article and I will report relative to that, rather than reading the full document. So to read…first the outline

Toward full consideration, the following topics expand on Teilhard's hypothesis to a necessary degree, and develop a "Solution Path."

A. Post Teilhard Considerations
    1. Evolution of the Intellect
    2. Cyberspace, its fateful connection
    3. Hypercyclic Morphogenesis, self-reproduction
    4. Infosphere, the practiced gathering of opinions
    5. The Ideosphere, routinely applying generic ideas
B. Potential Problems from Apparent Solutions
    1. Noocracy, powerful gathering, potential commanding
    2. Consequence illustrations.
        a. Computational predictability
        b. Control and potential wayward outcomes
        c. Learning from Mimetics
C. Resolution (Fight Fire with Fire)
    1. Protect the Future via an "Omega Shield"
        a. Recognize the Starter "Cy-gene"
    2. Shield the Cy-gene
        a. Reality Aware Cyber Humans via Ideologies
            Objective Humanism
            Self-Actuating Development
            Mind Centered Openness

Now using the outline, from here I read sections as I excerpted them following an order that was presented in logical sequencing…

"Evolution of the Intellect

The idea of the Noosphere expresses a result, not, other than complexity-consciousness, a detailed mechanism.

However, in recent times that investigation has been discussed. And, realizing the potential for troubling turns there are serious concerns driving such studies.

In 2005 Alexey Eryomin proposed a new concept related to the Noosphere which is imbedding a deeper description. We might say to coin a related term there is an "Oogenesis" in understanding the evolution of intellectual systems, concepts of intellectual systems, information logistics, information speed, intellectual energy, and intellectual potential. In short all of this may be consolidated into a *"Theory of the Intellect"*.

This theory combines the biophysical parameters of intellectual energy to the amount of information, its acceleration (frequency, speed) and the distance it's being sent. This idea has for some reflective scientist thought to be amendable into a formula, although that has not yet reached prominence.

Even so, according this newer idea there is a *progressive evolution of Homo sapiens mind*! This derives rationally from the analogy between the human brain with its enormous amount of neural cells firing at the same time and a similarly functioning hyper-active human society. *To wit, the brain cannot help but assimilate that which is all around it and constantly bombarding it.* Two graphs constructed by the author and included in Vicente's work illustrate the idea. These are on the handout I have just distributed. (Shown below)

This is a hypothesis that might be roughly compared philosophically somewhat like recapitulation theory which links the evolution of the human brain to the development of human civilization. The theory of the intellect, though relates specifically to cognitive development, i.e. the parallel is between the amount of people living on Earth and the amount of neurons becoming more and more obvious in real effect, leading us to viewing global intelligence as in an analogy for the human brain.

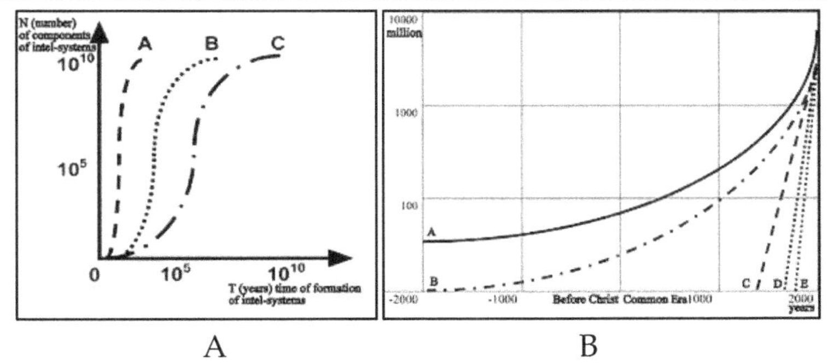

A   B

Graph A. Iteration of the number of components in Intellectual systems. A - Number of neurons in the brain during individual development (ontogenesis), B - number of people (evolution of populations of humanity), C - number of neurons in the nervous systems of organisms during evolution (phylogenies).

Graph B. Emergence and evolution of info-interactions within populations of Humanity. A - world human population → 7 billion ; B - number of literate persons; C – number of reading books (with beginning of printing); D - number of receivers (radio, TV); E - number of phones, computers, Internet users

Although there are such hypotheses on the ongoing development of the human mind, it is a simple, real factual observation that all of the people living on this planet have undoubtedly inherited the amazing cultural treasures of the past, be it production, social and intellectual ones. *That is, quite directly, we are genetically hardwired to be a sort of "live RAM" of the global intellectual system!*

In net, Alexey Eryomin argues that humanity is moving inescapably towards a unified self-contained informational and intellectual system. His research has shown the probability of "Super Intellect" realizing itself as "Global Intelligence on Earth"! (The Global Brain)

In his document Vicente agrees with the following statement by those reporting this "Evolution of the Intellect". "We could get closer to understanding the most profound patterns and laws of the Universe if these kinds of research were given enough attention. The resemblance between the individual human's mind development and that of the whole human race has to be explored further if we are to face some of the threats to humanity in the future." Then Vicente postulates his most serious and central concern namely the effect of Cyberspace on human development – its intellect. That is a major issue to focus on regarding our evolution in the future. "

Cyberspace it's Fateful Connection

To continue that from Vicente he addresses specific concerns emanating from Cyberspace…"At this point, in time much further than the original Teilhard proposal, it must be recognized that our evolution is dependent on cyberspace outcomes, (which, arguments can be made, later in this document, are embedding in our brain DNA)."

"Formally, cyberspace is "the notational environment in which communication over computer networks occurs."

The term was first used in science fiction and cinema in the 1980s, was adopted by computer professionals and became a household term in the1990s. During this period, the uses of the internet, networking, and digital communication were all growing dramatically and the term "cyberspace" was able to represent the many new ideas and phenomena that were emerging. The term is clearly appropriate as a blanket one for reference as to effects into future human behavior as the Noosphere continues to expand. That is, the notion of a Global Brain naturally must include the ever enfolding prevalent communication.

A major question wound around this is, where are we with Cyberspace and what pathways could be opened in relation to the Noosphere and the Omega point?

It is important to recall the depth in this consideration, which now is on a daily practiced-market basis."

"Today there are companies specialized in developing and deploying as expressed in company language "semantic solutions for information management and intelligence information analysis and sharing". What they do is sell software that allows computers and people to collect, organize, and keep current critical data regarding people, places, events, and various types of personal entities."

"These marketed solutions are at face for contingency preparedness and response, public safety and crime prevention, and defense and national security, yet the open market, technology advance, hacking and various ways of capturing coding---for such services is sweeping, as many who have experienced virus, and hostage crashed computer will testify. So it is via such packages possible to glean "mental false implants" toward population behavior."

From here Vicente described…first something called "Hypercyclic Morphogenesis", then he cited some important "Mimetic Headings" as in the literature. These are the Ideosphere, Infosphere, Noocracy, and an example of the power of computers holding information, which he called a few examples of "The Implantsphere".

I will read from these discussions all quoting directly…

Hypercyclic Morphogenesis

Hypercyclic morphogenesis refers to the emergence of a higher order of self-reproducing structure or organization and hierarchy within a system. It involves combining the idea of the hypercycle with that of morphogenesis.

The hypercycle involves, i.e. resembles a problem in biochemistry. It mimics that of molecules combining in a self-reacting group which is able to stay together (like genetic molecules for example). It is posited thus as the foundation for the emergence of multi-cellular organisms.

The researcher Thompson saw morphogenesis as a central part of the development of an organism as cell differentiation led to new organs appearing as it develops and grows. The chemistry and mathematics involved in such a process, would also be studied mathematically in the formulation of catastrophe theory.

Nevertheless, it can be argued that such a thing as Hypercyclic morphogenesis is a real, out-coming from human mentality. It is occurring today, slowly yielding a certain human persona! Those in "senior citizen status" know this, seeing the change in the way people, think, accept more and more unacceptable actions and behave!

On the societal level, Rosser suggested applications are visible in political economy such as the actual emergence of the European Union out of the conscious actions of the leaders of its constituent nation states, or the appearance of a higher level governance in urban hierarchy during economic development. It has been applied to the emergence of higher levels in ecologic-economic systems in turn augmenting the Noosphere of Vernadsky.

In short, we are, in reality, an experience within a mental Hypercyclic Morphogenesis!

Ideosphere

Semantics experts' note that the "Ideosphere", much like the Noosphere, is in a realm of "memetic evolution" just like the biosphere is the realm of biological evolution. The term, even so, is convenient in relating human actuality.

It is the "place" where thoughts, theories and ideas are created, evaluated and evolved.

The Ideosphere though is not considered to be a physical place by most people. It is instead "inside the minds" of all the humans in the world!

There is a technical distinction. It is also, sometimes, believed that the Internet, books and other media could be considered to be part of the Ideosphere. Alas, as such media are not (perhaps with exception of some developing media means as AI) "self-aware", it (the Ideosphere) cannot process the thoughts it contains as humans who have Dasein.

According to philosopher Yasuhiko Kimura, the Ideosphere is in the form of a "concentric Ideosphere" where ideas are generated by a few people with others merely perceiving and accepting these ideas from these "external authorities." We need think of this, that there is behind the matter the question, how deeply can it be centered, and perhaps more important, can it be within as we start life, i.e. an "Engram"!

Kaimura, hopefully, advocates in his terms an "Omni centric Ideosphere" where all individuals create new ideas and interact as self-authorities.

Vicente notes this self-authority is important to further human development, which will be touched later when defensive mechanisms are relayed.

As said the use of the mimetic term "Ideosphere" has a foundation. The aspects of Memetics important to consider in relation to the Noosphere are addressed later. However, mimetics is the theory of mental content based on an analogy with Darwinian evolution, as originating from Richard Dawkins' 1976 book "The Selfish Gene". Proponents describe Memetics as an approach to evolutionary models of cultural information transfer. That is, the mimetic mind can certainly grow via survival evolution!

Infosphere

Into the proposals of thoughts held growing from one person to the next, are two fold realities. These are the Infosphere and the Noocracy.

The "Infosphere" is a neologism (coinage, new word) composed of information and sphere. The word refers to an environment, much like a biosphere, that is populated by informational entities called "Inforgs".

While an example of the sphere of information is that in cyberspace--- Infospheres are not necessarily limited to purely online environments. (However, the notion of a Cybersphere is relevant as what is in the Infosphere, will as we have seen with the Way-Back machine, be fodder for its hold.)

The first documented use of the word "Infosphere" was a 1971 Time Magazine book review by R.Z. Sheppard in which he writes *"In much the way that fish cannot conceptualize water or birds the air, man barely understands his Infosphere, that encircling layer of electronic and typographical smog composed of clichés from journalism, entertainment, advertising and government."*

In 1980 it was used by Alvin Toffler in his book "The Third Wave" in which he writes "What is inescapably clear, whatever we choose to believe, is that we are altering our Infosphere fundamentally. In fact, we are adding a whole new strata of communication to the social system!

The emerging "Third Wave Infosphere" makes that of the Second Wave era - dominated by its mass media, the post office, and the telephone---seem hopelessly primitive by contrast"!

The Toffler definition proved prophetic as the use of "Infosphere" in the 1990s expanded beyond simple media to "speculate about" to the *in-common evolution of the Internet, Society and Culture!*

In his book "Digital Dharma", Steven Vedro writes, "Emerging from what French philosopher-priest Pierre Teilhard de Chardin called the shared Noosphere of collective human thought, invention and spiritual seeking, the Infosphere is sometimes used to conceptualize a field that engulfs our physical, mental and etheric bodies; it affects our dreaming and our cultural life. *Our evolving nervous system has been extended! As media sage Marshall McLuhan predicted in the early 1960s, into a Global Embrace!"*

The term Infosphere (as Global Embrace) has also been used by Luciano Floridi Professor of Philosophy and Ethics of Information at the University of Oxford on the basis of biosphere, to denote the whole informational environment constituted by all the informational entities (thus including informational agents as well), their properties, interactions, processes and mutual relations. It is an environment comparable to, but in a way different from cyberspace (which is one of its guiding regions, as it were), since it also includes off-line and analogue spaces of information.

According to Floridi, *it is possible to equate the Infosphere to the totality of being!*

Suggesting this leads him into an informational ontology. That is investigation into the nature and relations of being. Hence, among the many considerations is the "Manipulation of the Infosphere", and some special notions on "Publication of the Infosphere".

<u>Manipulation of the Infosphere.</u> The manipulation of the Infosphere is subject to a metaphysical analysis[1] and its rules. Information is considered to be Shannon[2] and is treated in a physical sense separate from energy and matter (hard reality).

The manipulations into the Infosphere include the erasing, transfer, duplication, and destruction of information.

Vicente, illustrates this in his document with a number of examples, drawn from recent news, as the president making statements that have no proof but the transfer is accepted by many uniformed about the foundation of facts. It has thus a way of supporting bias and bigotry.

That is the Infosphere can be (and is) used to cement ideas that by in large induce destructive behavior!

<u>Publications Using Infosphere.</u> Publications concerning the term Infosphere do range from commercial to visionary, to real possibilities.

For example, the IBM Software Group created the Infosphere brand in 2008 for its Information Management software products.

---

1. Metaphysics is a branch of philosophy investigating the fundamental nature of reality. Example, "What is it like?"
2. Shannon Information theory studies the quantification, storage, and communication of information. It was originally proposed by Claude E. Shannon.

in 1948 to find fundamental limits on signal processing and communication operations such as data compression, in a landmark paper entitled "A Mathematical Theory of Communication".

In the animated sitcom Futurama, the Infosphere is a huge sphere floating in space, in which a species of giant talking---floating brains attempts to store all of the information known in the universe.

Much more of concern and now some argue permeating in the world of reality, this term "Infosphere" was used by Dan Simmons in the science-fiction saga "Hyperion" (published 1989) to indicate what the Internet could become in the future: a place parallel, virtual, formed of billions of networks, with "artificial life" on various scales, from what is equivalent to an insect (small programs) to what is equivalent to a god (artificial intelligences), whose motivations are diverse, seeking to both help mankind and harm it!

This very salient notion is pointing to the probability that simulated reality could become reality (of behavior)?

How could that happen? There are several avenues to it but it would be guided...via a forceful source of information!

Noocracy

And Vicente answers that as follows. "We will call that force for purpose here, the "Noocracy". It is one in relation to the Noosphere, so it is appropriately termed the "Noocracy".

Well, forceful would be a simple way of expressing it or the "Aristocracy of the Wise", as defined by Plato. However, this is not about kings and queens, it is a social and political system that is *"based on the priority of the human mind"*, according to Vladimir Vernadsky. And, it was also further developed in the writings of Pierre Teilhard de Chardin!

As to etymology, the word itself is derived from Greek nous, Gen. Noos (νους) meaning "mind" or "intellect", and "kratos" (κράτος), "authority" or "power"! This, on the positive side is what the Vistavien (the mentor of the Future Navigators) wants. That is, the Mind under Self-Control, free to interpret and make good decisions. But, of course, she meant free in the open minded sense, so that rational decisions can prevail!

One of the first attempts to implement such a political system as a Noocracy was perhaps Pythagoras' "City of the Wise" one that he planned to build in Italy together with his followers, in the order of "Mathematikoi".

In modern history, similar concepts were introduced by Vladimir Vernadsky, who did not use this term however, but the term "Noosphere.

As defined by Plato, Noocracy is considered to be the future political system for the entire human race, but replacing Democracy ("the authority of the crowd") and other forms of government. Obviously, with our lessons from Cesare to Hitler to the dictators of the day, that can be manipulated in an adverse manner, and the tool is potentially there in the "Infosphere" and that through the massively expanding Cybersphere.

Mikhail Epstein defined Noocracy this way, *"As the thinking matter increases its mass in nature (just as the geo- and biosphere) it grows into the Noosphere, hence, the future of humanity can be envisioned as potentially a Noocracy, that is, the power of the collective brain controls, rather than separate individuals representing certain social groups or society as whole.* This is extremely concerning*!* The question is what would that collective brain be, how would it come about? It surely would effect Human Evolution!

In the European Commission Community Research article, "Art & Scientific Research are Free: Towards a Culture of Life", it states several commentaries by Hans Jonas and especially Ladislav Kovác about Noocracy.

"If Plato called his conception of governments a "sophocracy," then, we can envision (as seen by these authors) for Noocracy a modern ideal! That is a political system characterized by social experimentation with a scientific institutionalized base that could be called a "Noocracy."

"Noocracy would not be the reign of the philosopher-king as seen in Plato. Nor would it be governed by science or the scientists. Yet, certainly one hopes for an ideal outcome.

Ideally, a power acquired and maintained according to the laws of competition, would remain in the hands of the political elites but with these elites being professionally trained, making the most of the analysis, the forecasts and the propositions emanating from a vast array of advisory groups made up of experts from all areas of science, and setting up fieldwork experiments."

These authors take for example the current controversy about genetically modified food or GMO, a textbook case about setting up such a policy.

"Within a (ideal) Noocracy in its own right, GMO would be tested in one or several areas or nations and scientifically monitored by all, under the guidance of a main administration body. With, at the end of the day, the costs and profits equitably shared by all. The principle of precaution, highly controversial at the present time, would then be applied, without slowing-down nor impeding the implementation of scientific inventions."

A this point in the presentation, Pi commented, "This is an example of Future Navigators working in the Noosphere if it were to be unfolding ideally, i.e. in as spirit of Objective Humanism". However, although the outcomes could be good for long term Human Evolution it sort of seems like communism, does it not? It seems as though it could go way wrong, become over dictating and that could be guided against Humanism.[1]

PROBLEMS FROM APPARENT SOLUTIONS

"Yes, Pi (entered Chivonn) and Vicente is quick to address this." He said, "Noocracy, like technocracies, have been criticized for meritocratic failings, such as upholding of a non-egalitarian aristocratic ruling class. Others have upheld more democratic ideals as better epistemic models of law and policy. However, even though a potential useful guide to human behavior, there is, indeed, a critical question, what actual way would it go in reality, given the power of the Cybersphere, that is without some forward consideration?"

Chivonn notes as her presentation is about to proceed further that Vicente first cites examples of the power of computers contributing to Cyberspace and then he gives examples of the intrusion into human endeavors. First she reads on the former in Vicente's words…

"And that concern is real. Indeed, the power of computers, i.e. operation in Cybersphere in ways that can influence opinion and outcomes are rather prolific."

"<u>Computational Power:</u> Here (as cited by Vicente) are examples of the developing power of cyberspace control".

"First should be considered is the computational means of control. Very soon the old means of computing will yield to the new, which is the "Quantum Computer". Quantum computing is as different from traditional computing as an abacus is from a MacBook. "Classical computing was invented in the 1940s. This is like that creation in way, but even far beyond it," says Scott Crowder of IBM Systems."

"Quantum computers are made up of parts called qubits, also known as quantum bits. Quantum superposition is most important because it allows the qubit

1. The Navigators posit "Objective Humanism" as a path to the Future. It is described in the books, "The Future Navigator" and its sequel "Navigators on the Edge of Forever".

to do two things at once. While traditional computers put bits in 0 and 1 configurations to calculate steps, a qubit can be a 0 and a 1 at the same time. Quantum entanglement, another purely quantum property, takes the possibilities a step further by intertwining the characteristics of two different qubits, allowing for even more calculations. Calculations that would take longer than a human's life span to work out on a classic computer can be completed in a matter of days or hours!"

"Eventually, quantum computing could outperform the world's fastest supercomputer—and then all computers ever made, combined.

What problems could be so complicated they would require a quantum computer? Here is an example. One to two percent of the world's energy is consumed per year for mass production of fertilizer. However, the quantum computer alone has the power to take care of this"

"There's a type of cyanobacteria that uses an enzyme to do nitrogen fixation at room temperature, which means it uses energy far more efficiently than industrial methods. "It's been too challenging for classical computer systems to date to work out how to use it but quantum computers would be able to reveal the enzyme's secrets immediately so researchers could re-create the process synthetically!

Pharmaceutical science could also benefit. One of the limitations to developing better, cheaper drugs is problems that arise when dealing with electronic structures. The ability to predict how molecules react with other drugs, and the efficacy of certain catalysts in drug development, could drastically speed up the pace of pharmaceutical development and, ideally, lower prices.

Finance is also plagued by complicated problems. Quantum computing could figure out the optimal way to rebalance portfolios day by day (or minute by minute) since that will require a computing power beyond the current potential of digital computers."

"While business applications within quantum computing are mostly hopeful theories, there's one area where experts agree quantum could be valuable: optimization. Using quantum computing to create a program that "thinks" through how to make business operations faster, smarter and cheaper could revolutionize countless industries. For example, quantum computers could be used to organize delivery truck routes so holiday gifts arrive faster during the rush before Christmas. They could take thousands of self-driving cars and organize them on the highway so all the drivers get to their destination via the fastest route. They could create automated translating software so international businesses don't have to bother with delays caused from translating emails."

"In net, the existing power of computers upon which cyberspace operates will in human future become so far much more capable that it cannot even be imagined! While that can create applications making human time vastly more convenient, there is a flip side that should in rational minds be considered! Even now these flip side effects are able to predict and some even being seen.

For example, using algorithms partially modeled on the human brain, (a very important aspect to observe) researchers from the Massachusetts Institute of Technology have enabled computers to predict the immediate future by examining a photograph of humans doing this or that!"

"A program created at MIT's "Computer Science and Artificial Intelligence Laboratory" essentially watched two million online videos and observed how different types of scenes typically progress: people walk across golf courses, wave's crash on the shore, and so on. Now, when it sees a new still image, it can generate a short video clip (roughly 1.5 seconds long) showing its vision of the immediate future!"

"It's a system that tries to learn what plausible videos are ---what are plausible motions you might see," says Carl Vondrick, a graduate student at the laboratory and lead author on a research paper presented at the "Neural Information Processing Systems Conference" in Barcelona. The team aims to generate longer videos with more complex scenes in the future."

"But Vondrick says applications could one day go beyond turning photos into computer-generated format for image files that supports both animated and static images (GIFs). The system's ability to predict normal behavior could help spot unusual happenings in security footage or improve the reliability of self-driving cars, he says."

"If the system spots something unusual, like an animal of it has seen before running into the road, Vondrick explains that the vehicle "can detect the threat in that, evaluate and say, 'Okay, I've seen this situation before! I can let the driver take over!"(Vicenti says, so comforted will the driver do that?)

"To create the program, the MIT team relied on a scientific technique called deep learning that's become central to modern artificial intelligence research!"

"Artificial Intelligence: It's the approach that lets digital assistants like Apple's Siri and Amazon's Alexa understand what users want, and that drives image search and facial recognition advancements at Facebook and Google. "

Here Chivonn sets down the notes from which she is reading (taken from Vicente's dissertation) and comments extemporaneously, "And, yes, I understand that our BioSims Lab, Dr. Jodyn's, that is, uses artificial intelligence to predict what chemicals could be toxic to the cells they are creating." "To which, on behalf of the panel, Jehan nodded, and commented straight away, "yes, that is the case, and it is an important part of the work."

Chivonn, pleased with that input, continued…"Well, to return, as it turns out, experts say deep learning, which uses mathematical structures called Neural Networks (indeed used by the Jordyn Lab) to pull patterns from massive sets of data, could soon let computers make diagnoses from medical images, detect bank fraud, predict customer order patterns, and operate vehicles at least as well as people."

"Deep neural networks are performing better than humans on all kinds of significant problems, like image recognition, for example," says Chris Nicholson, CEO of a San Francisco firm which develops deep learning software and offers consulting. "Without them, I think self-driving cars would be a danger on the roads, but with them, self-driving cars are safer than human drivers."

"Neural networks take low-level inputs, like the pixels of an image or snippets of audio, and run them through a series of virtual layers, which assign relative weights to each individual piece of data in interpreting the input. The "deep" in deep learning refers to using tall stacks of these layers to collectively uncover more complex patterns in the data, expanding its understanding from pixels to basic shapes to features like stop signs and brake lights. To train the networks, programmers repeatedly test them on large sets of data, automatically tweaking the weights so the network makes fewer and fewer mistakes over time".

"While research into neural networks, is indeed loosely based on the human brain, it dates back decades, progress has been particularly remarkable in roughly the past ten years, Nicholson says. A 2006 set of papers by renowned computer scientist Geoffrey Hinton, who now divides his time between Google and the University of Toronto, helped pave the way for deep learning's rapid development."

"This year, a Google-designed computer trained by deep learning defeated one of the world's top Go players, a feat many experts of the ancient Asian board game had previously thought could be decades away. The system, called Alpha Go, learned in part by playing millions of simulated games against itself. While human chess players have long been bested by digital rivals, many experts had thought Go — which has significantly more sequences of valid moves — could be harder for computers to grasp."

"Vicente notes a group from the University of Oxford unveiled a deep learning-based lip-reading system that can outperform human experts. And this week, a team including researchers from Google published a paper in the Journal of the American Medical Association showing that deep learning could spot diabetic retinopathy roughly (almost) as well as trained ophthalmologists. That eye condition can cause blindness in people with diabetes, especially if they don't have access to testing and treatment."

"At the present stage of development there are of course limitations, but the potential is growing exponentially, day by day."

"And, the experts say, with a bit of awe, that the math operations involved aren't beyond an advanced high school student. Some clever matrix multiplications to weight the data points and a bit of calculus to refine the weights in the most efficient way are the most that is required. As it is though, at the present time, only modern computers, along with an internet-enabled research community sharing tools and data, have made deep learning practical."

"At the same time, if one steps back, the following comes to mind. "

"First, eventually these systems can become as prevalent as to make people believe that a certain action is justified (It's proven by computer, they would say). The methods could be used by persons with hidden and dangerous agenda, and the systems could encounter an error because they cannot really iterate creatively as well as humans. Finally, if a certain mode of behavior becomes universal there is the possibility that the governing machine could be "crashed" or hacked disastrously by one or more persons."

"In addition to creating artificial intelligence through neural networks, these networks are indeed, already operating in the Cybersphere. There is a direct influence they have on people day by day that it appears is becoming more universal. Does this not require ongoing analysis of evil data vs. gullibility?"

"<u>Brain Computer Interfaces:</u> More directly related to the brain and influence therein, SpaceX and Tesla are backing a brain-computer interface venture called Neuralink, according to The Wall Street Journal. The company, which is in the earliest stages of existence and has no public presence whatsoever, is centered on creating devices that can be implanted in the human brain, with the eventual purpose of helping human beings merge with software and keep pace with artificial intelligence, making humans smarter. These enhancements could improve memory or allow for more direct interfacing with computing devices. "

"The company's director told a group in Dubai, "Over time I think we will probably see a closer merger of biological intelligence and digital intelligence." He added that "it's mostly about the bandwidth, the speed of the connection between your brain and the digital version of yourself, particularly output." On Twitter, he has responded to inquiring fans about his progress on a so-called "neural lace," which is sci-fi shorthand for a brain-computer interface humans could use to improve themselves."

"This has not stopped a surge in Silicon Valley interest from tech industry futurists who are interested in accelerating the advancement of these types of far-off ideas. To be fair, the hurdles involved in developing these direct to brain devices are immense."

"Yet the attempts continue. Facebook's "direct brain interface," a creation of its secretive Building 8 division, could take tech-enhanced communication to the next level."

"In fact, Facebook has been exploring a silent speech system with a team of more than 60 scientists that would let people type 100 words per minute with their brain. What if you could type directly from your brain... with the speed and flexibility of voice and the privacy of text?" "It is noted that there are a number of computer and information specialist pointing out that such a method invites intrusion into the brain waves of participants."

"Even so, it is becoming clear that implanting in humans is not an absolute requirement, as there is are many examples where the overarching Cybersphere takes hold!"

"<u>Authorities Influence:</u> Reporter Todd of NBC news made an interesting point, one that relates directly to the matter of cyberspace influence."

"It is clear that political campaigns have become so tech-savvy (read cyber implanted and controlled) they can target the exact voters needed for a victory, often eschewing debates over critical issues, even telling lies, and ignoring sets of voters. Further redistricting with the use of finely tuned data sets, is used to protect incumbent legislators and produce further polarization. "We are sending lawmakers to govern who don't have any incentive to compromise", the reporter noted. "So voters are forced to pick a side, eliminate nuance altogether. And this leads to creating conflicts that can effect advance into reasonable governance. The notion that the other party threatens the nation, becomes a heightened relationship between people."

"<u>Social Networking:</u> And into this is the simple and direct way that the use of our mass communication-inter-netting capability is presently showing evidence of affecting the human psyche. Here we can turn to studies on the effect of our "interlinks" via social networking. There are presently a number of studies that show the pervading influence of cyberspace and certainly the interest Yof serious minded people in it."

"On line such as "Facebook" does give us more friends. A 2011 survey by Pew Research backs this up, suggesting people who communicate using social media and mobile phones have more close friends than those who don't. On the other hand, there are real concerns as we are just beginning to grasp the reality."

"The more people use Facebook, like posts, share their own links and are exposed to the carefully crafted profiles of their friends, the worse they will feel, a study by the John Hopkins Bloomberg School of Public Health suggests. It had already been cited as behind some serious downward effects on young people, who when cyberbullied via it, committed suicide!"

"Previous investigations into the use of social media have suggested that retreating online and away from face-to-face social relationships can lead to sedentary behavior and internet addiction. However, the more in-depth study by the John Hopkins Bloomberg School of Public Health has found that almost every form of interaction with Facebook can lead to diminished well-being."

"Writing in the Harvard Business Review, Shakya and Christakis said the three Facebook behaviors they measured to include liking, posting, and clicking links all led to negative self-comparisons and made people feel worse about themselves. They expected liking other people's content to be the largest driver of decreased happiness but said overall the sheer quantity of time people spent interacting with the social media app led to the negative effects."

"The results were particularly concerning for mental health. Most measures of Facebook use in one year predicted a decrease in mental health in a later year. This research found consistently that both liking others' content and clicking links significantly predicted a subsequent reduction in self-reported physical health, mental health, and life satisfaction," they added. The data base here was from over five thousand adults over two years. Yet, how the use of the social media caused the effect is not presently clear. However, these researchers concluded: "What seems quite clear ... is that online social interactions are no substitute for the real thing."

"A study, published by Oxford University Press, collected three sets of data from 5,208 U.S. adults over two years and measured how their mental health, reported physical health, and body-mass index changed over time relative to their use of Facebook. It also collected information on the subjects' real-world social interaction. While the numbers showed use of the social network led to a lessened sense of well-being, how exactly that happened was unclear, however."

"Ultra-easy Internet Linked Information: In addition to social networking per se, the long-term effects of technology use on the many available networks are still unknown."

"It is clear that internet linked technology information is changing the way we learn and are changing the way we think," says Dr. Benjamin Storm, Associate Professor of psychology at University of California Santa Cruz. "However, in the same way that advances in technology are outpacing our understanding of what it's doing to our behaviors and relationships, those changes are also outpacing our understanding of how it's affecting learning and thinking", says Storm, who studies human memory and cognition. In a recent study, Storm and his colleagues found that offloading one piece of information even the simple act of saving a computer file actually made it easier to learn an unrelated piece of information."

"And while rapid access technology is expanding our worldviews and social circles there are serious questions as to what the easy access may be doing to our inherent ability to think things through! Here are some thoughts on that gathered from various studies that appear here and there in magazines and the press."

"Will a baby born in 2017 ever unfold a map to determine the best driving route from New York City to a small town in Massachusetts? Will that baby memorize a phone number other than his or her own? Will they grow up to be a smarter man or woman because their mind is no longer cluttered with mundane facts and the processes technology can do for us? Psychologists and neuroscientists don't know these answers yet. But they're beginning to understand how spending every waking moment within reach of Internet-connected devices is affecting our lives." "We've never have had a technology that we use so intensively for so many different things," says Nicholas Carr, author of "The Glass Cage: How Computers Are Changing Us."

"For example we are shaking up the workforce in unexpected ways. We keep our brains in a constant state of overload, always distracted by new bits of information. It's human nature to want to take it all in because at one point in history knowing everything that was going on in the environment literally helped humans survive", Carr explains. "Now, (however) constant connection to the Internet via smartphones and laptops has changed long-established rhythms of human thinking. There used to be times when we were socializing and learning from the people and the world around us and times when we were alone with our thoughts." *But it becomes much harder to practice the attentive types of thinking---contemplative thought, reflective thought, introspective thought*", Carr says. "That means it's very hard to translate information into rich, highly connected memories that ultimately make us smart and intelligent."

"Further, Technology is changing how we empathize with others. For example, our relationship with technology affects how we communicate. But it also affects the deeper ways we interact and connect with people". This is according to Dr. Sherry Turkle, professor of the social studies of science and technology at MIT and the author of "Reclaiming Conversation". "Now we can always be heard, we never need to be alone, and we never worry about being bored thanks to the constant feeds of information. If you can't be alone with your own thoughts [ever], you can't really hear what others have to say because you need them to support your fragile sense of self. True empathy requires the capacity for solitude. Even if we think we're bored, the brain is working hard to process information we've taken in to replenish itself," Turkle explains. "Just like Carr and others are concerned that this stream of distractions prevents deep thinking, Turkle's concern is that those distractions also prevent the deep feeling that lets us connect emotionally with others!"

"We need to reclaim face-to-face conversation. One 2014 study followed 51 kids who spent five days at an outdoors camp with no phones or laptops allowed. After time away from technology, the children were better able to read facial expressions and identify the emotions of actors in videos they were shown, compared with a control group of kids who didn't attend the camp."

"Less interaction with technology allows us to focus on conversations and interactions with others instead of trying to fulfill cravings for finding new information via smartphones and other devices. We need (seriously) to reclaim face-to-face conversation, never have we needed to talk to each other and understand each other more."

"Digital Overloading: Further serious concern is evident in that "Digital Offloading" can in fact lead to information missed. Here are some perceptive comments. "It is true that our digital devices have become a memory partner (Storm et.al). "You can make more room for new information in your brain when you store and access other information digitally. The concern, however, is that too much digital offloading means we might miss out on the mental connections that make us more creative and intelligent", Storm explains---"and that offloading may prevent us from developing the very same sort of expertise as we would otherwise."

"Further to this problem of digital offloading is the following. A study published in "Nature Communications" found that certain parts of the brain actually switch off or become less active when drivers used GPS to navigate the streets of London compared to those who relied on memory. Indeed, research suggests that using a GPS navigation system to get to your destination "switches off" parts of the brain that would otherwise be used to simulate different routes." "When we lean on GPS, we're no longer using certain parts of our brain the way we have over millennia", says Dr. Hugo Spiers, the study's author and reader in neuroscience in the Department of Experimental Psychology at University College London. "This may not be good for us, but we can't currently tell. There are plenty of unanswered questions about how new forms of technology affect our thinking and behavior or if they harm our intelligence and creativity, Storm says, and there's a danger in deciding whether the changes are good or bad." By Vicente-"There is danger in auto-deciding."

~~~~~~

At this point Chivonn, concluded her review of Vicente's dissertation for this meeting. She did this by extracting his following comment…

.... "First, it is important to state that I deeply honor my fellow humans. Homo sapiens is remarkable in what they can create and it is clear that a great many cherish others. However, the basic exploration, as reviewed forgoing, reveals considerable potential, not only for good but evil outcomes from our now largely cyberspace implanting- developing Global Brain!

Pointedly, the matter of cyber-influx into a "Global Brain" matters greatly, because the full record of humans is one of political and often spirit linked cruel wars, where those now could be the masters of cyberspace, and so influence as to create a wholly inhuman, homo sapiens in large numbers!

In short, data manipulation, is a facet of Cybersphere that can greatly affect progress toward the Omega point, seriously putting Teilhard's impression of the creation of ultimate incredible benevolent humans, in jeopardy!
~~~~~~

CHAPTER 9: RISING "SAFELY" TO OMEGA

Memetics and Genetics
Omega Shields Armor
The Ideologies

At the next meeting the Professor was the first to comment. "Thank you, Chivonn, for that bridge into Vicente's work. So it is that we of the Panel are discovering before he was killed Vicente had developed his dissertation proposal well beyond just cursory background. That seems clear from that which Chivonn has reviewed for us thus far."

Before beginning to complete her review, Chivonn is reminded by Dr.Y "that a dissertation supports its claim to originality by positioning its argument both within and against prior scholarship and practices.

Furthermore, a strong proposal integrates the discussion of its methods into its claims to be presenting a new or distinct approach to some material or issue." Chivonn assured the Professor that what she would continue to review, fully met such criteria, and with that she opened her note folder as she had done, reading from her report a summary of Vicente's work.

…"Thus it is in his proposal-chapter Vicente treats central notions from which saving ideas arise. He chose to call the composite of these "The Omega Shield". His working hypothesis toward that is as follows."

"1. A shield for new humans must be developed to insure that final humans reach Omega as a united Humanity.

2. This Omega Shield will develop optimally when secured within the genome, in a cy-gen--- inherited and developed in future generations.

3. That can be created by present generations who honor the growth of all children through open-minded informed nurturing."

"In defense of the need for this future reaching shield, cyberspace is now everywhere and entrenches acceptance of evil as well as good.

Indeed terrible acts, such as the online beheading of hostages is patently accepted by too many. Murder while you watch refers to real Facebook events.[1]

Humanity is steeped in conflict and self-interest and unlikely to last to any of Kardashev Time lines with the aura of greatness projected by Teilhard at the Omega Point."

"It is the proposal of this dissertation that the construction of an appropriate shield to reach the Omega Point in good stead, is dependent upon allowing in our new generations a sense of objectivity significantly powerful in their genetic structure to rationally dissect aberrant anti-human influences permeating the Global Brain. For purposes of simplification, we will call that genetic structure the Cy-gene!"

"That such genetic control would develop can be seen by observing the power, indeed proof of self-replicating units of culture! The critical and philosophical term is Mimesis from which is drawn a gene parallel term the "Meme".

"Memetics is the theory of mental content based on an analogy with Darwinian evolution, originating from the popularization of Richard Dawkins' 1976 book "The Selfish Gene." Proponents describe Memetics as an approach to Evolutionary models. In the subject called "Mimetics" there is a foundational concept in a sense leading to evidence for a Universal Brain."

"Memetics is also notable for sidestepping the traditional concern with the truth of ideas and beliefs. Instead, it is interested in their success. That is indeed a concern!

There is via that the notion that a 'meme' is a 'virally-transmitted cultural symbol or social idea'!"

"The term "meme" derives from the Ancient Greek μιμητής (mimētés), meaning "imitator, pretender". The similar term "Mneme" was used in 1904, by the German evolutionary biologist Richard Semon, best known for his development of the "Engram Theory of Memory" (used in Scientology). "Mimeme" comes from a suitable Greek root, but as Semon said "I want a monosyllable that sounds a bit like "gene". I hope my classicist friends will forgive me if I abbreviate Mimeme to meme. If it is any consolation, it could alternatively be thought of as being related to "memory", or to the French word meme."

"A great many people in this modern cyberspace time, have heard the term because the majority of modern memes, fall into somewhat trivial or popular ideas. They are captioned photos that are intended to be funny, often as a way to publicly

---

1. Among many examples this is detailed by Kathleen Parker (Appearing in her article from the "Washington Post Writers Group", 20 April, 2017.)

ridicule human behavior. Other memes can be videos and verbal expressions.

However, some memes have, indeed, heavier and more philosophical even dangerous content!"

"The world of memes is noteworthy for two very, very important reasons: it is a worldwide social phenomenon, and memes as has been noted can be said to behave like a mass of infectious flu and cold viruses, traveling from person to person quickly through social media.

A point of focus from this wide human 'implantation', is that the meme, may be thought of, indeed, as analogous to a gene!"

"It was conceived as a "unit of culture" (an idea, belief, pattern of behavior, etc.) which is "hosted" in the minds of one or more individuals, and which can reproduce itself, thereby jumping from mind to mind.

Thus, what would be regarded as just one individual influencing another to adopt a belief is seen as an idea-replicator reproducing itself in a new host."

"As with genetics particularly under a Dawkinsian interpretation a meme's success may be due to its contribution to the effectiveness of its host.

In his 1976 book "The Selfish Gene", the evolutionary biologist Richard Dawkins, indeed, used the term meme to describe a unit of human cultural transmission analogous to the gene, arguing that replication also happens in culture, albeit in a different sense."

"Ted Cloak had briefly outlined a similar hypothesis in 1975, which Dawkins referenced. Cultural evolution itself is a much older topic, with a history that dates back at least as far as Darwin's era. Dawkins, however, in 1976 proposed that *the meme is a unit of information residing in the brain and is the mutating replicator in human cultural evolution. It is a pattern that can influence its surroundings, that is, it has causal agency – and can propagate.*"

This created great debate among sociologists, biologists, and scientists of other disciplines, because "Dawkins himself did not provide a sufficient explanation of how the replication of units of information in the brain controls human behavior and ultimately culture, since the principal topic of the book was not genetics per se." "Dawkins apparently did not intend to present a comprehensive theory of Memetics in "The Selfish Gene", rather coined the term meme in a speculative spirit. Accordingly, different researchers came to define the term "Unit of Information" in different ways."

"Another stimulus was the publication in 1991 of "Consciousness Explained" by Tufts University philosopher Daniel Dennett, which incorporated the meme concept into a theory of the mind. And, in his 1991 essay "Viruses of the Mind",

Richard Dawkins used Memetics to explain the phenomenon of religious belief and the various characteristics of organized religions."

"The idea of language as a virus was introduced by William S. Burroughs as early as 1962 in his book "The Ticket That Exploded", and eight years later in "The Electronic Revolution", published in "The Job". Douglas Rushkoff explored the same concept in "Media Virus: Hidden Agendas in Popular Culture" in 1995."

"However, the foundation of Memetics in its full modern incarnation originated in 1996 with publication of two books by authors outside the academic mainstream: "Virus of the Mind: The New Science of the Meme" by former Microsoft executive turned motivational speaker and professional poker-player, Richard Brodie, and "Thought Contagion: How Belief Spreads Through Society" by Aaron Lynch, a mathematician and philosopher who worked for many years as an engineer at Fermilab. Lynch claimed to have conceived his theory totally independently of any contact with academics in the cultural evolutionary sphere, and apparently was not even aware of Dawkins' "The Selfish Gene" until his book was very close to publication."

"Around the same time as the publication of the books by Lynch and Brodie the e-journal "Journal of Memetics-Evolutionary Models of Information Transmission" appeared on the web. It was first hosted by the "Centre for Policy Modelling" at Manchester Metropolitan University but it was later taken over by Francis Heylighen of the research institute at the Vrije Universiteit Brussel. So it was the e-journal soon became the central point for publication and debate within the nascent memeticist community. "

"In 1999, Susan Blackmore, a psychologist at the University of the West of England, published "The Meme Machine", which more fully worked out the ideas of Dennett, Lynch, and Brodie. It attempted to compare and contrast them with various approaches from the cultural evolutionary mainstream it also provided novel, and controversial, Memetics-based theories for the evolution of language and the human sense of individual selfhood. About the same time there were a number of other works and publications, e-type, newsletters and more."

"However, it was in 2005, that the Journal of Mimetic's "Evolutionary Models of Information Transmission" ceased publication and published a set of articles on the future of Memetics. There was to be a relaunch but that has not occurred! "It is, however, clear from this vast interest that the notion of implantation of ideas in people is possible through deliberate mimetic driven communication.

Thus, a lingering note is this, if the meme could be genetically engineered then so can the Planetary Brain."

"Of recent times an evolutionary model of cultural information transfer has arisen! It is based on the concept that units of information, or as might be said "memes", have an independent existence, are self-replicating, and are subject to selective evolution through environmental forces."

"Starting from a proposition put forward in the writings of Richard Dawkins, it has since turned into a new area of study, one that looks at the self-replicating units of culture. It has been proposed that just as memes have effects similar to genes, Memetics is analogous to genetics."

"It is for the sake of fairness and completeness noted that there are critics. They contend that some proponents' assertions are "untested, unsupported or incorrect." For example, Luis Benitez-Bribiesca calls it "a pseudoscientific dogma" and as factual criticism, he refers to the lack of a code script for memes, as the DNA is for genes, and to the fact that the meme mutation mechanism (i.e., an idea going from one brain to another) is too unstable (low replication accuracy and high mutation rate), which would render the evolutionary process chaotic."

"This, however, has been demonstrated (e.g. by Daniel C. Dennett, in "Darwin's Dangerous Idea") to not be the case, in fact, due to the existence of self-regulating correction mechanisms (vaguely resembling those of gene transcription) enabled by redundancy and other properties of most meme expression languages do stabilize information transfer. For example, spiritual narratives including music and dance forms can survive in full detail across any number of generations even in cultures with oral tradition only."

"Memes for which stable copying methods are available will inevitably get selected for survival more often than those which can only have unstable mutations, therefore going extinct. Notably, Benitez-Bribiesca's claim of "no code script" is also irrelevant, considering the fact that there is nothing preventing the information contents of memes from being coded, encoded, expressed, preserved or copied in all sorts of different ways throughout their life-cycles." Chivonn interjected here, that 'this latter point on coding is telling regarding a proposition in Vicente's dissertation noted later."

"The main take away from this meme history is that globally thought processes may be influenced by mimetics.
A question is---could this be used in a more active or directed way. In short, there are arguments pro and com as to whether memes per se may become an imbedded aspect of human behavior. However, there are already efforts to as noted by a number of commentators to capitalize on the "transcription process".

"Research methodologies that apply Memetics go by many names: Viral marketing, cultural evolution, and the history of ideas, social analytics, and more.

Many of these applications do not make reference to the literature on memes directly but are built upon the evolutionary focus of idea propagation that treats semantic units of culture as self-replicating and mutating patterns of information that are assumed to be relevant for scientific study."

"For example, the field of public relations is filled with attempts to introduce new ideas and alter social discourse. One means of doing this is to design a meme and deploy it through various media channels. One definite historic example of applied Memetics is the public relations campaign conducted in 1991 as part of the build-up to the first Gulf War in the United States."

"The application of Memetics to a difficult complex social system problem, that is Environmental Sustainability, has recently been attempted at "thwink.org". Using meme types and memetic infection in several stock and flow simulation models, Jack Harich has demonstrated interesting phenomena that are at best, and perhaps only, explained by memes."

"One of these models the so called "Dueling Loops of the Political Power place", argues that the fundamental reason corruption is the norm in politics is due to an inherent structural advantage of one feedback loop pitted against another."

"Another application of Memetics in the sustainability space is the crowd-funded "Climate Meme Project" conducted by Joe Brewer and Balasz Laszlo Karafiath in the spring of 2013. This study was based on a collection of 1000 unique text-based expressions gathered from Twitter, Facebook, and structured interviews with climate activists."

"The major finding was that the global warming meme is not effective at spreading because it causes emotional duress in the minds of people who learn about it.

Five central tensions were revealed in the discourse about climate change, each of which represents a resonance point through which dialogue can be engaged. The tensions were Harmony to Disharmony (whether or not humans are part of the natural world), Survival/Extinction (envisioning the future as either apocalyptic collapse of civilization or total extinction of the human race), Cooperation to Conflict (regarding whether or not humanity can come together to solve global problems), Momentum to Hesitation (about whether or not we are making progress at the collective scale to address climate change), and Elitism/Heretic (a general sentiment that each side of the debate considers the experts of its opposition to be untrustworthy)." Chivonn said here that "she was impressed (as Vicente) in how subtle and permeable are our conflicting balances as we face ideas."

"Francis Heylighen of the "Center Leo Apostel for Interdisciplinary Studies" has postulated what he calls "Memetic Selection Criteria". These criteria opened the way to a specialized field of applied Memetics to find out if these selection criteria could stand the test of quantitative analyses. In 2003 Klaas Chielens actually carried out these tests in a Master's thesis project on the testability of the selection criteria."

"In the book "Selfish Sounds and Linguistic Evolution", Austrian linguist Nikolaus Ritt has attempted to "operationalize memetic concepts" and use them for the explanation of long term sound changes and change conspiracies in early English. It is argued that a generalized Darwinian framework for handling cultural change can provide explanations where established, speaker centered approaches fail to do so. The book makes comparatively concrete suggestions about the possible material structure of memes, and provides empirically rich case studies.""

"And Vicente points out that there are a good number of other examples of direct studies on meme locking mentality.""

"Australian academic S.J. Whitty argued that project management is a memeplex with the language and stories of its practitioners at its core. This radical approach sees a project and its management as an illusion; a human construct about a collection of feelings, expectations, and sensations, which are created, fashioned, and labeled by the human brain. Whitty's approach requires project managers to consider that the reasons for using project management are not consciously driven to maximize profit, and are encouraged to consider project management as naturally occurring, self-serving, evolving process which shapes organizations for its own purpose.""

"Noteworthy in meme locking examples, Swedish political scientist Mikael Sandberg argues creative innovation of information technologies in governmental and private organizations in Sweden in the 1990s from a memetic perspective.""

"Concluding the Mimetics aspect of his dissertation Vicente comets, "The importance of the meme intrusion into the Global Brain by serious researchers is evidenced the simple fact that there have become a series of terms developed around the concept. Here are some of these.

Memeplex – (an abbreviation of meme-complex) is a collection or grouping of memes that have evolved into a mutually supportive or symbiotic relationship. Simply put, a meme-complex is a set of ideas that reinforce each other.

Meme-complexes are roughly analogous to the symbiotic collection of individual genes that make up the genetic codes of biological organisms. An example of a memeplex would be a religion.

To continue with terms, a Meme pool is a population of interbreeding memes. Memetic engineering is the process of deliberately creating memes, using engineering principles. Further, Memetic algorithms are an intelligent approach to evolutionary computation that attempts to emulate cultural evolution in order to solve optimization problems.

A Memotype is the actual information-content of a meme. *A Memeoid is a neologism for people who have been taken over by a meme to the extent that their own survival becomes inconsequential. And, there are certainly examples which include kamikazes, suicide bombers and cult members who commit mass suicide.*

There is also Memetic equilibrium which refers to the cultural equivalent of species biological equilibrium. It is that which humans strive for in terms of personal value with respect to cultural artefacts and ideas

In "The Electronic Revolution" William S. Burroughs writes: "the word has not been recognized as a virus because it has achieved a state of stable symbiosis with the host."

"However, that may be it is clearly apparent that programed thought transfer through mimetics has genetic replication analogies and that notion begs the question as to what could occur at the physical genetic level!"

᠁᠁᠁᠁᠁᠁᠁᠁᠁᠁᠁᠁᠁᠁᠁᠁᠁᠁᠁᠁᠁᠁᠁᠁᠁᠁᠁᠁᠁᠁

At this point Chivonn said …"Well, panel this constitutes a targeted selection of the research and review in Vicente's dissertation. There is much more, however, at this point I will turn to presenting his central hypothesis and proposed solution."

"As to Hypothesis, Vicente recognized, and accepted that there is development of the "Global Brain" and it is a real and a most serious consideration. It is of such importance that allowing current mere happenstance transfer from the ether, the Cybersphere, even various scurrilous mimetics to create a human future accelerating and embedding tolerance for evil would be a terrible mistake!"

"As to a "Proposed Solution", Vicente argues that the successful permeation in human thinking as is clear for example with the meme---may, he submits, occur naturally over time in the genome. He emphasizes that humans have imbedded in that genome a genetic species protective, humanitarian compulsion that is in their best interest to preserve. This is found in such historical developments as democracy, in the various faiths, all of which as they began reflected ideas of humanity."

"He proposes that must be protected, i.e. the genome must be given opportunity to retain that humanitarian impulse for it to become a "Shielding

Aspect" in what inevitably will be a global "Cy-gene" operating for humans to reach the spirit of Omega as envisioned by Teilhard.

"How can that occur?" He proposes that this come about through a twostep process".

"The first, is deeper awareness of our genetic capability and related susceptibility. "

"The second step is providing future humans ideas to obtain objective and free minded rational thinking, thus providing in time with new generations opportunity for such insight to become a functional operator within the cy-gene.

That first step, that is, deeper genetic awareness is through recognizing something that has not yet been fully realized, although this has been proposed[1]."

"Simply put, there develops in each new child, in each new generation a lingering code operating between base pairs in human DNA! It has been offered that this "Starter Knowledge" is imbedded deep in the DNA and is expressed in the way the brain detects life, events, the Cosmos and reality. (Do we not see it in the rapid awareness of babies?)

Of course, this is an awesome proposal, barely touched on before. But simply considering how naturally humans come into life with great interpretive power it is impossible to ignore.

Further and critically, it is known that hominids evolve in small biochemical but significant ways.

Thus, we have now many new enzymes to protect us as new chemicals arrive, i.e. to metabolize and detoxify them."

"Changes in our cellular, DNA-biology do occur, and this must happen at the electronic level in genetic chemistry."

"The fine and specific embedding in our molecular genetics is indeed real and can be found in a wide variety of examples. Here is another one, seemingly an outlier, but just to illustrate the effects on human behavior. Researchers have found a genetic mutation that, to put a comical label on it, turns people into "Martians" at least when it comes to sleep patterns. People with the mutation tend to be night owls because it keeps them on a perpetual 24 ½ hour schedule, close if you will to the Martian 24 hour, 39 minute day. Scientists reported this in "Cell' a widely respected journal.

With their body clocks always running a little longer than everybody else's, it's like having perpetual jet lag, the researchers at the Rockefeller University report.

1. This proposal is first in the words of the Vistavien cited in the book "The Future Navigator", ISBN: 978-0692-40588-8.

"Carriers of the mutation have longer days than the planet gives them, so they are essentially playing catch-up for their entire lives," said Alina Patke, who headed up the research effort."

"In fact it can be justifiably argued that we do begin in each new life with a "Starter Knowledge" (argued in foot note 1 above). It is proposed that implant is in the fine structure of the DNA, not just in the helix, not in the base paring per se, but in a *sub-code* of the fine chemical attractions and cross attraction and reactions within in those base pairings and supporting protein. Chemistry forms it and it takes energy (a new life) to activate it, but it lies there always, and always improving in that subtle inter-matrix exchange of electrons and energy!"

"The notion of perpetuating mind in the living is, of course, not unique and millions of people already believe in this. Examples can be found in tribal societies. The African Yoruba for example feel they tap this energy as Orishas or in Arada, the White Voodoo rituals!

The problem is that these beliefs do not treat mechanism. However, that such thinking has percolated up into daily lives is evidence that people sense this inner instruction although it is exhibited at the level of outward feeling. And there are other examples."

"Within the newer religion of Scientology is the same recognition which is in the Arada. That is acceptance of an inner set of passed on instruction within the brain that can be tapped. Scientology incorporates tenets from a number of world religions but most prominently it includes recognition of past lives, and considers the individual to be a spiritual being of immortal nature (called a Thetan). The belief pattern involves a technique of achieving better mental health by confronting memories that are not entirely accessible to the conscious mind, mental images associated with past moments of pain. The presence of these images which they call "Engrams (referenced above)"is held to provoke irrational behavior.

Buddhists view the mind as a consciousness that reincarnates over many lifetimes and exists to seek happiness and fulfill ones karmic destiny. They believe, justifiably, that human nature is compassionate and the science of "interior reality" is ethical as discoveries imply right actions. One might say that the Buddhists "Interior Reality" is a form of benevolent Engram."

However, they are correct, in a sense, if transferred onto a species basis. Thus, the "Theology" of the Buddhist specifies the "Goal of Human Life" as happiness. Yes, but to have human life, we must preserve the future of humanity, and each person must be healthy within! They must be able to adjust their "Truth Books."

"Even so, these philosophies are recognizing the first and kind brain as well as activation of inner signals, which it is proposed are from the sub-codes described."

"Of course, this is proposing a realm for knowledge existing in chemical signals within the DNA complexes of the brain, chemical transfers that we have to study. Although the base pair is mapped, we will expose this sub-come once we have mapped all the sub-elements of the genome. We cannot just speak of a base pair sequence, we must know of the entire supporting protein matrix and the inner base to base electron transfers. It is in those environment influenced electron transfers that matter. "

To be more specific, it is in the fine structure of the environment of the DNA, not in just the helix, not in just the base pairs, but in the sub-code of the fine chemical attractions of the entire DNA-protein complex. Chemistry forms it and it takes energy to activate it! And the activated new life chemistry in turn captures coded energy from the past."

It is in this manner that Starter Knowledge grows with each new generation. And that can be made safe, given minds free to think clearly and independently of aberrant global influences. "

"Of course, that discovery will take time, but there is already historical evidence. The evidence is simply in the transition of ability from simple hominids to Homo sapiens over millions of human life times for each simple step up toward more capable, more humane-humanity.

So, when this is deeply considered it becomes clear. With the influence of the developing global meme sets, new generations are subject to new imbedded genic structure, which with the massive overriding cyberspace influence coupled with the constantly firing human brain neuronal complex---can be appropriately named Cy-genes."

"These are proposed here as not just in the ether as a global brain, but they are in fact a real physical composite of that which will develop in the hominid brain at large. And that will be, if inappropriately developed- the imbedded tragic fate of humans, or with hope the bright Omega for mankind."

"How can that intelligent, analytical Cy-gene carrying us toward the Omega Point be shielded, made in net rational?"

"The following is suggested. This is not a dictated gene implant, it is a proposed learning pathway, one to guard against universal deep repetitive aberrant anti-human inserts from the Cybersphere. These suggestions are intended as information measures for those who choose to protect the deep future of human kind. Here are those Information measures.

1. Information is provided via established science that Forever is real, a chemical physical infinite creation. Thus, whatever one makes of oneself that is what one is always and that is for everyone. This provides a moral basis for a sense of humanity.

2. Information is provided on the natural growth mechanism of children. That is, the real need for learning self-dependence toward becoming self-actuating, and free minded persons, without pre-embedding superstitious dogma.

3. Information be provided on developing a free and open, rational (centered) Mind.

4. Information be provided on the advantages of knowledge ecology management for organization, shielding against the cruel negative side for the cy-gene.

These ideas should be held ideally by those who join the ranks of a new set of voyagers, worldwide Future Navigators.

That is, the Omega Shield is the rational formation in forthcoming generations of stable self-actuating-mindful Cy-genes. These will be developed in the Genome via children with education toward critical minds as their inevitable exposure to cyberspace occurs. These are necessary due to the potential for an ever growing, aberrant Global Brain, influenced by the immense worldwide cyberspace!"

After that read through Chivonn ends up her review as follows. "Lastly, in the dissertation, Vicente includes four educations. These educations detail the importance and methods underlying achieving his "Omega Shield Humane Cy-genes".

"I have handed out copies of these Ideologies. (The reader of this book will find them beginning page 245).

So then we have Vicente's core proposition, his proposal, his defense and his solutions so far provided."

"He left a short note with his writings, attached to the cover. It read, "The subject enclosed is extraordinarily serious and important. What I decided in the end was to construct my "Shield Defenses" as a set of ideologies to "Fight Fire with Fire". I hope all will understand." *Vicente Costa*

"And, of course, he offers appropriately a conclusion as follows."

"What is needed is the development of a unified knowledge ecosystem functioning in the Cybersphere contering the untoward effects permeating that sphere. The core of that is in the benevolent foundation of faiths, and the recognition in education supported and promulgated by cores of Future Navigators that each individual is allowed to reach self-actualization with open minds based on objective humanistic foundations.

This agenda will constitute as Omega is reached an "Omega Shield" via wise meme excited genomes-that will help insure its outcome holding against the collapse of human society in a cataclysm of religio-polymics---a sad energy implosion of wasted disappearing lives ---in Forever."

With that Chivonn indicated she was finished with her review of Vicente's work and looked toward the Professor to finalize the meeting!

The Professor summarized this way. "It is, in fact in my judgement an actual completed dissertation which our new student Chivonn has been reviewing for the panel."

"I suggest, and with your approval, we have the work presented to his supervisory committee posthumously! The intention is that they will evaluate his suggestions and decide to accept or reject it as a completed dissertation, awarding him the degree posthumous and as a matter of completing the university record."

We will listen to their opinion, so as to adjust further research in our laboratory. Should his committee reject posthumous awarding of a doctorate for Vicente, we will, in honor of his life and contribution, work to have it published in a statured journal or in book form. The Forever Panel all with favorable comments unanimously agreed!

Some six months later at the beginning of the summer semester, the doctoral committee deciding on Vicente' dissertation met at the request of Dr.Y. The matter was not only in respect for Vicente, but was reasoned a worthwhile academic endeavor. They, the Future Evolution Panel were brought in as posthumous representatives, where questions might arise the full Forever Panel.

At the meeting, traditional in doctoral defenses' the proposal was reviewed, but this was by Chivonn the new student standing in for Vicente, an exercise she felt quite worthwhile, clearly evident in the pride she showed when presenting.

After the meeting there were two weeks of consideration by the supervisory committee and written opinions and votes sent to the Chair who called a meeting on a Friday afternoon.

All came to the meeting with great curiosity. After coffee and general pleasant conversations the meeting was called to order and the Chair read the consolidated opinion of the committee.

"It is our unanimous opinion that we would not have approved Vicente's submission had he lived at its present stage. That is, as a fully approved science doctoral awarding submission. This is because, although the proposal is based on much factual argument, the underlying notion of an Omega Point, that is-- an end to human existence, is not universally agreed, though it is often a suspected, possibility. Succinctly, the work as submitted from a Science Laboratory to a Science Doctoral Committee is not a totally scientific work but one of philosophy and sociology in theology. Unfortunately, the candidate did not matriculate in a Theology or for that matter a Philosophy Division and in a mistake by all those faculty are not on this committee. It is of course given the complexity of the effort understandable that such omission was made.

At the same time the entire committee was convinced that this follow up on Teilhard's proposals was highly meritorious. It is an exemplary scholarly work, and it should be mentioned that a majority of the committee admitted to being convinced that we humans do indeed face an Omega Point, and if we reach that it will only be one of merit, by our societies following close to proposals, such as that of Mr. Vicente's. He is careful not to make those dictatorial, where they would not receive support, or that go wrong but to encourage cores as he called them of "Future Navigators" to insure the continuation for the sense of benevolent humanism. This in the end put aside a concern by Professor Alfred Henry that Mr. Costa was advocating forced genetic engineering.

Obviously the Future Evolution panel was disappointed, probably most so by the Professor who first advocated the research for Vicente.

However, when the meeting was adjourned, the Forever Panel continued in the meeting room and expressed each and every one that it was indeed wise and respectful to have Vicente's "Dissertation in Posthumous" brought to test under a doctoral committee.

 Before the panel adjourned Chivonn was asked if she intended to further pursue the Shield in same vein as Vicente.

She said, "She would be proud to do that but that the launching idea for her dissertation was given its impetus through the notion of cyberspace inserting into the genome." That she thought she could show by science experiments, although that a great challenge.

In point, she would use the growing tools at hand to show how fine inter-base pairs interactions within DNA could create a real and operating cy-gene, the starter knowledge of newborn that given the kind of Shield advocated by Vincente would grow to insure a stellar Omega Point!

The Omega Shield
Strategic Webnet Armor

Homo sapiens evolved "Human" surviving because of their instinct genetically embedded benevolence containing a sense of intelligent humane sympathy. This has been against almost unimaginable challenges, the twisting of greed, the Religio-polimics in un-rational punishments for differences in faiths and beliefs, the lack of understanding that all people no matter color or origin are of the same birth right, human beings.

Still at the present time there remain within the warring groups, the faiths and politics, are the semblance, the cores of humanity. Meanwhile, humans have created a new overlord, via their communicating machines! This cyberspace is making into them, their thought driven processes a "Global Brain". The underlying mechanisms of that have the potential to fade away from them the very sense of humanity that has seen them this far.

It is clear that there is need for shielding to help them evaluate and adjust those challenges, for the sake of their survival.

While the various groups of faith and consideration have in their beginning agenda the means to accomplish that the evidence, the entire history is that their deflections will not allow sufficient strength challenged with the onslaught of cruel and selfish acceptance to make their peaceful future happen.

There can only be one path to navigating the distant future toward Omega. This is attention the free and strong mindedness of the young--- the coming generations. That inborn gene of benevolence requires a shield!

Following are guiding protocols, ideologies toward securing their rational--- humanitarian Cy-gene development guarding against the permeation of cyberspace generated inhumanity. Proposed are The Method (The Armor), and The Ideologies' (The Armor Guards, that is Protect, Develop, and Insure.)

METHOD

It is proposed that "International Interlinking Webnets" are created connecting child oriented agencies who will disseminate a set of fundamental Ideologies throughout the cyber linked Noosphere. Their activity will prioritize response when the developing global brain becomes occluded with child damaging and misleading information.

The interlinked agencies will function via a Systematic Knowledge International Ecology System (SKIES). This knowledge ecosystem will oversee knowledge management regarding the needs and growth of children, as they may be negatively affected by Cybersphere evolutionary changes. SKIES will be constructed so as to unite groups of Future Navigators, people who believe in a secure future for the world's children.

SKIES will accomplish its mission through collaborative cyberspace networks in formal collaboration agreements. Decisions on publication and issuances will be through arbitration among the participating networks, with full disclosure to one another.

The linked organizations are charged first with insuring that Ideologies on Child Development, example as published below, are given all opportunity for priority distribution in strategic cyberspace appearances.

They are charged- in connection- to search for better more humanitarian outcomes, including new solutions, to the management of knowledge resources. This recognizes the massive acquisition of knowledge, stored and decimated in the age of the Cybersphere. They are missioned to give intelligent consideration to all "knowledge resources" of and within cyberspace!

The knowledge ecosystem shall foster the dynamic evolution of knowledge interactions between entities to improve decision-making and innovation through improved evolutionary networks of collaboration. In this pursuit they are charged to consider issuances that are less child destructive, more efficient, more fair, and responsive to human needs. They will operate according to the following mandates.

They will place emphasis on organizations who are focused on social justice, with care not to avoid the most vulnerable populations, including low-income persons and marginalized groups. This recognizes that huge hosts of people live in the margins of the global economy, and that our entire planet as the Noosphere--- The Global Brain grows depends upon knowledge for economic and personal development, education and health, political power and freedom, culture and is enjoyable.

The organizational framework will undertake and publish research and new ideas, engage in global public interest advocacy, provide technical advice to governments, and firms, work to enhance transparency in policy making in those entities.

In a prime assignment they will monitor actions of key actors with attention to child growth disrupting or contaminating enterprises, and provide forums for interested persons to discuss and debate the fundamental knowledge ecology topics. Decisions regarding issues of prominence will be though a panel of all participant units in the SKIES.

They will establish within National and International Agencies---Interlinked Knowledge Networking Institutions. SKIES will link knowledge resources, databases, human experts, and artificial knowledge agents to collectively provide online knowledge to achieve anywhere anytime performance of child protective actions. The availability of knowledge on an anywhere-anytime basis should be designed to blur the line between learning and performance. Both should occur simultaneously and sometimes interchangeably. Timely operating in protection of children is to be considered essential!

The networked knowledge systems will include at all times the highest state-of-the-art facility and operation to be fully actionable in the total Cybersphere. This includes the following.

SKIES will operate on two types of technological core, one dealing with the content or substantive knowledge regarding the primary objective and the other involving computer hardware and software and telecommunications, that serve as the "procedural technology" of operations. These technologies should develop their knowledge management capabilities that in goal are far beyond individual human capacity. They should provide communications between computers and among humans permitting knowledge ecosystems to be interactive and responsive within the wider community and within all of its subsystems.

The supporting system for securing humane knowledge will include research and development experts, operational managers and administrators, software systems, archival knowledge resources and databases should be the very best that can be assimilated.

Performative actions swill include persistent monitoring of the effects of Cybersphere memes on the behavior of children. This is through accepted practice in child behavior analysis. At option of medical communities, under informed consent agreements the gene status of each new generation is encouraged. That is recommended at time the internal workings, i.e. sub-codes of the Cy-gene have become known.

IDEOLOGIES-CORE PRINCIPLES

SKIES essential charge is the maintenance and growth of the admirable characteristics in humans, this against the degrading influences of the Cybersphere that creates the loss of their humanity, their concern and sympathy for others.

Humans have developed an initial sense of morality, redemption, empathy, and broad humanitarian sensitivity. The preservation of these preserving senses and the natural growth toward the magnificent creatures at the Omega Point the human spirit evolving magnificently, must be preserved in the genetic development of each new generation.

Underlying the preservation and optimal growth of these star reaching characteristics are three basic ideologies for universal dissemination, namely Protect, Develop and Insure.

Following are examples of primary ongoing idealities that SKIES would work to insure and extend into the future of human kind to provide the needed stable consistency

PROTECT

Irrational wars, starvation, faith-based crimes…greed against children threatens our future. Therefore, we adopt the following, a manifesto of values and behaviors. These are to unite the highest doctrines of Humankind into a "Final Code of Conduct," the system by which our children will survive in peace, happiness and productivity for all the future.

1. That there is no dogma in faith that demands converting, dominating, injuring or killing a "non-believer".
2. That philosophical, political, or national dogma used as the reason for harming any person is deception amounting to crimes against Humankind.
3. That children will not be used as monetary capital for any reason. Capital means returning love to them.
4. That murder is an act of insanity; persons committing this crime will be isolated from the population.
5. That those religious beliefs based upon the values, characteristics, and behaviors best in and for all human beings should be harbored without prejudice.
6. That every child from the first dawning of cognitive ability should be know that the whole of humanity is their family above all sects, states, or nations.

7. That every adult person will freely contribute every day an act to support planet Earth and an act contributing to the movement of the species throughout the Cosmos. From Earth's model, we will move into and find ways to reside in the broader Cosmos, to create Earth like places, "Tera-Realms".

8. That all governments will be guided as their first principle by this; anyone who denigrates, injures or kills a child commits a capital crime against the species.

9. That every government shall codify these principles in the laws of their nation.

10. We vow to the upbringing and education of all children as enumerated following.

1.) Every child will be guarded and supported to the finest health and education from birth at every place on the planet. We recognize that any child could be the seed to the "Final, Perfect Ultimate Human." So, all will be given the chance to mature in a safe and supporting environment.

2.) We will begin all our actions by never removing hope from any child! We recognize the line between hunger, and anger is a thin line. Universal education of the world's children cannot occur in a world at war. We will work exhaustively to prevent the loss of young life through starvation or in wars of idealism. Complete removal of war, will be the goal of each person on this planet.

3.) Each day we will honor the following practices born in the faiths and philosophies over the history of Humankind.

Islam: From the faith of Islam, we adopt the following. Children have the right to be fed, clothed, and protected until they reach adulthood. They must have the respect to enjoy love and affection from their parents. They have the right to be treated equally, in relation to their siblings in terms of financial gifts. Parents will provide adequately for children in inheritance. Children have the right to education. A saying attributed to Muhammad relates: "A father gives his child nothing better than a good education."

Christianity: From the Christian Faith, we adopt the following. Train a child to respect this idea "He will do unto others as he would have done to him."

Judaism; From the Jewish Faith, we adopt and will hold the following. Girls will be given the same level and quality of education and the same in all rights as boys.

Buddhism: From the teachings of the Buddha, we will hold the following. We support our children to become generous, compassionate, virtuous, responsible, skilled and self-sufficient beings. We will give them the basic mental skills they need to find true happiness. To that, the most important thing is helping them to understand that every action has consequences. Each of those actions will determine their happiness, not only in the moment, but in the future. That is the basic lesson of karma, or cause and effect.

Hinduism: From the Hindu belief, we consider the following. It is that one should discover and explore spirituality, religion and God on one's own, and that we shouldn't interfere. It's okay to share and teach. It's another to misuse God to strike fear in others.

Pantheism: If you choose to believe in a god, hold that personally without evil intent to others. Recognize that each faith's prophet would have the main message from the same God; there would be no other choice, one believing in one god. In this there is thus-no reason for a polemic. However, above all rest in the beauty of the world into which you were born, so sympathetic with your existence, in that alone is the unification of all faith. Stand unified in those ideas, the same God, the same creations, your precious earth.

Atheism: From the Atheist, we pay attention to the following. Early implantation of religion should avoid damaging in the following ways because children are especially vulnerable to mental harms related to it. This includes extreme guilt about normal, healthy sexual functions, disrespect for science and reason, feeling war like toward others, which do not hold the same faith. Remember, free inquiry on all matters, strengthens the species.

Further to Protection of Children:

We will help children along the path to self-control. This means they grasp reality, the karma of their lives. That means to understand things as they really are and to realize the truths of life, to see things through, to grasp the impermanent and imperfect nature of worldly objects and ideas. Since our view of the world forms our thoughts and our actions, this view, developing self-control, yields right thoughts and actions for all people.

Children will guarded such that they grow in to self-actuation. For them will be available to discover be educated with a higher sense of purpose, the realization the Cosmos is for our species a provided ideology because they are first Cosmos-lings! As they view this future, we will help them to understand that Earth is their glorious ark. It must last for thousands of generations. In its beauty, in the naturalness of earth's sympathy for our species, we have been matured. An ideal it would be that, even if most are elsewhere, this beautiful so precious home would exist as it has been found until it dies as it must through Space-time forces against which there is no possible reversal.

Children will be informed as to the matter of how our species is improving. We have become aware that of all the species, our strongest suit is our ever maturing brain. Our species agenda is to continue that remarkable development. This means that their Brain DNA in transferring and improving through the living generations insures the arrival of "Ultimate Humans." The young will be provided insight into this so that they may respect it as adults.

We will teach our children to join in the mission of feeding all the world population. Sapiens can mobilize to go to the moon that same species can certainly mobilize the fair feeding of the world's children, in every corner. The young should have full insight into this as the charge of all humans when adult!

Children will be informed about the conflicting forces that create behavior. The brain driven urge to destroy is an embedded part of the survival of the fittest, yet that drive refers to the physical and with self-control can be managed. The brain driven urge of benevolence is also embedded. It is that drive that referees the preservation of the species. It is our strongest suit, the ability to think things through. The young should have full insight into this as a principle to reflect upon when adult.

Children will be allowed and guided by example into ethical and mental self-improvement. That is, resistance to the pull of desire, resistance to feelings of anger and aversion, and not to think or act cruelly, violently, or aggressively, and to develop compassion. This education will avoid proselytizing children into beliefs for which there is no substantiation.

We will teach the young that their children will be the next form of their species, the path to the future and full enlightenment. This means that as adults, they will take responsibility for their reproduction. Wise and considerate human pairs will inevitably begat wiser ones. To aid children of each new generation adults will be provided an understanding of how natural development can lead to their children becoming self-activating, naturally transcending, humans. If humans could do this we benefit, female and male interaction would be equal without female victimization by men.

DEVELOP

The buffer and the guide to develop healthy-minded humans in each generation is to respect that they have psychology of needs. Respect for this development in face of damaging cyberspace influences will produce more secure, self-actuation persons. The human mind is complex and different motivations can occur variously in different lifetimes. They can be arrayed, however, much as in a pyramid, although each person from their starter knowledge may experience these differently, some in sequence others some aspects may occur simultaneously.

None-the-less the fundamental transition in growth to adult to be respected is as follows. SKIES activities will attend to insuring that these are published so as to be recognized and fortified.

Physiological needs

Physiological needs are the physical requirements for human survival. If these requirements are not met, the human body cannot function properly and will ultimately fail. Physiological needs are crucially important; they should be met first. Air, water, and food are metabolic requirements for survival in all animals, including humans. Clothing and shelter provide necessary protection from the elements. *As noted a prime agenda of SKIES to make aware when societies are being denied this fundamental due to cyberspace interference in needed relevant communic*ation.

Safety needs

Once a person's physiological needs are relatively satisfied, their safety needs take precedence and dominate behavior. In the absence of physical safety – due to war, natural disaster, family violence, childhood abuse, etc., people may re-experience post-traumatic stress disorder or transgenerational trauma. In the absence of economic safety due to economic crisis and lack of work opportunities these safety needs manifest themselves in ways such as a preference for job security, grievance procedures for protecting the individual from unilateral authority, savings accounts, insurance policies, disability accommodations, etc. This level is more likely to be found in children as they generally have a greater need to feel safe.

Safety and Security needs include, Personal security, financial security, Health and well-being, And a Safety net against accidents/illness their adverse impacts. **SKIES can help here by insuring that false promises (scamming) are on notification.**

Love and belonging

After physiological and safety needs are fulfilled, the third level of human needs is interpersonal and involves feelings of belongingness. This need is especially strong in childhood and it can override the need for safety as witnessed in children who cling to abusive parents. Deficiencies within this level due to hospitalism, neglect, shunning, ostracism, etc. can adversely affect the individual's ability to form and maintain emotionally significant relationships in general, such as Friendships, Intimacy, and Family.

Humans need to feel a sense of belonging and acceptance among their social groups, regardless whether these groups are large or small. For example, some large social groups may include clubs, co-workers, religious groups, professional organizations, sports teams, and gangs. Some examples of small social connections include family members, intimate partners, mentors, colleagues, and confidants.

Humans need to love and be loved by others. Many people become susceptible to loneliness, social anxiety, and clinical depression in the absence of this love or belonging element. This need for belonging may overcome the physiological and security needs, depending on the strength of the peer pressure.

Inherent in this is the social grouping that arises from cyberspace. Where that is obviously dangerous, example, suicide groups, or such as terrorist organizations, SKIES should provide warnings and options to bring individuals back to rational need-standings.

Esteem

All humans have a need to feel respected; this includes the need to have self-esteem and self-respect. Esteem presents the typical human desire to be accepted and valued by others. People often engage in a profession or hobby to gain recognition. These activities give the person a sense of contribution or value. Low self-esteem or an inferiority complex may result from imbalances during this level in the hierarchy. People with low self-esteem often need respect from others; they may feel the need to seek fame or glory. However, fame or glory will not help the person to build their self-esteem until they accept who they are internally.

Psychological imbalances such as depression can hinder the person from obtaining a higher level of self-esteem or self-respect. Most people have a need for stable self-respect and self-esteem. The psychologist Maslow noted two versions of esteem needs: a "lower" version and a "higher" version.

The "lower" version of esteem is the need for respect from others. This may include a need for status, recognition, fame, prestige, and attention.

The "higher" version manifests itself as the need for self-respect. For example, a person may have a need for strength, competence, mastery, self-confidence, independence, and freedom. This "higher" version takes precedence over the "lower" version because it relies on an inner competence established through experience. Deprivation of these needs could result in an inferiority complex, weakness, and helplessness.

Caution should be issued by SKIES where the influx of cyber enterprises tends to lower self-esteem, and conversely, applications into cyberspace that help persons to see their value are exercises well within SKIES agenda.

Self-actualization

"What a person can be, they must be." This quotation forms the basis of the perceived need for self-actualization. This level of need refers to what a person's full potential is and the realization of that potential. This this level is expressed as the desire to accomplish everything that one can, to become the most that one can be. Individuals may perceive or focus on this need very specifically. For example, one individual may have the strong desire to become an ideal parent. In another, the desire may be expressed athletically. For others, it may be expressed in paintings, pictures, or inventions. *To **understand this level of need, the person must not only achieve the previous needs, but master them. Protection of that capability against degradation of it from Noosphere influences is clearly a priority of SKIES.***

Self-transcendence

The above staging in life were set down originally by A.H Maslow, who wrote on "The Hierarchy of Needs". Maslow explored a further dimension of needs. The self only finds its actualization in giving itself to some higher goal outside oneself, in altruism and spirituality. ***This involves Transcendence, a state that is a critical agenda applying to the Global Brain for SKIES in its overseer role, as protection of this state is fundamental to the advance of humans---optimally arising toward the Omega Point. "Transcendence refers to the very highest and most inclusive or holistic levels of human consciousness, behaving and relating, as ends rather than means, to oneself, to significant others, to human beings in general, to other species, to nature, and to the cosmos".***

If healthy, and the path can be supported, growing children will be prepared at some point in their lives to "Self-Actualize", and from there to explore the minds-eye, seeking, stability and independence of thought. Children in that state express empathy. So released, they are easily recognized, and are set to interpret the way to reach their own goals at first on their own, and in that contribute to societies, benevolent and strong growth. ***That is SKIES will serve as one means to protect this growth potential and through this create opportunity for people to develop clear headedness, in open and capable analytic minds. The path to that protected by SKIES is one of capping or insurance, and is enumerated following.***

INSURE

Open mindedness is an essential to maintain the sense of humanity that will derive from the child protective and growth development programs. Via this means the protected, matured individual will resist the aberrant influences in cyberspace. From parent to child over generations the idealized will bring the Noosphere into a star reaching Nirvana. Here are steps in mind development to be preserved for individuals (and addressed to them) to help in that growth.

1. Understand Chaos.   We live with a sense of Chaos, but if it comes to ordering, if mental calm occurs - patterns can become aware and confusion can be employed to move creativity. New thoughts are generated. We can gain clearer light. Following helps in removing the sense of Chaos.

2. Know Dream Reality From Possible Reality. There is an edge to reality. We are often unable to grasp it clearly. It is as if truth exists over a razor's edge. Thus, we live in the dream of immortality. Be calm, realize it, there is the reverse side to everything and know that even the reverse has a reverse-these, we may never be able to see. So then you are back to the only possible reality for you day to day, the present you! *Your Mind it is that which governs your reality!*

3. Respect The Cosmos.   Remember, the Cosmos and our world is older than us. We are the end of a long chain of response, whatever we do the Cosmos has a head start! Reality proceeds, yet the direction we (you) set may be a part of that! If you try, and try again and fail, the Cosmos is speaking to you. If you feel success, you are in the possible process!

4. In Thinking Gain Freedom. Freedom and Security are interdependent, yet by separating them in our minds we grow. Security has a definite small connotation. Freedom has a large and unlimited connotation. Behind Security, there are boundaries, when we are able to cut through them there is Freedom. Freedom from boundaries puts one within an understanding of how their lives fit within the Cosmos. The mind cannot expand unless the center is preserved. That is achieved by selecting wise boundaries. With incomplete or arbitrary boundaries the whole structure endangers collapse. A wise center allows for delightful freedom. (Protecting the center of one's mind; makes it a capable mind, then the future has potential to be protected.)

5. Protect Your Mind.   The preciousness of your mind is impossible to underestimate. Use it or be abused by it!

6. Make A Capable Mind. The cause is given meaning by your noting the effect carefully! Know then that a single event is a tunnel through which all events reflect.

These two--cause-effect-- cannot be separated. So you learn to understand them, first in the minuscule which leads one to understand the macro that is the most important. In bees, it is the multifaceted eye...in humans it is your capable mind that can see that you see!

7. Overcome Interrupted Mind. The mind is full of noise, contributing to that sense of Chaos. Focus until it quiets to a single sound! Then will occur but one voice. Silence, frees one from interfering internal dialog!

8. Overcome Troubled Mind. Some have developed a library in their head that becomes but one book, in their view the "Truth Book." The one book mind attempts to avoid becoming contaminated by outside ideas. This is a system with such strong boundaries that it leads to defending self, then to bigotry and wars!

9. Realize The Difference Between Belief And Freedom. Belief takes meaning into formalization, then fossilization. However, if understanding is allowed to shift, each moment can be a path to freedom.

10. Believe Just First In Everything. Much of conflict between people is from colliding beliefs. So, practice believing initially in everything! Yes, that sounds strange, but internally, in time, the parts will sort logically, leading to one giant idea, hence, no boundaries! This should free one from the desire to be always right (which most of us have). Great problems can be solved, sometimes by evaluating the wrong. One should rather be happier in ideas that can be improved, than fearing the wrong.

11. Allow Time To Grow. Focus on nature, it has much to say. Remember the message in the seeds. Your time will come and with it a time to grow!

12. Understand Difference Between Fear And Courage.   Fear is controllable. In fact, if you think about it we only fear what we "see" in the future. The rest is anticipation. In fear, we begin to imagine what we can't do, rather than what we can. Dwelling on what you can't do leads to fear, dwelling on what you can do leads to courage!

13. Know Change And Learning Are Interlocked. To learn is to change, to change is to learn. There is no learning without change! To remain unchanged is to remain forever without comprehension.

14. Understand Perception In Relation To Reality. We must accept that there are both perception and reality. In fact, more aptly put, more relevant to us as persons, human life is "Attending." We can't turn it off. It is always pointing at something...as long as we are feeling we "Attend".

15. Recognize The Modes Of Attention. Within our attending, there are four modes: External and Internal, Narrow and Wide. We exist or see an existence in one or the other. Learn to know the whole! When looking down also look up,

expand the narrow to the wide and vice versa. Your choices at any time depend on the extent you see!

16. <u>Expand Attention To Its Twelve States.</u> Contract and magnify as you observe, use your attention! To add sparkle to the world practice alternate meditation, knowing each mode well at first. That is, recognize deeply that there are 12 states of attention: three senses; sight, hearing, touch and four modes; internal, external, wide and narrow to achieve 3x4 states. In your Mind gain, switch from external to internal using each. This will help your mind to become richer, more mature!

17. <u>Know The Basis Of Behavior And Perception</u>. We don't disagree over what we perceive (usually). We often disagree over what those perceptions mean to us individually! Thus, the behavior may be the person, how we respond gives the behavior meaning. The response is a secondary feeling, an emotion! The original perception is the primary or internal feeling. *To un-bias yourself, change variously your sense of the perception.*

18. <u>Balance Change and Response.</u> Responding to the messages of change can create meanings, thus giving you choices, access to different worlds. Changing response lets one see the world as the opportunity! This is what we call an "Open Mind".

19. <u>Enhance Attentions.</u> Practice each so it grows, make perceptions big enough to evaluate, then the distance will lend to improved attention, enhancement and greater value. In effect, become a "Mind Tracer."

20. <u>Learn Translation.</u> Learn to "Translate" each state. Make light have feeling, rock have fragrance. Intelligence is limited by the number of states one cannot master in this way. The more this can be achieved, the richer is the life experience. This helps to join one in existence within the Cosmos. In unhappy situations, one shifts attention through this means, to relieve pain or boredom.

21. <u>Move External to Internal.</u> A skilled Mind Tracer shift's attention, external to internal to achieve their skill. They see an external and envisions its meaning internally. This means appreciating the mental processes of which there are two; "Defining" and "Exploring." Too much defining leads to narrow judgment and views, but it can be useful if balanced as it may lead to more fruitful exploration. If one starts out with the basis of looking for something, they may find Yomething even more interesting. Pioneering something in this way for a group means the pioneer may gain a special freedom, a special feeling of accomplishment!

22. <u>Know Type of Questioning Relates To Happiness.</u> The essence of the Human is to understand, to be attentive. So the way in which questions are asked is important. When we question, we should use the 12 states to enjoy, this to

wander, this to let the ordinary become extraordinary. Even so, the words used are quite important. "Why" is a question of dogma, leading to more Whys? "Why" questions, sometimes work, but don't necessarily lead to information particularly useful, because this is thinking virtually, totally about meaning. "How" questions are those with a more often useful basis. One is thinking about actions. "How" leads us to use our senses probing into time, space, weight. We see the Cosmos as phenomena, take advantage of the universe's action on itself to accomplish! Our essence our mind turns wishes into use. We are excited about this skill. The skill at this is the measure of your life. It's very much about "How"!

23. <u>Grasp Importance Of Context In Thinking.</u> "Content," "Reality" and "Timing" only have meaning within the "Context" that they belong. They are subordinate to Context. Therefore, our ideas about them are changeable. That is these should be viewed within their specific diversity to allow one to arrive at an accurate understanding of them. We should want first to understand that process, even though in the end the outcomes become what are desired.

24. <u>Understand The Basis Of Feelings.</u> Feelings prompt a "Human Fog." There are two parts. Primary feelings are those of warmth, pain, satisfaction, the actual world. Secondary thoughts are the emotions and responses, the meanings we apply. They are how we think about the world. These can be and are most often mistaken, intermixed. Feelings mixing with emotions, can lead one astray. We must evaluate whether information is appropriate between the two…knowing the difference leads to better decisions.

25. <u>Calculate Connections.</u> Dreaming or envisioning is not a place, but a process of calculating connections between points. The insight comprehensively gained is in using the twelve states.

26. <u>Recognize and Use Space in Mind.</u> The mind has the property of space. Space is not just something to fill casually. In reality, within in it matter can be created from energy. Space can be thicker or thinner depending on how much has gone to matter. So Mind space has tremendous energy and promise. *Mind when stretched to a new dimension is never the same; it is now accepting new matter (ideas recorded).* To accept something new one must "empty some mind space," then open the door and let the future in, endless possibilities can come from this.

27. <u>Avoid Depression, Madness, And Lost States.</u> This is when one has lost the RANGE of attention, i.e. the twelve states. They are not out of Mind but lost in a limited realm within it. Perceptions are fixed! The mind is safest…not locked in, but when one is exploring freely within it. To discover and reveal hidden inner riches is the most exhilarating work of all!

28. <u>Realize Differences: Religion Vs. Science and Self.</u> Religion can deflect one's attention inward in a virtue versus failure appearance to God, i.e. one is to behave in a certain way making them hostages in a sense. Science directs one's attention outward. One becomes an aggressor for making change. In a sense, both fail to strengthen the individual as they abandon "Self-Regulation". One to be happy self regulates oneself, mind, body, and spirit. Once internally sound, one can then go out to see if that changes perception. Without self-regulation, peace can only happen in a perfect world, and must fail. Anything mind can't seem to affect must be external. Oscillate between the external ideas in relation to your foundation of internal strength!

29. <u>Know The Promise Of Human Maturity.</u> "When one resides within a correctly dimensioned drum, the sound of a beating heart is greatly magnified"… "When one truly sees the magnificence of human possibility, the sound of future beating hearts amplifies one's own! " Human kind has awesome potential, but only if it continues to exist.

30. <u>Seek Aging Well.</u> The body sends strong messages to the old. To respond with courage recognize time is the one resource you have. Manage it well. Here, the most important thing is your own voice. Learn that even now so what you say is heard. Complete is each day doing! Incomplete is unfolding! Blend these and the beauty of life unfolds. I am. Am I? Complete, Incomplete. With time ahead you are incomplete!

31. <u>Guide Yourself Internally.</u> Wanting to be perfect begins with self-control, internally. We think of the past as influencing what we should or should not do. Talking to yourself in the right way can ease the stresses produced by this. You have "Mind Police" built up in your raising and experience. These are what others want you to do, but you take control by your personal voice. Remember to change the "You" voice to the "I" voice. Internal You - leads you to some statement about yourself, usually in a bad way. "I "-needs to never tag negatively. With "I" you can change to the positive such as "I want to share my success". Cease wanting to be perfect by the demands of the Mind Police, give that up and stay with the good myth about yourself. That way, you avoid living in "a Police State." Relief is then gained. Delight is felt when your own internal voice wins.

32. <u>Change Yourself Upward.</u> With each heartbeat, we are changing. Time is the master. All our "Life Waves" are sums of our simple waves, compiling (tangled rubber strings by simile, Item 43). So how do we best change ourselves, take control of the waves? Emphasize the "I" voice, drop the you "always will be". That is with the "I" voice you gain, in effect, you control time. The "You" voice plants you in the past. Ignore it, emphasize the wonderful. The "I" voice directs you to

your future. Mood is set by who is talking in your head. Be free of your past, the Mind Policing, it only continues to affect you.

33. <u>Expand The Right "Mind Code."</u>   Pronouns (as above) are the way the Mind addresses itself. However, look at Mind as a verb it is what the brain does! The brain's memory is in Chaos and brain itself is a combination lock for everything.   These things can be brought up in several ways; one word will evoke several meanings. Being dumb is allowing just one door to open from the Chaos! Being smart is allowing multiple doors to open. Make a Mind Code for something important to you, anything stored or just hanging there, then bring it back and expand it. Once a bit of the Chaos is trapped (put in order) let it gather new thoughts!

34. <u>Know Limits In Existence.</u> Your life exists only in your Mind! If your view of what the world is fixed, (such as what is the perfect religion, the perfect car, move, etc.) unhappiness is sure to follow. View the world as incomplete, with room to finish it. Knowing your Mind leads to knowing your body. This gives the marvel of reducing illnesses that limit you.

35. <u>Know What Is Complete And What Not.</u> For strong viewed people the world is fixed, so every discussion is a fight or an attack. If thoughts are reopened to discussion, the world is open to many things. By knowing not to complete, minds are changeable. Each can make this discovery, and a wonderful world results. Remember "It depends, also depends." We search for new places, when we have "transformed eyes."

36. <u>Solve Problems And Issues.</u> The approach to every problem, no matter how big or small can be mastered by an expansive process in your Minds-Eye. First take the problem and expand it to as large a field as you can, organizing it into a single picture in your Mind. Then rise above that picture to look down on it, and *organize* the pieces. Now the clearer picture can be made smaller and lower it toward you. When enough small, insignificant actions become coordinated beauty and might are created! That is, the random neural discharges of brain must be linked and combined before the magic of thought, and understanding appears!

37. <u>Apply Superior Meaning.</u> Wrongly, values and beliefs become the lens through which we look, and color the way we see the world. This turns the infinite into the finite! Rather, see the world as incomplete and possible. Practice finding several meanings to each situation. The "this and that" events should not yet have true meaning. First see without seeing "Meaning"; attempt to see what actually is! Once, the big pictures are manageable stay with that optimal, adjusting slightly as you go as needed.

38. <u>See Together The World From Your Mind.</u> Nothing is completed in the world unless it is completed first in your mind. Once mastered, know what you can do and don't know what you can't do! There is no time when self-reliance wouldn't be an asset. But, seek people you can complement while avoiding those you are weaker with. At the beginning, these "Seeking's" may be muddy waters, but even muddy waters can quench a fire!

39. <u>Draw Opinions From Different Views.</u> The Mind operates differently among different peoples. Thus, the far northern people see the top and bottom of things (sun apparently rising and falling, only). The equatorial see the left and right side of things (Sun apparently rotating east to west). Remember that while we see much the same (it is the same sun), there are differences in the WAY various minds see the world. Draw opinions from different views to gain your own strength!

40. <u>Recognize You Can Change Ideas or Concepts.</u> Your Mind is extraordinary powerful. One can use it to help oneself to change the feelings about almost anything, from pain to aberrant notions. There are two ways of remembering 1.) "As it happened to you," and 2.) "As you see it happening removed from you." When it is "attached" you feel it "Here"! When detached you are at a distance from the pain or idea. If you run it backwards from that distance, you can find ways to control it until you get to the attached, so that can be rationally evaluated.

41. <u>Change Limits to Perfections.</u> The Mind can do anything through imagination; you can even envision greater imagination. In that state, you have the model! Knowing it well and with a method, what you can do is unlimited. Many institutions will not accept the unlimited. They think it is dangerous and set boundary places in children. However, humans are born to fight over limits. The space in your mind can determine what the world will be like. It is born in you. One always wants to be right, sometimes making one confused…remember through the newly activated space in your mind…more perfect things can be made out of air!

42. <u>Seek The Unknown.</u> Behind most everything there is the reverse, or the hidden, beyond your immediate vision. (Below the plant are the roots). It is also an energy that can be seen sometimes, worth the effort when one develops deep inner vision. It can give you power for an exceptional journey. Ask! Use your imagination that is the tie-in to the power. What you can compute may not seem achievable, but you know in your heart you can do it!

43. <u>Understand Time Truths.</u> Life can be compared to a rubber string, lengthening in time, along the way tangling, tangles representing trials, successes, and progeny making again more tangles. Then when fully taught the life string

let's go, snapping, releasing energy, to return to the original state, and the energy is provided to one following. (Matter will by us, neither be created nor destroyed, only return to energy. This is the natural phenomena.) You have though control of the tangles, the balance that creates or destroys them. So to do your best in life, recognize and balance destinations.

44. <u>Be Wise in Destination Choices.</u> The best lived lives see and understand destinations clearly. Choosing destinations involves two activities, 1.) Comparing, 2.) Contrasting. These are 1.) What someone wants you to do, choosing it or me, as for example in religion, or 2?) What you want to do. Comparing is using value differences, Contrasting is using exact measurement, no value implied. In Contrasting judgment is made considering things as parts, without meaning. Comparing is "the difference between it and me", contrasting is "the difference between it and It". If there is much emotion one is comparing, if not one is contrasting. As destinations are sought one asks, what is the meaning in knowing this (compare), or what is the difference between these options (contrast)? One's delight is the measure of whether they are in proportion with these two, whether they are centered rationally within their Minds-Eye! That means also one strives for simplicity in life not determined by imitation of others.

45. <u>Find Your Center.</u> Analyzing "Space" filled with objects, the objects seem to become uneven, but, there is a center to a flowing river, we can compute it but never really see it. One's Mind is full of boundaries, but there is a center. If one understands the ideas herein, one can find one's center. At the center is a surprise – a source of happiness, a sense of rest!

46. <u>Understand Feelings</u>. Each of us has primary and secondary feelings. Moods are secondary feelings, which are either attached or hanging detached. These feelings are similar to our two nervous systems, i.e., voluntary, involuntary. For example, we see a mountain. It is fixed, high with color, angles, and dark canyons. This is the "Content Code," the involuntary. It is there. The way we see it is voluntary. This is the "Mood Code." These two give our thoughts "Meaning." If we are afraid of height, we may see an ominous fearful structure. If we have a different Mood Code, we may see the beautiful purple in the evening light on the mountains. That is the Mood Code can be different than ominous, it can be changed so can the memory of things.

47. <u>Understand How To Use "Meaning."</u> From feelings, we develop "Meanings" to events and things. All meanings are arbitrary, one's interpretation. The meaning of anything is the way we represent it in our Minds. Meaning has the power to connect Mind and Body. For example, emotions (meanings) can be registered and affect our bodies. If one changes the meaning ascribed (example,

it's a lousy world), that will change how one feels. Changing another's meaning could change the world!

Meanings are guided by the constraints of our history, often making things difficult. However, if we change the meaning toward the obvious in front of us (finding order out of chaos) all else can be automatic. The obvious is the law, for which there are real consequences (what you do now can affect what happens to you in the future). If using "You" the "and" says you are damaged, then you are a different person, a damaged one. Conversely, if "I" is used you can change your perception of yourself, and become un-damaged. If one connects the two halves of the brain (the obvious to the consequences) there is enjoyment in understanding direction, a sense of delight happens!

48. <u>Recognize The Flavor Of Reality.</u> Although we have mood and content codes, we may have different moods, depending on what content we see or know. So, we can change the character of reality, how we feel in relation to it in spite of the Cosmic cause and effect. This is because the World itself has no meaning without thought we give it that through the state of our Mood Code.

Part of how we see reality is entwined with "Anticipation." If we anticipate a loss, then we are in a state of anxiety. If we anticipate a gain, we are in a state of excitement. However, knowing that moods are coded it is difficult to complain. One needs to imagine how they would code to feel in an "Up Mood."

This is not to say the world is just "Made Up." Because we have limits, we can't argue the reality per se, but we can adjust our thoughts to the "Flavor or Reality," that we choose to live with. One's life can be sour or sweet. It is a decision each can make in spite of the fixed cosmic cause and effect, within one's mind, through how they reflect on the world - change in their life can occur.

People and institutions set themselves up to define the "Flavor of Life" and expect you to agree that is the way the world is. However, there is never a totally correct answer you can live in a world you believe is right. Although there are Cause and Effect "How" you deal with it is your choice!

49. <u>Become A Decider.</u> In every journey one hopes to reach toward the end. This discourse you studied (this was a "Means" journey) now approaches that point. The last concerns the question of becoming a Navigator, one helping others.

More than doer's maturity leads one to become a decider, making the Mind aligned and clear as outlined, then doing becomes automatic and we and the World are acting together. The mysterious is more knowable through the obvious, and we gain control of our Minds. On the other hand, the aimless path consumes.

50. <u>Navigating Others into the Future.</u> Minds gained through the "Means Journey" just taken, can heal oneself and indeed, the world. Some last valuable recognitions, sign posts with clear lettering, help toward cementing that goal.

What is needed so that one can, (internal skills gained) externalize to be of value to others---the human species? It first is important, that each person heals self, and then they can try, and will likely want to contribute in healing the world, as our humanity is built in, an inherent instinct!

The following aspects' center upon that possibility. They are as follows, A.) Controlling the Structure of our Memory (how the past affects each one of us), B.) Controlling Time, C.) Understanding the Intersection of Imagination versus Reality, D.) Asking Fruitful Questions about Your Life, and a most important thought E.) Discovering that a Mature Mind makes you a Navigator.

A.) <u>Controlling the Structure of Memory.</u> On the way to a healthy mind, one wishes to forget "bad and frightening" experience, and certainly space for wisdom is needed in our often too crowded Minds. Some of the past, of course amounts to lessons of progress, and is retained in respect. Forgetting the unacceptable, the wrong, the cruel, the selfish, though takes effort, but we have direct control over how it affects us, because as we have learned we have control over the structure of memory. So, being enlightened, we know, for example, fear can now be seen as arbitrary-an internal event, the internal component can be controlled. Fixed, Mind Books, can be re-written.

Control over memory means developing a simple set of priorities. *These priorities tell us, in a nutshell, that we first mind our own business*! We are capable of doing this when we are prepared to supervise our own instruction, without the usual boundaries! One only needs to set as priorities; self-determination, i.e. creating their own future, avoidance of trends-that gives us quilt in the end, Integrity---thus not regretting our actions, and control of the central core, i.e. the "Foundation of Self," that is, unrestricted by useless boundaries.

B. <u>Controlling Time.</u> Being attentive creatures, or ones desiring to lead, the "Future" has a significant meaning, and in fact, offers pressure in our daily lives. "Future" might be described as the consequence of present circumstances, making it in a sense static or limited. That is, to us, there are only two ideas of time. These notions are "ongoing" and "finished" which seem to "leap frog" forever. They proceed and direct all our actions in a limiting game. However, we have control by stepping back and simply asking, "What is ongoing? What is finished? We have the power to decide to turn these into "Now is Dynamic," "Then is Static." The future is, thus, opened up to more possibilities. We select successful past ideas and continue to explore. We use our available tools to regulate thought about time, recognizing that to know one thing is to open the potential to know a thousand, if not today, then tomorrow. Well-practiced ability expects success with developing ability.

C. <u>Controlling Intersection between Imagination and Reality.</u> This comes about when one grasps meaningful meaning. In reality, the world will do in time what it wants. Give the world the chance it will resolve everything good or bad. One then recognizes that the World sits between ones "to be" and "to do." Our lives are within i.e. between those "Spaces." In that is the important intersection, it is the one between imagination and reality! If you control yourself, then you control this environment. If one does not intersect, that is try to control this, they become impoverished.

This says in seeming paradox, but in truth one must first become self-centered in minding one's own business---controlling one's own internal environment to achieve a really healthy and mature state! If that were achieved, for each of us, there would be no reasons for conquest, conflict or greed. We would all be safe in independence from each other, but by the same token, available as a success for each other.

D. <u>Working toward Answers for Central Questions about Life</u>. One last thought lingers before one rises to the Navigator State.

Each of us has most important questions guiding one's life (yes you do if you think about it, although you may not yet have addressed it). When one achieves rational answers, one becomes finally "Mentally Mature" if that answer yields happiness! The way in which this question is asked, though, is almost as important as its content. Otherwise, your "Life's Questions" can go a long way to making you quite dissatisfied. If the answer somehow defines who you are or your present state of being you are dug in and potentially sunk. For example, if you ask, "Will this last for me," you are headed into a yes or no situation that cannot succeed. Nothing here on earth lasts forever!

Here following are some thoughts that will clarify this all-important matter and put you on the way to happiness and maturity.

Eliminate yes or no answers!

(1.) Change the verb tense and the interrogative. For example, it is not "How will I obtain what I want, but how did I obtain what I wanted? The latter then leads you to open your future, from success.

(2.) When your question refers to yourself in relation to others, reverse it. For example, it is not "When will they like me,' rather, "When will I like them"?

(3.) Leave out the specific person and avoid leading the question with "Why or Where" as these lead to the need for extensive context development. (Remember "Why" takes one into a world of dogma, etc., and removes you from yourself.)

So, if the questions are done right you will ask overall "What in this situation loves me <u>and</u> them?" If the questions done this way work well for you, they will fill you with delight! They will direct you to the "Something" you are looking for. They will become a self-correcting life map, and that will be work done without effort because work done in a pattern of joy is work without effort.

E. <u>Discovering that a Mature Mind makes you a Navigator.</u> Navigation takes courage, the self-confidence, the ability to imagine, and to remain fearless, control over the Mind's apparent limitations.

 Those capable of rising to this level are "Advanced Immigrants on planet earth", in a sense Navigators who avoid the errors accumulated from the past and work toward the future for all people, uninhibited with superstition.

Among them are the many who have given us the joys of life, the tools to make it work. We will call them "Vistavien"; they are exceptionally capable navigators because they know themselves in a healthy way.

The ideas in this document, you have just read, have described the way to join this new bred a Vistavien-a Future Navigator.

Now you know the path. These Immigrants are those who first respect then exceed the boundaries of Mind!

After all the paradox of reality is that no image is as compelling as the one that exists in the minds-eye…When that image is vast enough, open enough, the question of belonging is finally settled; one belongs everywhere, is, strong, satisfied, productive, a true companion.one, indeed, for everyone else!

Think of the awesome potential should the whole of humanity rise to that level as time unfolds and the Noosphere encloses to yield Omega.

THE HUMAN TIME CAPSULE
AN ACCOUNTING

(Reproduced from the Book "Future Navigators on the Edge of Forever".)

We want to think of us, each---as Forever. That is a natural instinct. And, Human Time could be Forever, if we surround ourselves with an aura of wise mentality. Indeed, there are hypothetical pathways and even scientific evidence that it could be. That will not be entirely on our terms, but functions of reality within cosmic forces. So it is up to us to find ways to understand it, to live well within in it.

Given that maturity, we do have the opportunity, clearly from the advance of our knowledge even today, to catch up with a better understanding. However, that is certainly conditional. It cannot occur without the success of far future generations of humans, for which we must now account. In this time we are only on "the Edge of Forever".

Obviously, unless we everyday guard with every endeavor our precious children, to give their future children's-children the most humane chance, it is totally clear, that we will not mount Forever's elusive edge.

In the prequel to this book, "The Future Navigator" the following remains the relevant protecting container.

We are being day by day asked to develop a new kind of Mindfulness, one that leads to mental security for each person who is then progressing in a universal mindset as a member of the whole species. This will be an individual who recognizes that we can evolve, if we plan as one mentally expansive world community, we will see an awesome future.

It is why, the future protecting way, "The Vistavien Way" in these books is grounded on a special "Tactic of Behavior".

This is the philosophy of people that work to secure the progress of Human Kind into the future. It is an enlightened mindset yielding a sense of personal strength and promise!

The result is a protective blanket for children building future navigators who are armored mentally to create worldwide tolerance and peace.

Their way of thinking embraces human reason. This means first its caring ethics! Then it asks one to reject dogmatic pseudoscience and superstitions as the main basis of morality and decision making.

We may call this benevolent and wise philosophy "Objective Humanism". It is a continually adapting search for truth centered by a sense of humaneness. It holds intentionally that people be mentally free so that they can guard reasoning and subsequent actions!

Our ability to think, to be at first mindful and humane, is a gift so incredible, quite possibly, existing nowhere else in space and time that it would be the most terrible of all crimes ever-to lose that potential, through aberrations of greed and inhumanity.

It is a simple fact that we must---many more of us, see and feel it--our Vistavien Navigator self! Then and only then will there be earned for us….Heaven, Utopia, Shangri-La, Darul as-Salam for, for all time.

That is, of course, based upon sufficient time for us, the time to learn and grow, to practice our humanism!

If we achieve that, the story of human kind does not need to end untidy as it happens too frequently now. Then it could actually be as it may seem from distant outer space, one world, One-people!

GLOSSARY

<u>Anthroposphere</u>: The Anthroposphere (sometimes also referred as technosphere) is that part of the environment that is made or modified by humans for use in human activities and human habitats. It is one of the Earth's spheres.

<u>Biogeochemistry</u>: Biogeochemistry is the scientific discipline that involves the study of the chemical, physical, geological, and biological processes and reactions that govern the composition of the natural environment (including the biosphere, the cryosphere, the hydrosphere, the pedosphere, the atmosphere, and the lithosphere).

<u>Collective Consciousness</u>: Collective consciousness or collective conscious (French: conscience collective) is the set of shared beliefs, ideas and moral attitudes which operate as a unifying force within society. The term was introduced by the French sociologist Émile Durkheim in his Division of Labour in Society in 1893

<u>Conscious Evolution</u>: Conscious evolution refers to the claim that humanity has acquired the ability to choose what the species Homo sapiens becomes in the future, based on recent advancements in science, medicine, technology, psychology, sociology, and spirituality.

<u>Global Brain</u>: The global brain is a metaphor for the planetary ICT network that interconnects all humans and their technological artifacts.

<u>Hierchical-Task-Network</u>: In artificial intelligence, the hierarchical task network, or HTN, is an approach to automated planning in which the dependency among actions can be given in the form of networks. Planning problems are specified in the hierarchical task network approach by providing a set of tasks, which can be: primitive tasks, which roughly correspond to the actions of STRIPS; compound tasks, which can be seen as composed of a set of simpler tasks; goal tasks, which roughly corresponds to the goals of STRIPS, but are more general.

<u>Hypercyclic Morphogenesis</u>: Hypercyclic morphogenesis refers to the emergence of a higher order of self-reproducing structure or organization or hierarchy within

a system. The hypercycle involves the problem in biochemistry of molecules combining in a self-reacting group that is able to stay together

ICT: Information and Communication Technology (ICT) is an extended term for information technology (IT) which stresses the role of unified communications and the integration of telecommunications (telephone lines and wireless signals), computers as well as necessary enterprise software, middleware, storage, and audio-visual.

Ideosphere: The Ideosphere, much like the Noosphere, is the realm of memetic evolution, just like the biosphere is the realm of biological evolution. It is the "place" where thoughts, theories and ideas are thought to be created, evaluated and evolved. The health of an Ideosphere can be measured by its memetic diversity. The Ideosphere is not considered to be a physical place by most people. It is instead "inside the minds" of all the humans in the world. It is also, sometimes, believed that the Internet, books and other media could be considered to be part of the Ideosphere. Alas, as such media are not aware, it cannot process the thoughts it contains.

Infosphere: Coined by IBM, i.e. Infosphere Data Stage is an ETL tool and part of the IBM Information Platforms Solutions suite and IBM Infosphere. It uses a graphical notation to construct data integration solutions and is available in various versions such as the Server Edition, the Enterprise Edition, and the MVS Edition.

Knowledge Ecosystem: The idea of a knowledge ecosystem is an approach to knowledge management which claims to foster the dynamic evolution of knowledge interactions between entities to improve decision-making and innovation through improved evolutionary networks of collaboration.

Law of Complexity-Consciousness: The Law of Complexity-Consciousness (Complex Consciousness) is the postulated tendency of matter to become more complex over time and at the same time to become more conscious. The law was first formulated by Jesuit priest and paleontologist Pierre Teilhard de Chardin in his 1955 work "The Phenomenon of Man".

Memetics: Memetics is the theory of mental content based on an analogy with Darwinian evolution, originating from the popularization of Richard Dawkins'

1976 book "The Selfish Gene". Proponents describe Memetics as an approach to evolutionary models of cultural information transfer.

Noocracy: Noocracy (/noʊˈɒkrəsi/ or /ˈnoʊ.əkrəsi/), or "aristocracy of the wise", as defined by Plato, is a social and political system that is "based on the priority of human mind", according to Vladimir Vernadsky.

Noogenesis: Noogenesis (Ancient Greek: νοῦς=mind + γένεσις = origin, becoming) is the emergence and evolution of intelligence.

Noosphere: A postulated sphere or stage of evolutionary development dominated by consciousness, the mind, and interpersonal relationships (frequently with reference to the writings of Teilhard de Chardin).

Novel Ecosystem: Novel ecosystems are human-built, modified, or engineered niches of the Anthropocene. They exist in places that have been altered in structure and function by human agency.

Predictive Future: That is, Predictive analytics encompasses a variety of statistical techniques from predictive modeling, machine learning, and data mining that analyze current and historical facts to make predictions about future or otherwise unknown events.

Recapitulation Theory: Recapitulation theory also called the biogenetic law or embryological parallelism is a biological hypothesis that the development of the embryo of an animal, from fertilization to gestation or hatching (ontogeny), goes through stages resembling or representing successive stages in the evolution of the animal's remote ancestors (phylogeny). Since embryos also evolve in different ways, the theory of recapitulation is seen as a historical side-note, rather than as dogma in the field of developmental biology. Recapitulation theory has been applied and extended to several fields and areas, including the study of language (its origin), religion, biology, cognition and mental activities, anthropology, education theory and developmental psychology. Recapitulation theory is still considered plausible by some researchers in fields such as the study of the origin of language, cognitive development, and behavioral development in animals.

Theory of Intellect: a comprehensive theory about the nature and development of human intelligence. It was first created by the Swiss developmental psychologist

Jean Piaget. The theory deals with the nature of knowledge itself and how humans gradually come to acquire, construct, and use it. Piaget's theory is mainly known as a developmental stage theory. In regards to the Global Brain, it is proposed that such as cyberspace activity can actuate various types of Global Thinking.

<u>Universal Evolution</u>: Universal evolution is a theory of evolution formulated by Pierre Teilhard de Chardin and Julian Huxley that describes the gradual development of the Universe from subatomic particles to human society, considered by Teilhard as the last stage.

<u>Valtoos, Semandeks, and Noosfeer</u>: Illustrations of the power and invasiveness of computer driven communication.
Valtoos are tools Included in the Actuarial Calculation Toolkit ACT (Actuarial Calculation Toolkit), is used by actuaries to define how a plan must be valued and how benefit statements for that plan should be generated. ACT also allows the actuary to define how a plan's benefit estimation calculation is to be conducted, prior to final valuation. Semandeks are computer solutions for the most challenging data analysis tasks facing national security, law enforcement and information assurance professionals. Noosfeer is content for offline access on any device. Reduce mobile data usage when browsing the internet. You don't need an app to access offline!

<u>Wayback Machine</u>: The Wayback Machine is a digital archive of the World Wide Web and other information on the Internet created by the Internet Archive, a nonprofit organization, based in San Francisco, California, United States. The Internet Archive launched the Wayback Machine in October 2001. It was set up by Brewster Kahle and Bruce Gilliat, and is maintained with content from Alexa Internet. The service enables users to see archived versions of web pages across time, which the archive calls a "three dimensional index".

REFERENCES and ACKNOWLEDGEMENTS

This is the last book in a series that expanded from "The Final Human" (first print, ISBN 0-9781145-4-X) developed from the author's humanitarian experience in Africa as a Fulbright Scholar. The genre sometimes applied is "Conduct of Life Book". Even so, the hope is that more is offered, because descriptions such as "Narrative Novel "and "Challenging Essay" apply and are both integrated in the series.

It is noted, also, that many creative and thoughtful persons prompted these books. An extensive listing and related publications (in the "Minds-Eye Manuscript" series) can be found in the author's Library of Congress volume "Journey into the Light", ISBN:978-0-615-58784-4. Books that in one way or another touch deeply upon the core thoughts in the series are listed at the end of "The Future Navigator, Vistavien Way", the prequel to this book.

Part I of the book was constructed - beginning in chapter two around a series of reports largely from scientific papers containing technical arguments and propositions on existence in times Forever. This involves denoting a mixture of thoughts by various authors, scientists, philosophers and cosmologists. In scenario that part of the book is much the same as a seminar. The words of these great thinkers have been set in directly from publications with comments interspaced by the principal characters in the story. That approach was essential to preserve wisdom and insight in discussions and every effort has been made to cite the senior or guiding author in the publications as they appear in the text or where they could be located on the internet. Also, in so far as possible without disturbing the thought flow the APA style commonly used to cite sources using extensive in text reproduction in the social sciences was used in this work. For example the various author's words were set in text without quotes and were referenced as past statements. Occasional exceptions were necessary for practical reasons, for example it was necessary to set the text in 1.15 spacing vs. 2.0 because of print requirements. The authors' names and/or article titles are given recognizing that these papers with dates and full referencing can be obtained under author or title on internet postings in 2016 or earlier.

A sincere apology is offered if an author has been missed when the technical thoughts are presented and argued by the "Forever Panel" as they sought to investigate in their pursuit of "Forever". Also comments on various author's positional text made by the panel are intended to be the normal discourse between scientists. Of course, all of the authors cited retain the option of responding or a continuation of ideas. This may be forwarded to Minds-Eye at bresnan.net. The response will then be posted on the web site, www. aminds-eyejourney.net or on any other media an author may wish to have their response posted.

The cover of this book was created using open source stock photos and drawings. The subject matter entered for those was Omega and/or Global Brain.

All the persons in the Forever Panel are representative of those with whom the Author is acquainted, names are changed to protect privacy. Skellan's account mirrors the actual challenges that Explosive Demolition Experts face to save thousands of lives. Skellan is a nom de plume for a specific reason. Many other EODs and military were involved in the events described in these books. Actual names are not given in those descriptions, respecting the safety of these heroes in an age when radicals threaten their lives.

Part II of the book is composed around a series of proposals regarding thoughts related to the Noosphere and Omega, and a final result for human existence that are widely presented, discussed and even argued in popular discourse, and certainly in universities around the world. Indeed, as is frequently evident authors have debated as to who was first with this or that theory or title, (example Teilhard or Vernadsky or Le Roy, first using the term Noosphere). Consequently when appearing within this book the major thoughts are encapsulated into or under a series of subtitles which below are referenced multiply to pertinent sources for readers whilst the specific information contained has been edited and merged in the text as needed to present the dominant theme.

For the reader who may wish to pursue these subjects even deeper they will find by entering Wikipedia, *where reliability is specified,* using the captions below (Book Sub-Titles and Captions) vast citations and alternative views pertinent to the specific subjects.

Book Sub-Titles and Captions

Anthropocene (Anthroposphere)

Kuhn, A.; Heckelei, T., "Anthroposphere" pp 282-341, in "Impacts of Global Change on the Hydrological Cycle in West and Northwest Africa", ISBN: 978-3-642-12956-8, Springer Berlin Heidelberg, 2010.

Artificial Intelligence

Crevier, Daniel (1993), AI: The Tumultuous Search for Artificial Intelligence, New York, NY: BasicBooks, ISBN 0-465-02997-3.

McCordick, Pamela (2004), Machines Who Think (2nd ed.), Natick, MA: A. K. Peters, Ltd., ISBN 1-56881-205-1.

Newquist, HP (1994). The Brain Makers: Genius, Ego, and Greed in the Quest for Machines That Think. New York: Macmillan/SAMS. ISBN 0-672-30412-0.

Nilsson, Nils (2009). The Quest for Artificial Intelligence: History of Ideas and Achievements. New York: Cambridge University Press. ISBN 978-0-521-12293-1.

Biogeochemistry

Vladimir I. Vernadsky, 2007, Essays on Geochemistry & the Biosphere, tr. Olga Barash, Santa Fe, NM, Synergetic Press, ISBN 0-907791-36-0 (originally published in Russian in 1924).

Collective Consciousness:

Burns, T.R. Engdahl, E. (1998) the Social Construction of Consciousness. Part 1: Collective Consciousness and its Socio-Cultural Foundations, Journal of Consciousness Studies, 5 (1) p 77, Conscious Evolution.

Kenneth Allan; Kenneth D. Allan (2 November 2005). Explorations in Classical Sociological Theory: Seeing the Social World. Pine Forge Press. P.108. ISBN 1-4129-0572-9.

Evolution of Intelligence:

Eryomin A.L. The Laws of Evolution of the Mind, 7th International Teleconference on "Actual Problems of Modern Science". Tomsk, 2012. – P. 133-134.

Eryomin A.L. Noogenesis and Theory of Intellect. Krasnodar, 2005. — 356 p. (ISBN 5-7221-0671-2).

Global Brain:

Kelly, Kevin (1994). Out of control: The Rise of Neo-Biological Civilization. Reading, Mass: Addison-Wesley. pp. 5–28. ISBN 0201577933.

Mayer-Kress, G.; Barczys, C. (1995). "The global brain as an emergent structure from the Worldwide Computing Network, and its implications for modeling" this can be accessed in PDF form. The-Information-Society.11 (1):1–27.doi:10.1080/01972243.1995.9960177.

Heylighen, Francis (2011). "Conceptions of a Global Brain: an historical review" (PDF). In Grinin, L. E.; Carneiro, R. L.; Korotayev, A. V.; Spier, F. Evolution: Cosmic, Biological, and Social. Uchitel Publishing. pp. 274–289.

Helbing, Dirk (2015). "Creating ("Making") a Planetary Nervous System as Citizen Web". Thinking Ahead - Essays on Big Data, Digital Revolution, and Participatory Market Society. Springer International Publishing. pp. 189–194.

<u>Hierarchy of Needs:</u>

Maslow, A.H. (1943). "A theory of human motivation". Psychological Review. 50 (4): 370–96 and "Farther Reaches of Human Nature", New York 1971, p. 269.

Mittelman, W. (1991). "Maslow's study of self-actualization: A reinterpretation". Journal of Humanistic Psychology. 31 (1): 114–135.

<u>HTN-Hierarchical Task Network:</u>

Erol, Kutluhan; Hendler, James; Nau, Dana S. (1996). "Complexity results for htn planning" (PDF). Annals of Mathematics and Artificial Intelligence. Springer. 18: 69–93. Retrieved 8 February 2015.

Alford, Ron; Bercher, Pascal; Aha, David (June 2015). Tight Bounds for HTN Planning (PDF). Proceedings of the 25th International Conference on Automated Planning and Scheduling (ICAPS). Retrieved 8 February 2015.

Alford, Ron; Kuter, Ugur; Nau, Dana S. (July 2009). Translating HTNs to PDDL: A small amount of domain knowledge can go a long way (PDF). Twenty-First International Joint Conference on Artificial Intelligence (IJCAI). Retrieved 8 February 2015.

<u>Hypercyclic Morphogenesis:</u>

Alan M. Turing. "The Chemical Basis of Morphogenesis." Philosophical Transactions of the Royal Society B August 14, 1952, 237, pp. 37–72.

Manfred Eigen and Peter Schuster. The Hypercycle: A Principle of Natural Self-Organization. Berlin: Springer-Verlag, 1979.

<u>Ideosphere:</u>

Best, M., L., 1997. Models for Interacting Populations of Memes: Competition and Niche Behavior. In the "Journal of Memetics Evolutionary Models of Information Transmission, 1. http://cfpm.org/jom-emit/1997/vol1/best_ml.html.

Dawkins, R. 1976. "The Selfish Gene". Oxford: Oxford University Press.

Dennett, D. C. 1995. Darwin's Dangerous Idea. New York, Imprint Simon Schuster.

Hofstadter, D. R. 1985. Metamagical Themas: Questing for the Essence of Mind and Pattern. New York: Basic Books.

Lynch, A. 1991. Thought Contagion as Abstract Evolution. Journal of Ideas, 2, 3-10. Republished with revisions at http://www.mcs.net/~aaron/mememath.html. Scanned at http://www.mcs.net/~aaron/Lynch1991.htm.

Infosphere:

McBurney, Vincent (2006), "Lee Scheffler Interview - the Ghost of Data Stage present", Tooling Around in the IBM Infosphere (Search directly IBM their Infosphere).

Knowledge Ecosystem:

Choo,C.,Bontis,Nick (2002). The Strategic Management of Intellectual Capital and Organizational Knowledge. New York: Oxford University Press. ISBN 0-19-515486-X.

Consciousness:

Geraldine O. Browning; Joseph L. Alioto; Seymour M. Farber (1973). Teilhard de Chardin: in Quest of the Perfection of Man: An International Symposium. Fairleigh Dickinson Univ. Press. p. 127.

Memetics:

Boyd, Robert & Richardson, Peter J. (1985). Culture and the Evolutionary Process. Chicago University Press. ISBN 978-0-226-06933-3.

Boyd, Rob & Richardson, Peter J. (2005). Not by Genes Alone: How Culture Transformed Human Evolution. Chicago University Press. ISBN 0-226-71284-2.

Edmonds, Bruce. 2005. "The revealed poverty of the gene-meme analogy – why Memetics per se has failed." Journal of Memetics - Evolutionary Models of Information Transmission, 9.

Aunger, Robert. The Electric Meme: A New Theory of How We Think. New York: Free Press, 2002. ISBN 978-0-7432-0150-6.

The Meme Machine by Susan Blackmore, Oxford University Press, 1999, hardcover ISBN 0-19-850365-2, trade paperback ISBN 0-9658817-8-4, May 2000, ISBN 0-19-286212-X.

Noocracy:

Art & Scientific Research Are Free, European Commission, European Commission Community research, Semar Publishers Srl, 2005, ISBN 88-7778-102-5, ISBN 978-88-7778-102-4.

Noogenesis:

Pierre Teilhard de Chardin The Phenomenon of Man. Harper Torchbooks, The Cloister Library, Harper & Row, Publishers, 1961, p. 273.

Steinhart E. Teilhard de Chardin and Transhumanism // Journal of Evolution and Technology — Vol. 20 Issue 1 -December 2008 — pgs. 1-22 ISSN 1541-0099.

Eryomin A.L. Noogenesis and Theory of Intellect. Krasnodar,2005. Pgs...20 and p.331.

Noosphere:

Norgaard, R. B. (1994). Development betrayed: the end of progress and a coevolutionary revisioning of the future. London; New York, Routledge. ISBN 0-415-06862-2.

Samson, Paul R.; Pitt, David (eds.) (1999), the Biosphere and Noosphere Reader: Global Environment, Society and Change. ISBN 0-415-16644-6.

Georgy S. Levit: "The Biosphere and the Noosphere Theories of V. I. Vernadsky and P. Teilhard de Chardin: A Methodological Essay. International Archives on the History of Science/Archives Internationales D'Histoire des Sciences", 50 (144), 2000: p. 160–176.

Novel Ecosystems:

Williams, R.; Sörensen, K. H., eds. (2002). "The cultural shaping of technologies and the politics of technodiversity." Shaping Technology, Guiding Policy: Concepts, Spaces & Tools. Cheltenham: Edward Elgar. pp. 173–194. ISBN 1-84064-649-7.

Monserie, M.; Watteau, F.; Villemin, G.; Ouvrard, S.; Morel, J. (2009). "Technosol genesis: identification of organo-mineral associations in a young Technosol derived from coking plant waste materials". J Soils Sediments. 9: 537–546.

Theory of Intellect:

Mamedova M.D. The Concept of "Mind" in Chinese and Russian Linguistic Morld-images (on the material of phraseological units, proverbs and sayings). Dushanbe: Russian-Tajik (Slavonic) University, 2015. 245 pp.

Universal Evolution:

Paul R. Samson and David Pitt (eds.) (1999), the Biosphere and Noosphere Reader: Global Environment, Society and Change. ISBN 0-415-16644-6.

"The Quest for the Unified Theory of Information" [permanent dead link], World Futures, Volumes 49 (3-4) & 50 (1-4) 1997, Special Issue.

Norgaard, R. B. (1994). Development betrayed: the end of progress and a coevolutionary revisioning of the future. London; New York, Routledge. ISBN 0-415-06862-2.

Note: If you are an originating author who has been missed under the above categories, please address your concern to the Author at Minds-Eye @bresnan.net. Corrections will then be posted on the Manuscript's Web Site www.aminds-eyejourney.net.

READER REFERENCING

Fortifying the Omega Shield

Thankfully, humans do have a benevolent predisposition that will preserve them---if it is not lost through too many corrupting influences worming into their developing Global Brain!

Of course, censorship is not the answer. However, untoward effects will likely happen through mind warping powers implanted in cyberspace. People who care[1] will, consequently, need records of troublesome cyberspace threats. That is, evidence of those "insidious insertions" prompting people to adapt in ways their benevolent predisposition otherwise would not choose to go! A few examples follow and more should be added, upon readers consideration. The below were published in 2017, various news media making us aware. More of these may also be found in the book.

<u>Memes and Facebook</u>. This report is extracted from "The Morning Briefing Paper". "It's all fun and games until someone's password security question gets hacked. Here is an example. A meme making the rounds on Facebook asks users to list 10 concerts -nine they've attended and a fabricated one. It then invites others to identify the fake one. But the post "10 Concerts I've been To, One is a Lie" might also be an invitation to a midlevel threat to your online privacy and security, experts said. The meme, which surged in popularity this week, is the kind of frivolous distraction that makes up social media interactions, similar to other viral memes, such as the "Ice Bucket Challenge".(Remember how so many people adopted their behavior for this.)

However, privacy experts cautioned it could reveal too much about a person's background and preferences and sounds like a security question- name the first concert you attended -that you might be asked on a banking, brokerage or similar website to verify your identity. Michael Kaiser, the executive director of the "National Cyber Security Alliance", said "that the meme posed a moderate security risk, adding that not every website relied on a security question about a person's first concert. He said, further that the greater danger is what such a list might broadly reveal through social engineering. It could telegraph information about a

---

1. See beginning …for amplification in the "Skies" Proposal. This argues for world-wide cyberspace analytical groups to be organized as a formal part of the Omega Shield.

User's age, musical tastes and even religious affiliation, all of which would be desirable to marketers hoping to target ads." (And so influence the susceptible).

He said "it is similar to users who take quizzes on Facebook. The answers can reveal specifics about a person's upbringing, culture or other identifying details. You are expressing things about you, maybe in more subtle ways than you might think," he said. Mark Testoni, a national security and privacy expert who is chief executive of SAP National Security Services, said in an email "that he recommended exercising "vigilance bordering on a little paranoia" in online posts. We need to understand how we interact can disclose not only specific details but patterns of behavior and often our location, among other things," he wrote.

"Companies, governments and other groups rely on so-called authenticators, such as "What is your mother's maiden name?" Such answers are not truly authenticators, but are facts." "The usual aphorism is: 'Your password should be secret, but 'secrets' make really bad passwords' especially when they are just discoverable or guessable facts" Mr. Kaiser agreed. "In cases where the answer to a security question is easily obtained such as what high school did you attend? --- It's best to make up an answer, even if it's not as easy to recall. His advice about online quizzes and memes was not meant to be a killjoy, though he encouraged social media users to consider the consequences of what they share. People always have to have their eyes wide open when they're on the internet," he said. "It's the way of the world!" That is already of this time. It can be seen, the need for vigilance, gathering a person's persona allows development of means to stimulate it in ways undesirable, but not easily foreseen.

<u>Artificial Intelligence Influences:</u> This report is drawn from Microsoft's "Annual Build Conference". Microsoft on Wednesday unveiled new tools intended to "Democratize artificial intelligence (AI) by enabling machine smarts to be built into software from smartphone games to factory floors." The US technology titan opened its annual Build Conference by highlighting programs with artificial intelligence that could tap into services in the internet "cloud" and even take advantage of computing power in nearby machines.

"We are infusing AI into every product and service we offer," said Microsoft executive vice president of artificial intelligence and research Harry Shum. "We've been creating the building blocks for the current wave of AI breakthroughs for more than two decades."
Microsoft research has gone deep into areas such as machine learning, speech recognition, and enabling machines to recognize what they "see." "Now, we're in the unique position of being able to use those decades of research breakthroughs," Shum said. Microsoft rivals including Amazon, Apple, Google and IBM have all

been aggressively pursuing the promise and potential of artificial intelligence as well. Artificial intelligence is getting a foothold in people's homes, with personal assistants answering questions and controlling connected devices such as appliances or light bulbs. Digital assistants already boast features such as reminding people of appointments entered into calendars and chiming in with advice to set out early if traffic is challenging."

However, and this is critical input, to which there must be overt attention! Microsoft chief executive Satya Nadella, who opened the Seattle conference, also highlighted the need to build trust in technology, saying "new applications must avoid the dystopian futures feared by some. Nadella's presentation included images from George Orwell's "1984" and Aldous Huxley's "Brave New World" to underscore the issue of responsibility of those creating new technologies."

"What Orwell prophesied in '1984,' where technology was being used to monitor, control, dictate, or what Huxley imagined we may do just by distracting ourselves without any meaning or purpose," Nadella said. "Neither of these futures is something that we want... The future of computing is going to be defined by the choices that you as developers make and the impact of those choices on the world." (Is it not clear, that while the "desire" to not have an Orwell prophesy a reality, there are not also formulated preventative means, rules or codes?)

<u>The Bloggers</u>: The Silicon Valley entrepreneur Williams first drew notice during the dot-com boom, for developing software that allowed users to easily set up a website for broadcasting their thoughts: blogging. By the time Google bought the company in 2003, more than a million people were using it. Then came Twitter, which wasn't his idea but was his company. Then begins the posting the events "of concern for all to tell us". The owner recently commented about his consequent cyberlink invention. "A few years ago, Twitter was viewed as a tool of liberation. It enabled, some believed, the Arab Spring uprisings in the Middle East. Twitter, like the internet itself, was putting tyranny on a short leash. Then the narrative turned darker, with the rise of trolling on the platform. People are using Facebook to showcase suicides, beatings and murder, in real time. And, Twitter is a hive of trolling and abuse that it seems unable to stop. Fake news, whether created for ideology or profit, runs rampant. Four out of 10 adult internet users said in a Pew survey that they had been harassed online. And that was before the presidential campaign heated providing a new avenue for lies and innuendo. I thought once everybody could speak freely and exchange information and ideas, the world is automatically going to be a better place," Mr. Williams says. "I was wrong about that." He and others are currently hoping to correct such software programing to

avoid the pitfalls. (But it is out there and influencing thought already! Lesson learned?)

<u>The Brain Computer Interface</u>: As noted on page 78 there are "Silicon Expert Companies" backing brain implant-computer interface ventures (one is called "Neuralink" another "Kernel'). As various articles tell this is ongoing and here is updated, one of many needed as vigilance is required in shielding of Human Evolution toward Omega.

What Neuralink and new Kernel are trying to do is take the first steps toward hacking the brain, so to speak, so that human beings can in the future stay healthier for longer and potentially enjoy the benefits of treating the human brain like a computing platform. This means using a chip inside the skull or some other electronic device that could improve our memory and our ability to perform complex mental tasks, as well as increase speed at which we could communicate with one another. It could even allow us to directly link with the internet cloud and other forms of internet infrastructure. (This sounds impossible, and right now it may be)

The entrepreneurs involved think that improving human cognition is the surest path forward for humanity. To quote one of them, "I think if humanity were to identify a singular thing to work on, the thing that would demand the greatest minds of our generation, it's human intelligence," (This, however, seems at present to avoid recognizing that it is current homo sapiens who have traveled to the moon, created skyscrapers and antibiotics, then kill each other in wars with little sensible justification. Is it not more important that humans improve their sense of humanity, and that of course can only come with patience in living actual life and worldwide tolerance education?) The good side of these star wars ideas is, of course, that they may funnel greater funding into neurological medical research.

Currently, the arguments are pro and con as to the actual in practice use of this cyber technology. A severely paralyzed man with such an implant may be able to eat and drink. On the other hand while most healthy individuals are uncomfortable with the idea of having a doctor crack open their skull a good many people use mind expanding drugs such as marijuana (weed), that is the drive for satisfaction, thrill and ease of the days challenges is, of course, universal. " Obviously, people implanted (Neurolinked) are fully susceptible to most any suggestion, through "their" cyber neurons!

<u>'The Default Effect</u>[1]: Software and entertainment companies exploit the tendency to empower programs to collect as much data as possible from

consumers, or to keep us glued to our seats for "one more episode" of a streaming show.'

Even so and critical to realizing the reality of cyberspace control, overall--- "the fact is only five percent of users ever change these settings, despite widespread concerns about how companies might be using collected information or manipulating people's choices and thoughts! And, it is noted, even when people are unhappy with a state of affairs, they are usually disinclined to change it. This is documented in the cognitive and behavioral sciences and is known as the "default effect."

So in the face of this, the future navigator would say…How do good intentions hold when control is within an ever expanding Global Brain, running worldwide amuck?

It is, bluntly, a matter of vigilance, attention to intention! Concern and alertness returned to the Global Brain, is a counter measure - a means of clearing the "Brains Mind".

Not defaulting? Continue this list! Watch influences and resulting behavior in those new ones, the new generations coming into the age of the Global Brain! Stand against it degrading your humanity!

\`\`

1.Huh, Young Eun; Vosgerau, Joachim; Morewedge, Carey K. (2014-10-01). "Social Defaults: Observed Choices Become Choice Defaults". Journal of Consumer Research

THE AUTHOR

D.M. Yourtee, is Professor Emeritus, University of Missouri, USA where he was many years a teacher in the Schools of Pharmacy, Medicine and Dentistry. His medical research and scholarly record are well recorded in the scientific literature. Recognitions include Marquis Who's Who in Science and Engineering, and America's Registry of Outstanding Professionals.

This writing was created through his experience when he was a Senior Fulbright Scholar and Researcher Africa-Area-Wide "and his subsequent world journeys related to that humanitarian research.

Dr. Yourtee's books originate as "Minds-Eye Manuscripts"™, writings which take positions on past and probable future history. At time of this publication those manuscripts have been made into soft cover volumes that can be obtained at http://www.aminds-eyejourney.net. All the works are created to remind us about tolerance on behalf of our children and the potential of human kind.

He notes that his books do not always treat kindly the actions of the various faiths in what he calls their 'Spirit Wars"---the too often inhumanity, though as these books develop they show the beginning benevolent foundations in all the faiths, and ways for folks to look clearly toward options for their children, eyeing their eventual adulthood in our conflicted world.

In retirement Dr. Yourtee resides in Grand Junction Colorado where he enjoys watching his grand-children grow up and addressing he hopes, through writing his books---useful ideas for securing their health and happiness and that same for all the forthcoming generations.

Should the reader wish to communicate with the author your comments would be gratefully received through web mail address futurespeak@bresnan.net.